THE
HISTORY
BOOK

THE
HISTORY
BOOK

HUMPHREY HAWKSLEY

WARNER BOOKS

NEW YORK   BOSTON

Copyright © 2007 by Humphrey Hawksley
All rights reserved.

Warner Books
Hachette Book Group USA
237 Park Avenue
New York, NY 10169

Visit our Web site at www.HachetteBookGroupUSA.com.

Printed in the United States of America

First Edition: August 2007
10 9 8 7 6 5 4 3 2 1

Warner Books and the "W" logo are trademarks of Time Warner Inc. or an affiliated company. Used under license by Hachette Book Group USA, which is not affiliated with Time Warner Inc.

Library of Congress Cataloging-in-Publication Data

Hawksley, Humphrey.
The history book / Humphrey Hawksley—1st ed.
  p. cm.
"Kathleen 'Kat' Polinski—burglar, hacker, undercover agent—is out to avenge her sister's murder, and save the world from an international conspiracy as well"—Provided by publisher.
ISBN-13: 978-0-446-52744-6
ISBN-10: 0-446-52744-0
1. Computer hackers—Fiction. 2. Sisters—Death—Fiction. 3. Conspiracies—Fiction. 4. Undercover operations—Fiction. 5. United States Dept. of Homeland Security—Fiction. 6. Washington (D.C.) —Fiction. 7. London (England)—Fiction. I. Title.
PR6058.A95H57 2007
823'.914—dc22

2006025780

For my father, with love and respect

THE
HISTORY
BOOK

ONE

Saturday, 2:10 a.m., Eastern Daylight Time

Kat, you there? What do you see?"

She touches her earpiece. Streetlights cast a skittish beam into the room that has the feel of a ghost town. A sick feeling sweeps through Kat, like a cold mist spreading through her limbs from the center of her chest.

She had gone through a night like this before and come out with the chemical tastes of a mortuary in her mouth and memories that clung to her like thorns.

In the silence, just past two in the morning, she stands inside the doorway of the second-floor, open-plan office and looks at each of the six desks, taking in family pictures, coffee cups, computer monitors; no drawers or filing cabinets open; no papers strewn about; no desks disturbed; nothing smashed or strewn on the floor. As far as she can see, nothing's been touched.

The only thing that stands out is the five bodies.

"Kat. Speak. What do you see?"

Kat takes a deep breath to keep her voice steady.

"Two females, young, Asian-looking. Both wearing jeans. One is wearing a red blouse, the other a blue tank top. They're holding hands. They must have slid down the wall when they were shot. There's blood all down the wall right by them."

"Anyone else?"

"An Asian male, young, skinny, in a blue button-down shirt, under the desk, all twisted around."

"Dead?"

Blood's soaked into the carpet. "Yes."

Under the chair lies a pair of loafers, a head on the floor next to it, a young guy, longish dark hair, as if catnapping with his shoes off.

At the next desk, head resting on folded arms, is an older woman, long, gray hair tied back in a clip, blood dried around. A lot.

At one end of the room is a long window lit by the glow of a Washington streetlight. At the other, a window looking out into a courtyard, light enough to see a drainpipe. On the wall hang holiday posters of people skiing, horseback riding; in the middle, a portrait of the president; on the other side, more pictures, of oil rigs, pipelines; and a map of the world. Behind Kat is the door she's locked, with a bulletin board displaying embassy regulations, fire escapes, and other notices.

The air-conditioning's off. Humidity's clinging inside her lungs. But it's her nerves, not the air, that she's got to control. The killer's been and gone. She's sure of it. It's Friday night, Saturday morning, so she might have all the time in the world.

On the other side, near an ornamental clock hanging lopsided from the wall, Kat sees a woman's foot, tights, and a black shoe with a buckle and a heel.

"No one's supposed to be here, right?" says Kat into her mouthpiece.

"Kat, get out," orders Cage. *"Right now."*

From the street, she hears traffic. From the ceiling, the hum of old fluorescent lights. The ticking of a cuckoo clock from her right. She picks up a buzzing sound, stays where she is until she sees a wasp flying back and forth into the back window. She closes her eyes to check she's seeing right. When she opens them, nothing's changed.

She catches movement against a wall, a desk away from where the older woman's been killed. She grips the flashlight like a gun. Cage wanted her to take a weapon, but if she had, she'd end up shooting someone and be back in jail. All she has in the way of weapons are a cell phone taped to her right ankle, and a fiberscope and a can of Mace in her pants pockets.

Kat lets her breath out slowly. The movement is light from a computer screen. It flickers and goes dark again.

"Surveillance still out?" she asks.

"Abort, for Christ's sake."

"Answer me."

"Affirmative and no intercepts."

For the past couple of months, Kat's been breaking into embassies—China, Venezuela, Nigeria, a whole bunch of them—on behalf of the American government. But for tonight's job, she had to look up exactly where Kazakhstan was, a huge place in between Russia and China, an environmental shit-hole with oil, gas, mountains, and ski slopes.

The office she's in belongs to the trade secretary, Aliya Raktaeva, who Kat guesses must be the woman with the stylish shoes, lying about ten feet away from where the screen saver's spitting out colors. Kat walks over, pulling off a cotton glove and putting a latex one in its place. If you want to steal secrets, get them from where they're kept, usually a computer hard drive in a secure office.

"Kat, you don't abort now, you're back inside."

She glances at Aliya Raktaeva. The way she's fallen is graceful, lying half under her desk, like she's snatching an afternoon nap.

What would Kat have done? Stared at the killer while he shot her? Tried to run? There's something horrible, personal, but serene about the room.

There's also a hollow thumping in her chest that won't go away. It's not fear, although that's around. It's not horror, although that's with her, too. Something like embarrassment that she's invaded the intimacy of death, and guilt that if she hadn't been coming, they might not be dead.

But if they died because of her, then Kat's going to get what she came for. Cage wants her to stay, she tells herself, but is covering his ass. The jail threat's for the audio playback, not for her.

The screen saver's a lighthouse on an outcrop of rocks. A ship's foghorn blasts out from the speaker, volume down, but it sends through a rush of extra adrenaline. Kat taps the Return key. The screen saver goes away, and a security window pops up. Kat types in the password and PIN that Cage gave her. She slips a five-gigabyte jump drive into the USB port. The computer whirs.

A photograph comes onto the screen. A woman is holding a pistol to a man's head. It must be cold. She's wearing a knee-length down jacket, black leather gloves, a blue hat pulled down over her ears.

"Bill, you there . . . ?"

"*You're compromised,*" says Cage's voice. "*Are you still in the building?*"

"Yes," says Kat, studying the image.

The backdrop of the picture is a flat, vast landscape of snow disappearing over the curve of the horizon. At the edge of the frame is the wingtip of an airplane with a logo she doesn't recognize. Underneath the wing stands a jeep with a crest on the door. The driver carries a U.S. military-issue M16 automatic rifle.

"*Someone's in there.*"

"Where?"

She flips to the next picture. The man lies dead on the ground, a pool of blood by his head.

Kat ejects the jump drive, slips it into a plastic bag and into her pants pocket. She pulls out a high-resolution fiberscope with a tiny lens at the end. She doesn't look at the bodies as she crosses the room.

Kat isn't a tall woman, five-foot-four in sneakers, and she's dressed to look as far from feminine beauty as her imagination allows. No makeup, dark hair cropped short, black T-shirt, baggy black pants with big pockets, and a set of contact lenses to conceal her eyes from iris scanners.

Kat lies on the floor, bends the fiberscope cable like a coat hanger, and pushes it under the door. But with the contacts, she can't see anything except a blur of night-vision green. And she can't take the contacts out, because she has no idea where the scanners are. Stupid.

"Bill?"

"*We've lost surveillance.*"

"Where are they?"

"*We don't know.*"

Kat gets out her Mace can and opens the door. The corridor runs maybe 200 feet, the length of the building. It's lit by fluorescent lights, one bulb gone, another flickering. At each end are windows, one looking out to the back, one onto the road, the arc of streetlight streaming through the glass. The doorways to the room are recessed from the wall, leaving a space about the width of a closet, enough for Kat to take cover in.

A shot splinters wood above her head. Kat takes in a breath. She hurls herself across the corridor. Another round smashes into Raktaeva's name-plate. The shot is loud, not silenced. Whoever's shooting is there legiti-mately. Or they didn't have time to silence the weapon. Or they're crazy.

Kat ends up in another doorway, closer to the stairs.

"Don't shoot." She feigns a Spanish accent. "I'm only the goddamn cleaner."

"What's going on?" says Cage into the earpiece.

"A gun on the first floor," she whispers.

"Didn't get that. Repeat."

Oh sure, and get my head blown off if I speak any louder.

She tries the door to the office. It's locked. She watches for shadows. She can see in a semicircle to the two doors on either side of her. The shooter's not there yet.

But where?

The text message on her cell phone is preset, but she takes a long time to send it because her hands are shaking. The text message goes, but the shooter must have seen her, caught some movement. The second shot is so close, she feels the air in her ear, a high-velocity round that gouges out wood and plaster the size of a fist.

A shadow crosses the light, slow, confident. The shooter's taking his time, as if he knows Kat doesn't have a weapon. She calculates what she's going to do once he sees her. You don't miss a head shot by less than an inch unless you've come in for the kill.

Kat doesn't plan on getting shot. Her father died violently, and that's put her where she is now, and it would be dumb, so dumb, if she ended up get-ting killed stupidly like John Polinski, just because she was reacting to him getting killed.

Kat's strung taut like a bow, but when the streetlight flickers, flashes, and goes black, she does a double take. It's not the shooter. Wrong direction.

The window thumps, distorting the other lights from the street. Again. Again. Rapid shots against bulletproof glass.

The shooter's distracted, as surprised as Kat. She tries to see him, take in who he is, but can't register anything properly in the sudden change of light.

Kat pushes herself up against the door and drops the phone into her pocket. The shooter turns away from Kat, weapon raised toward the window. Kat runs at him. He senses her, twists back, fires. Misses.

She dives for his legs, tackles, arms around knees. He goes down like a felled tree, but he's wild-animal strong, throwing her off him, smashing her back against the wall. She's down. He's on his feet. It's registering with him that she's a woman. He wets his lips, lets a grin play over them, makes a show of dropping his gun on the floor.

A scar runs down from his right eye. His hair's black and matted. She can smell deodorant.

Just as he kicks, Kat shifts sideways. His foot goes into the wall. He curls his finger, beckoning her to his feet, and kicks again, aiming at her crotch, before she's steady. She turns, and it catches her buttocks, throwing her off balance. She hears him laugh.

"Stop, please," Kat whimpers, and he relaxes; his next swing is careless. She comes back up and hits him hard with her elbow above the mouth. He grunts, flailing at her, blinking, and Kat follows up with the heel of her hand into his nose, feeling it break like an eggshell. She hits him again, both hands locked, under the jaw.

He falls. She picks up the weapon and runs.

She zigzags down the corridor, around to the elevator bank, down the stairs, until only a turnstile stands between her and the front door. She stops, still inside the building, standing silently under the high ceiling of the foyer. Like an echo, the throb of quietness is a barrier to her moving any farther.

"Cage," she whispers, but gets only a rush of white noise in the earpiece. She curls her hand around the butt of the pistol, a military-issue 9mm Beretta. She sees normal traffic through stained-glass windows. The embassy's an ugly Gothic building, bulging with pregnant bay windows and peak-tile towers.

Spotlights show up lawn and flower beds outside, then a dark patch, then the Carnegie Institution, draped with posters and light.

A shadow crosses the wall and makes Kat drop, legs buckling, flat down. She turns on the drop, catching the frame of the shooter, exposed halfway down the stairs. She fires once, both hands around the butt, elbows jammed against the floor. She aims at his heart, but hits the stairwell banister. He steps back.

"*Stop shooting.*" It's Cage, in her headset, followed by the clicking of metal on metal as a round moves through the breech of a weapon.

"What the hell . . ." Kat's eyes fix on the emptiness of the stairs. He's better than her. If she stays, he'll get her; if not this second, the next.

She springs up, jumps the turnstile, runs at the front door, punches the green button to release it, pushes it open, checks the different hues of light, hears the alarm start, and cuts left into the blackness created by a bay window, down into the dampness of summer-mown grass.

"Cage?"

High across the street is the streetlight that Cage shot out to save her life. A flatbed truck goes past. It's getting late, and traffic is thin in this run-down part of town, where only poor countries keep their embassies.

The door opens. The shooter's standing at the top of the steps, one hand on his face, blood seeping through the fingers. His head tilts down, his right hand coming out of his pocket, looking straight toward Kat. She fires twice. He cries out in a foreign language, two single syllables, like *Bit* and *Ach*, sinks to his knees, and topples forward, head cracking on the steps below him.

Kat's on her feet, sprinting along the front of the building, braced for a shot from across the street, but sensing it won't come, because if anyone were there, they would have fired by now.

In the dark street ahead, two more streetlamps have been shot out, glass shards hanging—Cage's work. A green lamp shines from the embassy wall, illuminating a side door. Just beyond that, the wall is set back, and that's where Kat sees Cage's head, pushed out into view.

"Freeze, there." English with an accent. He has blue overalls like the other one, short-cropped hair, and a brooding face. And he has a gun to Cage's head, a hand around his throat.

She slows a step, thinks again, and runs away from the building into the empty street.

A clock keeps one time, the human mind another. Kat's movements take barely a second, but her thoughts run faster.

She runs in a looping curve, keeping herself in his line of sight while he makes his choice. If he kills Cage, Kat kills him. If he moves to kill Kat, either Kat or Cage kills him. He hasn't banked on Kat risking Cage's life, and that's why in an assassin's game, he's screwed up badly.

Kat detects the turn of the wrist, the hardening of the grip on Cage's neck, the shift of the sneakers.

He operates, as Kat hopes, on instinct, to attack the attacker. She lets him move the weapon a hairsbreadth from Cage, then she fires, keeps her finger on the trigger for four rounds, until the gunman's down, the green light showing blood smears on the wall.

Kat lowers the gun, lets her head hang, too, squeezing her eyes closed and open, wishing her heart would stop flapping inside her chest.

Cage gently pries the Beretta from her fingers.

"Thanks," he says, touching her lips with his finger. His hand trembles. His skin looks like wet chalk. He goes back to the corpse, runs his hands through its pockets looking for ID, but gets nothing.

The face of the guy she shot is lined and bloodless, long-boned with skin stretched tight and eyes ice white and open. A chill starts somewhere deep inside Kat and spreads through her limbs.

"No," she says sharply as Cage stands up. "You need to search more."

Cage steps back, draws a hand down his face, his expression tired but curious.

Kat squats by the corpse. She shuts her eyes and puts her hand underneath his shirt. His body hair is coarse on her palm. She sweeps her fingers around, chest, crevices of the neck, groin, thighs; all warm but going cold.

She breathes in his body sweat, feels a retching deep in her throat, holds it down. She takes out her hand. She's shivering, but she won't stop now. Rushing. Rushed. Breathing, not thinking. Trying to breathe, not think.

She opens the dead man's mouth, single index finger, probing, inner cheeks, roof of mouth, through the latex of the glove, feeling saliva cooling with death. Roof of the mouth. Worth a try. She's hidden stuff there herself.

Nothing.

"Over here," she says quietly, walking quickly around the front of the building, letting Cage follow. The body of the first man she shot has fallen headfirst down the steps, face upward, blood spilling from the mouth. This time Kat goes straight there, prying open the jaw, and finds it against the hard palate on the roof of his mouth, a tiny metallic object, wafer flat, protected by plastic wrap.

"Always good to learn what people give their lives for," says Kat blankly, holding it up to show Cage, then slipping it into her pocket.

She peels off the glove. Blood smears onto her hand. She sees a rain puddle around a drain blocked with leaves and rinses her hand in the filthy water; street dirt's better than corpse's blood.

A black Lincoln Town Car comes around the corner. Kat walks in the opposite direction.

"Over here," shouts Cage.

"Real discreet," says Kat. She keeps walking.

Cage runs to her, takes her arm. The Lincoln stops next to them.

"Get in," says Cage. Kat hesitates, then follows.

Doors closed, Cage says, "Kat—"

"Enough," she cuts in. "I just killed two people, okay? Give me some space."

A few blocks away, she hears a police siren. She peels off her dark wig, shakes her head, and runs her hand through her short blond hair.

TWO

◇

The car leaves them outside Kat's apartment on the corner of Olive and 29th Street in Georgetown.

It's a ground-floor unit in an expensive neighborhood, bought with trust-fund money after her father's death. The rooms are big, with high ceilings, and Kat's draped the windows with translucent, colored fabrics. She's divided the front room with a Korean partition screen. On one side, she hangs out on a low, white cotton–covered sofa with a TV, a sound system, and a pile of paperbacks. On the other, she keeps her workbench that stretches the length of the room, with a couple of desktops, a laptop, software manuals, and work gadgets.

Inside, Kat pulls two beers from the fridge and tosses one across the kitchen to Cage, who catches it.

"You know stuff I don't," she says, "so tell me."

"I'm trying to piece it together."

She rolls the wet, cold glass in her hands, feeling it slippery on her skin, then pries off the cap and drops it in the trash. The beer feels good.

"They'll deal with it," says Cage.

"Clean up our mess?" She's drumming one finger on the kitchen counter, the other hand fingering the jump drive in her pocket.

Cage pushes himself off the wall, comes up to her, and takes the beer out of her hand. Like a reflex, her hand is on his. Cage is tall, with a thin face, and when the light catches it in a certain way, like now, she sees Asiatic features, a smoothness in the way he moves, some kind of inner peace that Kat hasn't managed to find.

"Why don't I make us some coffee?"

"Sure," she says. "I'll be a couple of minutes."

The bathroom's off the bedroom, from which French windows lead onto a patio, messy with summer's growth and early-fallen leaves.

She runs the water to cover the sound of her movements.

She brings out the jump drive and lays it on the ledge, where her hair dryer is. She opens the back of her cell phone and takes out the SIM card. The phone's Subscriber Identity Module is half the size of a postage stamp and, in truth, is a tiny computer that can store massive amounts of information.

Government agencies have ways to store data in even less space, in microdot clusters the size of pinheads. But Kat doesn't like relying on anything. If she needs a SIM card, she doesn't have to ask. She buys one.

Kat swaps the SIM card for a blank one, links it to the jump drive with an infrared connection, sets the phone to take in the data, and covers everything with a towel.

Every time she does a break-in job, she does the same to protect herself against Cage.

Three years before, on the eve of her 21st birthday, Kat was arrested for illegal Internet hacking. But the government, spotting her talents, offered Kat a deal.

For five years, she would work under Bill Cage for a department in Homeland Security called the Federal Containment Agency. If she stayed the course, she could leave with a clean record. If she backslid or failed to follow orders, she would go to prison.

Kat agreed, and Cage trained her to crack into the databases of foreign embassies, sometimes even to break into the buildings themselves. Every operation Kat does, she copies the stolen information to use as insurance, in case Cage or his superiors ever go against her.

She has her jump drive and the SIM card from the dead man's mouth. She suspects that both contain the same data. He copied it first, but didn't know how to erase the file from the computer. Then Kat turned up and copied it, too. Or some of it.

Eyes closed, she splashes water on her face, lets it run down, drip off her chin, and wet her clothes. She flushes the toilet to keep up the flow of bathroom noises.

When a tiny red light tells her the transfer is done, she repeats the process with the dead man's SIM card. Once that's done, she checks the data on the cell phone screen, letting the pictures run through of the woman with the pistol and the dead man on the ground. She repeats it with the other copy. The data is exactly the same.

She has two originals for Cage and two copies for herself. She wraps each in kitchen plastic wrap, then in self-adhesive, waterproof polyethylene. She tapes one to the small of her back, slips the other into her pants pocket.

She smells coffee. Cage is sitting on a kitchen stool, legs crossed, waiting for her.

"You should've taken a shower," he says, glancing at her dry hair and same clothes. "Coffee? Another beer?"

She stretches past him and turns off the coffee machine. "You need to go home, Bill. And I need to be alone."

He moves back, giving her space. "You sure?"

"Been a tough evening." She smiles quickly. "You know little Kat. Not much good at sharing emotions. Tough for you, too, nearly getting your head blown off and everything."

He hesitates. "I think I should stay. You being alone isn't good."

"Alone's what I need," she says, steel in her voice. From her shirt pocket she produces the jump drive and the SIM card.

She drops them in Cage's hand.

"You did well," he says. "I owe you. We all owe you."

Instead of responding, Kat escorts Cage to the door. As he walks out, she calls his name. He stops and turns.

"Bill," she says, "are *you* okay? I mean, can you call Sally or anyone? Someone to talk to?"

His hand's on the edge of the door. "Sally's in Egypt. Paul's with her for a couple of weeks. But thanks for the thought."

Kat walks over to him, stretches up, kisses him on the cheek. "But you'll be okay?"

"I'll be fine, and you'll be fine. It's how we're made. Call me when you feel like that coffee."

She sees the Lincoln Town Car waiting for him, sees men watching the street. He gets in the car and waves, like he's dropped her off after going to the movies.

THREE

---◇---

One side of Washington, where Kat was raised, is wealth, fine wines, and power; the other side, where Kat's going, is violence, drugs, and poverty.

She gets out of the cab by a dirty, white Baptist church with a broken window. Across the street, outside a shut-down liquor store, five, maybe six guys share their gaze between Kat and the taillights of the cab. One lights a cigarette, flicks a match into the air. No one else is around; no cars, either.

Two guys break off from the group and walk to the edge of the sidewalk. A sudden breeze carries the smell of sweet dope.

"What'ya doin' on Dix Street?"

Kat says nothing.

"Answer me, girl. Show a brother a little respect."

Kat keeps walking along the road. They watch her, see where she's heading, and drop away.

Anywhere else, the low-rise houses with fenced gardens could have been plucked from the American Dream. But it's never worked here; no one ever thought it would.

Ten houses along, she lets herself through a garden gate. The front window's cracked and taped. The door's padlocked. Beer cans, cigarette packs, and candy wrappers lie on the front grass. Kat taps on a window, then goes around the side.

At the back, a floodlight snaps on. A basketball hoop hangs off the wall. A mattress, soaked with rainwater, slumps next to a side fence. Kat steps into the lamp's light.

A tall black man opens the door, a towel around his waist, big shoulders, no shirt, his eyes wide with surprise. A black woman, rake-thin, rumpled hair hanging past the shoulders, her body draped with a sheet, steps across behind him. Her eyes meet Kat's to let her know that she won't be leaving, but she won't interfere.

"How are you, M?" says Kat softly.

"I'm good," he says. He kisses her full on the mouth, his huge hands encircling her head. His mouth tastes spicy with hashish. His skin has another woman's smell.

They used to be lovers, and Kat made the house on Dix Street her home. Then, just as quickly as she arrived, she left, and hasn't seen Mercedes Vendetta since.

"You one bad girl, Kat," he says, breaking off, leading her into the house. "You disappear like that, even I get worried."

"Yeah, well . . ." The room hasn't changed, sheets rumpled, damp in the ceiling corner, mirrors on the closet and bathroom doors.

Vendetta stoops down, picks up the other woman's jeans, panties, and top from the floor. The towel rides up his leg, and Kat sees the scar from the gunshot wound on his right thigh.

"After you gone, one morning, two guys come, asked questions about you. Government men."

"What did they ask?"

"Whether you'd been here. Showed me your picture. Took a look around."

He lays the clothes on a chair.

"Long time ago," says Kat. "You missed me?"

"You were good for my life."

Kat goes onto tiptoe, kisses him, then touches the knife scar on his face just under his left eye. "Thank you, M, for being here."

Kat's never known Vendetta's real name. He calls himself Mercedes because he likes the car and doesn't give a damn that it's the name of a Spanish woman. Vendetta is a message that he won't forget anyone who crosses him.

Vendetta Mercedes runs petty-crime rackets. His dad shot his mom, then turned the gun on himself. When it comes to dead relatives, he and Kat have common ground.

Kat pulls the copied SIM card from her pocket. "I need your help," she says, holding it out.

"You got it."

"Put this somewhere no one will find it."

Vendetta looks hard at Kat's face, runs his knuckle down her cheek.

"You okay?"

"Anyone comes here again and you don't hear from me, give it to my sister, Suzy."

"She back? I thought she run out on you."

Kat brings out a card with two phone numbers on it. "That's my number at the top and Suzy's underneath. Suzy's in England. Okay?"

The day Suzy left for England was the day Kat walked ten miles from Georgetown to Dix Street and found Vendetta. It was four years ago, just after she'd turned nineteen. Their father had just died in a plane crash. Their mother reacted by taking her own life. Both Suzy and Kat went crazy in their own ways.

Ten years older, Suzy is a role model whom Kat fears she'll never match. Kat's impetuous; Suzy is quiet. Kat's raw; Suzy is self-composed. Suzy is elegant; Kat's a street fighter.

It took Kat a long time to forgive Suzy for going to England, and while trying, she lived on Dix Street, a rich white girl in a black gangster's bed, in a place where everyone had dead and runaway relatives. It was good. No one expected anything from her.

Her cell phone vibrates. Vendetta stops her from answering it.

"They've got people listening in on everything I do."

Kat nods as if she should have known. Silence drops between them, business done too quickly, too much else to say. Kat reads the phone screen, but there's no caller's number.

She sits on his bed, and he sits next to her. She takes his hand. "You killed people, right, M?"

Vendetta looks straight at her, their faces an inch apart. "Long time ago."

"What'd it feel like?"

"Depend on the killing. Once it was for cruelty. That still eats me. Other times, for self-defense. It still don't feel good. Better it didn't happen."

"I just did it."

"First time, yeah? Someone trying to kill you?"

"Me and a guy."

He squeezes her hand. "Don't go battling guilt, and you'll be fine."

Kat gets up, straightens her top. "Can I, like, call you? Drop around sometime?"

"I'm always here."

She points at the SIM card in his hand. "Keep that safe. Okay?"

He stays sitting on the bed. Kat lets herself out.

FOUR

$\longrightarrow\!\!\Diamond\!\!\longrightarrow$

Saturday, 5:58 a.m., EDT

A haze of dawn summer light hangs over Dix Street. Kat walks up to the intersection. The guys by the liquor shop have gone. Across from the Baptist church is a private parking lot protected by an iron gate sagging on its hinges. A man's undoing the padlock, looks up, sees Kat, and points back at half a dozen cabs inside. Kat nods. Six o'clock in the morning on Dix Street is when the cab shift starts.

The vehicle that comes for her has a cracked windshield and smells of whiskey.

She tells the driver where she wants to go, then checks her cell phone and finds a new message.

"Kat, it's Charlotte. Call me. I've sent you an e-mail. Okay? Love you." It's Suzy, except ever since she went to England, she's called herself Charlotte; Charlotte Elizabeth Thomas to be precise, with credit cards and ID to go with it, as if, ever since their parents' tragedy, Suzy wants to pretend she isn't who she is.

Kat's cell is programmed like a racehorse: streaming video, credit card payments, Internet access, fingerprint recognition. But the signal makes it slow to decrypt Suzy's e-mail. By the time Kat reads it, they're close to Georgetown, driving down Massachusetts Avenue.

Kat, call me, please. It's about Project Peace. I need your help. You're always on my mind when I'm staying incrementally one step ahead. These past four years, about Mom and Dad. Remember Dad saying they claim to defend us by creating tyrannies. It's all connected. Tonight will be lajb lslhnc

Moist beads gather on Kat's forehead. Suzy's message seems out of character. Kat's lips move silently, reading it again, repeating the sentences. What does she mean by "incrementally ahead"?

What's up, Suzy? You're not one to be confused.

Project Peace has been all over the media. It's the slogan used for an agreement being negotiated called the Coalition for Peace and Security, or CPS. It's aimed at securing energy supplies, with the United States, China, and Russia as the big players. A lot of Kat's embassy break-ins have had to do with CPS.

The cab's on M Street, about to cross Rock Creek into Georgetown. She tells it to stop, gets out, starts walking toward her apartment, dials Suzy's number, and gets an answering machine.

"It's Kat," she says. "Just after six in the morning, Washington time."

Back in her apartment, she tries again. Three rings and it picks up, a man's voice. Kat says, "I'm sorry, I got the wrong number."

"Maybe you haven't. That you, Kat?"

"Yeah, who's . . . ?" Then she recognizes the voice. "Nate?"

"Yeah, it's me."

Nate Sayer used to work for her father. After her father died, Nate got himself a job with the State Department and ended up in the U.S. embassy in London. She and Suzy have never liked him.

"What are you doing with Suzy's cell?"

"I'm taking care of it. It was ringing and—"

"No, stop. Where's my sister?"

"She's not here."

"Where is she?"

"Suzy . . . There's been an accident, Kat. Your sister . . . she's dead."

"Accident? What sort of accident?" Kat's looking at a picture by her bed of the four of them, Mom, Dad, Suzy, and little Kat. Nate's telling her she's the only one left alive.

"We're still trying to find out—"

"No, Nate. Tell me everything. What sort of accident?"

"We've only just heard ourselves. I'm sorry, Kat, I really am."

"Please, Nate," says Kat, trying to temper her voice. "Just tell me."

"Nancy and I are here for you," he says. "We feel for you, Kat. Believe me, we do."

Kat breathes out slowly. "Just tell me—"

"Are you at your landline?" Sayer cuts in. "We'll call as soon as we—"

"Was she hit by a car? Was it a drive-by shooting? How did it happen? Young, healthy women don't just die."

"We don't know." His voice hardens. "We didn't even know she was in London. She was living under a false name."

"But you have her phone?"

"We're in her apartment, Kat."

"How could you, if you didn't even know where she lived?"

Sayer speaks softly and precisely. "The embassy was notified of the death of a U.S. citizen. I said I would handle it. The victim's name was Charlotte Thomas. She turned out to be Suzy. Nancy and I have known Suzy since she was a baby. She's your only sister. Why don't you give us all some time to be sad and confused?"

Kat looks away from the photograph. Tears have made her face wet, and she can't see clearly. But looking away isn't enough. She picks up the photo frame and throws it against the wall.

"What's that?" asks Sayer. "Are you all alone there?"

"I'm fine." Broken glass is scattered across the floor, some as far as the bathroom. "I'm coming over."

"No. Stay where you are. I'll have Nancy call you. You need your strength for later. We'll come there. We'll bring Suzy back with us."

FIVE

Saturday, 9:17 p.m., British Summer Time

Breathing in the smell of aviation fuel, Kat shuffles off the plane onto the Jetway. Rain has leaked through, and she gets a bite of the wind. It's supposed to be summer in England; a chill cuts through her.

She downloaded the latest entry key for Suzy's apartment and printed out the bar code. She got Cage to get her a new, encrypted phone with a six-digit tag code in which the figures change randomly every thirty seconds. Cage drove her to Dulles.

Inside the terminal, Kat used it to call Vendetta, let him know the new number. When she told him Suzy was dead and that she was going to London, he didn't speak for a while, then said, "You're doing the right thing. If a person like you stays still at a time like this, you'll end up dying, too."

"Thanks, M," she said.

She joins the line for immigration control, with its choice of a fingerprint or iris scan ID check. One notice warns VISITORS MAY BE SELECTED FOR RANDOM BODY SCREENING.

Another says INFORMATION DERIVED FROM DNA SAMPLES MAY BE EXCHANGED BE-TWEEN SIGNATORY GOVERNMENTS AS AN EXEMPTION FROM THE DATA PROTECTION ACT.

"Kat! Kathleen Polinski. Over here." The voice is familiar—from way back in her past. And she should have expected it.

Nancy Sayer, in an olive green woolen suit, is flapping a white handkerchief at Kat to attract her attention. Nancy is Kat's godmother and the wife of Nate Sayer. With Nancy, the world is always fine, and anything bad can be turned to good. Nancy is Kat's height, with grayish blond hair tied sensibly back, and skin stretched tight across her face, making her cheekbones jut out like polished wood.

An immigration official unclips the cordon rope, asking Kat to step out of the line.

Nancy touches Kat's cheek. "You poor, poor child," she says. They embrace, and Kat remembers the smell of her godmother from childhood.

Kat holds Nancy until she's managed to fight off tears. She pushes herself away. The two women stand back from each other, and Nancy picks up the question in Kat's eyes. She nods sadly. "I'm so sorry, Kat. First your parents, now this."

"Is it true? Really?"

Nancy's eyes glisten. "It's true."

"But how? What happened?"

"I don't exactly know. Nate's been with the police."

"But what's he told you? I mean—"

"Best to wait." Nancy squeezes her hand and keeps holding it.

"Okay," Kat says, her grief fading into anger. She pulls away and looks back at the immigration line.

"Don't worry about that," Nancy says. "Nate fixed it . . . customs, immigration. There's a car."

"I don't want Nate—"

"That's fine," Nancy says quickly. "We'll just go ourselves."

"What I need to do," she says, "is get to Suzy's apartment."

Suzy's place is a stunning converted boathouse, with floor-to-ceiling windows and a terrace on the upper floor, overlooking the river. The building is set back from a narrow street separating the boathouse from the river. The front door leads into a gym and garage on the ground floor, where Suzy kept a silver Mercedes coupé. Past that, another door opens to a staircase, which leads up to the living area.

By the time Kat and Nancy get there, the wind has dropped. The moon hangs in a sky about to go dark from the long twilight. The night's become warm.

"Just think—Suzy was here all this time without letting us know," says Nancy, looking around her.

Nancy sits at the dining table by the big window to let Kat wander the apartment alone. The bedroom is airy, light, and textured, with a patterned quilt of blue cartoon elephants almost exactly as Kat remembers Suzy having at home. On the dressing table is a collection of ornamental pigs and a tiny stand-up chest of drawers, which Kat opens to find Suzy's jewelry. Some she recognizes, like their mother's butterfly brooch, so over-the-top with clashing colors that neither of them would wear it.

Suzy had made the second bedroom into her office, complete with shelves of books, a desktop computer, and a view of a tiny patio garden and wall to the house next door.

Kat shouts down to Nancy, "I'm taking a shower, okay?"

"I'll fix something."

"Coffee's fine."

Nancy's not telling her anything. Kat's pushed and gotten nowhere. So she's talking to keep things calm, as if nothing's happened.

Kat draws the curtain across the bathtub and steps in to take a shower. Suzy's been using a scented soap, suds dried on it, with a watermark on the wall next to the tray. The towel, decorated with elephants, had been hurriedly hung over the rail, creased and untidy.

Kat lets water run down her face, closes her eyes, and sees a static image of the man trying to kill her in the corridor of the Kazakh embassy.

Breath becomes tight in her throat. Her knees weaken. She's been expecting a physical reaction at some point, but the surge of it, only now, surprises her.

She opens her eyes, tilts her head back, and closes them again, only to be hit by another image. Two women, her age, are at work on a Friday evening. Someone with a gun tells them to move over to the wall and stand underneath a picture advertising vacations. Suddenly, they know they are going to die. But they obey, because every second they're alive is a chance. They hold hands. The next person who sees them is Kat, but by then they've slid down the wall, leaving only blood spatters to show where they stood.

Water hits the plastic shower curtain. The light coming through it is dim and distorted. She can't see or hear properly. She leans against the shower wall, turns off the water, steadies her breathing, draws back the curtain, gets out of the bathtub, slips on the floor tiles, finds her balance, snatches the towel off the rail, and wraps it around herself.

Two pairs of Suzy's sandals, one made of straw from Hawaii and one rubber, lie haphazardly between the bathroom door and the shower. A red T-shirt, blue jeans, and a pair of white panties are draped over the back of a chair in the bedroom.

Through the window, the moonlight splays across the river. Kat lets down the blind, bringing a chill to the room, and feels goose bumps rise, as if something cold, like a knife blade, is being drawn across her shoulders.

"Kat, you okay?" Nancy calls softly with a tap on the door.

"Fine," says Kat. She turns toward the bathroom again and sees a photograph of Suzy with a bunch of people outside Buckingham Palace, maybe a dozen faces, none of which she knows.

She checks CNN on her cell phone, then *The Washington Post.* There's nothing on the Kazakh embassy. Cage has done his job.

Kat's carry-on bag is on the bed. She flips it open, puts on a white top, jeans, and a fresh pair of socks, and opens the door to the aroma of freshly brewed coffee coming up from downstairs. When she's halfway down the staircase, she also picks up the sweetish smell of dying flowers.

Nancy is back at the table by the window, pushing down the plunger of a pot of coffee. "You're looking just fine," she says.

"The police—" Kat begins.

"It's okay. They've been here," says Nancy, as if she was talking about an electrician coming to fix a lightbulb. "Nate knew you'd want to come here first, so he made sure they did everything they needed already."

Kat sees the flowers in a vase on the floor next to a fireplace. They're orchids, as she'd expected; Suzy's favorites. She takes the vase, dumps its dirty water down the kitchen sink, lifts the trash can lid, and drops the orchids inside.

Nancy stays exactly where she is with her coffee. "Nate's waiting at the hospital," she says.

"Morgue, you mean?"

"Suzy's actually in the hospital mortuary. When you're done there, come back and spend the night with us. I have a bed made up and . . ." Kat's godmother's voice trails off.

Kat is standing across the table from her. "You know, Aunt Nance," she says, "I really don't want to deal with Uncle Nate right now. You know how . . . ," she hesitates, ". . . sometimes we don't exactly see eye to eye on things."

"I know," says Nancy. "It's tough. Tough on everyone."

As a child, whenever Kat looked into the face of her godmother, she saw happiness, far more than in her own mother. Kat looks at Nancy and realizes she's hoping that something like that will come back.

"Nate's difficult, but he's a good man." Nancy tries on a smile. "You need good people with you right now."

"I just want to be with Suzy by myself," says Kat.

"I know, and Nate knows," says Nancy. "That's why he managed to get her body back to London."

"Back? From where?"

SIX

———◇———

Nate Sayer stands behind a gurney. On it lies a body draped in a white sheet. Kat stops in the doorway of the mortuary. They look at each other in silence.

Sayer is solid, his hair still thick. He's in a green cotton shirt, a polo, arms bulging through the sleeves. He must have started lifting weights, except his stomach shows he's losing the battle. Stocky, broad-shouldered, he runs his hands through his thick gray hair. He's wearing dark, military-style pants, immaculately pressed.

He gives a half wave, moves toward her, arms out to embrace, smile awkward. All Kat's body language says *don't touch*. "Hi, Nate," she says.

"Kat, I don't know what to say . . ." His arms drop to his sides.

"Where are the police?" she asks. "And why are you here?"

"They're coming." He points his finger down the corridor behind her. "They're getting the paperwork ready. As her sister, you'll have to sign some papers."

Kat's eyes search the room. On the wall, Suzy's dental X-rays hang slightly askew in a light box. She swallows, takes a few steps inside, lets the door swing shut behind her. Sayer's distorted reflection shines out of a line of cold body boxes on the back wall.

"How'd she die?"

"The police will fill you in."

She draws in a breath, swallows again. The air's laden with chemicals, wetness, the brutality and stench of a mortuary.

"It is Suzy, right? No mistake?"

Sayer nods. "I've checked, and I've known you both since you were born."

Kat touches Sayer's elbow. "Nate, before the police come, can I please have a minute alone with her?"

"This isn't a good place to be alone."

"I'm better like that."

Sayer knits his brow.

"I don't ask many favors," presses Kat.

"Okay," he says softly. "If you need me, I'll be out there with Nancy."

She watches him head down the corridor. Nancy appears, takes her husband's arm, and leads him out of Kat's view.

For the briefest of moments, Kat lets herself imagine that they've screwed up Suzy's ID and that, in a last-minute miracle, she'll discover they've got the wrong person altogether.

Eyes closed, she pulls down the sheet, not just a bit, but the whole thing in one long movement, bunching it up in her hand, holding the soft cotton to her face.

People talk about looking peaceful in death, and someone's clearly prepared Suzy, because she looks just like that. Her blood-drained face looks up at Kat, her eyes dull blue and empty, her lips slightly apart. She must have just had her hair done, short, blond, slightly spiked, with dark lowlights in it.

Kat could have been looking down at her own dead face. Ten years might have separated them, but Kat and Suzy looked so alike that people got them mixed up all the time. As she turned from her twenties to thirties, Suzy was flattered by being mistaken for her kid sister. Kat tries to imagine her sister's face as far back as she can, maybe twenty years ago, but still as it always was—gentle, secure, looking out for her little sister.

Suzy's right leg is slightly bent, with a plastic toe tag hanging off her big toe. Kat spots needle marks in her neck and groin, where they've taken out the blood. Her left leg is ramrod straight, as are her arms.

She picks up Suzy's right hand and feels the coldness of the fingers against her cheek. There's a patch of charred skin on the shoulder. The fingers are curled like crab claws. On her left hand, the ring finger is doubled back on itself, broken.

The ring, which Suzy rarely took off, is missing. It was their mom's, and Suzy had worn it since their mother died.

Since a shoulder burn and broken finger don't kill a person, Kat looks away and back again, hoping she'll see something different. She doesn't.

Kat brushes the hand, trying to sense something of Suzy. She wants to pray, recite a poem, or cry. But she's too angry and confused for anything to come. She tucks Suzy's hand next to the cold skin of her thigh and takes a step to kiss her on the forehead.

As she leans over, she sees a tiny, dark red mark on her sister's brow that someone's tried to hide with makeup. There's dried blood in the corner of one eye.

Kat touches it gently and is about to lift up Suzy's head when she lets out a scream and steps back. The back of Suzy's skull has been blown away. Nothing's there, just jagged, blood-dark edges of bone. Suzy's face, propped up by hospital bedding, stares at the ceiling like an empty mask.

SEVEN

◇

Through the thunder of blood in her ears, Kat hears the door open.

"You okay, Miss Polinski?" It's the voice of someone English, older than Sayer.

"Are you the police?" she says, her back to him.

Footsteps come up beside the gurney. She sees a hand picking the sheet up off the floor.

"Wait," snaps Kat. "Can you just back off for a few minutes?"

"It's okay . . . I'm sorry." A different voice, not Sayer's, either. It's younger, cultured, somewhere between Boston and an ancient part of Europe.

She looks up at the wall of stainless steel and, in the reflection, makes out a tall figure, thirties, dark hair but fair complexion, and after that the image gets distorted. Beside him is an older man in a light raincoat, with sandy gray hair. Behind them both is Sayer. Her eyes return to her sister's body.

"I am Assistant Commissioner Stephen Cranley from the London Metropolitan Police," says the older man softly. "With me is Detective Inspector Max Grachev. And you know Nate Sayer from the U.S. embassy."

Kat takes back the sheet and folds it. She wants Suzy to stay uncovered. She turns to face them. They're standing back, giving her space.

Under his raincoat, Cranley's wearing a dark uniform. He has eyes that could silence a room. The last time she saw such authority in a face—zero doubt, but no arrogance, either—was in her own father's.

Max Grachev looks less assured but better dressed, with a jacket, tie, and showing just enough cuffs to reveal inscribed cuff links. He's about the same age as Suzy, a shade over six feet, with a high forehead created by a receding hairline, and unsteady brown eyes, absorbing and reacting all the time.

"My sister was shot," says Kat flatly, looking at Cranley. "It wasn't an accident."

"Yes. She was murdered," says Cranley. "Anything at all you have that might help us—"

Kat cuts in, "How does Suzy rate an assistant commissioner handling her murder?"

"It's possible your sister fell victim to a wider criminal operation," Cranley answers. "Charlotte Thomas, or Suzy Polinski as we now know she is, worked closely on setting up the Coalition for Peace and Security. As an international lawyer, her job involved standardizing legislation surrounding the CPS." He glances across to Grachev. "There are loose ends. Why did she work under a false name? Why did she not let the U.S. embassy know she was in London?"

Cranley's sharp blue eyes do not move from Kat as he asks each question. "Did she run afoul of an interest group that will lose out when the CPS comes into force? If so, did they originate here, in Britain, or—more likely—somewhere else?"

He glances over to Grachev. "This is why I've asked D.I. Grachev to help with the investigation. He's on loan to us from a special criminal intelligence division in Moscow with expertise in international organized crime."

Grachev points to the sheet, then to Suzy's body. "Perhaps we should?"

His voice with its blend of Europe is gentle, like her grandmother's. Kat lets him take one end, and together they drape the sheet over Suzy's body, leaving the face uncovered. "Would you like to talk here, or—"

"Here's fine," says Kat.

Grachev nods. Cranley's hand is on the door. "I have some paperwork to go over with Mr. Sayer," he says. "We'll be down the corridor."

Kat says nothing. Cranley and Sayer leave. Grachev moves around to the other side of the gurney so it's between them.

"She was shot by a single, very powerful, high-velocity round, which made a tiny incision in her forehead and destroyed her skull on exit," he says, shifting his head slightly, settling his eyes on Suzy's face. "We did some preliminary tests to check if she'd been sexually assaulted. She hadn't been."

Kat stays silent.

"We haven't found the killer and have no clues as to who he or she might be. There's also the complication of her false identity. In the United States, she was Suzanne Anne Polinski. In Britain, she was Charlotte Elizabeth Thomas."

He brushes down the sheet over the body, makes sure it's hanging right.

"When was she killed?"

"Friday evening around 9:30. We're still talking to—"

"9:30 British time?"

"That's right."

Kat performs a mental calculation. "Then she knew she was in danger."

Grachev's brow creases. "I'm sorry?"

"I got a voice mail and e-mail from her the next morning."

"I don't understand."

"She would have recorded the messages and set them to send then. Maybe in case she wasn't around to do it herself."

He cups his hand around his chin. "What did she say?"

"Like your boss said, it was about the Coalition for Peace and Security. But only a line of the message made it. The rest got cut off."

She studies Grachev, working out how much to tell. Grachev says nothing. He takes his hand from his chin and rests it on the edge of the gurney.

"Where was she killed?" asks Kat.

"She was attending a classical music concert in a village called Snape about a hundred miles northeast of London."

"She was shot in the middle of a concert?"

"During the intermission, she walked from the concert hall along a path that leads down to a river. She was shot there."

"Who was she with?"

"As far as we know, she was alone."

"Why was she there?"

"We don't know, Miss Polinski. There are still many things we are trying to ascertain."

"Yeah, well, Suzy didn't even like classical music."

Grachev eyes Kat sharply. "She didn't?"

"The only music I ever knew Suzy to have was an iPod playlist an old boyfriend put together for her for the car."

"Thank you again." Grachev's an expressive man. Every thought seems to show—in his eyes, his brow, a movement of his hands.

His gaze shifts to the corner near the door, where he's left a briefcase. "Mr. Sayer tells me he and his wife are long-standing family friends."

"His wife—Nancy—she's my godmother."

"That's good, at a time like this."

He draws the sheet over Suzy's face, and Kat doesn't stop him. Grachev walks around the gurney, picks up the briefcase, opens it, and pulls out a padded envelope. "These are some of her things."

Kat takes the envelope, opens it, and looks inside. There are keys, credit cards, photographs, the things any woman carries in a purse.

"Is her ring in here?" She picks up Suzy's left hand from underneath the sheet. "She wore a big ring on this finger. Finger's broken, ring's missing."

"Describe it," says Grachev, bringing a notepad out of his jacket pocket.

"It's big. You wouldn't mistake it," says Kat, determined to be as detailed and accurate as she can. "There's the ring, which is silver, and on top of that is a square, made out of pressed tin. Four tiny diamonds, one on each corner, with lines—they look twisted, like a rope—linking them to a sapphire in the middle; a figure eight, meaning infinity."

"She doesn't look the sort of person to wear—how do you say—ostentatious things," says Grachev. "Her clothes—we're still examining them—they are stylish, but discreet."

"It's a family heirloom," presses Kat. "From Poland. Our granddad gave it to Grandma, who gave it to my mom, who gave it to Suzy. The lid lifted up and underneath it, Suzy kept a picture of the family. Mom, Dad, Suzy, me, and our grandma. That's why she wore it."

"Thank you," says Grachev, writing, then putting his notebook away. He points to the envelope. "But it's not there. I'm sorry."

"But who would want to take a ring?" she says, using the question to stop her eyes from filling up. She moves her hands to her hips and puts an expression of determination on her face. "You don't kill someone like that for a lousy family heirloom."

Grachev clasps his hands in front of him. "If you know of anyone who didn't like your sister, any enemies or—"

"I don't," Kat cuts him off.

Grachev gives her a measured smile. "I understand," he says. "Mr. Sayer said you planned to stay at your sister's apartment tonight."

"That's right."

He takes a sheet of paper from his inside jacket pocket. "Your sister was due to go to this event tomorrow evening," he says, unfolding it and holding it out to her.

It's from the classified-ad section of a magazine. Kat takes one corner, Grachev holds the other. A section is circled. "I'd like to call you about it later," he says, giving her his card. "And this is my number. Any time, twenty-four hours, if you think of anything."

EIGHT

◇

Sunday, 12:32 a.m., BST

They are at the dinner table, just the three of them, in a big room that is both the living and dining room. Kat recognizes furniture and pictures from the Sayers' Georgetown house.

They've kept their Georgetown house on R Street because Nancy likes going back every couple of months. She's not taken by London. The checkpoints are getting worse, and the weather's been unusually hot. The windows are open, but there's no breeze.

"The English and air-conditioning are like the English and showers," says Sayer, wiping sweat off his forehead with his wrist. "They just don't get what they're all about."

On the wall hang photographs of Nate Sayer, on the edges of meetings with important people around the world. John Polinski is in a lot of them; group snapshots at the end of visits with cocoa growers in Africa; in tribal shirts on a Pacific island; bundled up against a below-zero winter in Moscow, when he and Sayer went over to look at working conditions in Soviet factories; another in Russia, hunting out in the wilds, one of their hosts holding up a brace of duck for the camera; and a picture Kat has known ever since she can remember, taken at the fairground in Lancaster, Ohio—one of her dad's arms is around Sayer's shoulders, and he's holding Kat's hand. Kat is barely five years old. It was taken the day he opened the orphanage he'd set up in Lancaster for the kids of migrant workers who'd died or become disabled in factories, quarries, or meatpacking plants. Kat made a lot of friends there.

Sayer used to be her father's chief investigator. Early on in their partnership, Kat's father represented the family of an undocumented Brazilian worker who cut himself during a night shift at a midwestern meatpacking plant and died from blood loss. By posing as a drifter, Sayer infiltrated the plant and came out with pictures of the floors, dark red with cattle blood, of workers unprotected from spiked meat hooks and knives, and stories of illegal workers being injured and killed. They made a good team; Sayer's roughness and arrogance was a foil to John Polinski's idealism.

But neither Kat nor Suzy ever trusted him. Sayer is a man with a chip on his shoulder. While his father was a decorated Vietnam War general, Sayer barely graduated from West Point and only made captain before leaving the army. Nancy was Kat's mom's best friend, and Suzy always said their dad took Sayer on as a favor to Nancy.

When Kat's parents were buried, side by side, almost four years ago to the week, at the cemetery of the United Methodist Church in Great Falls, Virginia, Nate and Nancy sat at the front of the church, acting as family and guardians to Kat and Suzy. They held the show together, Nancy staying with Suzy and Kat. Sayer moved between colleagues, business people, politicians, and family, the other relatives ashen with shock, their eyes glassy, unable to take in what had happened.

Kat pushes her chair back, both hands on her plate, the light salad barely touched.

"Thanks, Aunt Nance," she says. "It was great, but you know . . ."

"I've made a bed up in the guest bedroom for you," Nancy says. "I'll clear the dishes. You and Nate, you have some stuff to go over."

Nancy goes to the kitchen and closes the door. Kat walks to the window.

"Where are we?" she says, her back to Sayer. "Like, is this central London? Uptown? Downtown?"

"As central as it gets," says Sayer.

Suzy's murder lingers between them, unspoken. He has an envelope on the table and is drawing papers from it. "The U.S. embassy's three blocks away. That big road a block from here is Park Lane, and on the other side of that is Hyde Park, which is their equivalent of Central Park. But I prefer it. The English do parks well. The business district, that's about three miles farther east. Theater district is close by, a ten-minute walk."

"So Suzy's place, is it not in the center then?" Kat puts her head outside the window to catch a bit of breeze. She's three floors up. The street below is narrow and pretty empty, not surprising, since it's past midnight.

"Suzy was a little way out," says Sayer, changing Kat's tenses. "This is Zone One. She was in Zone Two. Not far."

"These zones, they're like in Washington?"

"They're based on the transportation zones, but a few years back, after London had bombings, they also became security zones. If they think there's likely to be an attack, they set up checkpoints on the zone boundaries. Britain's not as secure as back home. It's more in the middle of things, so to speak."

"Does that have anything to do with Suzy's murder?" says Kat, coming in from the window and moving over to the table.

Sayer shrugs. "The police believe it may be linked in some way. The signing of the Coalition for Peace and Security is coming up. They call it Project Peace over here. It's divisive. A lot of people don't want it."

It's the same line she'd heard from Cranley. "And Suzy never got in touch with you?"

"Both of you pretty much dropped out of our lives."

"I guess that's true," says Kat.

"We had a Charlotte Thomas registered with the embassy, but I had no idea it was Suzy. She was working for an international law firm, and from what I can make out, her job was to make sure multinational firms met their global obligations under CPS guidelines, the sort of work your dad and I did."

On the table, Sayer separates the documents into three piles, leaves the pen beside them, and steps back. "I know you don't want to, Kat, but you've got to sign these."

Kat folds her fingers behind her head, stretches her back. "My brain's kind of blown right now," she says. "Can't it wait till morning?"

"Best to get it done."

"This whole thing," she says edgily. "It's not about documents, you know. It's about finding who killed Suzy."

He must have caught the anger in her eyes, but went the wrong way about calming it. "Suzy would want you to."

Kat becomes rigid, checks herself, and says nothing.

"This one here says you've identified the body." Sayer walks around the table toward Kat and lays a form in front of her. It has the State Department seal on the top. "This one is the same, but for the British. I said I'd get you to sign it for Detective Inspector Grachev." Kat watches as Sayer places it neatly on top of the first one.

"And this is to release the body for transfer back to the United States. I can get these processed tomorrow. Nancy and I will come back with you and Suzy's body on Monday."

Kat stares at the forms. She doesn't reply. She leans on the table, splaying her fingers. "Suzy's okay where she is," she says at last. "As cold rooms go, it looks fine."

Sayer shakes his head. "It's not that simple."

"Not that simple that you can send the body of a murder victim back before the investigation's even begun?"

Sayer shifts his feet, rubs his eyes with the heels of his hands, then gathers up the papers. "Maybe you're right. Maybe we should do this in the morning."

Kat picks up her bag off a chair by the door and walks out of the living room into the hallway. Sayer reaches for her elbow. "Kat, you can't go back to Suzy's tonight."

"I'm going," says Kat, knocking his hand away.

"Best you stay with us," insists Sayer.

The door to the kitchen opens. Nancy appears, drying her hands on a dishcloth.

"If she wants to go, let her." Nancy hands the cloth to Sayer and fumbles under her apron for something in her pocket. "I'll see you downstairs and put you in a cab."

The old elevator, with its polished metal gate and arrival bell, takes forever to come up. As they wait, Nancy says, "If they ask you at a checkpoint, show your passport and entry stamp." She presses money into Kat's hand.

Nancy turns to leave as the elevator arrives, but Kat holds the door.

"Wait," Kat says. "Aunt Nance, can we go for a walk somewhere?"

NINE

———————◇———————

Streetlights show the dampness on the trees. Low mist is settling in the garden square across the street, and even past one in the morning, the English summer air is humid. They are in a street that slopes down to a side road of yellow and white painted houses behind clean black metal fences, with garbage bags dumped on the sidewalk, bicycles chained to lampposts, and expensive cars at meters.

Nancy leads because she knows Kat wants to talk. They walk silently for a few minutes, then onto a cobbled street with ethnic restaurants, tables outside, sounds of laughter, even after one in the morning. The night heat creates a bead of sweat on Kat's upper lip. The walk calms her.

"There was a time you called me when I didn't call you back," says Kat. "It was the day I saw Suzy off at Dulles. The cab dropped me back at Olive Street. You'd left a message on my answering machine, but I couldn't face talking to anyone. I didn't call. Instead, I locked the apartment and kept walking, walking, and walking until I got to a place called Dix Street. Same city, but worlds away from Georgetown."

They wait for the light to change, then cross the road to a square, where sparkling lamps decorate the trees in a small garden in front of them.

"You want to know what Dix Street is like? Imagine the filthiest, most run-down neighborhood, a place breeding crime, breeding drugs, breeding despair—and I mean *breeding*, because no one can ever get rid of it. You can't kill it, you can only let it multiply, and try and control it. But that's never going to work, because the place reflects the souls of the people who live there. They like it. They get wired up by it because it's their mirror. I don't know if I'm explaining myself, Aunt Nance, but I've never told this to someone who knows me as well as you.

"I was Kat Polinski, a spoiled little rich kid with a private education and a nice wardrobe, smart as hell, raised next door to you in a neighborhood wealthy like where we are now, and I rented a room in a house on Dix Street because I thought it helped me know how I really felt after Mom and Dad's death."

Kat runs her fingers backward along the garden railings and lets them hurt her knuckles. "The reason I'm telling you is because I was living with a black guy there, a small-time gangster who called himself Mercedes Vendetta."

She stops to take Nancy's hands, and when she looks into her face, she sees something from way back in her childhood that makes her feel good.

"You know, to this day, when I'm backed into a corner, I find myself talking like Mercedes, grinding my sentences, like they do on Dix Street. It's self-protection, I guess."

"I understand," says Nancy. Beneath her makeup and nip and tuck, Nancy's age shows, and there's strain, too, from her long, childless marriage to Nate, and Kat wonders if Nancy knows about Nate as Kat does.

"Mercedes always said that when other people have the power, you have to run with it. He said, 'Don't stop. You just go with it till you got the momentum to escape.'"

Nancy says nothing, but her expression tells Kat she wants her to continue.

"I feel now, Aunt Nance, with Suzy, that everyone else has the power. But I'm not stopping, and I'm not walking away. I can't just go back with you and Nate and bury her."

Kat falls quiet and resumes the walk.

"I was the only white person around the Dix Street area. But they got to know me, some of them even liked me, though they didn't know what I was, and curiosity's not a popular habit in a place like that.

"I made a good living as a criminal. I ran a whole operation from Dix

Street. Wrote software. Set up proxy IP addresses all over the world—Toronto, Jakarta, the Isle of Man. Dozens of them. I sold firewalls, then broke through them. Set up my own satellite antenna. I was good, Nance. I made a lot of money, which I didn't need, because I had Dad's trust fund.

"Some days I'd catch a cab back to Olive Street, call Suzy, tell her about my law school classes, have Starbucks cappuccino, then head back to Dix Street. I didn't feel bad about my double life. I mean, Suzy was living as Charlotte Thomas. If she could do it, why couldn't I?"

They shift to single file to make way for two men in tuxedos talking loudly and smoking cigars, Kat inhaling the smoke as they pass, enjoying it.

"One afternoon Mercedes and I were in bed," she says. "The closet door was open with a big full-length mirror on it. I had my head turned to one side, watching us in the mirror."

She hesitates and consciously folds her arms. "Is this okay, you know, I've never talked about these things with you before?"

Nancy replies with a tight laugh. "Don't worry about me. I'm fine with racy stories."

"Mercedes and I, we both had good, firm bodies; me white, him black, him tall, me five-foot-four; me on top; his hands on my waist, making me feel real good. Mercedes is good in bed; nothing wrong with him in that department. Only up here," Kat taps her head, "he's a little unhinged in the mind, and I was thinking that our reflection in the mirror was more real than us actually having sex on the bed. You know why? Because I was so angry. I was filled with it. Anger and self-loathing, like I wanted to set fire to myself and burn it all away, because deep down, I didn't like what I was doing with my Mercedes and my life, even though I was enjoying the moment.

"The thing is, Nance, I went to Dix Street because of what happened to Mom and Dad. I don't want to end up there again. You know? And it makes me frightened that Suzy's murder might send me back there again."

"I won't let it happen," says Nancy.

They walk back to Nancy's apartment in silence. When they get to the door, Nancy has her keys out, but she says, "You want to stay with us, or still go back to Suzy's place?"

"Suzy's place," says Kat.

Nancy hugs her. "Thank you for being truthful with me," she says. "I know you too well, Kathleen Jane Polinski. I know you need your space; that you handle bad times best by being alone. Your mother had high spirits and willfulness, just like you. She put so much good into people's lives, mine included. She showed me a lot of sunshine, Kat, and you have many of her qualities. More than Suzy had. Suzy was a lawyer like your father, seeing all sides of an argument and working out all the details. You're too impatient for that. Not to say that's wrong. You go ahead and listen to that advice from Mercedes, and keep moving, but do it with Nate. I know you sometimes shoot sparks off each other, but deep down, my husband is a good man, and he has your best interests at heart."

Kat kisses Nancy on the cheek. "Thanks, Aunt Nance," she says, and disappears into the night.

TEN

—————◇—————

Kat stays on the narrow street outside Suzy's front door, watching the cab's taillights disappear. She sees a policeman, arms resting on the river wall, his eyes following the moonlight along the river current. A twist of summer fog comes up from the river.

As she steps into the small front courtyard, two motion-operated lights rigged onto the roof terrace come on, startling her before she realizes what they are. Straight in front of her is the garage door with a side door on the right to let her in. She rifles through her bag to find the key and takes a while to get it working. Suzy's Mercedes coupé sits inside, to the left of a path of red terra-cotta tiles leading to steps up to the apartment.

She knocks the car's side mirror as she passes, pauses to put it back in place, then pats the hood above the headlight and says out loud, "Very nice, Suzy girl. You must have been doing well for yourself."

Like most modern apartments, Suzy's has a two-tier entry system; fingerprint ID for herself and a rotational bar code that she can use for the housekeeper or friends. Kat runs her bar code under the scanner, and the door clicks open.

Inside, she heads straight for Suzy's bedroom, lies on the bed, and calls Cage.

"Where've you been?" he says. "I've been worried sick."

"It's been busy. But not nice."

"I'm going to have to call you back—on the landline."

A simple statement telling Kat a boatload: the cell phone's compromised, and people can listen in.

The Federal Containment Agency, for which Kat and Cage work, was created in 1958, during the Cold War, after the Soviet Union threatened to move into West Germany. Technically, it was run by the State Department. But, after 9/11, as the intelligence community was reorganized, the FCA was brought under the umbrella of the Department of Homeland Security. Its specific task is to keep watch on diplomats from hostile governments who are stationed in the United States. Because of its resources, Cage can encrypt the call to Suzy's landline by pressing a few buttons on his own cell phone.

The phone rings within forty seconds.

"Nate wants me out of here with my sister on Monday morning," says Kat. "Suzy's lying in a morgue with her skull shot out. The police say they have no idea who did it, yet they're happy to send the body thousands of miles away to another country."

"I'll make some calls," says Cage gently. "You should rest up. There are a couple of things I need to check out in the meantime."

"What 'couple of things'?"

"Hunches."

"No. Not just hunches. Speak to me, goddamn it."

"Fine," Cage shoots back at her. "Like you said, it's not making sense. An American citizen gets murdered in London, which we're told is one of the most secure cities in Europe—"

"Suzy didn't die in London. It happened a hundred miles northeast."

"Okay, fine, good," says Cage patiently. "But it's a murder, and have you seen anything in the press about it? Isn't it a story the press would cover?"

"Five diplomats get gunned down in the Kazakh embassy," snaps Kat. "Two corpses left outside. Have you seen anything in the press about *that*?"

"I'll call you in a few hours," he says.

———◇———

Kat lines up Suzy's cards: frequent-flier card, credit cards, driver's license, a toll road receipt for passing into a zone called East Anglia. They are all in the name of Charlotte Thomas. But there's nothing really personal—no clothes, no tissues, no tampons, no makeup, no nail polish.

Next to them she places the torn page Grachev gave her with the classified advertisement from a magazine called *New Statesman.*

BRITAIN and PROJECT PEACE

Will Project Peace become Britain's written constitution? Will it bring peace? Who will lose from it? Who will gain? Speakers include Dr. Christopher North for the government, and Frank Hutton for the opposition. Audience participation will challenge ideas both supporting and opposing the creation of the Coalition for Peace and Security and Britain's policy towards it.

Hosted by International Policy Focus.

Free entry. *Linton Community Hall, Prince of Wales Drive, London, SW11 4BH*

A note written next to the advertisement says, "Hope to see you there, Liz xxx."

She dials the number on Grachev's card. He picks up immediately. "Are you back?" he says. "I'll come round."

His clothes are rumpled. There's stubble on his face. His shoes are scuffed. Grachev's been working and still is. He walks in without curiosity, because he knows Suzy's apartment. It's part of the investigation. He goes across to the table and points at the magazine advertisement.

"Only two types of people will go to this lecture," he says. "Those who support Project Peace . . ." He breaks off. "Sorry, what do you know about Project Peace?"

"You tell me," says Kat.

"Project Peace is what the British press call the Coalition for Peace and Security. It's a deal to make sure Russia doesn't play politics with its energy supplies. Russia's the big hitter. The United States, China, and others need what it's got. This lecture is part of a campaign to sell Project Peace to the public. The people who'll be there are either big supporters or big opponents."

His finger hovers over the clipping. "So who's Liz, and why is she meeting Suzy there?"

Kat doesn't answer.

Grachev turns his eyes directly to her. "She'll be looking for Suzy. You look enough like your sister for her to take a second glance. Then tell her who you are, and see what happens."

"Where will you be?"

He pulls a set of car keys from his pocket.

"Take Suzy's Mercedes. Liz might recognize it. If she suggests a coffee, something, do it."

"Where will you be?" repeats Kat.

"Watching. But if we go into the hall itself, she might not show up."

"Why?"

"And don't use Suzy's vehicle navigation system," he says, ignoring her question and gesturing toward a bookcase by the side of the fireplace. "There's a street map in there. Don't use your cell phone in the car." He pauses. "Will you go?"

"Yes." Kat stops asking things. She's not making conditions.

"Okay."

When Grachev leaves, Kat turns off the light and goes to the terrace window. He's driving alone, an Audi sedan. The taillights are melting into the river fog when Cage calls.

"There's a pissing contest going on," he says. "The British want to keep Suzy's body for the investigation. We want it back."

"Why?"

"I'm checking."

Kat asks Cage to check out Max Grachev. She tells him about the lecture.

"Go," says Cage. "But keep it from Nate Sayer."

ELEVEN

—◇—

Sunday, 7:22 p.m., BST

Kat's in Suzy's Mercedes with the satellite navigation turned off, as Grachev instructed. She takes a few wrong turns, and by the time she gets there, the lecture's been going on for almost an hour.

The Linton Community Hall is a corner warehouse across the river, butting onto a wide road with a dark, red-brick apartment block on one side and a park on the other.

In the foyer, Kat hands over the driver's license of Charlotte Thomas to a woman with spiked red hair in her early twenties, who swipes it. A machine prints out a CHARLOTTE THOMAS badge like an airline boarding pass.

"First floor, if you can get in," the woman says, returning the card.

Kat walks across the entrance hall. The door in front is locked. She looks back. The woman's watching a soccer match on TV.

"Where exactly?" she asks.

The woman points toward the staircase. "This is the ground floor," she says, irritation in her voice. "So up the stairs would be the first floor, wouldn't it?"

Kat climbs up stripped-wood stairs and comes to a spacious landing. To her left are two open windows that lead to a balcony. Straight ahead is a set of double doors, ajar. Kat squeezes through.

The room is crammed, big windows thrown open to the evening, doing nothing to cool the heat of so many bodies.

". . . forfeiting powers which any nation-state should hold," says a young, blond man sitting at a trestle table on the stage. The nameplate in front of him says FRANK HUTTON, OPPOSED. "The big issues will no longer be decided by us," he says.

A murmur of disapproval spreads through the room. A man next to Kat fans his face with a leaflet. On the front of it, there's a photograph showing the other speaker, Dr. Christopher North. North's wearing sagging beige pants and a crumpled shirt with a loosened tie, his jacket over the back of the chair.

In between North and Hutton is Jane Thompson, using a pen held between her fingers like a military baton to pick members of the audience for questions.

"Rubbish," shouts a heckler from the front. Hutton cups his chin in his hands and looks down, an expression of tedium on his face.

"They'll get away with it," mutters the man next to Kat. He sees Kat's looking at the leaflet. "Have a read," he says. "Biggest load of bullshit I've seen for a long time."

Kat takes it. "Dr. Christopher North," it says. "Author of *Project Peace— 24 Great Ways for Our World to Move Safely Forward.*"

Jane Thompson's voice carries through the hall. "Chris and Frank will take last questions. . . . This lady has been waiting for some time."

"She's a plant," says the man. His name tag says Tim Prescott.

The woman speaks in a heavy dialect. "So what you're saying, Mr. Hutton, is that if we sign up to this deal, we'll lose control of our destiny as a country, and what you're saying, Dr. North, is that if we do, then there'll be no more wars, we can live in peace, and they'll take the checkpoints down. Can you both say if I got your viewpoints right or not?"

Christopher North is on his feet, clasped hands rubbing in front of him, fired up with enthusiasm.

"Anyone who says there will be no more wars is a fool. But each of us knows that the causes of war are disagreements between powers, and from Pearl Harbor to Iraq, energy supplies have been the cause. Any agreement between foreign governments on this issue must be a step toward stopping conflict."

Applause thunders around the hall. Prescott peers at Kat's badge. "What do you think, Charlotte?"

"Really interesting," says Kat, giving the leaflet back to him, eyes hunting for a woman who'd be looking for Suzy.

"You're from the States?"

"Canada," says Kat. "We share the royal family."

From the front of the hall, a sharp female voice cuts through. "I would like to speak."

"Time's up," says Jane Thompson hurriedly, collating papers. "I'm sorry, but it's impossible to give time to everyone."

"No," says the woman. "I lost my son in the Thames River boat bombing. If this debate is about ending terror, I think I have a right."

"Another plant," mutters Prescott. "Terror victims have a big voice here."

"Of course," says Jane Thompson. "Go ahead."

"When the bombings first began in London, we heard a lot of talk about how if we hadn't gone into Iraq, we wouldn't have been bombed," says the speaker. Her voice is cultured and precise, the delivery practiced.

"In the months after Jason was murdered, I listened to it, but couldn't think about anything except losing him. It was so sudden; so random; so cruel."

A shuffling begins throughout the room. Kat sees the speaker now, a gauntly thin figure, could be thirty, could be fifty, blond hair cut to the shoulders, faded jeans, sneakers, and a red cotton tank top.

Prescott's attention is fixed on her. She pushes through the crowd toward the steps. Security guards in jeans, black T-shirts, and yellow armbands do nothing. She climbs up on stage and embraces North. "This is the man who knows how to keep families safe," she shouts, taking a tissue from her jeans.

"I'm sorry, I'm sorry," she says. "Sometimes, it just gets too much. If any of you had lost a son like I did, you'd understand what I am saying."

Jane Thompson is at her side, hand gently on her elbow, then embracing her.

"You're wrong," says Prescott loudly, breaking the sudden silence. He rips the leaflet in two and drops it on the floor.

"The session is closed," shouts Jane Thompson, her voice away from a microphone, and faint.

"No," yells back Prescott. "It's not closed as long as there are people here who want to listen." He pulls a chair toward him and stands on it. "I lost my wife, my son, and my daughter in the Oxford Street bombing. Who here will challenge me to shut up?"

The audience is turning toward him, their backs to the speakers on the stage.

"Oh, yes," says Prescott. "Anyone can play the victim card, but that does not make for sensible thinking. So I'll tell you something."

Guards move along the walls of the room toward Prescott. Jane Thompson steps away from the woman on stage.

"The woman who just spoke is Nicola Butterfield. Check her out. Her husband is an executive with the ACR Corporation, which stands to earn millions in share options once Project Peace is signed into law."

"*Enough.*" A guard's voice comes over the public-address system.

"Contracts worth billions of pounds will be issued without any of us knowing what the money is being spent on and why," continues Prescott.

Another guard kicks the chair out from under him. Three men frog-march Prescott from the room.

People press against Kat. She squeezes through to get deeper into the room. North is on stage, shaking his head, talking to Nicola Butterfield. Frank Hutton and Jane Thompson have disappeared.

Kat edges toward the side of the room. She hears different languages and accents. Five-foot-four isn't a good height for finding people in a crowd.

"Charlotte, great to see you here."

She's face-to-face with a black V-neck T-shirt, big mouth, and smile. So close, Kat takes in a breath of aftershave.

"That was dreadful, don't you agree? How could he make such accusations? Thank God they got rid of him."

"Yeah, really bad," agrees Kat, hand out, grasping his for a second. "I've got to catch a friend over there."

She keeps pushing through. She spots a ledge, six inches up from the floor, running beneath big windows. People are clustering there to get cooler. The sky outside is a deep blue.

Kat can imagine Suzy among these people—young, educated, international, and political, out to change the world.

Her shoulder is bumped by a kid with a face pockmarked from pimples. He barely notices her and keeps edging forward. Kat's within arm's reach of the wall. She wants to get up on the ledge so that Liz can see her.

"Excuse me," says Kat, smiling and pushing. "I have to get up here." Hand on the window frame, she pulls herself onto the ledge and gets a better look at how the people are mixing, those alone, those leaving, those flirting, those with the weight of the world on their shoulders.

"Charlotte?" It's a woman's voice. Kat steadies herself and turns, catches sight of a tall young woman, thin as a whip, with a red hooded T-shirt, moving away. Her hair is a mess, like she's gone for a saltwater swim and let it dry without combing it.

Kat jumps down. The woman has seen Kat, seen she's not Charlotte, and is moving away across the room, not looking back. Kat pushes through, catches up, and taps her on the shoulder. Her name tag says Liz Luxton. Her face is long, high cheekbones, high forehead; lots of brain. She checks Kat's name tag, looks up at her. Liz's eyes move separately from each other and can't keep still.

"S-sorry, I thought you were someone else," she says with a slight stutter.

She turns away, and Kat reaches out to grab her shoulder. "I'm Charlotte's sister," she says.

Liz shakes her shoulder free.

"I'm Kat," she says softly. "She might have mentioned me."

Liz shakes her head. It's not a no, though. Her eyes bob awkwardly. Her face isn't hostile, just suspicious. Or scared.

"Charlotte gave me an invitation and your name—"

"N-not true," says Liz.

Kat's hand reaches out again.

"No," Liz says, loud enough to turn heads, sidestepping away from Kat and slipping off. Her movements are awkward. Liz has a limp, and her hands are out of sync with how she walks.

Kat tries to follow, but a group lingering in the doorway blocks her, and Liz is gone. Kat heads back to the window. Down in the street a tall, burly man holds Liz's arm. A white van pulls up. The back door opens, and a hand stretches out to help Liz climb inside. Her body shakes with the effort of getting her balance right. She's helped by another man, also in a red hooded T-shirt, jeans, and lace-up boots. He's strong, either a manual worker or a gym junkie.

The van pulls away. Kat's not familiar with the make, and the plate number is unreadable, streaked with dirt.

Nearby, Tim Prescott's being pushed into a police car. But no one's following Liz.

TWELVE

$\diamond$

Kat's driving back toward Suzy's apartment. She wants time to think before calling Max Grachev.

With her stutter and limp, Liz has some kind of coordination problem. But she sure knew who Kat was. Hers wasn't the reaction of someone who'd just gotten a face wrong, and she wasn't part of any group inside the hall. Her people were waiting for her out on the street.

Navigating is tricky, especially with England's opposite-side driving system. Just when Kat thinks she's mapped a way back to Suzy's apartment, she hits a one-way street that narrows, causing traffic to pile up.

The evening light's gone, headlights are on. Kat emerges at an intersection with a four-lane highway and has to turn left. Wandsworth Bridge, about a mile up, will take her across the river.

On the bridge, a car comes up close behind, flashing its lights. Kat's going slowly in the passing lane. She changes lanes to let the car pass.

The sight in her rearview mirror becomes a stream of headlights. She keeps going straight after the bridge. At the end of the road, the lights turn from green to amber. Kat accelerates to catch them before they turn red, misjudges the power of the engine, and takes a tight left turn with a screech of tires. The other cars turn right.

A searchlight hits her eyes, and she stops dead. Two police cars are parked at an angle, hood to hood, cutting the road down to a single lane. Her hand goes up, shielding her eyes from the glare. An orange light flashes. Over a speaker comes, *"Turn off the engine. Engage the hand brake. Put your vehicle in neutral."*

"Okay," Kat mutters to herself. "Keep it cool."

"Turn slowly to your right, put your right hand, palm outward, flat against the window glass. At no time make us suspicious of your movements."

Kat presses her hand hard against the glass to give a palm reading. The United States doesn't share ID recognition with any other country. They won't have her palm print registered, but they'll ask why she's driving Charlotte Thomas's car.

Kat counts four cameras and two searchlights high up on separate lampposts. To the left is a trailer, emblazoned with red and black stripes over which is written STOP like the ones they have around the White House and the Hill. This one has a satellite dish on top.

Eyes moving, head still, Kat spots more cameras, one at bumper level to capture a clear image of the license plate, one at windshield level to record the badges and registration, and two in the road itself to check the undercarriage of the chassis. Fifty feet beyond that, a yellow barrier is embedded in the road. Kat's seen them all around Washington. They shoot up instantaneously to stop car bombers.

Kat keeps her hands steady. Police in flak jackets, bioterror masks hanging from their belts, train their weapons on her. No one approaches.

"With your left hand, release the bonnet and the boot."

Hood and trunk, thinks Kat. She hadn't checked either before she'd set out. She does it calmly.

Four streetlights have been switched off, making the checkpoint area dark. A blue light catches her eye from the rearview mirror as another car pulls up.

Out of the shadows comes Max Grachev. Holding up a badge, he walks right up to her car.

"Step out, so they can get a proper look at you," he says, arm on the roof, speaking to her through the window.

She opens the door. He taps a permit on Suzy's windshield. "This only authorizes you to drive outside Zones One and Two up until eight p.m. My fault. There was no way for you to know."

The temperature has dropped, and a chilly breeze zips through her.

Grachev's arm is on her elbow, guiding her onto the sidewalk. "Leave us for a moment," he says to the uniformed police. He's wearing sneakers, loose tracksuit pants, and a sport shirt. His hair's tousled in the front, as though he's come straight from the gym.

"Good job at the meeting," he says. "It worked well. But I must say, we didn't expect that kind of reaction."

"You know who she is?"

"We're checking." He turns and looks behind him. They're on a pleasant, residential street, a couple of shops, a bank, a bus stop, a little green circled by houses, curtains drawn, with families inside. "Do you understand what all this is about?" he asks, pointing to the barricade.

"I guess I don't, or you wouldn't be asking."

"London is not a safe city," he says. "It's crazy. Sometime soon, they're going to announce a date for the signing of Project Peace. A lot of people in Britain oppose it. Some are willing to use violence to stop it."

Grachev looks away from Kat toward the bridge they've just crossed. The light picks up his features, his hair still wet and shining under the checkpoint lamps, his face smooth and relaxed, but unreachable. His eyes run freely over her, one second weighing her as a woman, the next cold, warning her.

"A lot happens in a day," he says. "When I asked you to help us with Liz Luxton, I wasn't aware how . . . complicated . . . this was." He pauses, choosing his words carefully. "You won't want to hear this, Kat, but you ought to take Nate Sayer up on his suggestion, and go back to Washington."

Kat doesn't move, just stares him down. His voice remains quiet and measured. "Investigating your sister's murder is not a safe job," he says.

"Yeah, well, I'd like to help."

Grachev's look is sympathetic, but without compromise. "Impossible."

"You used me once. Use me again."

"It's too dangerous."

She waves toward the checkpoint. "Why? Because of this?" she says mockingly. "I don't know a city anywhere that doesn't have checkpoints."

"We've gone through Suzy's e-mail. It seems almost certain that her death is directly linked to the CPS."

"Even if it is—"

Grachev interrupts, voice raised. "What I would like is if you could keep your thoughts open and listen to me for a minute."

Kat says nothing, but holds his gaze.

Grachev leans against the hood of one of the police cars. "You saw how your sister was killed. She was murdered by a professional killer or killers. We're looking into the type of work Suzy did, the life she led. Who Charlotte Thomas was, or is." He pauses, making a line with his finger in the condensation on the windshield. "We don't have many leads."

"How does Liz Luxton fit in?"

"We don't see her as being able to have pulled the trigger on Suzy."

"You think she was her friend or enemy?"

"We're checking. We'll know by morning."

Kat shrugs. "Once we've found Suzy's killer, I'll get out of your life. Until then, I stay."

"Slow down. Suzy was killed Friday night. Today's Sunday. Your sister was popular, successful. But she wasn't who people thought she was. For your own safety, I'd like you back in the States."

"I want to see where she was killed."

Grachev shakes his head. "I'm sorry. That won't be possible."

"Why not?"

"It's far away. Forensics is still working there."

"What was she doing there anyway if she didn't like music?"

"There are a lot of unanswered questions," he says quietly.

"This zone thing . . ." Kat lets it hang, prompting a pique of curiosity in Grachev's expression.

"Suzy had a zone expressway receipt," says Kat. "Have you looked at the audience list for the concert, found out how many of them came from outside, like Suzy?"

"We're checking it."

"What d'you mean, you're checking it? It'd take five seconds."

He signals to the police that they're leaving and gestures at Suzy's Mercedes. "Drive behind me. I'll escort you back."

"Do you have an answer for me or not?"

He doesn't reply, and she follows Grachev's car to Suzy's apartment. They pass a roadblock, where the police have two men spread-eagle on the road with guns at their heads. Grachev waits for her to drive into Suzy's garage, flashes his headlights, and leaves.

Once in the apartment, she lies on Suzy's sofa, lights off, staring at the deep blue dome of the sky spread above the river. For a moment, and it can't be more than that, she lets the exhaustion of the past two days take her. Suddenly, she wakes, sitting straight up, hands reaching to answer the ringing phone.

It's Nancy. She's soft, persuasive. "We've been trying to get ahold of you," she says. "We wanted to have you over for a real meal."

"Yeah, thanks, Aunt Nance," Kat says, lets herself pause. "Sorry, you caught me napping. Must be jet lag. No, I'm fine. Guess I'll get an early night."

"Have you thought any more about Nate's suggestion? We can all go together in the morning."

"You, Nate, me, we're pretty good at doing funerals together."

Nancy gives it a second. "Let me come over, Kat. You need someone to talk to."

"Yeah, but not tonight. Maybe tomorrow. Tell Nate I'll sign all the papers he needs."

THIRTEEN

◇

Sunday, 9:17 p.m., BST

Kat curls her legs under her, pulls down the blinds in Suzy's bedroom, and closes the door. She doesn't want to see the river, the night, the distorted reflections of streetlights, the pattern of clouds in the humid night sky, cars driving on the left-hand side of the road.

She calls Cage. "I need you to call me back."

She cuts the line, holding the phone until it vibrates with Cage's call.

"You there?"

"I'm here."

"You okay?" he asks.

"I'm fine," says Kat.

Kat imagines Cage in his little study off his bedroom on P Street, blinds down, too, bathed in an emerald light, keeping his eyes on cryptic letter-number combinations flashing up at him on the screen. As long as they change smoothly and regularly, he knows no one is listening to their conversation. If he's suspicious, he'll prime one of the recordings he and Kat have on file and insert it into the signal so that the eavesdroppers hear the recording instead of the real conversation.

Cage's words will be secure, so he can talk in detail. But Kat's end may not be secure, so she must speak in generalities that would not catch the attention of eavesdroppers.

"How is it?" The vagueness of his question is a signal for her to proceed carefully while he tests the line.

"It's okay. I guess it's lonely more than anything. A detective called Max Grachev is investigating. He's a Russian, a specialist in organized crime, working with the British police."

"Hold a second, I have to take another call," he says, using another familiar code phrase. "I'll get back to you."

By hanging up, using the word "second," he's told her he's not happy with the security of Suzy's landline.

Kat lies on the bed, hands behind her head, staring up at the ceiling, ankle hooked over knee, waiting for Cage to finish.

Cage's title is senior operations officer. He's good at his job, better than many at higher pay levels. He's 53, but he has the energy of a man a generation younger. She saw Cage shirtless once, changing into a tuxedo in the back of a limousine, his torso strong, sinewy, not a ripple out of place, as if he'd relocated all his body's age and punishment into his face.

One night after a successful job, when they were driving through Washington's empty streets toward their separate homes, he told her that every middle-aged man at some time ends up looking at a younger woman who brings back memories of the person he thinks he should have married.

Kat liked him more then. Cage told her about a woman named Sally whom he'd never stopped loving, and their son Paul, who gave them a reason to stay in touch. Years ago, Cage and Sally had failed to make a home together. Now it was too late to do it with anyone else.

When the phone rings, she answers it casually.

"You've got two separate surveillance tracks on you," Cage says. "One is from the American embassy, which is being routed directly to the FBI. I know that system, so there's no problem with it. The second is less sophisticated, and I expect it's the British police. You may have to handle that one yourself."

"Okay." Her tone is measured. She sips coffee, letting its bitterness wash around her mouth.

"Every time you leave or enter the apartment, they're watching you. By morning, I'll know the blind spots and tell you a way out without being seen. I'll e-mail it to you."

"They want me to go home," says Kat in a non sequitur that will fit into what the eavesdroppers are hearing.

"It's best you're away for a few more days while the Kazakh embassy thing is properly cleared up. They're getting IDs on the two guys who tried to kill us. The Kazakhs are cooperating by not going to the press. The families have agreed. You and I are not involved."

The way he says it, so relaxed, makes Kat take a breath deep into her chest. Her throat is tight with the thought of Friday night. "Thanks," she says softly. "And thanks for being on the other end of the line."

"Now," he says. "I've got a bit on Tracy Elizabeth Luxton. If it's the right one, she turned twenty-seven ten days ago, on August 20. Father and mother are down here as Robert and Caroline. They used to run a seaside circus. Elizabeth went to school in Great Yarmouth in Suffolk, a county on the east coast. No college that I can see. No current address listed. She doesn't seem the type of people your sister would naturally have mixed with. The file is thin, which means either that she doesn't matter, or that she matters so much that the main file is held with an agency that doesn't share with us."

When Kat replies, it's as if Cage has been asking her about her evening.

"No, I got there real late. I ended up taking Suzy's car, remembering to drive on the left and everything, and I got there just as it was finishing. But it was worth it. Good to see the type of people Suzy hung around with, and to get in . . ."

She's hoping Cage will get the drift of what she's trying to tell him.

". . . I had to have her driver's license swiped at the door, so I guess that has everything on it, address, social security number."

"The system at Linton Community Hall is not listed here as being net-worked," Cage says tightly.

"It'd be great to get to meet some of her real friends," Kat replies innocuously.

Cage comes back immediately, a trace of irritation that Kat's being so specific. "Don't speak, just listen," he says curtly. "Hang up and do things as you normally would in the morning for at least an hour. I'm going to intercept the FBI's video surveillance and then feed your movements back into them. So go to the bathroom, shower, make coffee, look around Suzy's desk. Do them slowly. No rushing. Do not listen to the radio. Do not turn on the TV. Do not look out the window. Then go to bed. Leave a night-light on somewhere and the blind partway up so I can pick up the changing light of the morning. Make sure no clocks are in open view. Get up after full daylight. Sunrise is at 6:11. You should be safe at 6:45. As soon as you're out of bed, close the blind. That will be my signal to run the recording, and by then I'll know the safest way for you to operate."

Cage will know how many staff have been assigned to watch surveillance from Suzy's apartment, and he'll move in on the shift change. There's little chance the incoming shift will recognize that Kat is repeating exactly what she'd done the previous evening.

When she closes her eyes to sleep, she sees Liz Luxton, so determined, so surprised, so mistrustful, so desperate to get away, and, in the way she moved, so vulnerable.

FOURTEEN

◇

Monday, 6:50 a.m., BST

Sunlight pours through the open inches left under the blinds and hits her face, warm and hard. Kat is sleeping on her back, both arms across her chest, something she started doing years back, protecting herself.

She's in a pair of Suzy's elephant-pattern pajamas, and her sleep has been so deep and dreamless that it takes her a moment to remember where she is. Eyes blinking, she acclimates, reading her watch at 6:50, which means it's okay to start the day.

Kat plans to do two things. First, she will see if Cage has found how she can get out of Suzy's apartment without anyone seeing. Then, she will find Liz Luxton, which means going back to the lecture hall, getting into the desktop computer there, and finding her ID details.

She gets up, puts on loose blue jeans over shorts, opens the terrace doors to morning chill and sun, with whitish light, rising over the river.

A gust brings in river smells, a mix of dankness, summer leaves, and boat oil. Kat steps back inside and shuts the door.

On her cell phone screen, she sees that Cage has sent a file on surveillance in the apartment. He's countered the surveillance inside and marked the fields of view of the cameras in red and a safe path out through the apartment in green.

But the screen on the cell is too small to read it accurately. Suzy's desktop has a slot for SIM cards. She turns it on and it boots up without asking for a password.

She takes out the cell phone's SIM card, slips it in, and waits for Cage's antisurveillance route to appear. She memorizes the way out of the apartment.

She unwraps the SIM card she's had taped to her back to check on the Kazakh data file. Many sensitive data files have self-erasing programs written into them, and Kat has her own special program to counter it. Most times it works. Sometimes it doesn't. Sometimes the erasure is on a time mechanism that takes twenty-four hours to activate.

Kat sighs in relief. The Kazakh file is intact. She inoculates it, then flips through to the murdered man lying in the snow. She wants to go on, but tells herself to stop. There's no time to do it properly.

She goes into Suzy's e-mail. But there's nothing. Nothing in; nothing out. No copy of the e-mail Kat got on Friday night. She checks the recycling bin. Nothing. Either Suzy, knowing she was in danger, erased her own e-mails, or someone else did.

What's the computer doing there, anyway? It should be the first thing police take in a murder investigation. Why did Suzy not use a password?

Kat shuts it down, rewraps her SIM card, first in plastic wrap, then in sturdier polyethylene, and tapes it under her top to the small of her back. She also wraps her own software cards in polyethylene, zips them into her pocket, and puts a change of clothes, shoes, and a wig into a shoulder bag.

From a window in the utility room by the kitchen, she drops down onto the fire escape. Keeping flat against the brickwork, she walks down the steps into the small backyard. A wooden door, unused and partly hidden by an overgrown buddleia tree, is in the wall. Its bolts are rusted. It takes three kicks to get the lower one back. Rust flakes spill onto the ground.

The upper bolt is too high for her to reach. Kat hauls herself halfway up the wall on an overhanging tree branch, then wedges the toe of her shoe into the gap from a broken brick. But she can't go farther over the wall because of coils of razor wire.

She hits the upper bolt with the heel of her hand. It doesn't move. She hits it again. It begins to give. She keeps hitting it until it's free. She drops down, opens the door, and steps into an alleyway.

Ahead of her is a graceful, green iron bridge crossing the river, coming alive with workday traffic. Sunlight breaks through black clouds, then disappears again. Spitting rain hits her face.

Halfway across the bridge is a sign telling her she is leaving Zone Two and entering Zone Three. The road narrows, forcing cars to slow down enough for police to check who is inside. Kat watches the pedestrians, sees them showing IDs. She walks back, away from the river, toward an overpass and intersection.

She flags down a cab. "Prince of Wales Drive, Battersea, cross street Alexandra."

The driver examines her in his mirror, chewing gum, eyes flicking out to his side mirror. "You visiting?" he says as he pulls out. The wiper smears the windshield.

"How'd you guess?"

"Just that, if you were staying," he says eventually, "I'd tell you we don't do cross streets in London. We work with the numbers."

"Good to know," says Kat. She's counting out £350 and some loose change from the money Nancy gave her.

"You from the States?"

"Canada."

"Who are you lot supporting, now you're out of the football?" he says.

"England, I guess. Or maybe Brazil."

"Russia and China'll go in the quarterfinals," he says. "England will top Germany. Brazil will trounce France. The final will be England-Brazil, so why Brazil?"

"I used to know the captain, Javier Laja."

The cabdriver's foot leaves the accelerator as he turns in his seat to look at Kat, not in the mirror, but face-on. "Yer 'avin' me on."

"No. My dad ran a home for orphans. Javier was one of them." She's told no one this for years and now comes straight out with it to a stranger.

"You still in touch?"

"I thought about it when he became famous, but never did." Kat notices a white flag with a red cross pegged into a slot to the left of the windshield. "That's the England flag, isn't it?"

"The cross of St. George," he says pithily. "But they'll soon be telling us to fly a bloody Project Peace flag instead."

On the streets, people move quickly. They're busy, young, mostly, well dressed, earning money. But the sidewalks blow with litter. Concrete is cracked. They pass derelict buildings, stained and boarded up.

At a red light, just before they get onto a bridge to cross the river, the cabdriver turns in his seat and looks at her directly. "One road down from where I'm dropping you, you can't go no farther in a vehicle without a pass."

Kat shifts her gaze to the river, fast running and brown with the rain, the tide so high that a line of houseboats look as if they're sitting on the road.

"One moment and I think they're going over the top," he says. "The next moment, I change my mind. Since we haven't had no big bombs recently, they've got support. A lot of people reckon that once Project Peace is signed, things will get back to normal."

Battersea Park comes into sight, rain glistening in the trees. He stops just where Kat told him. Before he starts off again, he dials his cell phone.

Kat's on the sidewalk, looking at Linton Hall across the road. The cabdriver's talking, looking straight at her. Kat starts running. The cabdriver makes a U-turn and heads back the way they came.

FIFTEEN

◇

Monday, 8:13 a.m., BST

Kat looks for an entry to Linton Hall. She starts with the double doors. They're held by a dead bolt inside.

She walks down a street by the side of the building, which is set back, with a wall running along the length of it. She climbs the wall and lands lightly in an alley. She's hidden from the street, but the building has large windows, and she could be seen by anyone inside.

The paved ground of the alley has recently been swept. Broom marks run through patches of water drying on the concrete.

Kat hears a car slow and stop on the street. A flashing blue light reflects off an upper window of the building. From a distance, a siren wails, coming closer until it stops by the other vehicle. Two car doors open.

A radio crackles, *"We're looking around . . . yes . . . came in five minutes ago from a cabdriver . . . blond, twenties, sports clothes . . . checking the streets now."*

Kat moves quietly down the alley. Just before the end of the building, there's a standpipe faucet. A door's open next to it with keys hanging in the inside lock, and there's a broom and bucket in the doorway. She steps over them into a large, windowless storeroom, shelves on one side with cleaning materials and a vacuum cleaner, drills and tool kits stacked up against the wall on the other.

The door ahead is unlocked.

Kat steps into the corridor leading to the staircase. She hears voices above.

"Like I said, I'm the only one here." It's an elderly voice. "Next people due in are after eight-thirty. The place was rented out last night for a Project Peace function. They're coming to take the computer."

Kat follows the curve of the corridor away from the staircase until she comes to a second, smaller staircase. On the stairwell, one flight up, there's a fire door. She opens it an inch. Two cops are with the janitor, an old, short guy in a neat, brown uniform. He's still talking, but Kat can't make out the words.

She heads back down, gets an empty bucket from the storeroom, fills it with standpipe water, then sluices it along the corridor at the foot of the main staircase, making it look as if a leak has sprung from somewhere.

Back up at the fire door, she sees the janitor close the main double doors, glance at the computer on the reception desk, and head back down the main staircase.

The mess she made should hold him there for five minutes.

Kat turns on the computer behind the reception desk. While she waits for it to boot up, she goes upstairs. The doors of the lecture hall have been left open. Tables and chairs are stacked against the wall. The window shutters are closed and bolted. A microphone is on a stand in the middle of the stage. There's no trace of what was there 12 hours earlier. It's a rental hall, waiting for the next hire.

A minute later, she's down again, and the computer is ready. The screen saver shows the face of Dr. Christopher North and the banner of Project Peace. Tim Prescott was right. The lecture might have been sold as an open discussion, but it had been paid for by those pushing for Project Peace. That'd explain why Prescott was thrown out.

She touches the keyboard. In the center of the screen, across North's avuncular face, comes the narrow pop-up demanding the password.

Kat brings out one of the data cards from her bag and slips it into the computer. She types in six digits at random and waits for it to carry out its magic. No one except Kat knows the secrets of her hacking software. For every password rejected comes a hint of what might be acceptable. The design bombards the security system so rapidly that it's unable to tell when the quota of wrong guesses has been made. In less than five seconds, the hard drive is whirring.

Kat flips through the screen options and quickly pulls up Suzy's record. She does a double take at what comes up in front of her: the life of Charlotte Thomas, but with Suzy's picture, a mug shot from three angles. Everything is there to profile a person: address; picture of the outside of her river house; Mercedes registration number; driver's license; health insurance information. After that come boxes and boxes of details about Charlotte Thomas—mother, father, place of birth, education, work, race, sexual preference, political affiliation, travel, associates. Charlotte Thomas was raised in Colorado and Connecticut, in towns Kat has never heard of.

Kat tries *Tracy Luxton*. Nothing. She tries *Elizabeth Luxton*. Nothing. Then just *Luxton*. The file on *Tracy Elizabeth Luxton* flickers and settles on the screen. In the time it takes Kat to copy the record to her data card, she's memorized Liz Luxton's address.

She calls up a street map. It's four miles due south of the lecture hall, and Kat plans to walk all the way. She won't be taking any more cabs. She realizes now how much more efficient London is than the States when it comes to watching people.

SIXTEEN

Kat walks south.

Her cell phone vibrates. She already has three messages from Nate Sayer, and he's calling again. Once more, Kat decides not to answer. In all honesty, she doesn't know what to do about Sayer. She never has.

Kat wrote her first piece of software to get revenge on Nate Sayer, then perfected the art while living on Dix Street.

Her mom and dad had been hosting a lunch party at the house in Great Falls. Her dad was holding court, cracking jokes, winning support for his plans to change some important employment law. Suzy and Mom were inside, fixing lunch. Kat was swimming, climbed out of the pool, and while she was toweling herself down, her dad asked, "If you're going inside, can you get me the big blue law book sitting right in the middle of my desk?"

Kat ran into the kitchen, where the shade hit her like darkness; past Suzy, who was cutting up fruit; headed upstairs to her father's study; pushed open the door and stopped, fingers turning to white as they gripped the handle.

The window blinds were down. Slatted sunbeams across the desk mixed with the new shaft of light let in by the half-open door. The book was just where her dad said it would be, but the rest of the room took on a new shape as she stared straight into the eyes of Nate Sayer, who held her gaze, unyielding, when he could have looked away.

"Little busy in here right now," he said.

Kat didn't shift as her mother turned and wiped her mouth, looking at her daughter. Mom stood, adjusted her T-shirt printed with its image of a handcuffed Hispanic farm laborer, and walked toward the door, running her fingers through her hair.

Kat let go of the handle and stood aside.

Her mother's eyes darted everywhere, skittishly flitting to Kat. "Suzy needs me in the kitchen, doesn't she?" she muttered. A smile, a nervous laugh, she brushed past Kat.

Sayer buckled up his pants. "You know what was happening there, Kat?"

Kat stepped inside the room and closed the door. "Dad wanted that book," she said, pointing past Sayer to the desk.

Sayer picked up the book and handed it to her.

"Up until today, you might have thought the world's just as it seems. Now your mom and I have taught you that it's not."

Kat dropped her eyes, saw the bulge inside his pants. She caught the scent of him and nearly retched. Sayer bent over to look into a small mirror her dad kept on the side of the desk.

"Best to keep these things to ourselves," he said, checking his chin growth with the edge of his forefinger. "The fact is that truth hurts people, Kat. Your dad, Nancy, no one wants good people to get hurt."

"But you're Dad's best friend" was all Kat could say.

Sayer put his hand on her shoulder. She recoiled, stepped back. He patted the book in her hand. "Take that down to your dad. I expect they'll be wanting more beers and wine out there, too. You want me to give you a hand, or can you manage?"

"I can manage," she whispered.

Holding the tray like a waitress, squinting into the glare as she looked around for Suzy, Kat delivered the book on a tray of cold beers. Her mom came out and sat with Nancy and a few others, looking at the rose garden. Sayer was already at her dad's table, throwing his head back with laughter at some joke.

Her dad broke off to thank his daughter and to announce to everyone that while Kat had big plans to follow Suzy into law school, he thought she'd do better studying math. Sayer brushed her elbow as she put the drinks on the table. Kat headed straight for the diving board, put her hands together in front of her as if in prayer, and dived into the pool.

That evening she told Suzy what happened.

Suzy patted her bed for Kat to sit down. "Mom's not happy," she said, "and when women aren't happy, often they do things like that."

"Yeah. Well, I saw it," said Kat, challenging Suzy to make the call as to what she should do, because Suzy was twenty-five and had boyfriends and things.

"Nate's wrong, but he's right, if you know what I mean," replied Suzy. "He wasn't forcing Mom or anything, and it's what she does from time to time to fill some void in her life. Dad knows it. Maybe not about Nate, but he knows Mom cheats on him. Dad loves Mom. Part of what drives him are goals he can never reach. Maybe Mom's infidelity is part of it. And he needs Uncle Nate for his work. And Aunt Nance is Mom's best friend. She's your godmother. If you tell anyone apart from me, then all that might fall apart."

By the morning, it was too late to tell anyone. Kat remembered that day as the time she became Nate Sayer's victim. Whenever she was around Sayer, Kat felt humiliated.

Although a year later, Kat tried to get even.

This time, the party was at the Sayer house, with a quartet playing Mozart out in their courtyard garden, butlers moving through with canapés, laughter and political talk.

With a cell phone and a cable in her purse, she slipped into Sayer's study, a large, bleak room on a half landing with a narrow, high window overlooking the street.

Two maroon walls hung with five rows of pictures, always of Sayer, someone shaking hands, someone famous, a record of a life on the fringes, a man who hid inside a uniform, and then, when the uniform was no more, tailored suits, trousers sharply pressed, shoes polished like a mirror.

Sayer displayed his life like a peacock displays his tail.

The desk was neat, with two telephones, a pile of magazines, a legal pad, a yellow jar of pens, and an empty In tray and Out tray.

Kat had been in the study before and knew that Sayer kept the keys to the cabinet behind the desk in the yellow pen jar. Kat opened the door; the only thing inside was a safe.

Using a program she'd written herself, she attached a cable from the cell to the safe lock with a rubber suction cup like a stethoscope, covered the digital code light with a sensory fiber, punched in six incorrect digits, and waited for the cell to read the messages it was getting from the safe's software. For fifteen minutes, Kat went through a series of combinations until the cell lit up. She pressed the Open button.

Kat pulled out folders, closed the cupboard door, and fanned papers out on the carpet behind the desk like a deck of playing cards; bank statements, mortgage files, car and household insurance—all predictable matters.

It was too dark for Kat to see inside the safe. She felt around with her hand, tapping the cool metal walls, but found nothing more. She unhooked the cell and put it into the safe, resting it on her hand, turning it like a compass. Its infrared sensor picked up a beam. The dial lit up, asking Kat to accept it. When she did, the left wall of the safe slid back. A tiny light came on, and Kat brought out a file of papers.

She had also set off an alarm on Nate Sayer's cell phone.

New at the safe-cracking game then, Kat kept working. She didn't notice the drone of the party get louder for a second as the door opened, a band of light streaked across the carpet and the top of the desk, and Sayer slipped into the room.

She was absorbed in the documents in front of her. She simply couldn't understand it. Sayer was keeping evidence of himself handing over money and breaking the law. Photographs clearly showed his own face. Bank statements matched transfers and dates. Two files were of him having sex with named women, making Kat shiver with disgust. One showed charges from the sheriff's office of Lincoln County, Nebraska, where Sayer was accused of breaking into a meatpacking plant and lying about his identity. The next document was a photograph of Sayer handing out bribes to get the charges dropped.

Kat smelled Sayer's cigar smoke. The lights came on. Kat tried to make herself smaller behind the desk.

Sayer locked the door. "I don't know who you are, but get on your feet and walk out from behind the desk."

Kat stayed quiet.

Sayer took a key out of his pocket, opened a wall cabinet, and took out a pistol. He opened a drawer for ammunition. Kat heard metal on metal as a round went into the breech.

"Leave everything and just stand up, or I'll blow your head off."

She slid up onto her feet. "Uncle Nate, it's me, Kat. Don't . . ."

Sayer's face broke into a lazy smile as if he was dumb not to have expected it. He emptied out the rounds from the pistol, put everything back, and wiped sweat from his forehead with the back of his hand.

"Kat, Kat, Kat . . ."

She stepped back.

"Come over here," ordered Sayer.

Kat didn't move.

"What do you want me to do, call in your mother? Move away from my desk, so I can see what you were doing down there."

Kat stepped back and edged along the windowsill.

Sayer glanced down at the files, pulled open the cupboard door to see the open safe, peered in toward the inner safe. "How did you get in there?"

Kat shrugged. She wanted to appear defiant, but couldn't find words.

"You're a clever little bitch," he whispered. "Waste of talent, becoming a lawyer, I'll tell you that."

"Uncle Nate," said Kat, trying to sound as if everything was normal. "Why'd you keep stuff like that? You could go to jail."

She stepped farther away, as Sayer looked through the documents himself, for a second absorbed in his own past and what it meant.

Then his voice stopped her. "I'm going to tell you something you need to know," he said.

There wasn't harshness on his face; no kindness, either, or real surprise at what Kat had done. His eyes, though, had almost no color, nothing to judge them by.

"Like with your mom and me, it usually takes two people to do something wrong. The work I do with your dad, I break the law a lot, so I make sure that if I'm ever going down, I take others with me. That's how it works out there, Kat."

"Does Dad know?" muttered Kat.

"No." Sayer crouched down, put the files back into the two safes. "And don't you go telling him," he said, closing the door. "If a kid like you can get into this . . ." He didn't finish the sentence, but stared at the desk, chin in his hands.

Genuine curiosity kept Kat in place. "But why not tell him, if it's that important?"

Sayer actually smiled then. "Your father's a great man. He has big dreams. He just doesn't understand the bad things a person has to do to achieve them, and that's where I come in."

SEVENTEEN

$\diamond$

As Kat slips the cell phone back into her pocket, she realizes how bleak London has become, rain-washed, splattered with litter, claustrophobic with dark clouds, and no spring in the step of the people.

She's also being followed.

With most people, when she tests eye contact, she's met with suspicion. But she's just eyeballed her tail, and he reacted too quickly, one second at one with his environment, looking tiredly at a shop window, the next, when Kat hijacks his gaze, alert and calculating.

She's halfway to her destination in an inner suburb called Clapham.

If he's the primary tail, there could be others ahead, putting her in a box formation, meaning a primary tail, two farther back, two in front, and, if they have the resources, one or two on each flank.

Kat's used to being invisible, used to observing people without being seen. She doesn't like it the other way around. Surveillance in London might be different from that in Washington, but that doesn't mean Kat can't get around it.

She crosses a park that is more cut up and dirty than the one near the warehouse. Across the next main street, two giant television screens billboarded onto the sides of buildings are causing a crowd to gather under them.

Kat sees a way of giving her tail the slip.

As a kid, Kat remembers screens like this only in Times Square and other big places, but now they're commonplace. These days, there's no place you can't watch TV.

In England, they seem to be bigger and more planned. On most intersections, two screens are rigged side by side above the street, with a single caption running underneath both, explaining what's showing. The one on the left is dedicated to sports; the one on the right concentrates on politics and other news.

A growing crowd is looking up at the screen showing the wreckage caused by a car bomb that has just gone off in the Middle East. A smaller group's watching a soccer match on the other screen.

The crowd spills onto the road, causing traffic to jam.

Kat pushes her way through, jostling, moving quickly. Once she's ten deep in the crush, she turns to check. The primary tail is still behind her.

The sports screen shows the Brazilian soccer team's captain, Javier Laja, his jaw jutting out over a stack of microphones.

Next door is the U.S. president, James Abbott, a man her dad used to call a crook.

"Yeah, what's that prick Abbott got to say?" says a loud voice so close to Kat's ear that she jumps. It belongs to a heavyset black man, hands on hips, staring upward.

"What you get so worked up for?" retorts another black guy with him.

"How come he has so much power over here, yet we can't vote him in or out?"

"What's it matter? They do the job for themselves, not for no one else."

Squeezing through, Kat mistakenly knocks the elbow of a middle-aged man in white overalls, carrying a Starbucks cup. Coffee spills on his wrist.

"Sorry," she says.

He glances at it, ignores her, and keeps talking to a younger man beside him. "Things ain't as simple as they're making out."

"Yeah. Why not?" replies the younger man. "Your type makes everything complicated when it's not, which means you never have an answer to nothing. This Project Peace could be the answer, but you trash it and don't have the brains to think of anything else."

The older man keeps his eyes to himself. "If that's the world you want."

"What world's that?"

The older man brings out his driver's license, holds it tight between two fingers. "There's everything they need to know about you on this," he says angrily. "Soon, they'll issue them transmitting signals, so they can read it while it's in your pocket, who you spoke to, who you shagged, who you called on the phone. And supposing you do something wrong, anything, when they want, anytime they want, they'll get you for it. And if you don't carry it, then what do they do? Arrest you."

Everyone's talking, arguing. Whatever's been announced, there's not much happiness about it.

"Saturday's a bit much," she hears from somewhere, but by the time Kat starts looking for the face, a surge pushes her forward.

"If they can do it by Saturday," says a woman. "I know the football's important, but this is more important, don't you think?"

Kat ends up catching her eye. "Of course," she says, trying to do an English accent.

"We're all so sick of war, war, war," continues the woman.

On the screen, a television host in a white pantsuit appears against a backdrop of crowds waving British flags. Her voice is inaudible, but Kat reads from subtitles. "Give us your view. Do you support Project Peace? Text message us YES or NO on your mobile phone or on your interactive TV at home."

A teenager jabs his cell phone keys to vote NO, but an older hand stops him. "Press that, son, and they'll have you marked for life."

With the next announcement, Kat sees what the commotion is about. The signing of the Coalition for Peace and Security and the soccer final are now to be held on the same day—Saturday, September 2. A problem with President Abbott's schedule has forced the ceremony to be held then. Rain is forecast for Sunday, so the soccer final's been moved forward a day.

"In our time, you'd play football in the rain," says a man behind Kat.

"What about the roof over Wembley?" says another man next to him. "I thought they'd spent millions just for that purpose."

A woman behind Kat begins loudly. "The *whole* world will be watching the final."

"Not too loud," mumbles a man with her.

"But it's deliberate," she continues, her voice lower. "Billions of people glued to a football match, while Abbott, Rand, and their cronies stitch things up."

"Grace, let's go," insists the man. "Nothing we can do about it," he says.

"But don't you see what they're doing?"

"Yes." He's tugging her back through the crowd, his voice fading. "There's nothing we can do to stop it."

Javier Laja, a huge smile, right hand raised, points his fingers forward in a V, the victory sign.

Kat remembers Laja making the same gesture when he was a kid. The orphanage was a row of clapboard houses at the edge of the Lancaster Fairground, and Kat loved the bright colors, pictures on all the walls, the sound of kids running everywhere, and the grown-ups laughing and letting them do it.

With no siblings her own age, Kat grew up almost as an only child. She spent a lot of time by herself in the huge family house on Georgetown's R Street.

Laja's father, an illegal immigrant working at a meatpacking plant, was killed in a trade union fight with the police. The next day, the police came for his mother and shot her as she tried to run. Kat's mom heard about it, and both her parents brought along Kat to collect Javier from police protection.

Next to the sports screen, British Prime Minister Michael Rand stands in front of a display outlining the benefits of Project Peace. It scrolls down slogans—GREATER COOPERATION, DEMOCRACY FOR ALL, SHARED ENERGY, ALLIES TOGETHER.

Behind Kat, kids in the backseat of a car wipe the window with a cloth to see what's going on. The traffic's not moving, cars clogged up like river logs. People are getting wet, but there's no moving them.

"You only have to see how run-down everything is getting," a gray-haired woman is saying. "Look at the legislative process in Parliament, every law being postponed because of debates on the war. You can't run a country when laws aren't being passed."

The politics screen switches to a broadcast from the Kremlin. The sports screen shows how the quarterfinals and semifinals are being rearranged to meet the new date of the final.

The crowd has provided cover. She can't see the primary tail. But that doesn't mean he's not still there.

"They're not going to get away with this." A voice that's hardly a whisper, a young black woman Kat's age, thin like she hardly eats, angry eyes, hands on hips, and not caring whose space she's taking.

The dark eyes rest on Kat for a moment, with the beginning of a smile, which becomes serious when she sees Kat doesn't want to talk.

"Call it a democracy," she mutters. "They have no idea what the word means."

Kat starts moving, but the black woman catches her elbow. Quickly, Kat pulls away. Now's the right time.

She pushes through the crowd to a pub on the corner. Inside, the heat and noise hit her. She heads to the restrooms at the other end of the bar.

EIGHTEEN

---◇---

When Kat comes out, she's taller, wearing sneakers with heels, a light gray, long-sleeved, hooded T-shirt, black cotton pants, and a wig of brown hair falling long below her shoulders.

She skirts the crowds and keeps going south, hood up against the rain. The areas get even poorer—strollers, kids slung on backs, mothers shouting, cars with windows taped up, guys hanging around storefronts—a cab company, betting shop, pub—with nothing to do but watch and resent.

White, black, Asian—when hope goes, it doesn't matter what color you are. Dix Street was like this. Rainwater not getting drained away. No one fixing the broken pavement. Broken neon signs staying broken.

Greendale Road curves off slightly from the main road, with row houses on both sides. As Kat makes the turn, she sees no sign of being followed. Three kids swing around a lamppost at the bottom. Two black women in cropped tank tops and jeans walk past her, brushing her like she's not there.

The street's heavy with cars parked bumper to bumper, leaving just a single lane for driving. A red compact car is coming toward Kat, with an SUV approaching from the other way. They slow to a snail's pace, getting past each other by knocking side-view mirrors. She counts out ahead to number 49, walks straight up to it, and rings the doorbell.

She stands in a small front yard, its path overgrown with weeds, separated from the house next door by a knee-high brick wall. A television flickers at her through lace curtains.

Sharp and decisively, the door opens, and Kat's face to face with the guy who helped Liz into the van. He's powerful, thirtyish, huge shoulders, hair closely cropped, high forehead, red plaid shirt hanging from his jeans. He toes the doorstep with brown leather boots, laces hanging untied. He's like a horse, impatient in its stable. Before looking at Kat, his eyes dart around the street, taking their time.

His eyes settle on her, deep blue, which could have made him attractive but for the flatness in them. He doesn't speak; nor does Kat. She looks up at the sky, still oppressed with rain clouds. She hooks damp hair from the wig behind her ears. Drops of water fall onto her shoulders.

Still he doesn't speak. Nor does he move his eyes off her. He's inspecting her to see what threat she carries. He puts his hand up on the doorjamb, leaning on it. She finds she's biting her lower lip. He's standing there, making her socially nervous, which is exactly what Kat isn't expecting.

"I'm looking for Liz," she says.

He keeps studying her face; feet, hands, eyes, everything stays just the same as if she'd never spoken. She takes a deep breath and lets it out slowly. Nothing happens. He's the most arrogantly confident man she's ever met.

"Liz Luxton," says Kat. She swallows, can't help herself, knows he sees it, then picks herself up and hardens her voice. "Tracy Elizabeth Luxton. Age twenty-seven. Birthday August twentieth, nine days back, went to Hydeburn Comprehensive School, just around the corner from here. Is this her address?"

He shakes his head. "Not here." His voice is dull, like his eyes.

Kat shifts her head toward the window, but keeps her hands clasped in front of her. "Is this the Luxton family home?"

"No."

"How come?" Kat shifts her body weight forward and puts her hands on her hips. "This is the address she gave me last night."

He comes out the door, takes her shoulder, making his grip hurt, and walks her backward three steps.

"Hey," she says, reaching across to get rid of his hand. He takes it away before she gets there, turns his back to her, and is halfway back inside the doorway when she says loudly, "Are you the guy who blew my sister's brains out?"

For a moment, from the way the veins in his neck tighten, she thinks he's going to react. But she's wrong. Without looking back, he goes inside and shuts the door. He's in the television room, at the window fiddling with the curtain sash.

"Pity," she shouts. "I thought maybe we could be friends."

He meets her eyes with a look as flat as before. He closes the curtains.

Kat's certain now. He's the guy who helped Liz into the van. He knows who Kat is, knows about Suzy, why she died, maybe *how* she died, and why she called herself Charlotte.

Kat steps into the street, looks left and right. She pulls off the wig so he can see her, feels the cool air around her head.

The door of the house opens and he comes out, his shirt tucked in, his bootlaces tied, his eyes narrowed toward her, a cigarette half-smoked between his fingers.

He goes straight past her. "Walk with me," he says. She runs to catch up, the bag bumping up and down on her back. He stops for her at the intersection and says, "Whoever you're looking for isn't here."

"You were with her. Last night. I saw you."

"If you get picked up here, you'll be deported," he says. "If you cross a zone from here in a cab, he'll report it." He gives her a card with a magnetic strip on the back.

"It's a tube ticket. Walk straight up." He points back the way she came. "Not the first tube station, but the second, Clapham South. The iris scanner is broken. This ticket will see you in. Take the Northern Line northbound to Waterloo. When you get there, don't use the elevator. Take the stairs, where tickets are checked manually. The staff are on strike, so you'll walk straight out. Don't head for the street, but for the Eurostar train. If you've got enough cash on you, buy a ticket to Paris or Brussels. Then head back. You'll be inside the Zone One central cordon. If they're looking for you but haven't got your visual signature, it'll take them at least twenty-four hours to go through the material. No cabs, keep your head down, and you'll be okay."

Kat's listening, taking it in, waiting for him to finish. "What about my sister?"

"I'm telling you how to get back." He's looking somewhere across the road, where two screens hang and a dozen black guys are leaning against cars outside a private car service office. "You've got balls, so I'm helping. That's all."

"Then help me some more. I want to go to where Suzy, or Charlotte, was killed. Do you know that place? Can you take me there?"

He draws on the cigarette, drops it, and kicks the butt into a puddle.

"If you come here again, I won't be so nice," he says.

"All I want to know—"

"You angry because the world isn't fair?" he says derisively. "Big club to join." He glances down at the hissing butt being washed down a drain, turns, and walks away.

NINETEEN

———◇———

Monday, 3:43 p.m., BST

Kat does exactly as he's instructed. At Clapham South, technicians are up a ladder, working on a scanner. A notice at Waterloo Station says ticket staff are on a 24-hour work stoppage.

She's walking on the sidewalk of a wide riverside road toward Suzy's apartment when her cell phone alerts her to a new message.

Sayer's already sent five of them, and now Nancy's left a voice mail: "Kat, you've got to call. Please. Don't disappear like this."

But it's Cage she needs. And as she thinks it, the cell vibrates. She leans on the river wall, head lowered.

"They've ramped up Sayer's instructions," says Cage. "If he doesn't deliver you to Washington, they'll have someone else do it."

"Whose instructions?"

"Technically State Department, but it doesn't sound right to me. I'm hoping it's not connected to Friday night."

"Me, too." A tingling runs through Kat. She watches ripples from a wind gust push against the river wall. She tells Cage about her encounter.

"She has an older brother," Cage says. "Michael. He was raised to be a trapeze artist, which fits in with the family circus, and he did time with the British army in Iraq. That could be who you just met. Also, it turns out Liz works as a film editor at a place called Media Axis."

"What do they do?"

"Run twenty-four-hour news and sports channels."

"Okay. And Max Grachev? Anything there?"

"He checks out, but he's not your usual cop. Maximilian Yury Grachev. Thirty-six, St. Petersburg State University, London School of Economics, where he got a first-class degree in European economic history, then he went on to train as detective in Moscow. It gets better. His mother, Tiina Alekseevna Gracheva, is a Russian oligarch. That's a double *i* in Tiina, and Russian female surnames have an *a* on them. So her husband, Max's father, is Vadim Andreevich Grachev. Not particularly interesting, a time-serving apparatchik and loyal to his wife. Tiina runs a Russian oil and gas conglomerate called RingSet. They've got some business in the United States. She got the job after heading the American desk at the SVR, the Russian Foreign Intelligence Service. When I have more, I'll let you have it."

"What does RingSet gain from Project Peace?" says Kat.

"That depends how close Tiina is to the Kremlin."

"But there's an interest, isn't there? And that's what Suzy was working on. So it makes sense that Grachev's been brought in. And Media Axis, they're running promotions about Project Peace. Something's connected here, Bill."

A bus followed by two trucks rumble past, making her press the earpiece tighter in.

"Most things connect," says Cage. "But it doesn't mean they're right."

"Can you get me Max Grachev's home address?"

Cage says nothing. He doesn't want to do it.

"Bill, where does he live?"

"I can't let you break into his place."

"You don't have to let me do anything. We're totally unauthorized here anyway, Bill. A professional assassin took out my sister. You helping me or not?"

TWENTY

◇

Max Grachev lives in a ground-floor apartment on one of the most expensive streets in London. It is a four-story building with its white gray facade pollution-streaked around floor-to-ceiling windows that face the street.

Through white lace curtains, Kat's been watching two people move around inside. When she's certain one is Grachev himself, she steps up to the front door, presses the bell, looks full into the side-wall camera, and speaks loudly. "Kat Polinski."

A woman opens the door, older than Kat, with wet blond hair hanging loose, wearing a bathrobe and a towel around her neck. She jerks a thumb back behind her and smiles.

"Max, are you in?" she says loudly in a confident, East Coast American accent. "Or are you not receiving visitors this afternoon?"

She turns back. "Hi. You must be here for Max," she says, smiling.

Kat covers up the inevitable thought racing through her mind. What's this detective doing in the middle of the afternoon with this woman when he's supposed to be looking for Suzy's killer?

"I'm here on business for Detective Inspector Grachev," Kat says formally.

"She's here on business, Max," she says lightly, rubbing her hair with the towel. "Can I let her in?"

Her hair is dyed, dark roots growing out into the blond. Kat hears Grachev's voice from far inside. The woman steps back and tilts her head. She keeps her eyes steady on Kat all the time.

Kat doesn't challenge her gaze. This isn't about Grachev's private life. "Thanks," she says.

The woman lets out a friendly laugh, touches Kat's elbow as she passes. She has a long, graceful neck, swanlike. Just under her eyes are freckles, and a small reddish-purple birthmark runs down her left temple.

"Don't tell anyone, but it's not as exciting as it seems," she whispers. "I'm his sister, Yulya. So you're not disturbing anything."

The entrance hall of the apartment is high-ceilinged, with a dark wood floor. Grachev is in a large living room, standing, reading papers on a desk, barefoot and dressed in a white T-shirt and red shorts.

He glances up and goes back to what he's doing. Yulya walks smartly past Kat and speaks in Russian to Grachev, who replies curtly without looking up.

Yulya tops up a cup from a coffeepot on a table by the fireplace. "He's telling me to leave you two alone," she explains. "Max has always been rude and so serious."

Yulya disappears down a corridor. Grachev picks up a pile of papers, taps them together on the top of the desk.

"My sister," he says. "I have two. Lara's a dedicated archeologist. Delightful. And Yulya's a handful, but also delightful. She arrived this morning."

He slips the papers into a plastic folder, crouches down, and locks them in a cabinet. "But you haven't come to see me about that."

"No," says Kat, standing, arms folded, in the middle of the room.

"Then, if you don't mind waiting a minute, I have to get changed."

"It won't take a—"

"Just give me a minute," he interrupts, walking off down the corridor.

The apartment reminds her of the family house on R Street, like a big hotel suite rented for life, comfy red-striped sofas, thick soft materials, a coffee table strewn with magazines, peach-colored walls with pictures of Russia. Kat walks across to them, two prints and three original oils, all of wild, desolate landscapes, snow, a church and farm buildings, and people in the distance, far from any shelter.

Above the desk are a couple of photographs, one of Grachev with a group of cops, in summer shirtsleeves. They have glasses raised in a toast, and there's no way of telling where they are, except on a riverbank. Another is of him with his arm around a woman outside a chalet in woodland. Grachev's face is soft, completely at home. The woman's face is harder, as if she's doing it for the picture. Her dark hair, streaked with gray, is pinned up off her eyes and ears. She's in a blue business suit, older than Grachev, difficult to tell for sure, but probably his mother or an aunt.

Between the photographs is a framed newspaper article in English from about a year ago, a lifestyle piece on Grachev after he got to London. It's pretty much like Cage told her, but with more detail about his time as a homicide detective in Moscow and praising the way he took on organized-crime gangs there.

There's no mention of a wife, any kids, or a girlfriend. The other people in his life are his two sisters; his father, who is retired; and his mother, Tiina—as Cage said—who heads the Russian energy conglomerate RingSet, making Grachev an heir to billions. There's no other way a cop, whether British or Russian, could afford an apartment like this.

"Good, eh? My famous brother."

Yulya is behind her. She's changed into a dark, pinstriped pantsuit and has a briefcase hanging from her arm, while trying to tie back her hair.

"Don't worry, I'm going out. It's all a rush. I've got an evening of meetings."

She has a rubber band between her teeth.

"Turn around, let me fix it for you," suggests Kat, stepping forward.

She bunches Yulya's hair, smells jasmine and honeysuckle. "Here, give me the rubber band."

"Thanks," says Yulya, handing it back.

"What do you do?" says Kat.

"I'm learning the family business. Our mom got lucky in oil and gas, but wants to retire soon."

"But Max is a cop?"

"He's the brainy one. He takes a cut of the family dividends and does what he's always dreamed of doing. As a kid, he spent all day reading detective novels."

Yulya runs her fingers down her hair, adjusts strands at the front, puts on a floppy, bright red hat, and gets its position right in the mirror over the fireplace. "How's that? Knock 'em dead. What do you say?"

"You look great," says Kat.

Yulya's face becomes serious. "I know I am not meant to ask. But Max is homicide. He investigates murders. I mean . . . I hope . . ."

"My sister was shot dead on Friday night."

Yulya steps back, her hand on her mouth, eyes up at the ceiling, dropping back again to look straight at Kat. She holds out both hands, turning the palms upward. "I'm so, so sorry," she whispers.

Kat finds her throat rigid. She swallows, and deep in the pit of her stomach, she controls the sadness kicking at her. "Thank you," she says tightly.

She moves back. Grachev's watching them, zipping up his jacket.

"Take care," says Yulya, and leaves.

Grachev stays quiet until he's seen his sister go past the front window and out of sight.

"Let's take a walk," he says. "Stay behind me; don't catch up until I signal." He goes out the door, leaving it open for Kat.

TWENTY-ONE

$\longrightarrow\!\!\!\diamond\!\!\!\longrightarrow$

He's out in the street. He looks straight ahead, not acknowledging her, eyes on trucks and buses trundling past.

She follows.

He's at the light, about to cross the street.

The light turns green. Grachev crosses and walks right onto a footpath through a lawn decorated with flower beds.

Grachev stops and signals for Kat to catch up with him. He puts his hands on her shoulders, turns her toward him, takes a green cotton scarf out of his pocket, and drapes it around her neck.

"Keep your mouth covered, like this," he says, pulling it up gently. She now sees he has a scarf for the same purpose. He begins walking again. She falls into step with him.

"Are you wired?" he asks, putting the edge of his hand above his eyes to look at an aircraft in the sky.

"No," she says, irritated.

"No one sent you?" He brings down his hand and studies her face. The rain's stopped. The sun's out, and Grachev's worked it so she's looking straight up at it, squinting.

"I sent me."

He looks away from her and talks in a low voice. "Five days from now, on September second, they're signing the Coalition for Peace and Security," he says. "Project Peace, as they're calling it here. Do you understand what that is?"

"Yeah." Kat nods. "They moved the date up."

"Correct, and everyone's been taken by surprise. The closer it gets to that date, the tighter surveillance is going to be everywhere in London. We can't talk in my apartment because it's wired. So is the phone. So is my cell phone. Most times, I'm being followed. The scarves are important. They'll blow up the surveillance pictures and bring in lip readers, who'll go through them frame by frame."

Kat nods again.

"You are clever. You are stubborn. You have the confidence of youth," he says. "You were able to get around the surveillance on your sister's apartment because you have a friend in Washington. But make no mistake. They're good here in Britain. They'll break your encryption system. They may already have done so."

He cuts a look across her, part reprimand, part sympathy, meeting her eyes. She wants to mask how she feels, but her nerves make it difficult.

"So, it was you—following me?" she manages.

"I'm investigating your sister's murder. I told you I was using you to get to Liz Luxton. It's natural that I should put you under surveillance."

"But they lost me."

"Perhaps."

She smooths a loose end of hair around her ear and says nothing. "You're working against me with Nate Sayer," she challenges.

"No one's working against you, Kat. We're working with you. If we weren't, you wouldn't be let within a mile of your sister's apartment." He shrugs. "If you want to play clever, we can all play clever. But then you don't learn, and I don't learn."

"Once I have Suzy's killer, I'll be gone," she whispers loud enough for him to hear through the scarf.

"Walk with me," he says, taking her arm, leading her across the grass. She glances at him but can't read his face, which takes on the expression of someone who wants to be rid of her; who has judged her too difficult, but has decided to go on.

"Remember what I told you about Project Peace."

"Yes. The United States, Russia, and China doing an energy deal."

"The big opposition is here in Britain. The prime minister backs the United States and wants to sign. But he's pushing against public sentiment."

"What exactly has that got to do with Suzy?"

"Suzy was standardizing laws between the three powers. That was her job. From murder to bicycle theft, Suzy was checking that penalties came within internationally accepted guidelines. She was on the team that put together the Project Peace pamphlet you saw last night. Think about it, Kat, for the love of God, think about it."

She stops walking. The air in the park is cool, smells of flowers and freshly mown grass. "I am thinking about it. There must be hundreds of players like her, so how come they're not dead?"

"How do we know they aren't?"

An image comes immediately to mind. Then another, and another.

A man, shot through the head, his blood leaking into the snow on a windswept airfield. Two young women, holding hands in death, their blood thickly streaked down the wall; a young man dead under his desk; an elegant woman, shot, looking as if she were asleep . . .

She looks up at Grachev. "Go on."

"Suzy was shot on a marshland footpath during the intermission of a classical music concert, Tchaikovsky and Beethoven," says Grachev. "Why? Who? I don't know. Is there a bigger picture? Yes, certainly there is. And that's why I'm telling you this, because when we're finished, you will leave London. Go to the airport. Go back home."

He looks at her, and Kat meets his stare. They both hold the silence. Kat doesn't move.

"You're not investigating her murder, are you?"

"You're letting the past eat you," says Grachev.

"What the hell's that mean?"

"Like your sister," he says flatly, giving her nothing.

"You found anything on her computer? No. You haven't even taken it out of her apartment. You found anything from the audience list yet, from people who traveled through checkpoints to that concert? What the hell are you doing to find out who killed her?"

Grachev looks down at the ground.

"Give me the courtesy of an answer," says Kat.

He toes his foot into the grass. "To find a killer, you have to find a motive. Who would want Suzy dead? What I've learned about your sister is this: One, she was obsessed with how your father died. She believed it was not an accident. She believed the plane was sabotaged. Two, she was living under a false name."

Kat and Suzy had reacted differently to their father's death. Kat didn't want to think about it. She blanked out the reasons, blanked out detail, blanked out the list of John Polinski's enemies and found solace in Mercedes Vendetta. Suzy immersed herself in it, wanted to know everything as if she thought it was her job to find out exactly what had happened.

"How obsessed was she?" asks Kat.

"One morning, four years ago, almost to the week," says Grachev, "your father climbed into his Cessna Skylane at Fairfield County Airport after visiting your grandmother, Kathleen Mary Polinski, at her house in Lancaster, Ohio. The Cessna was only eighteen months old. It had just been through a routine servicing. Flying weather was not good, low cloud, rain to the east, but John Polinski had dealt with far worse. On the climb, at 920 feet per minute, something happened, and the plane crashed. Your dad's body was unrecognizable.

"John Polinski made a name for himself on class-action employment cases. He took on packers, canners, agricultural corporations, and got his first break on the issue of illegal migrant labor. About a year before he died, he decided to branch out and took on a case against an international energy consortium. Suzy believed that consortium sabotaged the plane and murdered your father."

Kat's hands have gone knuckle-white to control the rush of thoughts. "Is that what you believe?"

"I don't know yet. It's only three days since Suzy was killed." Grachev is frowning. "But I do know she kept tearing and tearing at the wound and wouldn't let it heal."

"She's not crazy," says Kat defensively, using the present tense. "She wouldn't go chasing ghosts. She must have found something."

"Perhaps," he says. "So let's assume she was right. If your father was murdered, it would have been done by highly professional killers. Now Suzy."

Suddenly, he turns away.

Two Muslim women, covered in black, walk past, each holding the hand of a little girl.

"Let's assume, then," Kat fires back. "Let's assume it is all connected. You're suggesting that I forget any of this shit ever happened?"

"Use Nate Sayer's air tickets."

"You got a problem with me? I'm too much of an addition to your workload?"

"Listen to me, Kat. Hear what I'm saying . . ."

"No, you listen. Suppose Suzy's right?" She walks into his space. "Suppose she's found out that my dad was murdered, and suppose the same people killed her? What are you going to do, Mr. Detective? Ignore two murders because they interfere with your real investigation? Just close the file and send me home like nothing's happened?"

Lightning fast, Grachev's finger is on Kat's chest, pushing her back hard. "Stop right there." He holds her chin between his fingers. "I made a mistake last night, sending you to the lecture. I've learned since then how dangerous this case is. I'm sorry."

There's no waver in his eyes. "If you hunt your sister's killers, you will die. Period. Go to Nate Sayer and ask him to get you back to the States. After this, you won't see me again."

He walks away. Kat doesn't follow. She watches him go, fast and purposeful, then loses sight of him as he turns onto the street outside the park.

Alone, she tears off the scarf. Her hands tremble as she fumbles for a tissue. Her eyes are moist, and her throat is tight. She walks toward the edge of the grass, screwing the tissue into a ball. She pulls out a compact, a thing she never otherwise uses, opens it, and uses the mirror to look around her.

Two women, looking like mother and daughter, have fallen into step behind her, chatting, laughing, alert. The Muslim women have finished their circuit and come out on the path in front. She spots a camera in a tree, its wire trailing. Two white guys, one in denim, the other wearing a leather jacket, sit on a bench, leaning back, legs outstretched, ankles crossed, staring at her. She sees another lens in a streetlight.

She closes the compact and walks quickly along the path toward the road. One of the white guys gets up, cuts across the grass, and jumps a flower bed toward the same exit.

Kat starts walking quickly, not caring who sees, turns, her glance catching a jogger coming right up behind her. She gets to the sidewalk before the white guy, and she's out of the park, hand raised, about to shout for a taxi, but then she drops it.

Kat runs.

TWENTY-TWO

---◇---

Monday, 5:23 p.m., BST

She runs south, past the Chinese embassy, a church on the left, a luxury hotel on the right. She concentrates on her breathing. Fresh rain falls on the sidewalk. The air is damp again.

Pedestrians slow her down at Oxford Circus, a big shopping area. She jogs in place until the lights change. Once across, she cuts down a side street on the right, where there are fewer people.

She recognizes the streets where she and Nancy walked on Saturday night. Too close to Sayer's apartment. She breaks out into a wide street, the Ritz Hotel up to her left and a park on the other side.

Inside the park, she falls into a walk. She's run a mile, maybe more. The whole time, she hasn't stopped thinking about her father. New details are falling into place, starting with the day her father died.

Kat was working at a coffee shop on M Street. Business was quiet. She had finished a year of law school, but she knew it wasn't working. Her mom and dad were fighting, or rather Mom was angry at Dad most of the time. Suzy's career was flying.

A shadow stretched across the sidewalk, and two Lincoln Town Cars drew up in the "No Parking" area in front of her workplace.

Kat remembers a TV on the coffee shop wall showing Jim Abbott launch his first campaign for the presidency. Abbott was talking about his slogan for global security—Safety for All. For some reason that Kat never fully understood, her dad would barely allow Abbott's name to be mentioned in the house.

From the front car, Nate Sayer stepped out with a couple of the bodyguards he'd hired after getting threats from a cattle company.

He came in alone. "Kat, can you turn that off for a minute?" he said, glancing up at the screen.

Sayer was the last person she wanted to see on any day. "Why?" said Kat. "You can't just walk in here and tell me what to do."

Sayer shrugged. He wasn't angry. Kat and Sayer hadn't talked much in the three years since she'd seen him with her mom. But now, he wore an expression Kat hadn't seen before. He wasn't scoring points; he was devoid of arrogance, devoid of that chip he carried around, devoid of agenda.

"Kat, your dad. He's dead."

Kat looked straight at the TV as if her head had been jerked up there by some fishing line. She saw Jim Abbott's face, then let her eyes rest on spilled cappuccino on the counter.

"The Cessna went down, just after takeoff. He was heading back after seeing your grandma."

Kat had been up in the Cessna with her dad. She tried to picture it; how it worked when a plane fell out of the sky.

"The weather wasn't too good. A guy at the airfield said he advised your dad against flying, but he wanted to get home. He told them he could handle it."

Sayer swallowed hard. His eyes were shining. He looked away; too much history with Kat for him to be the right person to tell her. Suzy was in New York. Her mom was with her family at Great Falls.

Sayer's eyes went sharply to the screen. Kat followed them and found herself looking head-on at her father on TV talking outside a courthouse, the camera tight on his face; plenty of lines, but not an ounce of fat, same deep blue eyes as Kat, high cheekbones that he got from his own father, and a stubborn forehead, creased in the lights from the stage.

"What are you saying?" she told Sayer. "There he is, there on the screen. He's fine."

Sayer, looking down, made out that he was rubbing a scratch off the counter with his fingernail. "Some people are saying he was murdered.

Some people are saying he took his own life. Most are saying it was just damn bad luck."

Kat tried to call her mother at home and on her cell phone, but got only voice mail. Suzy had taken a plane straight from New York to Ohio to identify the body.

"I'll find out what happened," Suzy said. "I'll be back later tonight. You going to be all right?"

"I'll be fine," said Kat. "Mom'll be here."

"Look after Mom, okay?" asked Suzy.

Kat was closer to their mom, Suzy to their dad. John Polinski had groomed Suzy for his work. She was a crusader like him. Kat had tried to follow Suzy into law, but she was no good at it.

"It may be that you're not suited to do what Suzy does," her dad had told her only a couple of days earlier. "It may be you have a different personality. It doesn't matter a dime what someone is—lawyer, farmer, senator, truck driver. What matters is the character of a person, so you've got to know, Kat, that there's nothing wrong with walking on the opposite side of the street from everyone else."

Sayer gave Kat a ride to her house on R Street. Kat didn't want to be with her mom and Sayer at the same time. When the car pulled up outside the house, Kat said, "I'm fine here, Nate. Thanks."

Sayer nodded and let her out.

Even if her mom hadn't gotten back yet, Angela, the housekeeper, would be there. Much of Kat's childhood had been spent rattling around the big house with Angela while everyone else was out.

In the past years, her mom's mood swings had become more unpredictable. One day her face would stream with sunshine; another it would be filled with so much anger that Kat needed to run.

Her mom came from a landed and wealthy family in Great Falls, Virginia, about 20 miles northwest of Washington, D.C. John Polinski was the only child of penniless Polish immigrants who'd settled in Lancaster, Ohio, after World War II. He became a pilot, then a Washington attorney, and made his name taking on corporations that mistreated migrant workers. Mom had fallen for John Polinski's idealism.

One day, after they fought, Suzy told Kat that their mom's parents never accepted their dad, and ultimately, neither did their mom. Suzy tried to make sense of it like a legal brief, as if that would make it okay.

"It's like this," said Suzy. "Mom thinks Dad puts his causes before the family. Dad says he's the luckiest man to have married Mom, and he would walk across broken glass for her. But Mom doesn't want that. She wants Dad to love her like a soul mate, someone who's flawed, human, and knows about limitations. But Dad won't do that. He wants to save the world all the time, and it drives her mad. That's why she cheats on him."

Kat walked across the lawn, around the flower beds her mom tended, and opened the door with her own key. She heard a cry from Angela and saw her, on her knees, looking up the stairwell.

Kat looked where Angela was looking, but didn't know what she was seeing at first. Even now, there's no image in her mind of that precise moment.

Like an automaton, Kat went to the kitchen, got a knife, gave it to Angela, and asked her to go up the staircase with it. When she had a good grip on her mother's legs, Kat told Angela to cut the rope.

Kat lowered her mother to the floor. The marble tiles in the hallway were cold and hard—she remembered that clearly. Angela grabbed a cushion.

Helen Polinski's collar was askew, and she had bruise marks around her neck. Kat found a note in her sleeve. "I loved my husband. I cannot live without him. I have no more life to live."

Later that night, Suzy called and said the Cessna's wreckage was scattered all over. There was no body, just flesh, clothing, burned-out things.

Kat finds herself sitting on a park bench and realizes her cell is vibrating. She gets up, walks, and listens. It's Cage. "The FBI is looking into the Kazakh embassy. They've questioned me. They want to question you."

TWENTY-THREE

---◇---

Monday, 6:06 p.m., BST

A surge of anger twists through her. "You said it was fixed."

"It's internal. And it's getting nasty."

"Did you give them the file I got?"

"No."

"Don't."

"It erased."

"What do you mean?"

"Thirty seconds into looking at it, and the whole thing was wiped clean."

"Did you see the woman, the dead guy?" she asks.

"Yes."

"People are being killed for that file."

She's standing on wet grass next to a line of deck chairs abandoned because of the rain. A guy, closing up a burger stall, glances at her. Two cops are talking by a bandstand, too far to hear what she's saying. One looks toward her.

A thought shoots through her mind. That morning, without thinking, Kat used Suzy's laptop to check the Kazakh file. The computer might have had trouble handling that much data in a single file. It would have fixed the problem by copying the data into a temporary file on its hard drive. Kat needs to go back and erase it.

"I need a few hours," she says calmly.

"How are you holding up?" says Cage, stumbling on his words. "I mean physically. Everything."

"Good," she says tightly. "Get me more on Max Grachev and his sister, named Yulya. She's with RingSet. And I need one more thing."

"Go ahead."

"Can you set up that countersurveillance again in Suzy's apartment?"

"Don't go back there."

"I have to."

A pause. "It'll work for five, maybe ten minutes before they realize," says Cage. "Text message me when you're going in. I'll tell you when to leave."

As she approaches Suzy's apartment, Kat stays out of sight of a policeman leaning against the river wall. A V-formation of geese fly parallel to the path, and the evening breeze, coming against the current, makes the river water chop up white.

She goes into the alley that runs behind the apartment building. The door she unbolted in the morning seems untouched. A vine has fallen onto it from a tree branch. She pushes open the door and goes into the patio. She steps across puddles of rainwater. Leaves clog the patio drain. She keeps to exactly the same route, moving along the angle of the wall, onto the fire escape. She texts Cage, waits a minute, and then lets herself in with the back-door key.

No one's been in. Nothing seems to have been touched. She rests her head against the glass of the roof-terrace door. She never imagined how quickly paranoia could eat into someone.

She boots up the computer. Temporary files don't have names, just long numbers. The only way she can identify the Kazakh file, if it's there, is by the time of activation and the size reference.

It's there, right at the top. But the time puts it at 2:01 today, Monday. Kat checks the computer's clock and sees that Suzy had it set on Washington, not British, time. It must be the right file. Kat used the computer just after seven that morning.

She opens it. The picture of the woman with the gun comes up. Erasing it won't do any good. An imprint might remain on the computer. Kat flips out the hard drive.

In Suzy's bedroom, she undresses. She stuffs her laundry into her suitcase, takes out a fresh set of clothes, dresses in jeans, a beige shirt, and sneakers. She puts another set of clothes in a waterproof bag. She checks her software and tool kit and slips Suzy's hard disk into the same bag.

She untapes the Kazakh embassy SIM card from the small of her back. It's damp with sweat, but the polyethylene and plastic wrap has held. She tapes it back again. She puts her passport, money, Suzy's ID, credit cards, and makeup case into a waterproof pouch, which she straps around her waist and pushes down the front of her pants.

She washes her face and brushes her teeth. She leaves the suitcase open on the bed, as if she plans to come back—which she doesn't.

She's been inside the apartment 30 seconds under five minutes and is moving through the kitchen when the doorbell rings.

The apartment has two intercom video screens, one by the front door and the other in the kitchen, exactly where Kat is. It takes a moment for her to read clearly the digital color picture.

Whoever's there has their head down. It's a woman, but she's too close to the lens to identify. Kat zooms the lens to wide angle. Across the street is clear. She sees the policeman at the edge. No other cops are around. Her cell phone's silent; no text message from Cage.

The buzzer goes off again, this time with a voice. "Kat. Kat. Are you there?" The woman steps back. She has a red hat in her hand.

Kat isn't like her father, who believed that everyone had some goodness in them. Nor is she like Suzy, who distrusted everyone until they proved themselves good. Kat's fault is that she suffers from curiosity, and from the moment she identified the woman at the buzzer, she knew she would have to confront her.

Kat doesn't respond. She leaves the way she came in, across the patio, through the door, then around the river pathway.

Yulya Gracheva's hand is back on the buzzer. Kat walks straight past. "If you want to talk, we have to keep moving," Kat says, not looking at her.

"Other way," warns Yulya. "They've got a zone control going on up ahead."

Two police cars are on the entrance to the bridge. Cars and pedestrians are being checked. Kat turns and keeps walking. Yulya falls in beside her. She's dressed the same, but her expression is tight, her lips pursed.

"I thought you had an evening of meetings," says Kat.

"Nothing will be agreed. They're all idealists fighting among themselves."

"So you just happened to drop by my sister's place?"

"Max told me exactly what happened to her. He's upset by it and worried about you, but there are limits to what he can do."

They're moving briskly down the center of a narrow road with cars parked half on the sidewalk. The houses are set back, up steps, with gates to protect them from tidal flooding.

"So?" Kat keeps the pace fast to put distance between herself and Suzy's apartment.

"He can't help you. But maybe I can."

"How?"

"Max is a cop, so he has to do what he's told. I don't. He explained the background, that your sister may have uncovered something to do with the CPS. I can help with that."

Kat keeps moving ahead.

"I'm no good at walking and talking." Yulya stops. "We're far enough away from them." She gestures back toward the bridge.

They slow, but Kat doesn't stop.

"Max told me the river was pretty safe," continues Yulya. "Especially in light like this. No camera across the river can get lip-readable images. And private residents don't like cameras on their property."

She stops, smiles, and blows a kiss into the air. "Don't you love England? When it comes to being watched, there's no place in the world like it."

They're surrounded by a blue twilight deep from the sky, lit by the after-glow of the sun. The river is high, lapping against the wall. Kat stops and leans on it, looks across to boats anchored in the middle and trees and scrub on the far bank. "All right," she says, not quite trusting Yulya, but even more curious than before. "I could do with some help."

Yulya leans next to Kat, elbows on the wall, not worried about dirt on her sleeves. "Those meetings I dipped into," she says. "They were about the CPS. That's why I'm here. My family company's actually pretty big. We're setting up joint ventures along CPS guidelines. Mom's the big hitter, and she's coming over for the signing ceremony on Saturday. I'm learning the ropes. From what I can work out, no one wants any problems before Saturday. So if Suzy's murder is really to do with the CPS, then nothing will be done before then."

"And afterward?" says Kat.

Yulya pushes herself off the wall, wipes grit from her hands. "Who knows?" She adjusts the shoulder strap of her briefcase. "But we're already looking into it and hope to know the answers *before* Saturday. We have a whole department whose job is to know what's going on with our competitors. If people are getting killed over the CPS, we need to know why."

Kat's listening, staring into swollen water, murky from the changing tide. If Yulya can be trusted, what she says makes sense. Private, commercial intelligence agencies are becoming better than government ones. And they're often more motivated.

"Max is off the case," says Yulya. "That's why he was so angry in the park. When he told me, I knew I had to do something, both for him and for you. I'm on my way to Moscow. The company plane's at Heathrow. There's a seat, if you want it. Tomorrow morning, I'll give you our best investigators to find out who killed your sister and why."

Yulya reaches out, takes both Kat's hands. Kat keeps her eyes lowered, arranging her thoughts.

"It's for me, too, Kat. Please. If your sister's murder has anything at all to do with the CPS, all of us need to find out, and you can help *us*."

Kat tilts her gaze up toward Yulya, who's backlit by a streetlight. She steps to one side so she can see Yulya's face better.

Then a number of things happen at once.

In the top pocket of her shirt, Kat's cell vibrates.

"I'll just check this," she says, dropping one hand from Yulya. She takes out the cell. It's Cage.

The hold Yulya has on her left hand tightens a fraction more than necessary. Kat catches an expression on Yulya's face, mouth half open, lips tight, eyes concentrating hard on something behind Kat.

Kat turns.

She sees four men walk toward them, two on each side of the road. One of each pair wears a light long coat, hands inside. The other is in an open-neck shirt, jeans, and sneakers. Farther back, where the road widens, two silver sedans are parked on the sidewalk, doors open, engines running, a driver waiting in each.

For a second, she can't place it. Just people on the road. Nothing unusual.

Then, in that instant, Kat understands. The grainy photo, the blue hat, the heavy coat—none could hide the essential features of the person before her. It's the way Yulya's standing, the certainty on her face, the cast of her eyes.

She's looking at the same woman who shot a man in the head and left him to die in the snow.

No one's said anything. Nothing's moved from normal. People are walking along a river path. Someone's calling a cell phone. That's all.

"Not important," says Kat, putting on a smile, dropping the cell back into her pocket. She tightens her own hold on Yulya's hand, calculating their positions. "Thanks," she says softly. "Thanks so much."

Then things move from normal.

Two men draw out weapons from inside their long coats. The two others sprint toward Yulya and Kat. Kat sees them. Yulya hasn't yet. She's turned slightly away.

Kat swallows, calms herself for what must come next. "What you say makes a lot of sense. So my answer is yes, please."

Yulya's lips loosen into a small smile. But her eyes stay the same. There's a flicker of uncertainty. She shifts slightly to check behind her, and as her concentration on Kat falters, Kat rips away her hand.

Yulya lurches forward. Kat kicks her hard in the sciatic nerve in the upper right thigh and begins using the movement to take her over the river wall.

But Yulya absorbs the kick. Her fingers become a vise, wrenching Kat back. Instead of resisting, Kat calculates the level of pull Yulya's using against her and lets her body go slack. Yulya steps back to compensate. But her fine balance has gone, and she knows it.

Yulya pulls Kat toward her and raises her hand to strike. With all her strength, Kat pulls back. Then, just as Yulya's compensating again, Kat lurches forward, ducks Yulya's blow, and head-butts her, first in the chest, then under the jaw.

As Yulya stumbles back, Kat puts her hand on the river wall and swings herself over.

The fading light has brought with it an evening breeze that runs across the surface of the water. Mud and debris knock against each other. The river surges back and forth against its banks. As she jumps, Kat sees the lights of high-rise apartments, undergrowth, darkness, and the flash of a pistol being fired at her.

The cold bites straight through her as she hits the river.

TWENTY-FOUR

$\diamond$

Monday, 8:38 p.m., BST

The water twists downward. Tidal currents drag her deep beneath the surface. She tries a breaststroke, swimming upward, opens her eyes to stinging, muddy water, and can't reach the surface before being drawn down again.

Mercedes Vendetta growls in her head.

"You ever want to know what's going on, you wait till you get so tired your eyes, your ears, your brain can't take any more. That's when you see what's real."

Kat's lungs are bursting. The water's sucking her down.

Another voice, her father talking to her as a little girl. "Your great grand-dad didn't make it. He was murdered in a place called Auschwitz. Your granddad crossed the Elbe River to escape the Russians. Before that, he'd crossed a river in Poland running from the Nazis."

She can't remember the river's name. She wonders if she'll ever get around to having kids and telling them how she escaped across her own river.

Her mind's getting weak. Her blood screams for oxygen.

Her cell phone's gone already. She tries to get rid of her shoes when, suddenly, the downward drag stops, and Kat begins turning slowly like a top. She kicks herself up, breaking the surface and gulping in air.

She's come up by the side of an anchored barge, exposed to the northern bank, where Yulya is. She ducks under again and swims around to the other side.

She hooks her hand around a rusting painter ring on the hull and lets her body go slack. The current is strong, pushing her feet in front of her. The water's cold, but she can stay in.

She pulls weeds from her hair, runs her tongue around her teeth, and spits out grit. Driftwood bumps her leg.

There's only one way she can go, downstream, which means she has to go through Zone One. Zone One seems like the Green Zone they set up in Iraq or what they have around Capitol Hill. It's quiet inside, but big on checkpoints to get in.

She will have to float out through the other side, the river her cover, and make landfall in the zone beyond and across, on the southern bank. She needs to find Liz Luxton but doesn't want to cross a bridge, where there may be a checkpoint.

She rolls onto her back, legs out in front of her, and lets go of the painter ring. The river washes around her, and the outgoing tide takes her fast. Her lips are pursed, eyes squinting against water surges.

If you work with it, a fast-flowing river is easier to handle than a slow one. Kat's hands bat back and forth like fins to keep her direction while the current moves her quickly along.

You don't fire a gun in a residential area unless things are bad. Yulya must have known Kat had the file that implicated her. But how? She must have assumed that Kat recognized her before she actually did. Why else take such risks?

Up ahead, Kat sees a cordon of four police boats strung across the river. At the jetties along the bank, there are more checkpoints for boats that dock. A helicopter circles.

A minute from now, Kat will be bobbing right under a police searchlight.

The cordon has created a bottleneck of river traffic, mostly tourist leisure boats. Searchlights penetrate enough to sweep underneath hulls. As she gets closer, she sees two police divers in the water.

A voice shouts out from a loudspeaker, but a sweep of water washes over Kat's head, and it fades like a radio tune.

When she comes up, she sees a policeman on a launch step out of the wheelhouse. He balances himself by holding the edge of the doorway, puts binoculars to his eyes, and points them straight toward Kat.

Kat goes down and tries to swim backward against the current. Her right knuckles scrape the hull of a passing speedboat. A roar sears through her ears, water pressure pushing up her nose. She's pulled along in the speedboat's wake and kicks against the hull to push herself clear.

Waves from passing boats hit her face. Kat ducks under but knows now how she's getting through.

She has to get the timing and the boat exactly right. Too close, and she'll get chewed up in the propeller. She chooses a slow-moving, midsize tour boat. The first deck has diners peering out of a light-dimmed restaurant. From the top deck comes music.

Like finding an air thermal, she maneuvers into its wake and grabs the bottom rim of a tire hanging on the waterline as a fender and hooks her arm inside.

The boat slows for the checkpoint. Up ahead, another tour boat has been pulled over. Police are on board, checking passengers' IDs. Searchlights play into the water. An orange inflatable raft bumps up against the side, and a diver on it jumps into the water.

Fifty yards back from the search, Kat's boat's propeller spins into reverse, throwing a gush of white water toward her. Kat takes a mouthful. River weed gets caught in her eye.

Music from the upper deck goes quiet. The propeller slows. Kat treads water. In all, two tour boats and a barge are being searched by police from the three launches in the cordon.

If Kat's boat is called in, she'll be found for sure. She snatches a glance at each bank. To her left, she recognizes the Houses of Parliament and the Big Ben clock tower. No landfall there. To her right, the London Eye Ferris wheel and a promenade. She twists around. There's no way she can swim back against the current.

If they pick her up, it wouldn't take long for the police to ID her. The first person they would call would be Max Grachev. If he's anything like his sister, he'll want her dead. If Kat asks for consular protection, Nate Sayer will turn up, and he wants her back in the States.

Someone blows a whistle. The engine on Kat's boat revs, and she's pulled forward again. She tightens her hold on the tire.

The music starts up. The boat gathers speed. Pitching and banging against the hull, the tire pulls her along, water gushing around her face, like she's a hooked fish.

TWENTY-FIVE

◇

Kat makes landfall when the tide is low enough for her to come ashore on a stinking beach of mud, rotting debris, and tiny stones. A night wind whips through her. She wipes water from her face, tries to pick weeds from her hair, but they're knotted in.

On the northern bank, London is alive with neon and moving cars. On this side, the area looks desolate. No movement. No voices. No city sounds.

Fifty yards farther on, a darkened barge is moored to a jetty, with a small, dirty motor dinghy banging alongside.

The beach stops at a 12-, maybe 20-foot wall; difficult to tell in this light. Metal chains hang down, but are too far apart to climb up. For about four feet from the base of the wall, there is an area of complete darkness, reached by neither the moon nor streetlights.

Kat steps in there, undresses, leaves the sodden clothes in a heap, and peels off the SIM card taped to her back. The fresh clothes she packed are damp inside the bag but wearable. There's underwear, jeans, a white tank top, a red cotton shirt, socks, but no shoes. She'll have to stay with the sodden sneakers.

She uses a leg of the jeans to dry herself a bit, but they're too coarse to soak up much. Despite the chill, she stands naked, letting the wind dry her skin while she checks the waterproof pouch with the SIM and Suzy's credit cards. They seem to have survived.

Her software cards and Suzy's hard drive made it through, too.

The cell phone's gone, and she remembers during the last seconds before she jumped into the river that Cage was calling.

She dresses while working through the questions.

Grachev's behavior now makes more sense. He's assigned to head up Suzy's murder investigation, yet he does nothing. Suzy's computer stays untouched in her apartment. Grachev stays in London, while the murder site is 100 miles away. The only thing he does is ask Kat to flush out Liz Luxton.

Suzy may have had a dozen different people to meet over the next few days. What's so special about Liz Luxton?

Then he warns Kat away. He must have anticipated that Kat would go back to Suzy's apartment, then tipped off Yulya, who waited outside either to abduct or kill Kat. Either way, Max and Yulya working together, along with a small team of gunmen, makes as much sense as anything else she can come up with.

But how does such a bent homicide detective get himself assigned to the case? Does it mean that the assistant police commissioner, Stephen Cranley, is also involved?

A more tenuous connection comes to mind: Suzy's murder coincided with Kat's breaking into the Kazakh embassy. They occurred on the same day. Was the break-in the catalyst? Or was Kat sent in there *because* Suzy had been murdered? Kat gasps at what this line of thought implies: could Bill Cage be part of this?

Kat's eyes sting around the rims. Wiping them doesn't help. Her legs give way, and she balances against the river wall like a drunk, barely managing to put on the damp clothes. Exhaustion takes her by surprise.

She squats by the wall, eyes closed, gathering her strength, focusing her thoughts on the single pinpoint of what she needs to do. She gets up and, carrying her previous outfit, walks to the jetty where the barge is.

The jetty ramp to the barge has two strips of thin red carpet. They are dry. The tide's going out, and it'll be hours before it comes back in again. Kat lifts up the carpets and lays one on the beach, directly beneath the ramp. She covers her sodden clothes with the other as a pillow and lies down.

Before sleep takes her, she sees an image of two Asian women, holding hands, leaving bloodstains on a wall as they slide, dying, to the floor.

TWENTY-SIX

◇

Tuesday, 6:32 a.m., BST

Day's first light reveals two tall tenement blocks on one side of the main street. Grass scrubland lies around them. On the other side, a derelict building has windows smashed and tiles missing from the sloping roof.

Graffiti has been sprayed onto a wooden fence with the faded logo of a security firm. RAND FOR PEACE, it says, with a cartoon image of the young British prime minister.

What Kat needs is *people*, crowds of them, distracted and pressing against each other. She sees no one.

Half a mile ahead is an intersection with traffic lights, but no vehicles. Across the road from her, just beyond the tenements, are five huge trash cans for recycling. She puts her sodden clothes in one and walks toward the intersection.

A white contractor's truck passes her from behind, slows at the lights, and takes a right turn. A red double-decker bus crosses the intersection, heading west. Kat spots video cameras on four lampposts and two yellow traffic detectors.

At the bus stop, she slows, but doesn't stop walking. The bus pulls up. A half dozen people get on. Two use fingerprint ID on board with the driver. Two flap open their wallets to produce electronic ID cards. One buys a ticket with coins from a machine on the street. One has a ticket already.

The driver has a bank of monitors in his cab. He wears headphones and an earpiece. One of the passengers pulls a hood over his head, covering his eyes to avoid iris scanners. TV screens, in pairs, surround the bus's lower and upper decks. Kat sees a broadcast of a soccer team filing onto a plane.

The bus is too empty to be of any use. What's more, no one's using a cell phone. She keeps walking.

More people are around. They walk purposefully, their expressions contradictory, angry, yet defiant.

Zone One is the area where people realize the benefits of state protection. In this zone, they feel victims of it. More cameras watch them. More screens influence them. The road is potholed, the buildings derelict, litter and graffiti abundant.

And, still, no cell phones for the taking.

A quarter mile farther along, outside a row of shops, she comes across two telephone booths that take credit cards, bills, and coins.

The landlines from the telephone booth would be vulnerable if targeted, which in an area like this, they might be. Kat plans to make a single call to Cage, to the one number she knows is secure.

Then, with a stolen cell phone, she will text him to call her. Because there might be triangulation detection on the stolen phone, Kat will need two, ideally three, to make it work.

She goes into one of the phone booths. It's broken, with prostitutes' calling cards taped to the glass. The next phone is working, and she feeds in a £50 note. A message comes up, PLEASE INSERT YOUR IDENTITY CARD OR CREDIT CARD NUMBER.

She presses the cancel button. Another message. THIS MACHINE CANNOT REFUND YOUR MONEY. PLEASE INSERT YOUR IDENTITY CARD, AND A REFUND WILL AUTOMATICALLY BE CREDITED TO YOUR BANK ACCOUNT. IF YOU DO NOT HAVE YOUR CARD WITH YOU, PLEASE INSERT YOUR PERSONAL ID NUMBER.

Then in big letters, like a cigarette pack warning, IT IS ILLEGAL TO BE WITHOUT YOUR ID CARD. MAXIMUM PENALTY—IMPRISONMENT.

Wise up, says Kat to herself. Why would anyone put in a £50 note, unless they were calling overseas? Chances are, it sounded off an alert.

A printed card comes out. On it is a photograph of Kat, a record of her fingerprint, and a note that she is owed £50 by British Telecom.

The final line says USER'S IDENTITY UNKNOWN.

She walks quickly along the main road toward Rotherhithe subway station. As she gets closer, she sees what she needs.

A crush of people is gathered under screens outside the subway entrance. The sports screen is split. One side shows an interview with the England soccer captain. The other runs replay highlights of the match with China. On the second screen, which no one is watching, two bearded men are paraded at an army barracks. The caption says KASHMIRI TERROR COMMANDERS CAPTURED.

Kat's thefts take less than five seconds each. One cell phone is hidden only by a scarf in a woman's bag. Kat identifies the second by its bulge in the side pocket of some overalls. The third has worked its way loose from a belt case whose covering flap is undone.

Kat breaks away from the throng and heads south. She turns the phones off to lower the risk of triangulation. She walks for more than a mile. Then, at a newsstand, she buys chocolate, a Coke, a hairbrush, and an *A–Z London* map book. As she's paying, she sees a stack of pocketknives and buys one, too. The newspaper headlines are of England's soccer victory over China.

Dr. Christopher North, author of the Project Peace pamphlet, is on the newsstand's TV. The volume is turned up high, the sports channel muted.

". . . coalition will feed the hungry," North is saying. "It will protect our homes and make the world safe for us to live in."

Kat gets her change and leaves. She's near a subway station called Surrey Keys. Liz Luxton's place in Balham is a long way to the southwest. It'll take a couple of hours to walk there.

Now she needs a place where lots of people are using their cell phones. On the map, about a mile south, is a soccer stadium. With England celebrating a big win, there might be some hope there.

All cell phones contain a built-in International Mobile Equipment Identity (IMEI), which automatically logs into the nearest base station whenever it is used. The phones' SIM cards, which can be swapped from handset to handset, carry an International Mobile Subscriber Identity (IMSI), which contains the billing number, including the international code for the country in which it's registered. If a phone's reported stolen, it's most likely this will be the number used to track it. The IMSI is also the one used to intercept and tap into cell phone conversations.

Cell phone receiving antennae can be on any tall structure, and at least three are needed to triangulate a call. The closest tower detects the distance of the caller, but it could be in any direction. The second tower defines an arc. The third pinpoints the location.

Some cells have devices that triangulate the phone so it can be tracked if stolen. Their cameras will automatically take pictures of the thief and send an iris ID to a police database. A phone's laminated cover can activate to absorb fingerprints and send them as well.

Kat has to find Bill Cage, organize a secure way of communication, and get rid of the phones quickly.

It spits with rain. She passes an intersection where the sports screen is broken and the U.S. president, Jim Abbott, is in the White House Rose Garden. The caption says ENERGY TREATIES CONFIRMED.

She finds the audience outside the soccer stadium, concentrating on the twin sports and politics screens. Javier Laja, the Brazil captain, is being interviewed, with sound being blasted from speakers in the stadium's wall.

"What will you do if you lose?" asks the interviewer.

Laja puts on a smile, his bushy, dark hair pulled back, big hands open. "I will find a beautiful woman and make love to her," he says.

Kat laughs out loud. She's eating chocolate, her body sucking in the sugar.

The host's reaction is deadpan. "If you win, your victory will be doubly historic because it will coincide with the historic signing of Project Peace."

Laja turns, spits on the ground, looks back straight into the camera, and says, "Project Peace is a trick—" The screen flickers to black.

"I thought they had a five-second delay," says a man close to Kat.

"It was deliberate," comes the answer from a woman next to him. "A lot of TV people loathe Project Peace, and no one can touch a man like Laja."

Kat hasn't seen Laja since she was about twelve, and even now she gets a little choked up when she remembers their first encounter, when they were both about eight. "I'm sorry about your mom and dad," she said to this Brazilian kid who'd lost his parents, both undocumented workers.

Laja stared in front of him, his right foot on a soccer ball, not saying anything, because he didn't understand English. Tears just tumbled down his cheeks.

He wrote her a letter when her own mom and dad died. Kat was too broken up to reply. As the screen picks up with the same pictures of the Chinese team getting onto a plane, Kat realizes that Laja's comment and the screen blackout have prompted people to make cell phone calls.

Kat melts into the sea of people and fires up one of the cell phones.

TWENTY-SEVEN

———◇———

Tuesday, 7:46 a.m., BST

It's me," she says.

Silence for a beat. Then, "You okay?"

"I'm fine."

"I called twelve hours ago. Then—"

"Aliya Raktaeva, the Kazakh embassy trade secretary," Kat interrupts. "Was she working for you?"

A pause. Then Cage answers straight. "Yes."

"Those men I killed. Are they from the same people who killed Suzy?"

"Yes."

"Did you know Suzy was dead when I went in?"

"No."

"Did you know the embassy had been hit?"

"No."

"Do you know what Suzy was doing?"

"I can't answer."

Kat lets it go. Cage can only say so much.

"What do I need to know?" she asks.

"Stay away from Nate Sayer and anyone in government," answers Cage quickly.

"Are you safe?"

"The next twenty-four hours will tell."

"Anything else I need to know?"

"Yulya Gracheva and her mother are bad. They're killers," says Cage.

"Max?"

"Don't know."

Two police motorcyclists, blue lights flashing, pull up outside the stadium, signaling people to stay on the sidewalk. A limousine with darkened windows turns into the road and accelerates past.

"You there?" asks Cage.

"Sorry. Yeah. Can you find Liz Luxton and tell her I need to see her? Now." Before Cage can answer, she gives him the address in Balham, then hangs up.

She leaves the crowd, walks half a mile until she finds an Internet café. Two guys in sweatsuits with hoods are checking in by signing onto a biometric fingerprint reader. They pay cash for a booth.

Kat needs to find a way around that detection system. She steps back out and keeps walking southwest in the direction of Balham. She examines the Internet access on the stolen cell phones. The problem lies with their embedded antitheft systems. If she were at home in her workshop, she could have neutralized them, but not on a London street.

It starts raining. She steps under a shop awning, removes the SIM card from the phone she used to call Cage, puts in one from another phone so that the SIM ID no longer matches the handset ID. It doesn't make it secure, but it buys her more time. She calls Mercedes Vendetta in Washington.

A siren flares up. At the edge of her field of view, an ambulance jumps red lights and makes a sharp right turn.

Someone picks up at Mercedes' end. She hears loud, rhythmic music and a woman's voice. It's the early hours of Tuesday over there. "M?" says Kat, hesitantly. The music fades. An English caller ID must have come up on Mercedes' phone.

He speaks away from the mouthpiece. "Give me a sec," he says. A door closes. "Okay, we're confidential," he says. "How's things?"

"Has anyone come to see you?"

"Not from your world. And what you asked me to do is fine."

"Thanks."

"Is this a new number to call you on, like if I get a visit?"

"No," says Kat sharply. "I'll call you again soon."

"You got time for advice?"

"Sure."

"Don't think confusion. Don't think mistakes. Don't think emotions—"

"I love you for that, M," interrupts Kat, "but I need you to do one more thing for me."

Kat tells him, then hangs up.

TWENTY-EIGHT

$$\longrightarrow\!\!\!\!\diamondsuit\!\!\!\!\longrightarrow$$

Tuesday, 9:46 a.m., BST

She finds what she needs in the third Internet café, part of a chain called Simple Net. The link between the central database and the fingerprint biometric sensor is broken. Rather than shut the store down, staff are swiping ID cards or taking an infrared record from cell phones.

Kat uses Suzy's ID, then pays cash for a PC with an extra hard drive in a private booth. They put Nancy's £20 note through a scanner, and it comes out clean.

At her computer, Kat logs into her encrypted personal storage file. While waiting for it to come up, she takes Suzy's hard drive out of her bag, puts it on the workspace, and plugs the cord into it.

Kat brings out her compact mirror, pretends to fish something out of her eye, sees there's normal activity behind her, and puts the mirror at a tilt on the glass desktop, so she can keep checking.

Her personal file lights up as active. She messages Cage and tells him where Liz Luxton can find her.

She waits for Suzy's hard drive to respond. She waits for Cage to get back to her. She Googles the Project Peace pamphlet she saw at the lecture. North's face appears, then fades to the logo of Project Peace with a caption under it, *The Secure Path Ahead.*

The pamphlet is ten pages long, with pictures of energy workers of all nationalities on oil and gas fields featured early on. Further along is a chart of terror groups and mug shots of their leaders. Then a map of energy supplies around the world, spread over two pages, and divided into oil, gas, nuclear, and others. On the two back pages is a bulleted list in alphabetical order.

- Apply yourself to the situation.
- Better yourself in the eyes of your peers.
- Create trust between neighbours.

Kat scans through until:

- Zealotry is destructive.

Set in a bold-type box:

> Suspicion is bad; skepticism is good. Ensure you know your neighbour. If he or she doesn't want to know you, *be skeptical.*

In another:

> Make a friend of a person of another religion. If they shun you, *be skeptical.*

The inside pages are a brief history—crusades, trade wars, discovery of oil, the 1978 overthrow of the shah of Iran, the Soviet invasion of Afghanistan, the 1991 Gulf War, 9/11, the Iraq war, Iran, Syria.

Throughout, the Coalition for Peace and Security seems to depend on being made credible by the omnipresent historian Dr. Christopher North.

Her eyes jig to the mirror. She sees backs of heads, glimpses of screens. She switches to Suzy's hard drive. Nothing. She gives it time. Still no data. Condensation from her river journey must have wrecked it.

Another glance behind her, then Kat peels the SIM card copy of the Kazakh embassy file from the small of her back and unwraps the plastic wrap and polyethylene. It's bone dry. The PC has no slot for it. She puts an unused stolen cell phone in front of her and lines it up on an infrared link.

She takes a flash card from her own software pack, praying that it's survived the river. The desktop recognizes it. Kat creates a protective cordon against being monitored.

The flash card emits a radio signal that jams triangulation of the cell phone's signal. It also throws out an electronic decoy screen, which deceives remote surveillance on the computer.

Kat splits the screen. On the left, she runs a video interview with North. On the right, she opens the Kazakh file.

Now she's certain, and it doesn't even require seeing Yulya's face. It's partly the way she stands, legs half apart and torso slightly twisted. It's the way the arms hang, too. Kat zooms in closer to look at the face and picks out the freckles and the birthmark that just appears at the rim of her hat.

She flips on further into the file. It's big. She can't look at it all, and she needs to know exactly what it's about.

She stops at a section of e-mails, most of them one-liners, arranged by date, with no company logo or reference. They are sent from AOL, Hotmail, MSN, servers where anyone can open and close an account in a minute.

They don't indicate who sent them and who's receiving them, and they're in three languages. Given more time, Kat could source them, but Simple Net café is not the place.

Figures for reserves in the Caspian Energy Region are incorrect.

Данные по запасам в Каспийском энергетическом регионе не соответствуют действительности.

Каспийдін энергетикалық эніріні коры туралы кужаттар шындыкпен сэйкес келмейді.

Where are the inaccuracies?

Ninety percent of reserves are within Kazakhstan's borders.

Declare only those outside.

You happy with that?

Our advantage.

See attached. Ballpark?

Twelve percent official. Seventy percent actual. Published Kazakh reserves are 17.6 billion barrels. Actual are 120 billion barrels.

Keep the lid on that.

Post CPS, no problem.

Kat recognizes the first language as Russian. She copies and pastes the second version into a search engine. It comes out as Kazakh.

Kat's only 24 years old and knows she's ignorant about a great many things. What she's looking at now is getting far too complicated.

Oil and gas reserves are being rigged. Prices are being falsely fixed.

Three languages mean at least three people know. The chances are that those three people also know about the photograph of a man lying dead, his blood turning snow to red.

She highlights the file and presses the keyboard to transfer it to her personal storage file. The cursor stays hourglassed. Then a message says "File too large for transfer."

She could try splitting it up, but when you tamper with data, you never know if it will erase itself or send out an alert.

In the compact mirror, she sees a face behind her, not peering at her screen, but looking straight at her.

He stands, resting his hand on the partition. The green light makes his skin look tanned and pockmarked. His eyes are a milky gray. She feels his gaze, but doesn't react, doesn't match it, keeps her eyes ahead of her, turns her screen to black, drops her eyes, and sees a scuffed boot.

"Hello, Mike," she says. "Thanks for your help yesterday."

"I was right then?" His tone sounds like he doesn't much care either way.

"Yeah. You were."

He doesn't answer.

"Someone told you I was here?"

He nods. "Liz. She was a good friend of your sister's."

Kat's not sure about the answer. She needs to know that Cage sent him.

She stands up and speaks with her voice lowered. "Which someone?" she asks.

"From Washington," he says softly. "And not Nate Sayer." He looks around. "You made a good choice coming here," he continues. "You're secure."

Mike Luxton moves into her booth. There's just enough space for the two of them. Kat edges back. Her hand covers the cell phone. Her thumb and forefinger unclip the Kazakh embassy SIM card. She examines Luxton's face. It's unshaven and creased, with the same dulled expression as before.

"Why do you want to see my sister?" he asks.

"She was supposed to meet Charlotte on Sunday evening."

"That's right."

"Why?"

"I said they were friends."

"Why at the North lecture?"

His expression changes, a smile at the edge of his mouth. His arrogance is naked, the threat cold, but there's something else. The way he makes her wary isn't just professional, it's personal. Mike Luxton has sexual power, and she's feeling it.

He drops a cell phone on the desk. Kat doesn't touch it. "To be honest, I'm not sure myself," he says. "Liz would come herself, but she has cerebral palsy. It affects her muscle control. The birth got screwed up and they took her out with forceps that rearranged her brain, so the messages to her limbs become mangled. She gets around slowly."

"I'm sorry," Kat says.

"Don't ever say that to her. Just give her time when she gets caught in a stutter."

Kat activates the PC's screen. Cage has messaged. "They're coming. They're trusted."

She looks across to Luxton. He's not a man she would like to see angry. She'd be wrong to think of his face as cruel. But internal scars are etched into it, giving him something untamed in his character, like with Mercedes Vendetta. She doesn't mistrust him so much as she finds Mike Luxton an interesting man.

"I need to see where my sister was murdered," says Kat.

"Understood," he says. "Murder sites give answers."

It's a struggle to keep her voice at a whisper. "Why was my sister there? Who was she with? What was she doing? Why was she at the concert? Who else was in the audience?"

"Good questions, but they're for Liz, not me."

"Where exactly was it?" presses Kat.

"A village called Snape. The concert hall's called The Maltings."

He glances at the cell phone he gave her. Kat takes the back off it, slides out the battery and the SIM card, casts her eyes over them, slips them back in again, checks the number of the phone, and commits it to memory. He watches her.

"After I leave," he says, "give it five minutes. Go outside, walk to the intersection. Watch the TV screens there until Liz calls you."

Kat waits until Luxton goes, collects her things, and shuts down the computer. In the bathroom, she wraps the Kazakh SIM card again in plastic wrap and polyethylene and tapes it to her back, then messages Bill Cage with the new cell phone number.

Then she steps out.

TWENTY-NINE

———————◇———————

Rain spits down past the TV screens on the street corner. Kat blends with people gathered there. They are people with time on their hands who are angry at life. They gaze at the digital images as if wishing for a miracle to fall from the sky.

She puts one of the stolen cell phones in a garbage can, slips the other into a woman's open shoulder bag, and keeps the one she hasn't used.

The cell phone that Luxton gave her beeps.

"K-kat?"

"Yes."

"Are you facing the ACR B-bank?"

Diagonally across the intersection, Kat sees ACR. High on its frontage are two more TV screens, and a pub to one side.

"C-cross over, go straight, leave the b-bank on your left and go right at the first turn. G-go round a curve, and you'll get to a railway. T-turn right and go in under the arches."

Kat walks, letting Liz explain in her own time. Her grandma, when she chose to speak, used her words so slowly it used to drive Kat mad with impatience, until one day, her father whispered in her ear, "Words are all she has now. You have to let her speak them as best she can."

She follows Liz's directions and finds herself at the start of a dead-end alley, a high-fenced wall on one side, an elevated railway line on the other, with dull gray brick arches underneath, each one housing a workshop: Chas Motors, Scrim Bikes, Heath Mercedes Specialists.

Up ahead, maybe 200 yards away, is a high, flat wall. In between, a reek of chemicals and engine oil, radio noise, men working in jeans and greasy overalls. Cars, hoods up, jacked up, clouded in spray paint, are out on the street.

She turns down the road, which becomes cobblestones. She slows, dropping the spring in her step. A car, three men in it, moves across the entrance, blocking her way out.

She hears a familiar song on the radio, gritty and soulful from her Dix Street days.

The three men look her over like people did on Dix Street. She's in a community that looks after its own. Kat slows but doesn't stop.

She sees Liz, her long arm shaking slightly, wrist raised high to attract Kat's attention, like they've agreed to meet all along, and this is just how it should be. Liz's hair is tied back, but not tidily, and she's wearing a floral, red and white summer dress. Mike Luxton is standing beyond the raised hood of the car, one hand on the roof, the other pointing angrily at his sister.

Kat gets closer and hears Liz shouting, not caring who hears. "If you strip them out, we're not taking it." There's no stutter; her irritation seems to suppress it.

"If you keep them in," says Luxton evenly, "you'll get picked up as soon as you leave London."

"Do you want us to get there or not?" challenges Liz. She balances her long, willowy body by holding on to the top of the open car door with one hand and the hood with the other. As her weight shifts, her muscles race to catch up. It looks like she could fall at any moment, but she manages to keep upright.

"I want you there, and you want to *be* there," says Luxton. "That's what all this is about." He clicks his tongue at the back of his mouth and takes a cigarette out of a pack in his jacket pocket.

"And don't you smoke while we're discussing this," says Liz.

Luxton pinches the bridge of his nose with his fingers. "We can handle the checkpoints."

"You handled them *once*."

"And it worked."

"Two *months* ago," Liz shoots back. "Have you noticed what's happened since Project Peace moved up? They've been upgraded."

Behind Kat, the three men are watching the main street, not Kat.

"You guys need some help?" Kat asks, hoping to lighten the situation. She comes up on Liz's side of the red Ford Mondeo, which is new and has a rental card hanging from the mirror.

Luxton is on the other side, his hands motionless on the hood, a brother being told off by his sister. Kat smiles.

Liz looks up. "H-hello. I'm Liz. Suzy was one of m-my best friends. She told me a lot about you. She loved you a lot."

"Thanks," says Kat, softly. "I thought you were running out on me the other night."

Liz offers her hand. It feels knotted when Kat takes it. The skin is coarse, with a scar running down from the thumb. Her fingers clench with different strengths, not able to work together.

Kat looks back at the open hood. "You got a problem here?"

"They've put a new roadblock up on the route to where your sister was killed," says Mike Luxton. "I don't know what you have over in the States, but here a car comes with three ID sensors, two on each number plate and one in the engine casing. Each emits a signal, which is picked up as you approach a checkpoint. If the car's sensors are working, they can run an immediate ID check on you. If they're not working, they detect that, too, and pull you over. Either way, it's risky."

"Is our trip illegal?"

"We c-can go," says Liz, staring down her brother. "It's just that we don't want them to *know* we're going. If we take the sensors out, they'll know we've tried to cheat them. If we keep them in, at least we're not doing anything illegal until we're pulled over. Then they'll know who we are."

Kat squats down by the front license plate and runs her fingers over the surface. A barely detectable transmitter stretches across the top of the lettering, similar to the type used in the States a few years back.

"In the rain, it's about a three-hour drive," says Luxton.

"The rain's stopping," says Liz.

"You got replacements for these?" says Kat, looking up at Luxton, her hand on the license plate.

He points to a worktable under the nearest arch, where two plates lie. Kat brings the cell phone out of her pocket. "Is this straight off the shelf?" Luxton nods.

Kat works on the Mondeo's front seat, setting the cell phone down next to her flash card, connecting them with infrared and loading a software program into the cell phone. She turns the phone back on.

"Run the engine," she says. Liz steps back, and Luxton starts the engine. Kat gets out, holds the cell phone a few yards away from the license plate, and summons Liz over.

"See here?" She points to the phone's tiny screen. "It's like our system in the States. The license plates give off the vehicle specs, service history, last mileage, registered owner. It's a static data chip that activates when the engine's running. Anyone can access it—police, tow truck drivers, anyone with the equipment. It's not encrypted."

She steps closer to the car. "Okay, Mike, cut the engine."

As it dies, the sensor's transmission signal also goes.

"This is a rental, so you'll be fine," says Kat. "I assume it's not under either of your names."

"Right," says Luxton.

Guiding Liz by the elbow, Kat leans into the engine. "That's where the really nasty one is, and you can't get to it. They embed it inside the engine metal like an airplane's black box. If they're suspicious of the car, they tune into it. They'll know who's in it, what they're talking about, where they're going. Everything. This is what we need to fix."

Kat knows about code-screening vehicles so no one can tell where they're registered or who's driving. Most times when they carried out an embassy job, she and Cage rigged at least two vehicles, a primary and backup.

"I'm going to override the engine casing signal with the cell phone," Kat continues. "It'll take about fifteen minutes. The override takes the make of the car, plate numbers, and registration details, but sends out a whole heap of false information so no one will know who we are, and in between checkpoints, they won't know where we are, either."

As Kat works, Luxton melts back into a workshop, and Liz perches on the hood. Kat can't help noticing a scar underneath Liz's right lower jaw. It matches the one she's seen on Liz's hand.

"Did they cut you up a few times to try and fix you?" she asks.

"W-when I was a child, they tried to loosen up my muscles." She's got one hand on the windshield to keep balance even when sitting. "It didn't work *very* wonderfully, but at least I can walk. And I can drive."

One set of fingers unfurls to tap her skull. "W-what I really want to do is g-get rid of my stutter. Even if I get my brain signals right, my tongue muscles are not coordinated enough to reach the right parts of my mouth to make words properly."

"You seemed all right when you were yelling at Mike."

One eye swims around in an orbit of its own. The other is sharp and shining. "Cerebral mystery, they should call it," she says. "You never know what might happen. A lot of people think it's a disease, but it's a condition, like having a broken leg."

"How did you know Suzy?" Kat asks.

"She found me. She was very clever." Liz holds her hands out in front of her. "You wouldn't think it looking at these, but I'm a video editor. I work at a production house called Media Axis, which does most of its work for the government. About a year and a half ago, I began work on the Project Peace video profile, you know that thing by Christopher North, where I saw you on Sunday. That's when I first met Charlotte—or Suzy, I guess. Her job was to check that everything in the documentary matched the line being put forward in the printed materials. An example would be that in China, say, they have special compartments in trains for minorities, like Tibetans or Uighurs. In Europe, we would call that racial discrimination. It was down to that sort of detail."

A light comes on in the cell phone.

"Does the car have a cigarette lighter in it?"

"In the d-dash."

Kat plugs in the cell phone. "Sorry, go on."

Liz's face is creased in thought. "But that's not really why Suzy was there. She knew a lot more about Media Axis than I did. Everything—and I mean everything—that's visually recorded comes into its database. It takes up three whole buildings in Docklands. Floor after floor, both above and below ground, are taken up with a digital computer archive. My tiny job on North's video was part of a huge contract to ensure that the Coalition for Peace and Security went ahead. Eventually Suzy told me that she'd found me because she wanted to prove that the CPS was a con."

"When was this, exactly?"

"Around Christmas, not the one just past, the one before that."

Kat thinks back, recalling that Suzy contacted her around that time, when they hadn't talked for months. They chatted like normal, big sister, baby sister, except Kat didn't tell her about Dix Street, Vendetta, or that she was working for the U.S. government.

Suzy asked for help, and Kat ended up writing software and then a key-logging program so Suzy could find passwords by recording users' keystrokes. Kat copied it onto a tiny jump drive and told her how to conceal it in a mainframe. It must have worked, because she didn't hear from Suzy again for a long time.

"And you went along with that?" says Kat.

"I was against P-project Peace. There are dozens of editors she could have worked with. But we managed to link up, and—"

"How?" Kat interrupts.

"I guess you'd say I'm just one part of a network of people who don't want the CPS being signed."

"How big is this group?" presses Kat. She climbs out from inside the car, stands up, and faces Liz.

"Not yet," says Liz, her stutter subsiding as her face flushes with what seems to be anger. She glances across toward the workshop where Luxton went. "All I can say is that we need your help. I'm not meant to tell you this now, but fuck them. I will. Suzy was on a mission to prove that four years ago, your father was murdered by the people setting up the CPS. They killed her because she got the evidence she was after."

THIRTY

Tuesday, 2:55 p.m., BST

You smell like shit," says Liz.

Kat's been dozing on and off. She pushes herself up in the seat. "I got busy. No time to shower." Kat doesn't plan on telling anyone about her river swim, not even Cage.

Liz Luxton drives leaning forward more than is natural, her eyes fixed on the road.

The shape of her head is elongated, as if it's been squeezed. Her mouth hangs open, and her hair, although tied back, is unkempt. Her fists show knuckle-white around the wheel as she overtakes a truck.

The cell phone, plugged into the cigarette lighter, bleeps its signal as if it is transmitting a text message.

They're on a curve in the road, in lush countryside, deep green leaves heavy on the trees, fields of bright yellow stretching back from the four-lane highway, harvesters bringing in crops, and a lone church far in the distance against a blue sky wisped with clouds.

"Where are we?"

"Ten minutes from the new roadblock." The car swerves suddenly, but it's just Liz settling it back into the inside lane.

"You're a terrible driver," Kat says.

"I'm d-disabled. I deserve to be," jokes Liz. She brakes, jolting Kat forward so much that her seat belt locks. Far ahead, Kat sees a truck slowing.

"Sorry. Shit driver, like you said."

Kat's eyes go out to fields rolling as far as she can see, some yellow, some green, some filled with purple flowers. When she turns back, Liz's expression has changed. Her tongue plays with a mole at the side of her mouth, and Kat recognizes a woman trying to hold back tears.

"I loved Suzy. She talked about you a lot. She worried about you. That's why I wanted to meet you, to take you where she was k-killed."

Liz sets her good eye level on Kat for a moment before looking back to the road in front. Kat reaches out, puts her hand on Liz's arm.

Liz's cell phone rings. It's Luxton. "Can you get it?" asks Liz.

"How far are you from the checkpoint?" asks Luxton.

Kat looks across to Liz, repeats the question. "Ten minutes," says Liz.

"Okay, I heard that," says Luxton. "They're pulling over rental cars. One of the cameras is logging every rental, so that by the time it gets to the checkpoint, they know chapter and verse about the car and who's meant to be driving it."

"Shit," says Kat under her breath.

"Might your system override the fact that it's a rental?"

Kat shakes her head. "It won't. They'll have enough time to bring up the data." Kat tells Liz, who moves across to the slow lane.

"Do you want to try again tomorrow?" says Luxton.

The way Kat's world is running right now, tomorrow could be a year away. She shakes her head, looks across to Liz.

"We k-keep going," Liz says, loudly enough for her brother to hear.

A pause at Luxton's end. "Okay. I'll see what I can do."

Liz pushes herself up in her seat. "I'm pulling up ahead," she says. "You drive. An American tourist and a cripple might do the job."

Liz stops on the shoulder and keeps the engine running. Kat slides across behind the wheel. Ahead, on high ground, she sees a shopping mall, PC World, Toys "R" Us, McDonald's. Liz uses a walking stick to walk around, climbs in, and slots the stick by the seat. She peers through the windshield, her good eye balled up in concentration, a line of sweat on her upper lip.

"M-move out and g-get over into the right lane," she says. Kat follows her instructions. The traffic is jammed up, stop and go.

"We take the signs to Felixstowe."

Kat edges forward. On a field across the road, a seagull flies around the back of a harvesting combine.

"S-see where that red container truck is?" says Liz, pointing across the rotary. "That's where the checkpoint starts. They're probably using exterior voice surveillance. Audio and lip."

"Why here?"

The traffic inches forward. "The port," says Liz. "It used to be owned by the Chinese, then the Russians bought it." She glances across. "About six weeks ago, there was a roadside bomb, like they use in Iraq, not in the port, but on the road leading to it. It wrecked a truck and k-killed the driver."

The traffic stops. Liz shifts in her seat and points again. "Over there, see, those iron posts on the side of the road? They're the audio filters. They bring in sounds from the car, filter out extraneous noises, clean up the audio stream, and feed our voices to their database."

The traffic begins moving again. Liz's finger swings down to yellow lines painted onto the road. "That's where it starts in earnest. Underchassis X-ray and some k-kind of thermal imaging which c-can read a person's heat signature through a vehicle chassis. Mike used something like it when he was with the army in Iraq. They can tell if we're armed, whether we're sweating with fear. They can see us actually *breathing*."

Kat brings her window down. A grass bank rises steeply. The wind's cool, smelling of rain about to come. Traffic fumes are mixed with the smells of damp soil and summer harvest.

"Who owns the port?" she says.

"A company called RingSet."

"That'd be right," whispers Kat to herself. What are the chances of Yulya reading Kat's mind, calling the checkpoint, telling them to bring her in?

"Do you know anything about them?"

Liz puts a finger to her lips.

With a belch of air pressure, the truck ahead releases its brakes and jolts forward. Slowly, they move around, like it's any jammed-up junction in the rain. Kat watches a couple come out of Toys "R" Us, lift a child out of a stroller into the backseat of a car.

She follows the truck onto an exit ramp sloping down toward a line of tall, concrete barriers set in the road to narrow traffic into one lane. Corrugated plastic stretches across the top of them as a roof, creating a dark area underneath.

Kat makes out four uniformed men, two on each side, two armed. The truck moves on. Liz's head is dropped, staring at something around the glove compartment, fingers drumming on her knee.

Every few yards, a different sign instructs drivers. TURN OFF MOBILE PHONE. NO INTERNET. NO RADIO OR TELEVISION. REMOVE CONTACT LENSES. REMOVE GLOVES. TURN OFF HEADLIGHTS. ILLUMINATE INSIDE OF VEHICLE. PREPARE WINDOW FOR PALM IDENTIFICATION. RECITE CLEARLY AND SLOWLY WHEN ASKED, STATING NAME, NATIONALITY, AND POST CODE.

Kat lets the car glide up to the checkpoint line. As soon as she reaches the covered area, a spotlight hits Kat's face.

"Do *precisely* what they say," whispers Liz, pushing the central control to lock Kat's window. The spotlight snaps off, throwing Kat's vision out. Illuminated arrows mark a route through the concrete blocks, green for the section Kat's in and red farther ahead.

From somewhere comes a male voice. "Place your hand on your side window glass. Look into the scanner above your head to your right."

A blue light comes on. A three-dimensional image of Kat's hand appears on a screen.

Liz is doing the same, hand on window, eye on scanner. God knows how it deals with the lazy eye. Liz gets a green light on both. Kat's are still being searched.

"Passenger Luxton, get out of the car."

Liz opens the door. She swings her legs out, heaves herself to her feet, takes a second to balance, grabs the walking stick, and heads unsteadily across to a booth between two concrete blocks and disappears.

An X-ray box comes toward the car from the ceiling and judders to a stop, like in a car wash.

"Driver, remove your right hand from the window. Put both hands on the wheel. Keep them in full view."

Sweat gathers inside the palms of Kat's hands. She closes her eyes to try to think. Could this be Yulya's doing? She and Grachev knew she wanted to head down here. Grachev has the authority to put out a bulletin for Kat. She's swept with a sudden sadness that it's all come to nothing. Suzy, her dad, her mom are all gone. And for Kat, it ends at a grubby roadblock a long way from home.

"Keep your eyes open at all times and look at the scanner."

A pause, then. "Be prepared to surrender your mobile phone."

Kat's eyes stay on the scanner, and the passenger door opens, with a new voice commanding her. "Keep your eyes on the scanner, and start the car."

She doesn't react. She recognizes who it is; the tone, the confidence of movement. He closes the door with a gentle click, buckles himself up, leans across her lap, and starts the engine. His breath smells of nicotine, his shirt of oil.

"Keep driving. They'll flash red lights. The guards will wave you back. Go fast. Don't smash, and don't stop."

Kat releases the hand brake, lets the engine go. A siren echoes around the concrete. She picks up speed, headlights on, or she'll hit the sides. A red laser hits her in the eye. She squeezes the gas, accelerates around a sharp curve.

Kat swerves out, overtaking the truck in front of her. She glimpses the side mirror and sees a guard with weapon half raised, face creased with uncertainty. She's around another curve, and she comes out into a stream of sunlight, blinding her.

Kat guns the engine. The transmission jumps down a gear and picks up the acceleration. There's a barrier coming down. Kat gets under it into a two-lane highway stretching far ahead, grass embankments on both sides, thin traffic.

Mike Luxton pulls a cigarette from a pack in his pocket and points with it between his fingers. "Keep going, over a bridge. On the other side, two miles up, there's a gas station. Pull up there."

THIRTY-ONE

◇

Tuesday, 3:22 p.m., BST

Luxton directs Kat to a parking lot. He unbuckles, opens his door, cups his hand against the wind, and lights the cigarette. Two parking spots over, she sees Liz by an SUV, pushing windblown hair out of her face.

The man who drove Liz is medium-built, wearing a tweed jacket with leather patches and a green polo shirt with a slate green scarf hung loose around his neck. A black Labrador, tongue hanging, sits in the back of his vehicle.

He spots Luxton, raises a hand in greeting, and comes over. Kat gets out, stretches, feels sun on her face.

"Tappler," he says, "Simon Tappler. I've heard a lot about you. Sorry you're with us in such difficult circumstances." He doesn't offer a handshake. Tappler has two fingers around the bowl of a pipe. He bends over, knocks the pipe against the heel of his shoe, and lets the burned tobacco drop to the ground.

"Biggest checkpoint I know of," he says. "Rotten luck that today of all days, they're pulling over rental cars. But you got them through, Mike. Well done." His hand grips Luxton's. "I'll be over there with Liz," Tappler says. "Come over when you're ready."

As Tappler walks back toward the SUV, Luxton takes a deep drag on his cigarette. "Like he says, well done."

"Who's this Tappler?" asks Kat.

"A helper. We're waiting for someone else. Then we'll join them."

Kat walks away from the car to a bank of freshly mown grass. She sits on the grass, picks a daisy, pushes her thumbnail in the stem and lets green juice stain her skin. Luxton's shadow falls over her and she looks up, hand over her eyes.

"What sort of helper?"

Luxton doesn't answer. He sits next to her, his arms hanging loosely over drawn-up knees.

"How did you work the checkpoint?" says Kat.

"Money, power, local knowledge." He takes the daisy from her. "Here, let me do that." He plucks another one and feeds the stem through the fingernail cut Kat's made in the first one.

"No," says Kat. "I mean exactly how did you get us through?"

"The people who man the checkpoint are corrupt," he says flatly, his fingers linking up the two daisy stems. "I paid money. The person who's coming to see us has authority in this part of England. It'll be a one-off; we won't be able to do it again."

"You did it for you or for me?"

Luxton looks ahead, squinting, where rain's sheeting down on a gray river in the distance, but above them the sky's pure blue, without a cloud. "I did it for all of us."

Kat leans back, lets the sun play on her face. "While we're waiting for this other person," she asks dreamily, eyes closed, "can you do me a favor?"

"Sure."

"Quit fucking around. Tell me who you are, who Liz is, what the fuck's going on, what it has to do with Suzy, and if you know who killed her, tell me."

Luxton lets her outburst hang. His shadow crosses her face again as he plucks another daisy stem. Kat opens her eyes, props her head up on her elbow, and changes tack. "Okay, here's an easy one: How come you're not doing the trapeze anymore?"

He stops for a beat. A smile flickers across his face. He feeds another daisy into the chain and lets out a small whistle.

"Yeah, good one," he says. "My specialty was the triple trapeze. That's when you have one artist at one end, one at the other, and I was flung between them and did a double somersault on the way. But to answer your question, I joined the army."

A silver station wagon pulls into the parking space next to the SUV, where Liz is leaning on the hood. There's something familiar about the man who gets out, but he's too far away for Kat to recognize.

Luxton looks up and points. "Like I said, I was in the army. Now I work for him."

Kat's about to ask who, when Luxton says, "Liz was walking home late one night near our home in London, and you know how unsteady she is. A police car passes. When they question her, of course, she stutters. She's nervous and she's swaying. They accuse her of being doped out and put a restriction order on her, which they have the power to do without going to court or anything. It took a month to get it lifted, for us to prove that Liz isn't a troublemaking drug addict." He adds another daisy.

"When it happened, I was in Iraq, in the south in Basra with the army. I came back on leave. Liz was distraught. I couldn't get any sense out of anyone, and I looked more into what was happening. Just about every week, the government was passing a new law of social control. They'd passed laws so that judges couldn't overturn them. I hadn't realized it before, because it hadn't affected me, but more and more, we were living in a police state, and the government sold it to the public by intimidating the media and talking about the terror threat. That's when I began to understand it.

"Like, in Iraq, we were doing a good job, trying to set up fair government, treating people equally, making the place safer. I could see why we were there. But alongside all that, a lot of people were getting very, very rich. Millions were being handed out for contracts without anyone checking what was happening to the money. One week, an American colonel came down from Baghdad and gave away twenty million dollars. Just like that. He made no checks that it would be spent properly, no checks on who he was giving it to, no checks that it wasn't going into a back pocket or foreign bank account. Why should he? The war had begun a huge, new industry. A lot of people benefited, but it wasn't about helping normal people. There was a whole other agenda. When I saw what they did to Liz, I checked more and found how much American and British companies were making from the security industry, iris scanners, ID cards, database exchange, and all that. You don't have to be a brain surgeon to know it's wrong."

He pulls a daisy through too roughly, and the stem breaks. "Shit."

The man who's just arrived at the gas station has brought out documents and is looking through them on the hood of the car with Liz.

"But what's the point of the government making an enemy of people like Liz?" asks Kat.

"In Liz's case, it was because of her job. They need Liz because she's good, but they also want her to know what they can do to her if she steps out of line."

"But . . ." Kat hesitates. "Well, she told me how she met Suzy."

"Yeah. But they went at her *before* any of that happened."

Kat likes Mike Luxton, the way he strips down politics to simple human motivation. If things ever got back to normal, she could see herself falling into a relationship with him.

Luxton laces his boots with double knots and tucks the lace ends into the side of the leather. His lips are tight together, playing into the hint of a smile, his unshaven face just a little too close, but not hostile. Their eyes lock, then he shifts his gaze over toward Liz, who's waving them over.

"Here." Luxton hands Kat the daisy chain. "It's from all of us." He leans forward, puts it around her neck, and straightens it. She lets his hands brush her clothes. "You look good in it."

"Thank you," she says, fingers on the stems, feeling the dampness from their juice.

Luxton gets up, brushes his pants off, and offers a hand to Kat. She takes it while he helps her up, then lets it go.

"Now this is what's going to happen next. You're going over to meet my boss."

"Who is he?"

"You met him with Max Grachev on Saturday night," says Luxton. He lets go of her hand. "He's Assistant Commissioner of Police Stephen Cranley."

THIRTY-TWO

Tuesday, 3:43 p.m., BST

Kat stops dead. She looks behind her for a way out. Luxton, half a step ahead, reaches back to take her elbow. Kat moves away.

"Do you have any idea what you're doing?" she yells, tearing off the daisy chain.

She works out how far she'll let him come toward her before striking him. She works out how she'll take him, what she's not going to tell him.

"You know who Max Grachev is? You know who runs that roadblock, which you got through so fucking easily?" She steps back, testing the unevenness of the ground.

Luxton's looking at the grass. "If you promise not to interrupt," he says evenly, "I will tell you. Like I said, first you will meet Stephen Cranley—again. He has something to tell you. It's about your sister. He's going to show you the documents that they're looking at over there. When you've read them, we want you to call Bill Cage, then you and Liz are going to the place where Suzy was killed, because that's where we need your help."

As Luxton talks, Cranley is walking toward her, tall, elderly, but fit, his face lined around his eyes and chin. He's wearing beige cords and a brown waterproof jacket. When he gets closer, his blue eyes seek hers, but not with hostility, not a man looking for an enemy.

Kat holds her expression. She plans to give nothing. Cranley holds out his hand. Kat doesn't take it.

"I was a friend of your father's," he says.

"Yeah, well, Dad never mentioned you."

"No, he wouldn't have."

"So how do I know?"

"Your father told me that Javier Laja once proposed to you," he says.

"So?" she says, and leaves it like that, but inside she's trembling. Cranley's picked a story she's told to only three people—all dead.

"You were a child in Rising Park in Lancaster overlooking the orphanage," says Cranley.

Kat picks up. "And Javier said if I couldn't find anyone else, he'd love to marry me. We were both about nine."

Cranley runs a hand through his hair, sandy colored with a streak of gray. A speck of black ash blows onto Kat's shoulder. She picks it off and sees fires burning stubble in a freshly harvested field.

"Okay," she says, taking a step toward him. "What now?"

Cranley's expression is half sad, half relieved. "I need to show you something. It's not nice, but it'll help what you're trying to achieve."

She walks with him to his station wagon, where he draws an envelope from his pocket.

"I want you to read this, Kat." He points behind the SUV to where Luxton and Liz have dropped back. "I'll be over there."

Kat holds the sheets steady on the hood of the car. It's the postmortem report on her mother.

The deceased is female, fifty-four, measuring five feet, seven inches and weighing one hundred and ten pounds. Definite ID of Helen Anne Polinski established through dental records. Visible distinctive marks include a mole on her nose. Clothing was in place and comprised blue denim jeans with leather belt, zippers and buttons fastened; blue Giordano shirt over bra, still fastened; Nike tennis shoes with socks, laces tied. Jewelry comprises ornamental pendant necklace, believed to be silver, gold wedding ring, and a large ornamental ring.

Examination shows single fracture of the upper thyroid horns, a fracture of a lower thyroid horn, and laryngeal soft tissue trauma. Macro-
scopic bleedings of the laryngeal muscles were also found.

Kat rushes her eyes along, looking for something fast and conclusive.

Defined and deep ligature marks are consistent with the nylon curtain cord found around the neck.

Kat flips over a page. She's seeing nothing that she doesn't know
already.
She scans over to the next page.

. . . carotid arteries are compressed; jugular veins are normal, consistent with suffocation and heart failure from suicide by hanging.

"What am I looking for?" She looks over at Cranley. Liz comes instead.

"M-most women who commit suicide don't hang themselves. Men do.
And they shoot themselves. But women usually slash their wrists or take a
drug overdose."

Liz leans across, turns over to the last sheet in the file, which looks like
a copy of the page Kat's just read.

"This is the original death certificate," she says. "Here." She points to a
line halfway down in the middle of a mass of medical jargon. "Sodium pen-
tothal, pancuronium bromide, potassium chloride. All these were found in
her blood."

"My God." Kat's chest goes tight. The back of her neck prickles. They are
exactly the drugs used for execution by lethal injection.

"Your mother was murdered."

"But why?" she says faintly, barely a whisper.

"Suzy suspected it from the start. Your mother didn't love your father
enough to kill herself for him. She was killed in case John Polinski had told
her what he knew."

A single tear runs over Kat's cheek, down onto her lip. She tastes the salt
on her tongue.

"And that's why . . ."

Liz nods.

Cranley joins them, but Kat turns her back and concentrates on a seagull flying behind a tractor in a field.

"The day you heard your father was killed, you went home to find your mother dead," he says. "Suzy went from New York to the mortuary in Lancaster. It was chaotic because of who your father was and the conspiracy theories running around about his death. The next day, you were both involved in dealing with your mother's apparent suicide. Suzy handled the paperwork. In the mortuary, she saw the original death certificate. When she was handed the false one, which said your mother killed herself, she understood exactly what was happening. Murder and cover-up meant that Suzy's own life was in danger. She had to get out of the country. She didn't know what to do about you. If you were with her, they might get both of you. But you weren't involved in your father's work, like Suzy was. You were young. If you stayed back home, she didn't think they'd go after you."

He walks around so that he's in Kat's field of view. Kat's fists are clenched hard.

"Suzy came to England and changed her identity because her life was in danger," says Cranley. "Your father and mother were murdered, Kat. Suzy was determined to fight, but she wanted to keep you from running into any harm."

Kat squeezes her eyes. She doesn't want to see Cranley, see anything, no light, no shadows even, no kaleidoscopic swirls of color. She tries to breathe slowly, but hears her heartbeat louder and louder. If she loses control, she will shriek and thrash about. She holds on to the discipline until all she sees is calm black. She inhales deeply, exhales, and feels the knives inside her chest withdraw. Then she opens her eyes again.

"Thanks," she says, "for letting me see that."

She calls out to Luxton, "You got a phone?"

Cranley has one in his hand. She takes it, walks away, and faces the gas station. Cars are driving in and out. Drivers pump gas. Moms take kids to the bathroom.

She dials Cage, paces, keeps her eyes on the distant stubble fire in a far-off field, watches smoke drifting straight up, then curling suddenly as it catches in the wind.

"Rain's coming," she says to herself. The call's on the fourth ring when it picks up.

"It's me," she says.

"You've met Cranley?"

"Yes. Does it mean we're authorized again?"

"No." His voice is soft and strained, and it's not like Cage to show trouble. "Things have changed. The pissing contest's over, and we lost."

"What's that mean?"

"You're taking the fall for the embassy killings."

"You said—"

"I know what I said. I'm sorry. It's a federal double homicide rap with mandatory death penalty."

"It was self-defense," she says hurriedly.

"All of them," says Cage. "The five inside."

Kat says nothing.

"Stick with Cranley. Don't go near Sayer. Don't go near anything connected to the American government."

THIRTY-THREE

◇

How can anyone who has learned what Kat has in the past few hours stand so tearless and alone under an ocean blue sky with barely anything interrupting her thoughts except the details of the landscape around her?

She draws clean air deep into her lungs, listening to the whispers of reeds knocked together by the breeze and the lapping of the river tide.

From where Kat is standing, through a screen of trees rising out of flat marshland, she sees patches of the concert hall, its square white chimneys stark against the sky.

Around her, she hopes, lie the secrets of Suzy's death.

She's on a narrow public walkway running an inch above marsh water. Farther ahead it drops to become a mud-soaked footpath that curves around the river's edge toward a church far in the distance. Along the way, seagulls dip and bank. The tide is low, the small boats grounded on mud.

Would Suzy have been a solitary figure as she walked across open marsh-land to the river, or had others been on the lawn? Did she know then that she was in danger?

Wanting to feel Suzy's presence in the last place her sister was alive, Kat squats, runs her hands softly through the reeds.

There is nothing to show that a woman has been murdered here. River marshes stretch away on both sides of the path, which is earth-cracked dry in some places and sloppy with mud in others. With water to the left and right, there's nowhere to go but the path.

She wonders if Suzy ever saw her attackers, which way she was facing when she was shot.

Kat is pretty certain that Suzy was killed by a hollow-point bullet. Nothing else would have blown so much of her sister's head off. There's a type of hollow-point known as the Black Talon, in which the copper jacket peels back into six claws to inflict maximum damage.

The image causes sweat to break out on Kat's neck, despite the breeze and chill from the weakening sun. She wipes her sleeve across her forehead and hears movement, different from the rustling of the reeds, and takes a moment to work out where it's coming from. First she thinks it's behind her, then what sounded like the sway of leaves becomes a dull hum, and in the dimming light, she recognizes aircraft lights in the sky, wings tipping after takeoff.

Friday night, when Suzy was killed, it was raining. Why would she go for an intermission walk in the rain? Was she dating someone? Was she killed by her date? Why was she even there? Suzy never went to concerts.

On the path at the edge of the grassland leading to the concert hall, at the edge of her vision, she imagines for a split second a tall figure with a rifle. Then she remembers that Liz is holding back, giving Kat space, and what she sees as a weapon is only Liz's walking stick. Luxton is returning the rental car and getting another one. Cranley has gone back to London.

Kat beckons Liz Luxton onto the walkway.

"Nothing's here," she says.

Liz points across the marshes to the river. "The p-police have put up a fake murder site over there," she says. "But *this* is where she was shot."

"How do you know?"

"Cranley's got to an officer who was here. He says he wouldn't lie."

"The police would go that far?"

"They do what the politicians tell them."

"But Stephen Cranley is in charge?"

"Exactly. He went along with it in order to stay in charge."

Liz's face glows in sunset colors. Kat might have half an hour of decent light at most.

"Where exactly was the body?" she asks, surprising herself by using professional terminology. Not *my sister* but *the body*.

"There." Liz points to a straggle of marsh reeds, thin trees, and mossy growth.

The impact of a bullet does not knock you back, as many people think. Her nervous system instantaneously wrecked, Suzy would have collapsed on the spot, at most fallen from the walkway into shallow water.

"Faceup or facedown?" says Kat.

"Faceup."

Feet firm on the walkway, Kat looks across the soft light green of the wet marshland bathed in the long rays of the sun. Between her and the concert hall is an expanse of low green yellow reeds, a hedgerow, a line of pine trees, but no cover for a close and accurate shot. Was the killer behind Suzy, following her, or in front of her, waiting?

Kat takes the pocketknife from her bag and steps off the walkway onto the soft, muddy bottom. Water, two inches deep, tepid from the day, seeps into her shoes. She wades forward, opening the knife. Her mind is on the burn mark on Suzy's shoulder. The killer was behind her, not waiting. He fired as she turned. The first round would have touched Suzy's shoulder, causing her to freeze just long enough to make the head shot.

Pushing aside the reeds, her pants wet above the ankles, Kat splashes toward a dead tree, its thick, gnarled trunk rising out of the water, the only object in range that could have stopped a slug. If it didn't, the slug could be anywhere in miles of thick reeds and mud, and she'll never find it. With the back of her wrist, she wipes sweat out of her eyes and runs her hand over the wood, caked with moss in some places, smooth as skin in others. She spends fifteen minutes examining the wood, knife blade open, probing for an embedded round.

Her eyes sting with grit fallen from the trunk. Her fingertips and knuckles are grazed. It could be there, and she'd still miss it. It would take a forensic team a day to cover what she's trying in fifteen minutes of fading light.

Liz sits cross-legged on the walkway, her walking stick across her knees and her hands resting loosely. The reeds, the water, the air are perfectly still. Only the color is changing as a bronze moon changes shift with the vanishing sun.

Gently, trying to stir the water as little as possible, Kat wades back and climbs onto the walkway. "I want you to go right back over there," she says to Liz. "Then walk toward me, as quietly and softly as you can."

Her back to the concert hall and Liz, she waits. There would still have been twilight, there would be a moon, and even in the rain, Suzy would've been able to see the walkway without a flashlight. No one would be around except her and the killer.

When she feels the vibration from Liz's footsteps, Kat shouts, "Stop."

Liz is maybe forty yards away, around a slight curve. Kat keeps her eyes level and without emotion as she walks toward her.

Hard green plastic runs down the center of the walkway, held in place by wire netting wrapped around the edges of the planks. On her hands and knees, Kat searches the surface around where Liz is standing. Then she lowers herself into the still, brackish water, closes her eyes, and eases her hands into the silt, washing it gently through her fingers, inch by inch.

It takes time and many false hopes, but at last she touches the piece of metal she's been looking for. With Liz holding a flashlight, Kat wipes it clean and rests it in the palm of her hand—the spent cartridge thrown out of the automatic weapon that killed her sister.

Kat's fingers curl around the cartridge. "Know somewhere we can get this analyzed?"

"Stephen can get it done."

Kat slips the cartridge into her pocket, and they start walking back toward the concert hall, but slowly because Kat doesn't want to reach the open ground just yet.

Low tide has stripped the river to a stream, leaving the marsh reeds in two colors, mud black at the bottom and moonlit yellow at the top. Two grounded boats tilt against the jetty wall, one with faded maroon sails tied to its mast like a Chinese junk. The other, bigger, with blue paint peeling, has a streak of smoke unwinding from a thin black chimney. No rain. No wind, either, out there. So bright is the moon now that Kat can still see the faraway church and gulls circling above the emptiness.

River smells cling to Kat like wet rust—this is the second time today she's found herself stinking of brackish water. She wants to shower. She wants to sleep.

Above the marshes, couched in the moon's glow, she watches an aircraft, lights flashing in and out of heavy blue gray clouds as it comes in to land on an airfield nearby.

"Where do these planes come from?" says Kat.

"Byford," says Liz. "It used to be an American airbase with the biggest runway in Europe. RingSet bought it, together with the port."

Kat gazes across the open lawn toward the concert hall, which is empty and unlit on a weekday night with no performance and made gloomy by scudding dark clouds overhead.

"No one looked at the audience list for Friday night?"

"Officially, yes. In reality, no." Liz looks at Kat, unblinking. "That's what we're hoping you would do."

A lone heron flies low over the yellow reeds. Two rabbits dart across the lawn. Wind blows strands of hair into Liz's face. She runs a hand across the base of her neck and checks her watch again. "Now it's almost dark," she adds.

Kat nods. After all, this is what she does for a living. "I'll go alone," she says at last. "You stay here. Wait for Mike."

THIRTY-FOUR

—————◇—————

Tuesday, 10:17 p.m., BST

The sloping roof of the concert hall stands straight ahead, with four square, ice white ventilation shafts standing symmetrically on the peak. In front are trees, a gravel driveway, a solitary sculpture, and dangerous openness.

Kat chooses not to cross the grass but rather to skirt around it through a bank of evergreens, across the empty parking lot, to the front of the complex, where she has a clear view of the box office door. In front of the door is a patio. Farther on is a wooden bridge across water, and there's another bridge between Kat and the concert hall.

It reminds her of one of the big restaurants on the banks of the Potomac, except more quaint and lacking the smell of money.

She runs silently across the parking lot asphalt, then across grass; then she's jolted by the loudness of her sneakers on gravel. She reaches a low wall before the steps, ten yards away from the box office door, which is wooden and windowless.

Once over the bridge, she stops, catches her breath against the wall of the concert hall, looks up, and thinks she sees a figure on the grassland ahead. For a second she stalls, until her eyes adjust, and she sees it's a sculpture.

On the side of the concert hall facing the marshes, small basement windows run the length of the building. The first three look into a kitchen. Through the fourth, Kat sees an upright piano and a camp bed. And the fifth is just what Kat needs; it's been left ajar. She squats, eases a finger underneath, and unclips the latch. It's a squeeze to get through, and she lands clumsily, knocking over a cello covered in a blue velvet cloth.

The door is unlocked, the corridor dark. She goes along to the end, where there's half a flight of stairs up to the ground floor, and at the top, sealed off from the outside by windowless wooden doors, is the box office.

She boots up the office PC, her flash card slotted in to silence any alarms. She sits cross-legged on the floor, the soothing whir of the computer bringing down her adrenaline level. She's staring at a poster displaying the summer schedules. Last Friday's concert, which Suzy saw, was the Youth Chamber Choir and Symphony Orchestra of St. Petersburg, conducted by the director of the Rimsky-Korsakov Conservatoire playing a selection of Tchaikovsky, including Symphony No. 5 and *Romeo and Juliet*, and Beethoven, including the Ninth Symphony. It started at 7:30 p.m., with a half hour intermission at 9 p.m., which is when Suzy was shot.

Suzy, she asks silently. *Why drive three hours, through the mother of all checkpoints, to come here?*

The computer screen settles, then dissolves again as Kat's software succeeds in punching in the correct password.

Kat types T-H-O-M-A-S into the booking search engine. It delivers three Thomases. Kat narrows it with C-H-A-R-L-O-T-T-E, and up it comes, just like at the North lecture, a whole data file on Charlotte. Suzy was sitting three rows back from the front and one seat in from the center aisle. The booking was made only for Charlotte Thomas, paid for by her credit card.

Charlotte is described as an employee of Eurojuste, the legal agency of the European Union.

Beginning with the back row, Kat skims down the list of those in the audience. She makes her way across and down until her gaze freezes on a particular name. She hits a key to go beyond and get the data file, makes sure her mind isn't playing tricks on her.

It flashes up ALERT; then comes CLASSIFIED. Kat punches the F5 key to reactivate her flash card. The screen goes black. A blood red warning uncurls: ATTEMPTED ILLEGAL ENTRY. The central processing unit clicks and whines down into silence.

Kat's eyes are on the darkening gray of the computer screen, at first ashamed, then motivated by the creeping dismay at what will now happen.

An alert is going out to every security agency signed up to protect the CPS. So powerful is the cordon surrounding the concert bookings that it's overridden all of Kat's software.

Kat flips out the flash card and runs back down the corridor, through the cello room, out the window, across the grassland, down a slope, and onto a path, eyes scanning the marshlands for Liz, but seeing only confusing night shapes.

On Friday night it had been raining, with none of the hazardous clarity Kat has to deal with now. The moon lights up the landscape as far as the broken horizon. Wherever Kat can see, she can also be seen.

Kat slows to a fast walk, checks behind her. She's in the marshes, but on a different walkway. There are no sirens, no lights blaze from the concert hall. She stops, hand on mouth. To her right, down from the walkway, are flattened reeds, cordoned off by a trail of yellow tape. One end is tied around the trunk of a dead tree; the other nailed into a post. The tape, taut and windless still, carries the warning POLICE CRIME SCENE—KEEP OUT.

This is the bogus murder scene, where no spent cartridges will ever be found.

Whoever came up with the idea that a bogus site be created knew Suzy's killer. Which means that Cranley might know as well. And to Kat, everything has become clear. When she asked Max Grachev about the audience list, he didn't answer. No wonder.

The name given to her by the concert hall database seconds before the system crashed was Max Grachev, sitting four rows back and on the other side of the aisle from Suzy.

The next sound Kat hears is real: a click of metal on metal.

THIRTY-FIVE

◇

Tuesday, 10:36 p.m., BST

Kat's facing the marshes and the river, looking into the blankness of a blue gray, moonlit night. There's a sound from somewhere behind her, where the path comes out of the marsh reeds to the open ground in front of the concert hall, marked by a sculpture on the lawn, and then the terrace, where the audience has drinks during the intermission of a concert. Beyond that is a parking lot, the village, the lives of ordinary people. Ahead lies wilderness.

Kat wipes her eyes with her sleeve, breathes in smells of pines and river water. Then she doesn't move. This is where people run to if they're being chased from the concert hall. Had Suzy seen Grachev and run, not to safety among the audience, but to the emptiness of the marshes?

The walkway vibrates with the pressure of slow footsteps. Not one person. At least two.

Tension tightens around her face, her neck; then it ripples down her back as if in preparation for a hollow-point bullet smashing into the back of her skull.

The footsteps behind her stop. Kat gulps a breath, puts her hands on her hips, turns, and faces Yulya Gracheva. Her hair is down. She's wearing a white leather jacket and jeans with leather boots. She's holding a 9mm Serdyukov SPS pistol, common in the Russian military. Her left hand's in her jeans pocket, and her face is soft, sympathetic, as it was when Kat first met her. Yulya keeps moving forward and stops about ten feet away.

"You've got to stop running," Yulya says gently.

Kat can't detect anyone else with her. Behind Yulya, she sees marsh reeds and the concert hall. There's nothing at the edge of her vision, either, just water glistening on the river's muddy flanks and boats leaning aground in the low tide. There's no sign of Liz or Mike Luxton.

Kat tilts her head. "You seen my friends around anywhere?"

Yulya doesn't answer. She shifts her position, right leg taut, left leg relaxed, looking more than ever like she did in the Kazakh file picture. She folds her arms, cupping her fingers loosely around the butt of the pistol.

"You want me to put my hands up or something?"

Yulya's expression doesn't change. It's friendly but firm. A keen intelligence radiates from her face. "I don't want you to waste your valuable life hunting down Suzy's killer."

Kat takes a step back. Yulya doesn't react. "I appreciate your concern, but aren't I facing her?"

"No."

"The real killer doesn't always pull the trigger."

"I like you, Kat," says Yulya. "I liked you the moment I laid eyes on you at Max's place."

Kat takes another step back. Yulya still doesn't react.

"Was it Max?" asks Kat.

Spits of rain fall on them. Yulya glances up—the moon and clouds play together like a spider, making cobwebs.

"Max isn't cold-blooded," she says. "That's why Mother moved him out of the business. To build up a company like RingSet in Russia, you need a ruthless streak. Max doesn't have one. Nor does my little sister, Lara. But I do. I was born with it. It's part of my spirit. My mother noticed it early on and encouraged me. She kept saying that without people like me, the human race would not have achieved as much as it has."

Yulya's accent doesn't sound as pure East Coast American as before. It has a European lilt to it. Kat keeps her eyes on her folded arms.

"So what do you want?"

"You're here because you want to know who killed your sister. I am here because I need the file you stole on Friday night. I propose an exchange. Then you can go home."

"Who killed Suzy?"

"He's a professional. In exchange for the file, I will give you his name. You can spend the rest of your life hunting him down. When you find him and kill him, you might feel better."

Kat shrugs. "And you can spend the rest of your life hunting down copies of the file so that picture of you with blood on your hands doesn't end up as someone's screen saver."

Yulya brushes raindrops off her shoulder. Kat might have penetrated a layer, but nothing yields in her expression.

"But it's bigger than that, isn't it," continues Kat. "They're rigging the oil and gas figures, pretending the price has to be high because there's not enough around. But there's plenty. RingSet's getting rich, buying up airfields and ports." She waves her hand in the direction of Byford.

Yulya's eyes follow, but she doesn't move. "Suzy was killed because she chose to walk over a cliff," she says. "The CPS is inevitable. Suzy didn't like it. She couldn't stop herself. But you can, Kat. I'm spelling it out and giving you a choice."

"I'm not cutting a deal with you," says Kat.

"I'm not asking that. I'm asking you to save your own life. You tell me one major change in history that hasn't involved people getting killed. It doesn't exist, Kat. This isn't about you, me, or Suzy. It's about something none of us can stop even if we want to."

"Says the killer," Kat replies.

"You shot two men on Friday night," snaps back Yulya, stiffening.

"Suzy wasn't a hired gun. Those men were."

Yulya's eyes cloud. "What are you, Kat? Think hard what you do for a living."

Kat says nothing.

"The picture in the file," says Yulya tightly, "was taken two years ago. The man I shot was about to kill not only me but others. You of all people should understand killing in self-defense."

Yulya takes a step forward. She's almost close enough for Kat to strike. Kat works out how she could do it in one blow.

"If your real purpose is to find Suzy's killer, then I can give him to you," says Yulya, leaning closer. "But if you're chasing a higher moral issue, like Suzy, then I will become your enemy."

"Is that what it is for you?" says Kat. "A high moral issue?"

Yulya swallows. Her voice drops. "Your father would have understood. These past years, you in the West have been getting richer. And we in the poorer countries have been getting poorer. That's the terrible evil the CPS is going to reverse."

The gun hangs more loosely in Yulya's hand. A strand of hair falls on her face. She hooks it back, waiting for Kat to respond.

Kat doesn't.

Yulya shakes her head. "If someone took a picture of you killing those men on Friday, you'd want it back. That's all I'm asking."

Yulya's eyes are rock steady. The position of her feet, balance, the casual way she holds the pistol signal that, like Kat, she's ready for violence at any moment.

Kat shrugs. "You know, Yulya, you've told me something. I want to tell you something. I've got a federal homicide charge waiting for me back in Washington for what happened on Friday. I have no place to go that's safe, and I'm pretty much alone here. So if you want to make a deal, we need to include me getting off that rap."

Yulya smiles nervously. "You think I have more power than I do," she says.

"Then use up favors, because it's no good for me to give you the file, then have nowhere to hide." As Kat talks, she imperceptibly shifts her weight to position a strike. But she must be tired, or Yulya's too good for her. Yulya's face tightens. Her fingers grip the pistol butt.

Kat continues, "I haven't got it. But I can get to it if you give me time."

Yulya half opens her mouth to reply. Kat moves a fraction to begin her attack. But Yulya raises her gun hand high above her head and two, maybe three people—difficult to tell in this light—appear from behind her.

Kat recognizes at least one of them from the bank of the Thames. Behind him, another man carries Liz Luxton along the walkway, her feet dragging on the slatted wood. Liz's hands are tied in plastic cuffs. Her mouth is taped. Two others carry Mike Luxton as if he were a corpse.

They drop him at Kat's feet. His hands are cuffed, too. Blood runs down his face. It's congealed around his nose. His right eye is closed. His left eye flickers, looking up at Kat, saying he's sorry.

THIRTY-SIX

$\Diamond$

Yulya hands her pistol to one of the men who carried Luxton. She walks straight into Kat's space and hits her across the face with the back of her hand. Kat absorbs the pain without moving.

"I gave you a very nice chance, Kat, and you lied to me. After how well you did on Friday night, I'm surprised at your choice of new friends. You're too good for them."

The gunman, holding Liz, keeps a weapon on Luxton. The two other men take Kat by the arms. One kicks her feet out from under her. They lower her to the walkway, lay her on her back, and spread-eagle her arms and legs.

"The two men you killed were Alex and Vadim. These are their colleagues." A gunman stands astride Kat and lets her see him put on a latex glove.

Yulya continues, "Vadim was the one whose mouth you probed and found the SIM card. A disrespectful way to treat the dead."

The man kneels across Kat and forces open her mouth. His breath is stale and smells of bars, tobacco, and linseed. His eyes are brown and expressionless. He's neither enjoying nor hating, just doing his job.

He puts his right hand under Kat's jaw. "Open," he says in a rough, accented voice. Kat obeys. His finger goes inside. She retches as muscle spasms fire in the back of her throat. He presses lymph nodes under her jaw. The pain is sharp and controlling. Kat goes quiet.

He probes more, finds nothing, looks to Yulya for instructions. She squats down, her face level with Kat's. Bile dribbles from Kat's mouth. She meets Yulya's gaze.

"Kat," says Yulya. "Meet Lev."

One of the other men hands Yulya Suzy's hard drive from Kat's bag.

Kat is thinking several things. Once Yulya finds the SIM card taped to her back, she will kill her, Liz, and Luxton, unless Kat can convince her that at least one other copy exists. The only other copy she knows of is with Mercedes in Washington. The version on Suzy's hard drive might be repairable, but not out here on the marshes. Either way, the longer Kat spins things out, the more time they all have.

"The drive's damaged, but I could fix it."

Yulya glances down to Kat, then across to Lev. "Is this the only copy?"

Kat nods.

"We'll check."

Lev squats down, his fingers pawing at Kat's waistband, pulling out her shirt.

"Viktor," says Yulya, signaling Kat's feet.

Viktor crouches, pulls off Kat's shoes, runs his hands over the soles of her feet, slots his fingers between her toes.

Lev tugs at her jeans. Kat slaps his hand back. He grips her hard. Another man holds down her shoulders.

"Twenty-four hours and you're all dead." It's Luxton's voice. Kat twists in time to see a boot kick him in the midriff. He goes silent.

"The more you resist, the rougher Lev will be," says Yulya.

Lev pulls up her shirt. She's damp with sweat underneath. The night breeze chills her. Lev holds her throat with his left hand and checks her torso with the right. His fingers push down on her breasts and run underneath. Fingernails scratch the skin. Kat lies completely still, eyes closed, and imagines the women holding hands in the Kazakh embassy as they were shot on Friday by men like Lev. Kat's glad she killed them.

Lev withdraws his hand. Viktor lifts her buttocks. Lev pulls the jeans over her hips. Kat resists. Viktor hits her hard in the face with the back of his hand. Lev hooks his fingers into Kat's panties.

Yulya crouches down by her and rests her hand with the 9mm on Kat's shoulder, the gunmetal on her neck. Yulya's mouth is next to her ear. Kat smells expensive perfume.

"They are men," Yulya whispers. "Let them do their work quickly, before they get excited."

She stands up and speaks in Russian. Lev and Viktor rip her jeans down to her ankles and turn her over onto her front. Her cheek presses against the damp of the walkway. The marsh breeze catches the sweat on her back, cools her, and brings a shiver. A hand rests on her buttocks. The tape holding the SIM card to her back is torn away. Viktor gives it to Yulya. Lev speaks in Russian, then in English. "Any more?"

Kat feels a hand move between her legs. She hears Luxton cry out. Then, barely a foot away from her, two shots ring out as slugs splinter wood on the walkway.

THIRTY-SEVEN

———◇———

Tuesday, 11:06 p.m., BST

A searchlight comes on and hits Yulya in the face. Kat hears a familiar voice. "If anyone touches her, they'll be shot."

Nate Sayer walks in under the glare. "Stand up, Kat. Get dressed."

Yulya squints with her hand up to shield her eyes.

The men move back from Kat. The light casts shadows of Lev and Viktor over her bare skin. Kat scrambles to her feet, pulls up her jeans, and smooths down her shirt.

"You okay?" says Sayer. His eyes have a look she remembers from childhood; impatience mixed with pity.

"Yeah."

"They hurt you?"

"I'm fine."

Yulya still has the 9mm. The SIM card is pressed between her palm and the butt. Her pupils are narrowed, her lips tight.

Sayer's wearing light cotton summer pants pressed like a knife, a pink striped shirt, and a double-breasted navy blue jacket. He has his back to the concert hall. Behind him stands a uniformed U.S. marine aiming the M16 that fired the shots.

"Help him up," says Sayer, looking down at Luxton. Two more U.S.

marines walk forward from behind the searchlight. They pull Luxton to his feet.

"You okay, son?"

Luxton doesn't answer. His bloodied right eye is enough to cause the marine with the searchlight to open a first aid kit.

Sayer picks up Liz's walking stick. "Let her go," he says to the man holding her. He obeys, steps away toward Viktor and Lev. Sayer hands Liz the stick. "You okay?"

Liz nods.

"You help your brother," says Sayer. He points to Lev, then to Yulya. "You, all of you, go stand next to her."

They move over. No one speaks. Sayer puts his hand gently on Kat's shoulder. "Do exactly as I say," he says, "and we'll all get out of this okay."

One of the armed marines steps forward and takes Liz's arm.

"They'll escort you out," says Sayer to Liz and her brother. "Once you get to your vehicle, go wherever you want. But do not return here. Do not contact Kat." He indicates to Luxton. "You okay to walk, son?"

Luxton's eyes are cleared. He stares at Sayer, but doesn't speak. A marine takes Liz's right arm. She shakes him off, jabbing her stick onto the walkway.

"This is British territory. You can't do this."

Sayer doesn't respond. He nods to the marine, who leads Liz along the walkway. Luxton follows.

The marine with the light disarms Yulya and her men while the other officer covers them. "You next," Sayer says to Yulya. "Take my advice. Get out of this country, and don't come back." Sayer moves to one side of the walkway to let them pass.

Yulya takes a step forward. She shows no resentment, no surprise on her face.

"I need the card," Kat says quietly, only loud enough for Sayer to hear. He doesn't reply and grips her elbow.

"Nate, she palmed the SIM card. She's got it there in her right hand."

"Kat, that's enough."

Kat stiffens. "What are you doing?"

"I'm saving your goddamn life."

"A lot of good people died for that card."

"And you're not joining them."

Sayer lets Yulya and her men through. Yulya looks Kat straight in the eyes. She walks with a sense of victory about her.

THIRTY-EIGHT

Tuesday, 11:18 p.m., BST

The searchlight snaps off. Sayer and Kat are left with the marine sergeant, whose name tag says Mason.

"They picked up Bill Cage in Washington," explains Sayer.

"What's going on, Nate?"

Sayer shifts his weight and checks his watch. "You're coming back to our place. Tomorrow, you're going to Washington."

"I don't mean that, goddamn it!" Kat tries to control her anger. "You cut a deal over Suzy's murder, didn't you? That's why you let her go."

Sayer rolls his eyes. "I don't know what they teach you in that agency you work for, but it's not common sense."

In the concert hall parking lot, Kat sees Yulya and the men get into vehicles. Engine sounds cut through the river quiet. Mason shifts the way he holds his rifle, ready to leave.

"You know what'll happen to me in Washington?"

"I heard." Sayer begins to take her arm to lead her out.

Kat resists. "What did you hear?"

Sayer hesitates and relaxes his grip. "That Bill Cage got you involved in something he shouldn't have."

"How bad is it?"

"It's bad. I was told seven people dead. But it'll get figured out."

A gust of wind bites through her clothes. *Right*, she thinks. *By pinning all seven on me.*

"Best come, ma'am," says Mason. His tunic sleeves are rolled up above the elbows, showing a Marine Corps emblem tattooed on his right forearm and the American flag on the left.

They walk in silence. At the edge of the reeds, the walkway drops gently to hard ground, with a path that leads back the way she came.

In the parking lot are two U.S. diplomatic cars. Kat sees the dimly lit shapes of the other marines.

When Kat reaches the first car, Mason hands over her bag. "Empty this, please, ma'am. Your pockets, too. Place all the contents on the hood of the vehicle."

She pulls her compact, pens, and the spent cartridge case from her pockets.

"Now raise your arms," says Mason. "Face your possessions while I pat you down."

She catches Mason's eye and sees a shaved head and steady eyes, a man with no agenda but his job. He searches her without being overintrusive, around her breasts, her crotch, across the small of her back, where he would have found the SIM card.

No one's threatening her. She's not cuffed. Mason picks out the brass cartridge shell and holds it up to Sayer. "You might want to look at this, sir."

Sayer examines it in Mason's hand.

"That's from the gun that killed my sister," says Kat.

Mason holds a flashlight on it. "It looks like a 7.62. From which weapon, it's impossible to tell."

"Bag it," orders Sayer. The order passes through Mason to the driver of one of the other cars, who walks up with a zippered polyethylene bag.

"I need to sign for it," says Kat.

Mason's already taking a notebook out of his tunic pocket.

"Say where it was found," she says. "A 7.62—"

"We don't know that for sure, ma'am," says Mason, pen top in his mouth, leaning on the roof of the car to write.

"Then write that's what it might be and that Kat Polinski found it."

Sayer's feet scrape the gravel. He shakes his head. "Your father would be proud of you," he says.

"Sign here, ma'am." Mason punches his finger to the bottom of the page. Kat signs. He tears off the bottom copy and gives it to her. "We will keep the computer-related materials. You're free to collect the rest of your possessions." He opens the rear door of the car.

Kat shoves things back into her pockets. She turns to Sayer. "I need you to ride with me, Nate."

Sayer pauses for a moment, then walks around to the other side of the car and gets in. Mason drives, but a glass screen divides them from him.

As they head off, Kat looks out the back window. In the darkness, with the tinted windows, she can just make out the shape of the pub and the boat with the ragged maroon sails.

Sayer leans forward and turns on the overhead light. "You look bad," he says, snapping it off again. "Have you slept, eaten, washed since you got here?"

Kat's eyes look straight ahead. Her fists are coiled against her hips.

"Whose side are you on, Nate?"

"It doesn't work like that," says Sayer.

She closes her eyes, lets her head go back. "Then how does it work?"

"I tried to stop Cage," Sayer tells her. "Way back when you were first arrested. I saw your name on the list. It comes up every month. Bright criminals the government wants to use. I pointed out that you were John Polinski's daughter. You were traumatized. These guys, Kat, they train you, use you, and when you're damaged, they feed you to the wolves, and that's what they're doing now. Total deniability. I don't know what happened on Friday night, but they've got seven bodies they have to blame someone for. You're it."

He shifts in his seat and drums the side of the door with his fingers. "You made wrong moves. Before Cage, you were only wanted for Internet fraud. You could have got off with a fine. Now it's multiple counts of homicide. They've even matched the weapon used to kill the embassy staff with the one you used to kill the two guys."

The headlights rise and dip on the hump of a bridge.

"They went down to your old place on Dix Street," continues Sayer. "They picked up a Leroy Jenkinson. You know him as Mercedes Vendetta. He showed them where you and he hung out. They took prints from there, DNA, traced the phone line from the apartment, and came up with more credit card and Internet fraud. They found an unlicensed forty-five and a Benelli M4 military shotgun, so they've got Jenkinson in custody on a firearms wrap. He's talking, Kat, building up a good profile on you for the prosecution."

Kat opens her eyes, turns to Sayer. "Is Yulya part of the deal?"

"Nancy and I tried to help after John and Helen died, but you put up walls."

Kat says again, "Is Yulya part of the deal?"

Sayer stops drumming. "I don't like it any more than you do."

"Like I said, Nate, whose side are you on?"

"Jesus." He sighs. "You think this is some big political conspiracy all about Kathleen Polinski? You're wrong. It's about guys like Cage getting out of control and—"

The ice in her eyes stops him cold. "Because if you're with the people who killed my family, you've picked wrong."

THIRTY-NINE

$\diamond$

Wednesday, 6:30 a.m., BST

A siren blares in the street below. Kat wakes, opening her eyes to a slatted blue light circling on the ceiling above her head.

"Did you manage to sleep?" asks Nancy, placing a steaming mug on the bedside table. Kat blinks, sits up, gets hit by a wall of sleep, and fights it. She remembers bathing, drying her hair, trying to stay awake, talking to Nancy. About what? Sleeping over. Nothing big. Nothing about what she needs to do.

Nate Sayer plans to send her back to the United States today to face homicide charges while Yulya and Max walk free.

Kat pushes back the covers, swings her legs out on the other side of the bed, goes to the window, looks through the blinds. Two police cars are parked at angles at each end of the street.

"What's going on?" she says.

"They've blocked off South Audley Street and Grosvenor Square, where the embassy is," says Nancy. "President Abbott's coming for the signing on Saturday, and there's been a bomb scare."

Nancy sits on the bed. "Here. Hot, milky coffee. Just the way you like it."

That was when she was a kid. Kat now takes her coffee strong and black.

She says nothing, takes the mug, and wraps her hands around it, as if it were winter. "It's early, right?"

"Just after six-thirty," says Nancy. "You didn't get here until three. You've been sleeping deeply."

Kat sips the coffee, looks up at the window.

"Nate's doing everything he can, Kat," Nancy says, her voice lowered. "He's afraid for you, here in London; you'll be safer in Washington."

I won't, thinks Kat, but she doesn't argue. "What time's the flight?" she asks.

"A car's coming at nine. The flight's at eleven-thirty."

Kat checks her watch. She's got two and a half hours to get out of the apartment. She sits down on the bed next to Nancy.

"Where's Suzy's body?"

"The British police are keeping her—"

"I thought Nate said—"

"Things have changed." Nancy's eyes are edgy, flickering. "Nate told me what happened Friday night. It's horrible."

"I didn't kill those people in the embassy," Kat says. "They were dead when I got there." Kat looks straight at Nancy, making sure her own face gives nothing away.

"I know. We'll protect you."

"Is Nate here?" Kat asks, putting the cup on the bedside table.

Nancy shakes her head. "He'll be back soon. He got called away for the bomb scare." Then, as if Nancy read Kat's thoughts, she puts her hand on Kat's knee and smiles. "And don't think about running. They've put a couple of guys outside. It's only because of Nate that you're not under lock and key."

Kat says nothing. She's good with computers and material things, not so good with people.

"Nate told me a bit about last night, too," says Nancy. "You've got to stop lashing out. Some things you can't control."

Kat squints her eyes and turns to face Nancy full on. "Do you think my mom killed herself?"

Nancy is taken by surprise and laughs nervously. "Why would you ask me that?"

Kat stands up again, leans on the windowsill, her back to the glass, looking into the room. "All this, and being with you." Inside, the butterflies kick. She knows where's she's heading, knows it'll be merciless.

"Helen was my best friend," Nancy says. She gets up from the bed, stands next to Kat, and takes her hand. Kat glances outside. A police car turns off its flashing light. A policeman speaks into his cell phone.

"But your mom wasn't an easy person. She had a dark side. I don't mean evil or cruel. She had no self-esteem. John never let her step down from that pedestal where he treated her like a goddess. Helen found that difficult, because with a man like that, you never know how he'll treat you when his worship stops."

Nancy frowns at her own memories. "Helen tried to become what your father wanted her to be. Not what she really was."

Kat eases her hand away, reaches to get her cup, sips it, and puts it on the sill. A second flashing light goes off. A police car door closes.

"I'm not saying anything bad about your father," Nancy says. "He was a strong man. Often, I wish Nate had his backbone. But your mom and dad were two people who didn't like to know about each other's weaknesses."

"So you think she did kill herself?"

"I think she did, Kat. Things get dark if you haven't been able to be who you really are for twenty years."

Nancy's face is soft. Her eyes are damp. She's wrestling with something. "Helen didn't understand what her real human spirit wanted. She was living a life not suited to her."

Kat looks out the window again. The police cars are moving away. "They're leaving."

Nancy follows Kat's line of sight. Traffic is returning to the street. "The bomb scare must be over. Nate'll be back soon, then. You'd better start getting ready."

Kat takes Nancy's elbow. "So what you're saying is the day my father dies, the day Mom can get her character back, she goes upstairs, ties one end of a curtain cord to the banister, the other around her neck, jumps over, and hangs herself." Nancy winces, but Kat keeps spelling it out. "And by killing herself, she's abandoning her children who on that day will need her more than ever."

She grips Nancy harder than she meant to.

"No one knows what went through your mom's mind," says Nancy calmly.

Kat touches the edge of her lip. She opens her arms toward Nancy and buries her head in her godmother's shoulder.

"Aunt Nance," says Kat, "you have to help me. Yesterday, I learned that my mom was murdered. The same people who shot Suzy drugged her, then they hung her and tried to make it look like suicide—"

"Stop," interrupts Nancy, patting Kat's back. "Don't start thinking those horrible thoughts."

"It's the truth," counters Kat, keeping her arms around Nancy, speaking softly, her mouth right next to her ear. "And you know it, don't you, Aunt Nance? You always have."

Nancy doesn't reply. She keeps holding Kat.

"If I go back to the United States, those people who killed Suzy, Mom, and Dad are going to get away with it, and they're going to put me in jail and tell lies about me killing people and try to get me executed with the same drugs that killed Mom."

Nancy lifts her head. "I love you like a daughter."

"Then you've got to help me."

"I can't."

"Because of me or because of Nate?"

Nancy pulls back. "I can't go against Nate."

"Even though Nate's been cheating on you for years?"

Nancy's head drops, her eyes wet. Her hand fiddles with a hair clip. She looks so old, suddenly. "That's just not true."

"No?"

"Don't try to come between me and Nate."

Kat draws back, puts even more space between them, and folds her arms. "You want me to tell you how he cheats on you, Aunt Nance? You want me to tell you what your husband and my mom did together? You want me to tell you what deals he's cutting with murderers? You want me to tell you what you already know about your husband but think you can keep hidden? How can you live in such a lie? You're a good person. Is that why Nate and you have no children, because you couldn't look them in the face and tell the truth about what . . ." Kat's fired up to go on, but she stops as Nancy's face turns white and skeletal. She reaches out for Kat to catch her balance.

Kat's broken her. She bites the inside of her cheek to control her own emotions.

It's done.

Nancy dabs her eyes. "You told me Saturday night about Dix Street and that man you lived with and how frightened you were about running away to a place like that again. I know the place I've built for myself is a hell inside my marriage with Nate. But it's a place I'm too afraid to leave."

There's no resentment in Nancy's tone. Only regret.

"I'm sorry," says Kat softly.

"I want to help you, Kat. I do. But if you leave Nate's protection, they'll kill you."

Kat's look hardens. "They won't know how to start."

Nancy nods, the decision made. "I'll show you how to get out of here."

FORTY

She's wearing clothes belonging to Nancy, low-heeled leather shoes, blue jeans hanging too loose on her, a short-sleeved red blouse, and a dark woolen jacket hanging over her arm, under which she's holding Nancy's Glock Model 38, registered on diplomatic license to the American embassy.

It might be a .38, but it takes a shortened .45 cartridge, which gives it more power. It seems from the way Max Grachev examines the weapon that he knows that, too.

Kat went straight to his place from the Sayers', and Grachev let her in. She leveled the Glock at him and asked him what he was doing at the concert hall the night Suzy died.

"As I expected, still picking at those old wounds," he says, relaxed, wearing a beige silk and cashmere suit and an open-neck red shirt.

"What the hell does that mean?"

"Don't worry. Russia has been doing it for centuries."

He stands in front of Kat, blocking light from the street-level window of his apartment. He's left the coffee table in between them, not invading her space.

He brings out three photographs and spreads them on the table.

One she has seen before, of Grachev, his arm around an elegant, older, unsmiling woman with the backdrop of a snow-drenched forest.

The second looks like the Grachev family around a dinner table, with a spread of drinks and food, everyone clinking glasses. The older woman again; a gaunt, thin-faced man with streaks of white in his hair; a younger Max Grachev, with a dark mustache, broad shoulders in an ice white T-shirt, his eyes mournful, almost poetic, staring somewhere far away; a pretty young teenager in a pink tank top, all her concentration on making a sketch on a paper napkin; and a taller girl, in her early twenties perhaps, with blond hair tied back from a high forehead and penetrating eyes taking an inventory of everyone around her.

The third photograph she's seen many times before. Her father had it. Sayer has it on the wall of his apartment. It is Kat's dad and Nate Sayer with a group of people in Red Square in Moscow.

"Now," Grachev says. "Are you beginning to understand what this is about?" He hasn't threatened, hasn't mentioned Suzy again. There's been no menace. Nancy's pistol hasn't worried him.

"No," she says bluntly. "I don't understand at all."

Grachev squats down so their faces are at the same level. His finger hovers over the first picture. "This is my mother. Her name is Tiina Alekseevna Gracheva. She did not want this photograph taken. That is why she scowls."

His finger moves to the second photograph. "This is my family. My stepfather, Vadim Andreevich Grachev, loyal to my mother, but when it comes to brainpower, out of his depth. My younger sister, Lara, totally beautiful. She is now an archeologist, one of the youngest professors at St. Petersburg State University."

He smiles proudly at Kat. "She's a little bit crazy, I always say. She's working on a project on the Luga River, a mysterious burial mound called Shumgora, outside the old city of Great Novgorod."

His face darkens. "And Yulya, whom you know. She is a nasty piece of work. I'll tell you how nasty. She dated a Russian student when she was going to Columbia in New York. Yulya cheated on him, and they split up. Then when he began dating again, she beat the shit out of his new girlfriend. My sister is not someone to cross."

"Is that how she got RingSet over you?"

"Ruthlessness is a trait we Russians admire, and she is better at it than I."

His eyes drop down to the photographs again, and he moves onto the third one in Red Square. "Here is your father; there is Nate Sayer, thinner with more hair; and here, slimmer in those days, is my mother. She was an interpreter working for the KGB, as all Soviet interpreters did. Your father was an employment lawyer then. He came over to see if there were any areas in which the two great superpowers could work together." He laughs, scratching his right temple in bemusement. "Anything to stop us blowing each other to pieces."

Grachev withdraws his hands from the table, stands up, and steps back. Kat stares stone-faced at the photograph of Tiina, a young woman, firm and elegant face. Blond hair hangs loose to the shoulders, and bangs straggle over her eyes.

"You don't believe me?" Grachev asks.

"There's nothing to believe, unless you tell me why it matters."

"Your father and my mother had an affair," he says without expression. "I am the result. Your grandmother in Lancaster, Ohio—she's my grand-mother, too."

Grachev's looking for a reaction. Inside, she compartmentalizes. Kat's outward expression registers nothing.

"Doesn't interest me, Max," she says casually. "There's no replacing Suzy with a half brother."

He points to the sofa. "This isn't easy. May I sit down?"

"No," says Kat. "Let's deal with this factually. First, you're not an English cop. You're on some sort of personal mission."

"Right. I'm a Russian cop, but I was also keeping track of you and Suzy—"

"How did you know Charlotte Thomas was Suzy?" interrupts Kat.

"My mother found out. She told me. I checked it out through our London embassy. Once confirmed, I worked on getting loaned out to the Metropolitan Police."

"Why?"

"To get to know her. To find out more about my real father."

"But you thought he was dead."

"Of course. I read everything in the newspaper. It was—devastating."

"How old are you? And what date was that photograph taken?"

"I am nineteen months older than Suzy, if that's what you're thinking. Our father—"

"Don't."

"I'll call him John, if it makes you feel better. In Moscow, that winter, John had just asked your mother, Helen Mitchell, to marry him, but she turned him down. When John and Tiina slept together, he wasn't cheating on your mother. John's love was still alive, but the relationship had broken up. A few months later, he asked your mother again, and she accepted."

Kat doesn't respond.

"Why did John fall for Tiina?" continues Grachev. "For sanctuary? For lost love? To relieve sexual frustration? Who knows, particularly as it was my mother's job in those days to seduce foreign visitors. How did she get pregnant? Why did she not abort me? These are not questions for a son to ask his mother."

Kat stays quiet. But she's examining Grachev. His long, handsome face and his contagious enthusiasm are like her dad's.

He sits on the sofa, eyes toward the floor, hands clasped between his knees.

"I want to tell you about your dad," he says.

"No." Kat, still on her feet, stares straight at the marble fireplace with fake coals in the grate. "You will tell me what you know about the last moments of my sister's life."

They're both caught by surprise as their eyes meet in the mantelpiece mirror. Kat detects a flash of fear in him.

"You want to peel the world like a fruit. But the world doesn't work like that."

"Why were you with her at the concert?"

"Kat, stop this."

Kat moves carefully to the high sash window looking out over the main road, keeping her eyes on Grachev and the gun in her palm. With the morning sun behind her, Grachev is seeing her backlit, in half silhouette, which is the advantage Kat intends to give herself.

"Why did you sit through the second half without her," she asks calmly, "when you knew she was missing?"

"Not like this."

"Yes, Max, like this."

"You asked about Yulya. You asked how she stole RingSet from me. Yulya is a new breed of Russian patriot; she has no morality except—"

"No, Max," interrupts Kat. "Don't change the subject. You, not Yulya, were at the same concert as Suzy. You were in row G. Suzy was in row C. You could see her. In the second half, you knew she wasn't there. But you sat through it."

"I stayed because I *knew* Suzy had been shot. If I had moved, I would have destroyed my cover."

"You're a policeman, Max," says Kat contemptuously, her back still against him. "It's your job to—"

He's on his feet, his expression hard. "I will spell it out for you," he says, his eyes flaring with anger. "And you will listen. My sister, Yulya, doesn't choose violence. She was born with it. She takes what she wants when she wants. She doesn't reflect. She studies people only for what she can extract from them. She uses killing, torture, and sexual promiscuity. She has her eye on one goal, and that is to control RingSet, because it is the creation of my mother, who protects her. Do you understand the complexity of the person I am talking about?"

"Sounds like your average serial killer to me."

"Kat, you've got to understand."

"No. I have to deal with her, not understand her."

Grachev's expression is raw; she sees pleading in his eyes.

"No one takes on our family company and wins," he says softly. "That's why Suzy died—because she had the power to destroy RingSet."

At that moment, Grachev's cell phone rings from the mantel.

"Excuse me," he says, walking over. He picks it up, checks the caller ID, and frowns as if he knows who it is. He presses the answer button.

The next thing Kat hears is a noise like a tidal roar. Then cracking like gunshots. She's already moving, but it's too late. From behind her, the huge window, glass, wood, and plaster, blows across the room.

FORTY-ONE

◇

Wednesday, 9:03 a.m., BST

Air rushes from her lungs. Her face is hot. She feels a sting of broken glass cutting her cheek.

A fireball rises up from the middle of the room, yellow, orange, and black, catching a vortex, blowing out the window, streaming above her, leaving a shadow of suspended black debris across the gaping hole in the front.

The mirror falls askew, glass tumbling out of it, and it crashes to the ground. Grachev is facedown on the floor, his right arm twisted around his back. He lifts his head, tries to get up, and collapses back again. Kat's hand is cut. Blood runs down beside her left eye. Out in the street, a car alarm is blaring insistently.

She breathes in air like burning paint and crawls toward him through the choking smoke on all fours.

"*Get up!*" she screams.

Flames from a curtain leap toward the sofa and catch. Blood dribbles down to the edge of her lip. She licks it into her mouth, along with plaster grit.

Grachev rolls himself over. His face is gashed, his left eye closed, his shirt torn to rags. He presses his hand onto the floor. Kat's hand is under his shoulders, heaving him up.

He grunts. She wraps his arm around her shoulders. He leans heavily on her and cries out as he puts weight on his right leg. She feels his breath on her cheek. It smells of blood.

Grachev's knees buckle. She's taking all his weight. His eyes have gone gray and cloudy. They roll up into his head, and Kat slaps his face. The heat is up to the ceiling, plaster cracking, chunks falling, hanging by electrical wires, flames licking up the walls.

Then there are other people in the room. A hand grips Kat's shoulder, prizing itself between her and Grachev. Grachev drops to the floor, his legs twisted.

She is being lifted up—a man on either side—she sees fireproof suits, masks. "*Stop!*" she screams hoarsely, her throat dry with dust. She tries to tear herself away. They're too strong, and they know where they're going.

Kat is suspended inches off the floor, as one of them kicks open the kitchen door. She is bundled out through the back door, down steps to a basement patio, through another door, already open, and then a small apartment, and out into the street behind the building, where it's calm, no shattered windows, just black smoke spiraling above the rooftops.

Quietness envelops her. Her ears ring, but all else is silent. She can't hear the engine noise. She's lifted onto a paramedics' stretcher and slid into an ambulance.

FORTY-TWO

$$\diamondsuit$$

A nurse fills in a form on a clipboard and hangs it at the foot of her bed. Kat sees a policeman's boot in the doorway. It's a private room, a split-screen TV on mute, and sunlight playing on her bedclothes. Kat's wearing underwear and a green hospital gown. Her clothes are folded on a chair in the corner.

Her body aches. Her cuts sting with antiseptic. Her mouth tastes of burning and medicines. After refusing an IV and a tranquilizer, she feigned sleep because she needed to get her thoughts in order.

Grachev knew who was calling him when his cell phone triggered the bomb. The explosives must have been planted by someone who had access to his apartment.

Seconds before, Grachev told Kat that they shared a father.

Does *she* care? No. Does *he* care? Yes. But people don't go hunting around the world for lost half siblings unless they've got too much time on their hands or something more is at stake.

Her dad's onetime lover, Tiina, heads the Russian RingSet conglomerate. Yulya, Tiina's daughter, is being groomed to take over RingSet. She's made sure that her brother, Max, and sister, Lara, have no part in it.

Yulya knows the identity of the men whom Kat killed outside the Kazakh embassy. Those men had just murdered five diplomats who were unlucky enough to be working a nine-to-five office shift.

So, if the gunmen attacked at five, at the latest, it would have been ten at night in Britain. The intermission at the concert was at nine. The chances are that Suzy was dead *before* the attack on the embassy.

Bill Cage asked Kat to break in at 12:30 on Saturday morning. Suzy and the Kazakh diplomats would have been dead for about seven hours.

One of the victims, the Kazakh trade secretary, Aliya Raktaeva, was working for Bill Cage. The Kazakh data file that Cage ordered Kat to copy was on her computer.

But Yulya was right. She could explain away the photograph of her with the pistol. And companies lie about energy reserves all the time. So what's in the file that's so important?

Through half-closed eyes, she sees a shift in the policeman's boots in the doorway. "An American national, sir," he says. "The embassy has been informed."

An image of Nate Sayer with his documents flits across her mind. She remembers that he wants her back in Washington to face federal homicide charges, that Yulya cut a deal with Sayer to keep the Kazakh file, and that Sayer has the cartridge from the weapon that killed Suzy.

The door opens wider, and the policeman stands aside. Stephen Cranley, in a civilian pinstripe suit, comes in and closes the door.

"They tell me you're bruised but otherwise unhurt." He's carrying a plastic bag, which he puts on the end of the bed before he takes a chair from under the window, lifts it to the bedside, and sits down.

"I bought you some clothes." He glances at Kat's clothes on the chair. "They're torn and have blood on them. I got as close to the originals as I could find."

Kat says nothing, glances around, worried about surveillance. As if he reads her mind, Cranley says, "We can talk freely. The cameras and microphones are off. The American embassy has been told you're too injured to receive visitors. For the moment, you're safe from Nate Sayer."

Kat props herself up in the bed. A pain stabs through her right side. She ignores it. "Max? Is he okay?"

Cranley nods. "Worse off than you. But you're both lucky. The explosives were planted under his desk, away from where you were. He's in good shape, considering. I've talked to him. The call that detonated the bomb was from Yulya."

"She must have planted it on Monday just before I got to his apartment." A week ago, Kat would have wondered about a sister trying to kill her brother. Now she finds there's nothing more to say.

"Mike and Liz?" she asks.

"Mike's angry and aching. Liz is composed and fine. They drove back to London and are still working with me."

She stares at Cranley for a long time. His suit is well tailored. He's wearing a blue shirt with a yellow tie, slightly undone at the top. He is in his sixties. He has authority, but also sadness. Her father was close enough to Cranley to tell him the story about Javier Laja. Not even Nate and Nancy knew that. Cranley knows how her mother died. He deals with Grachev and Sayer. He works with Mike and Liz Luxton. He can turn off surveillance cameras.

She takes a sip of water, wipes her lips with a tissue, keeps looking at him, and Cranley gives her time.

"Who the fuck are you?" she says finally.

FORTY-THREE

$\longrightarrow\!\!\!\diamondsuit\!\!\!\longrightarrow$

Wednesday, 12:27 p.m., BST

Cranley steeples his fingers. "I come from the tawdry world of intelligence-gathering. I met John when he was a young lawyer during the trip to Moscow. I was posted to the British embassy. Your father was a political innocent. He believed in visions. I didn't. When I accused him of being naïve, he countered by saying I was confusing naïveté with curiosity." He laughs lightly. "We got on straightaway.

"We never lost contact, but I hadn't seen him for years. Then suddenly, he flew over to London to see me. We met in Battersea Park in London, freezing cold but safe, because even then, London had more cameras watching its citizens than any other city in the world.

"After the first London bombings, I had taken up a job at Scotland Yard to help liaison between intelligence services. Later, after the port bombing at Felixstowe, I was posted to the east zone, known as East Anglia. That is why we were able to get you through the checkpoint. I still have some influence there, although probably not much past today.

"Anyway, when we met, your father asked if I could find out about a summit that had taken place a few years earlier in St. Petersburg. If it was anyone but John, I might have done nothing. But your father's . . ." Cranley seems to struggle for the right word. "His moral core, I suppose, persuaded me to help. I squeezed people whom I normally would have kept for a rainier day. I found out that the summit was held in secret between the presidents of the United States, China, and Russia. They were together for four hours and twenty minutes; no one else in the room except their interpreters. The topic was long-term energy supplies.

"There haven't been any big discoveries of oil since the early 1950s, and nothing really substantive since the 1970s, when the North Sea and Alaska's North Slope were opened up. The nub of the summit was that China and the United States need energy. Russia has it, but no one knows how much.

"The Middle East has about twenty percent of known reserves. No single country outside of there has more than about three percent. Russia is thought to have five percent. Central Asia perhaps another five percent. But since Russia's been backsliding, turning inward, you know, we can't confirm those figures."

Cranley pauses to make sure Kat's following. She nods for him to proceed.

"Well, U.S. intelligence discovered that reserves in Russia and the Central Asian countries were ten, fifteen, twenty times more than what had been published. Bottom line: There's more gas and oil there than anywhere else in the world. So in St. Petersburg, the three leaders made an agreement. The truth about those reserves would remain confidential, which would keep prices high. On the strength of the shared secret, the United States, China, and Russia would carve up the world between them, dividing it into spheres of influence, pretty much like it was during the Cold War, and that's what will happen on Saturday when the Coalition for Peace and Security becomes an international treaty."

Kat swings her legs over the side of the bed, grimaces at the twinge in her side, then walks across to the sink and splashes water on her face. "How did Dad know?" she asks, drying herself with a hand towel.

"John came to me after he'd been contacted by a contractor working on the Tengiz oil field in Kazakhstan. There had been a spate of fatal accidents, and because American companies were shareholders, the contractor wanted to know if John could take action through the U.S. courts. Before accepting the case, John made inquiries and heard something about St. Petersburg. By the time he accepted the case, the contractor had been killed."

Cranley grimaces. "John was like a terrier. He pressed me. He must have pressed others. When he found an injustice, a secret, you couldn't stop him."

"So Dad found out, and they killed him," says Kat. "And killed Mom, too, for good measure, and now Suzy."

To her surprise, a faint, knowing smile dawns on Cranley's face. "Kat, your father never died in a plane crash," he says. "He's still alive."

FORTY-FOUR

---◇---

Her ears still ringing from the bomb, Kat's not sure she's heard right. Her lips move without a sound coming out.

"We need your help to keep him alive," says Cranley.

But she's barely listening.

Still alive.

How many times has Kat imagined those last moments, the Cessna spiraling out of control, her father fighting to survive?

Still alive.

She grips the edge of the sheet. "Go on."

"John never got into the Cessna. Someone else flew it, put it into a dive, and parachuted out. The plane blew up on a timed explosion. John was kidnapped. He was taken to Columbus and flown in a chartered Boeing 767 straight to a military airfield in Kazakhstan at a place called Vozrozhdeniye Island. That's a mouthful, but it means Renaissance or Rebirth Island in Russian. In Cold War times, it was a biological and chemical weapons factory; Kazakhstan was then in the Soviet Union. In preparation for the CPS, Voz Island was declared a Special Economic Zone, with investment and tax concessions. In fact, it's a prison camp, outsourced on a forty-nine-year lease to RingSet."

"Tiina Gracheva," mutters Kat.

"Exactly."

"Who my dad had an affair with?"

"Yes. Max said he told you."

"But I don't get it. What's the point of keeping Dad alive?"

Cranley shrugs. "Tiina demanded it. From what I understand, Tiina accepted John's abduction and imprisonment as a necessity to ensure the CPS went ahead, but she refused to sanction his murder. It's a strangely human decision, but Tiina said that if John were harmed, she'd blow the whistle."

"But killing Mom was okay."

"It seems so."

"And Suzy."

Cranley lowers his eyes, doesn't answer.

"How's Dad living, then?" she says, keeping herself measured. "In chains? In a cell? Does he know Mom's dead?"

"Suzy was trying to find out," says Cranley, "but what she uncovered went far beyond your father. She was going to take down the whole rotten system. She compiled a dossier. It contains documents, including the falsification of the reserves, photographs of people actually being murdered, the people who work with Yulya. Suzy found a lot of the evidence in the Media Axis archives. Liz Luxton helped her put it together. She was transmitting it to Aliya Raktaeva in the Kazakh embassy on Friday night when she was killed."

"And Raktaeva worked for Bill."

"Yes. For the FCA."

"Did Suzy know I was FCA?"

"I don't know." Cranley plays it straight, like Cage, trying not to let Kat get worked up.

"Was it coincidence that Suzy and I were working on the same project?"

"Your separate skills made it happen. But when you were arrested for hacking, Suzy made sure you came under Cage's care and not Nate Sayer's."

Kat brings out the clothes from the bag. She tears the labels off as she looks at them, uses it to give her time and hide her expression. She swallows and keeps going.

"Who's doing it then? Who kidnapped Dad? Who's running this rotten system?"

"It's in the dossier, which I haven't seen."

"Then how come you're involved?" snaps Kat. She unfolds the jeans, deciding to dress here and not risk breaking the conversation. She slips them on under her hospital gown. Tight, but fine.

"Many don't agree with the CPS," says Cranley. "It's more divisive than the Iraq invasion, and its opponents are prepared to go further to stop it. The fight is not only between governments, but also between people within governments."

"And that's you?" says Kat, unfolding a red cotton shirt.

"Yes."

"And Liz and Mike?"

"Yes."

"And Bill Cage?"

"The whole of the FCA."

Kat pauses, reflects for a second. "But not Nate?"

"Nate follows government orders. He doesn't question."

Kat slips off the gown and doesn't care that Cranley's in the room. She puts on the shirt and buttons it. Cranley looks toward the bed, then out the window onto a tidy lawn and garden. Kat goes to the mirror. She hurts, but she's leaving. She runs a brush through her hair.

"You said you needed my help."

"Yes." Cranley pushes back the chair. It scrapes on the hospital floor. "Tiina is due here on Saturday. There'll be a signing ceremony, first with the coalition partners, then with the heads of the corporations. We've heard that as soon as that's done, Tiina will step down, and Yulya will take over RingSet. She's drawn up a list of prisoners from Voz Island and other camps who are slated for execution. We suspect that John's on it."

Kat's brush stops. In the mirror she sees Cranley, his back to her, his chin in his hands.

"Yulya has your copy of Suzy's dossier," says Cranley. "The copies you gave Bill Cage self-erased. The only other copy we know of is in Liz's computer in the edit suite at Media Axis. Liz secured it, but since then, another cordon has been put around it with a new password."

Cranley's bought her a light green windbreaker as well. She shakes it open and slips it over the shirt, then looks back at Cranley. "If you can get me in, I can get it."

FORTY-FIVE

Wednesday, 3:14 p.m., BST

It's sixteen minutes before the shift change that Mike Luxton and Kat will use to try to get into Media Axis.

A window poster in the café where she sits advertises a live question-and-answer show with experts on Project Peace. Through grimy windowpanes she looks across the street to a line snaking around to a gated entrance. Some hold a copy of Christopher North's pamphlet, reading it as they wait.

Inside the compound are three high-rise buildings protected by razor-wire fencing, with flags on poles, flying full in the strong wind. One with red etched on blue has Chinese characters—和平工程. Next to it, Russian—Проект Мир. Then English—PROJECT PEACE.

A huge banner is strung across the top of each of the three buildings. On the left, THE COALITION FOR PEACE AND SECURITY. In the middle, 平安联盟. And on the right, Коалиция для мира и безопасности.

On a TV screen in the café, the English soccer captain Gary Spooner, wearing a bright-red sports shirt, holds both hands with thumbs up against the backdrop of a banner with a multinational bank logo on it. A sports news strip schedules matches; quarterfinals Thursday, semifinals Friday, and the final, at Wembley Stadium, on Saturday.

The second screen shows three men crouched behind an upturned van and fires on a hillside in the distance, with the caption FRESH FIGHTING IN MACEDONIA; ANTITERROR SQUADS DEPLOYED.

The roaring inside Kat's head from the bomb began again when she left the hospital, but it's subsided to a dull throb, the ringing in her ears quieter. Her left ankle is weak. If she puts too much weight on it, pain screams toward her thigh and kicks a nerve somewhere in her femur.

She's been watching the screens for almost an hour. There's a tiny spot about a gas pipe explosion on Portland Place and a brief shot of the destroyed facade of Grachev's apartment.

From the hospital, Cranley took her to an office. Luxton was there. Apart from the cut over his right eye, he seemed fine. They photographed her, scanned her eyes, fingerprints, and palm, and made her an ID card for Media Axis, stripped secure by laser, and gave her a set of flash cards and USB drives. Her new name is Rachel Williams.

She's wearing light blue dungarees with MEDIA AXIS in yellow letters on her back.

Between the café and the Media Axis compound is a pedestrian area, then a bend in the Thames River. On either side are the high-rises of other multinational corporations.

Luxton comes into view, walking alongside the line. He's in the same uniform dungarees, and when he's level with her window, he unfolds his arms, which is the signal for Kat to join him.

Kat walks out and falls into step ten yards behind him.

"After Iraq, everyone was saying that American power had to be balanced, right?" A tall man, head shaved and his face laden with rings, is haranguing anyone who'll listen. "Well, that's what Project Peace is all about."

Luxton cuts to the left and goes through a revolving door. He waits for Kat in a foyer with stainless steel floors and ceilings, with a wall of television screens, at least 20 huge images.

It takes Kat a moment to separate out the familiar screens she sees on the streets; one with Spooner talking and playbacks of him as the England captain scoring goals. On the right, the story has shifted from Macedonia to Cuba.

BREAKING NEWS flashes in the top right-hand corner. A caption says HAVANA SIGNS PEACE TREATY WITH WASHINGTON. SANCTIONS LIFTED.

Luxton presses his pass against another revolving door. A green light comes on with a click, and he walks through. Kat's about to follow him when a security guard steps in front of her.

"Pass," he says, glancing at Kat and a row of clocks on the wall behind the reception desk. Kat flips her pass up to him. He checks it, looks at her again.

"What time does your shift start?" he asks.

"Now," she says softly, looking down, not eyeballing him.

"What kind of an answer is that?"

She sees Luxton through three different shields of glass, halfway up a flight of stairs by a bank of elevators. He catches what's happening and keeps going.

"My shift starts in four minutes," says Kat. She twists her wrist and checks her watch so he can see it. "Fifteen twenty-seven. Well, three minutes."

He says nothing, just nods. Kat slaps the card onto the ID reader, her heart pounding in the split second it takes for the green light to go on. She pushes the door and steps through as if she's been working in the place forever.

She follows Luxton down a corridor of plasma screens from which faces stare out, soundlessly, talking at her.

With each step, the screen face locks onto her, eyes following until she moves out of range and another takes its place. She recognizes some from watching in the street; one of them is of Prime Minister Michael Rand. The ceiling is pine, lit by crisscrossing image lights that project laser slogans onto the floor. Kat makes out words like *Trust* and *Values*.

Eyes down, she keeps Luxton in view. The corridor leads to another foyer, older, with a wooden reception desk and visitors sitting as if in a hospital waiting room, all staring at screens on the wall. Luxton turns left down a flight of stairs. He waits for Kat at the bottom, then opens the third door on the right and holds it for her to walk through.

FORTY-SIX

———◇———

The door swings shut behind her. The temperature is cooler and drier than outside. A stack of hardware, locked into frames, hums in a corner.

Liz sits in a high-backed chair in front of a semicircle of monitors, the center one showing a skirmish in Macedonia that Kat saw in the café a few minutes earlier. The shot pulls away to a road on a lush green hillside, where she sees that the upturned van is actually part of a three-vehicle collision.

"W-welcome to my edit suite," Liz says, wheeling her chair to one side and beckoning Kat to pull up an empty one.

Kat sits down.

"That's a pileup in Malaga in Spain," says Liz. "I g-get those pictures, put them with an armored car from Iraq, mix that with shots of the insurgency in Kashmir, and tell everyone the global terror threat has erupted into fresh fighting in Macedonia."

Her contorted fingers move incredibly fast over the keyboard. She flips the screen back to the scenes she has just cut. "See how I show those bodies? No faces. No distortion. No flesh ripped down to the bones. I call them the peaceful dead. And they're the bad guys. My job is to create images of sanitized war. Now look at this."

She brings up a shot of a baby with its neck half severed; a village razed by tanks; a child's hand protruding from underneath the rubble; three soldiers, their clothes torn off by a bomb, naked white limbs streaked with gore and one of them crying out.

"That's Iraq." She brings up another set of pictures. "These are the people in Russia who suffer under the control of companies like RingSet. See the children? The dullness in their eyes? That's pollution. That scab there." She points to a close-up of a boy swinging on a tire hanging from a lamppost in a concrete playground littered with plastic bags. "Malnutrition causes that. The food they eat is crap. The air they breathe is crap. The wages they earn are crap. All the money goes into RingSet's pocket."

The screen flips from one image to another and another—all scenes of dreadful poverty.

"They die. RingSet wins. Game over," says Kat softly.

"All of this is censored," says Liz. "For each story I edited for broadcast, Suzy and I edited another with the banned pictures. We loaded in the other evidence she collected, and that's what's buried somewhere deep inside here. Suzy called it The History Book, because it's historical fact not controlled by television networks. There's enough to jail Yulya, Tiina, and all the rest of them for life."

"Those types need the needle," Kat starts to say, then notices the shadow of someone passing outside. The door opens slightly.

"Something with the security guard who handled you at the door," says Luxton. "He's checking on Rachel Williams' ID. There are other checks in line, so it'll take him a few minutes, but hurry."

FORTY-SEVEN

$$\diamond$$

Wednesday, 3:52 p.m., BST

Is this where you and Suzy worked all the time?"

Kat's looking at a keystroke tracker, linked into the cable between the keyboard and the computer.

It's a tiny gadget that records every key used, including passwords that show up unencrypted. When a password appears on the screen as **************, it will show up on the keystroke tracker in the actual words, letters, and symbols.

"Most of the time. Sometimes we were bounced to another suite."

"When were the new security codes put in?"

Liz stops working on the computer and looks up at her. "I found out on Saturday morning, the day after Suzy was killed."

"You tried to get in?"

"Yes, and f-failed."

"Alarms?"

"N-no. Just refused access."

"What's the authentication code?"

"MC08/5783"

Kat notes it on a scrap of paper. Liz's images of fighting in Macedonia hang frozen on the screen in front of her. Chilled air-conditioning catches in the back of her throat.

"What's your user name?"

"L-U-X-4-6-8-3"

"Password?"

"I'm logged in already."

"Just give me your password," says Kat patiently.

"C-L-O-U-D-N-I-N-E"

"When did you change it?"

"Saturday."

"Same time you were denied access?"

"Y-yes."

"Do you have e-mail confirmation?"

Liz leans over Kat, opens Outlook, which shows her e-mail list, high-lights one, and opens it. "Job number SATAUG014/password change/L-U-X-4-6-8-3/operator MQuinn, HD."

"MQuinn?" asks Kat.

"HD means the IT help desk. Melissa Quinn works there."

"How many people would have been on shift with Melissa?"

"On Saturday? Three."

"If she changed your password, would she have also changed Suzy's?"

"She might. But Suzy was a client. She actually had a higher authoriza-tion than me."

"So could it have been changed by the client—from outside?"

"I don't know. But I've seen Suzy do it at the keyboard without register-ing with the help desk."

"When did you last work here together?"

"Thursday, until late. We left at two on Friday morning, actually."

Friday at 3:00, Suzy e-mailed Kat. In the evening, she was murdered. Kat points to the keystroke tracker. "How is this secured?"

"Any unauthorized access sets off an alarm." In the opaque lighting of the edit suite, Liz's face is creased with worry.

"Would Melissa be authorized?"

"I d-don't know."

"What about Suzy?"

"Her company might. But not here with me around."

Kat glances up at the clock. She's got a tough choice and no time to make it. Either she tries to attack a higher access level or she breaks into the keystroke tracker, pulls up everything from Thursday and Friday, and, amid the streams of text, identifies which one might be a new password.

If the password were made up of random keystrokes, such as gy&ltf*k, it might be easy to spot. If it were a familiar word, though, it would mean reading every sentence.

The keystroke tracker's data will be protected, so Kat types the address of the Web site that she uses to help devise her own hacking software.

With the Web site up, she concentrates on ascertaining the types of security cordons she's up against. Only two meet the level of security needed by a place like Media Axis. One, almost exclusively used in the United States, is known colloquially as Ball Blocker. The other is more global and operates under the licensed name of White Ice. Unless Media Axis has installed a military firewall, Kat figures it would almost certainly use White Ice—to which Kat, through one of her offshore companies, is a subscriber.

She types in c:\Program Files\Network ICE\WhiteICE\LICENSE.KEY, and clicks to get the White Ice log-in and password page. Kat puts in her personal code.

At the top of the screen, as her code is being checked, details come up of an organization providing security for Media Axis.

WEB-FRONTPAGE service.pwdSID959
参考 hacktrap,1205 考：
National Intrusion Computer Network Protection Center, Shanghai

She's never heard of the organization, which means it could throw anything at her at any time. Like many corporations that do not trust their own staff, Media Axis has outsourced its security. A shadow passes outside the door again, reminding her of Luxton's vigil outside.

Kat goes to the My Computer icon, selects the drive E, which takes her to a USB port, and types the keys to open the keystroke-grabber file.

The screen unfurls into a string of sentences and keyboard instructions.

"Okay," says Kat, breathing out slowly. She scans for a time and date reference, but can't see one. "Any of this Suzy's work?"

They read together through a stew of catchphrases, rewrites, updates, and other products of CPS's media campaign: POVERTY SUCH AS SEEN HERE WILL BE OBLITERATED THROUGH COOPERATION BETWEEN NATIONS. THESE PHOTOGRAPHS SHOW

MISERY CREATED BY TRIBAL CONFLICT AND TERRORISM. MEASURE BROUGHT IN BY THE CPS DEAL WILL END SUCH PLIGHP\\\\\ T = ..>>>>>

Spaces are shown with chevrons, backspaces are backward slashes. Mouse movements were not picked up, so the text constantly goes non sequitur into new documents and e-mails.

"Wait! This is what we were d-doing on Friday," says Liz. She touches the screen.

"What was Suzy's user name?"

"T-H-O-M-9-7-3-6"

Kat runs a search on it, and way down the data, the cursor comes to a stop. T-H-O-M-9-7-3-6 and right next to it without a space L-B-U-P-M-J-W-F.

She notes the password, scrolls down the text, and finds the user name again, this time with another password next to it: M-C-V-Q-N-K-X-F. The next time she does it, the password appears as L-C-W-S-Q-O-B-*. Once again, and it appears as J-Z-S-N-K-H-U-D. Then again and it comes up as F&6LUIT$, and finally F*SDLT*U.

One of those six passwords will give her access to Suzy's History Book, the dossier she and Cranley need.

As on the shooting range, you have to get balance, breathing, and concentration in line before taking the perfect shot. With code analysis, you do the same. The first three passwords seem to follow a pattern. The fourth with the star is difficult to tell. The last two look as if they have been thrown up by the system.

Kat reckons she'll have two, maybe three shots at it. It's like the chamber of a revolver loaded for Russian roulette. Each time a password is rejected, the system will note it. Too many rejections over too short a space of time, and it will signal an alert.

She types in F*SDLT*U. Since it was the last one to show up, logically she guesses it is the current password. But the window fades and returns. Above in red is the message INCORRECT USER NAME OR PASSWORD.

Strike one.

The next step is to try the first one. She types in L-B-U-P-M-J-W-F. The screen takes longer to react, a mechanism set up against password cracking. Each time a wrong password is entered, there's a longer delay before accepting a new one.

Kat's hands rest on either side of the keyboard, fingers splayed out to dry the sweat on her palms. The red message returns.

Strike two.

Kat holds back from typing in a third password from the list. She breathes deeply and asks Liz, "You were here at three o'clock, Friday afternoon, with Suzy?"

"Yes."

"How does it work? You editing and Suzy on the keyboard, sitting next to each other like you and I are now?"

Liz nods.

"So you wouldn't know what Suzy is writing, everything she's doing here?"

"That's right."

As Kat fires questions, her eyes skim ceaselessly over the keystrokes her sister left on that fateful night, then she sees KAT, CALL ME, PLEASE. IT'S ABOUT PROJECT PEACE. I NEED YOUR HELP. YOU'RE ALWAYS ON MY MIND WHEN I'M STAYING INCREMENTALLY ONE STEP AHEAD.

Oh my God. The solution, Kat hopes, is the word *incrementally*. Could the clue to decoding the password be *staying one step ahead*?

A moment of thought, and Kat gets it. Those five words must somehow point her to the correct password.

She begins playing the alphabet game with her own name. Kat spots the right one—L-C-W-S-Q-O-B-*. Suzy actually made it more obvious than she should have. *One step ahead* turns a K into an L. *Incrementally* means adding two letters to the next letter, three to the third, and so on, thus turning an *A* into a *C* and a *T* into a *W*.

Kat's name is represented by the first three characters; *Olive*, as in Olive Street, where she lives, is the basis for the last five characters.

In the password window, Kat types in K-A-T-O-L-I-V-E, disciplining a welling in her throat, stopping her eyes from misting so she can see properly.

"Got it," she says. Liz joins her, leans on Kat's shoulder.

"There," says Liz, finger clumsily jabbing the screen at a folder called The History Book.

Kat asks Liz to watch the door and tries to settle her mind. Kat opens the file and finds herself looking at Yulya again, her face cruel and untroubled, her victim's blood soaking into the snow.

She flips on to make sure it's all there. The next shot shows an airbase in a snowy wasteland that's completely stark and empty, like a white sea. Two transport aircraft are on the ground. Behind them stands a control tower amid a sprawl of low-rise buildings and a high wire fence.

Is that Voz Island? she wonders. If so, is her father still there?

Kat double-clicks the White Ice security software icon at the bottom of the screen, copies a symbol called On-The-Move, and pastes it into the History Book folder. She calls up the folder itself. The security software demands her code and password. Now she opens her own secure Internet file and copies over The History Book to the remote site where her private data are stored.

She inserts a jump drive into the USB port, copies it again. She's about to put in a flash card for good measure when Liz's hand grips her shoulder. Through glass at the top of the door, she sees Luxton, talking into his cell phone and shaking his head.

An image from the file automatically comes back onto the screen and catches her eye: A dead man's face is in the snow. Blood soaks all around his gray hair. He is wearing just a shirt, no coat, no scarf, no gloves. His corpse would be frozen within minutes.

Why would Suzy put it there, the first picture of the file, if that man is not their father?

"That's not your dad," says Liz, reading her mind. "But here." She zooms out to make the picture's panorama expand.

Behind the executed man stands a line of prisoners—there must be a hundred of them, all dressed in summer clothes although the ice on the jeep's windshield puts the temperature at well below freezing. What Kat had once thought was a U.S. eagle is, in fact, the RingSet logo: a bird of prey, wings outspread and beaked head turned slightly away. And the victim—was he just picked out of the line at random? Why?

Shaking, Liz's finger points to a man still standing in the line. "Suzy said that was your dad."

Blood rushes through Kat's ears like wind as Liz zooms back in on the man in question. He's hunched and looks racked with cold and hunger. He's trying to clasp himself warm, but is stopped by shackles confining his movement. He's the right height and age, tall and ungainly, his face blotched with blood sores, lips peeling, one eye infected and half closed. But he isn't defeated. Nor does he show fear.

Luxton taps on the glass, beckons them out.

"C-come on," says Liz.

"A second," says Kat. Why did the file reappear automatically? She calls up the copy in her own Internet file.

Only an expert, with an eye trained to detect, would be able to tell immediately that something is wrong with her secure site. Kat swallows hard, shoots a look through the door glass. Luxton's gaze shifts from inside the edit suite to something happening along the corridor.

The only excuse Kat can come up with is that she should never again mix computer work with being bombed.

She had been sure that the White Ice firewall would stop it. Or was that a rationalization because this was the only shot she had at saving her father's life?

Now, instead of seeing a copy of Suzy's History Book, she's looking at a pair of hands in cuffs.

参考：hacktrap,1465 考：

CAPTURED BY

National Intrusion Computer Network Protection Center, Shanghai

FORTY-EIGHT

$$\longrightarrow\!\!\Diamond\!\!\longrightarrow$$

Wednesday, 4:07 p.m., BST

Luxton opens the door. "Now!" he shouts. He's grabbing Liz's arm. Kat's not moving. She's punching keys to cordon off Suzy's dossier in its remote file and in the hard drive so that no one else can get to it and no one can detect her keystrokes on Media Axis's computer network.

Luxton's hand is on her arm. She shakes him free. "Go, go," she yells.

"Out, Kat." His voice is a whisper.

She's almost there, putting up a hall of mirrors between keystrokes.

She seals it with an ampersand and a pound sign, returning the file, with its evidence of killings and corruption, to its embedded sanctuary.

An alarm starts up in the corridor.

Luxton carries Liz over his shoulder. People jostle, running. Sirens blare right through the building. Crowds gather on the sidewalk, hands over eyes against the sun, looking for smoke.

On the curve of the corridor, past a screen where a host is explaining a graph of the global economy, Luxton pushes open a door. They go into a dimly lit stairwell. Luxton climbs up from the basement toward the ground floor.

"With luck, there'll be a vehicle waiting—" he begins to say, when a light from above hits him in the face.

He drops to a squat, gripping the banister to keep balance with Liz's weight. Kat judges there are two flashlight beams, two or three floors up.

"What floor do you need?" she says to Luxton.

"One floor up," he says.

"I'll stay and stop them. You take Liz out."

Luxton has a dead expression around his eyes, the look of someone who's stopped trying to find emotions. He knows what she's suggesting is the only way.

"I'll wait as long as I can," he says. "Door at the top, cross the road. It's a long white stretch . . ."

Footsteps are coming down, not fast, flashlights swerving all over. Liz hangs over her brother's shoulder; her face caves in on itself, as if by being carried, she has put Kat in more danger.

Kat looks at neither of them. She pushes past Luxton, takes two steps at a time upward, runs across the landing to the next flight, hand shielding her eyes whenever the flashlight catches her, keeps going. Just a few more steps, and she hears a voice, "Stop. Stop right there."

Kat turns her shoulder, shouts, "What the hell—"

She falls with a hand on the wall, lets her foot slip back a stair, and comes down on the edge of the concrete, cutting into her upper thigh, which ignites a nerve already made raw by the bomb. She cries out, hadn't meant to, but it works.

There are two of them, in dark blue uniforms, light blue short-sleeved shirts, the logo of a private security firm on the breast pockets. They're middle-aged, hesitant, not there to get her, just clearing the building.

One steadies a flashlight beam in her face, the other crouches down. "You okay?"

Kat holds her leg, teeth pressing into her tongue while the pain subsides. "How do you get out of this place?" she manages.

"We'll get you out, love," he says. "But they think it's a false alarm, don't they, Rick?"

His hand is on her elbow. "Can you balance on that leg?"

"I'll try," says Kat. It's like being with the dentist when the anesthetic hasn't kicked in. Her lips are tight, eyes closed. She feels a tug on the cord holding her ID card to her waistband.

"You'll be all right, Rachel," he says kindly and looks up toward Rick. "Rachel Williams," he reads off the card. "ID number 873289/f/MC/8005."

Rick pulls out a keyboard and punches in the number.

"Are you American?" asks Rick.

"Canadian," says Kat.

The guard reading her ID card is the more out of shape of the two; Rick has a steadier, meaner face, like violence is his hobby, and his day job's holding him back.

Kat strikes the out-of-shape guard just below the nose. Through the stairwell railing, the bladed beams of Rick's flashlight catch a sheen of blood on his face. She hits the man again, in the same place, then kicks hard into Rick's knee.

Rick's tough. He staggers, but takes her measure as if he has all the time in the world. He has a wiry face with sharp surfaces. He shifts to get his position right and brings the flashlight up, no longer a lamp, but a weapon.

Kat puts up her arm to block it, causing him to hesitate. She slams her foot into his chest, catches him just below the rib cage, and follows it with her fist. This time he falls.

Down one flight, she finds the door and pushes it open, gets across a corridor, and through another door is the street, where she sees a stretch limousine with darkened windows.

The sidewalk is crowded with evacuated staff, everyone standing in someone else's way.

She gets clear of the crowd, runs into the middle of the street, and sees a police barrier. Another one is set up behind her.

The limousine's brake lights come on. The back door opens, fingers around the inside handle, and another hand beckoning. Kat jumps in.

Luxton's driving. He accelerates, jumps red lights, and heads toward an overpass. Two policemen stand in the middle of the road, hands held high, ordering the car to stop.

They're going fast up the overpass, lampposts and street railings flashing past. The hood of the limousine rises up like a speedboat, pushing Kat back into her seat.

Through the top corner of the side window, Kat sees a large, two-engine military helicopter flying unusually low.

The checkpoint rushes toward them. A policeman fires at the limousine.

The windshield cracks but doesn't break. Another policeman is looking up at the helicopter, confusion on his face; neither their limousine nor the helicopter is meant to be there.

"That ours?" she says.

"Not ours," says Luxton, his arms tightening to take the pressure on the wheel.

The sheer weight of the limo, which must be armor plated, tosses police cars as if they're plastic cartons. Kat's thrown against Liz, then back against the door. Automatic fire frosts a side window but doesn't smash it. Luxton takes them up the overpass, makes a right-angle hand-brake turn at the top, heads down a side road, and stops.

"Switching cars," he says, throwing open his door. He's on the sidewalk, pulling Liz out.

"You. Out," he yells at Kat. "This side." She slides across and out.

A police van pulls up on the overpass. The back doors open. A rocket flashes from the skids of the helicopter, and the blue metal of the vehicle tears apart like a ripped sheet. Flames, fed by oxygen, curl underneath and catch on the clothing of the men sitting inside. Two men make it out, blazing, and fall to the concrete, rolling. Then the fuel tank catches, and the van disappears in a fireball.

Luxton opens the door of an old red sedan and lifts Liz into the passenger seat. Kat gets in the back.

Smoke blows toward them, shielding them from the checkpoint. She hears automatic weapons fire, and a new explosion buffets her eardrums, with a fresh surge of heat that clears the smoke. A rocket from the helicopter has destroyed their limousine.

"What the hell," she shouts to Luxton. "Is the military trying to kill us?"

Luxton, at the wheel, pulls out, his eyes half on the mirror, half ahead of him.

The helicopter's directly above them, descending so low now that Kat feels she could reach out and touch it.

The car jerks, and they're thrown forward. Luxton's eyes flicker uncertainly. His foot is hard on the gas, but nothing's happening except the whine of the motor. The car's roof creaks. The helicopter has taken the rear wheels off the ground with magnetic claws, which lift it a fraction, then clamp down and around the chassis to carry the full weight.

Hands off the wheel, Luxton turns in his seat. "Sorry," he says.

With preternatural calm, Luxton lets down his window and tilts his side mirror toward the sky. Claws stretch from the helicopter's underbelly like the legs of a beetle, clutching the sedan around its midsection.

Kat's stomach muscles tighten, and her body chills. She is filled with hatred so pure that it flushes all fear from her system. It makes what she feels about Sayer an irritation; her shooting of the men an unemotional necessity. It's as if every piece of anger she's experienced before is a preparation for how she now intends to use it. She will kill these people, and she will enjoy it. Nothing will stop her.

She breathes in the acrid smells of burning vehicles.

South of the overpass, the helicopter has lifted them high enough to cross above a high wire fence into a parking lot. Between rows of cars, many of them old and battered, the helicopter descends slowly until Kat feels the car's chassis touch the ground again.

The clamps are released, and the helicopter goes up fast again, its nose dipped.

A voice from a loudspeaker commands, "*All of you come out of the car with your hands up.*"

"No choice," says Luxton.

Kat opens her door. She has one foot on the ground when she senses rather than sees a faraway flash of yellow. She looks straight above to see the helicopter jerk in midair, like a horse rearing at a jump.

It swivels, and a jet of oil spurts, hitting the ground around her. The chopper's tail arches as if it's going to snap, making the aircraft spin out of control, with a grating sound of metal destroying metal, sending out columns of sparks.

"*Move!*" yells Kat. They both have Liz, carrying her, Kat's hands under her legs, Luxton's under her arms.

The helicopter, flames shooting from the fuselage, twists toward the ground. A rotor blade hits the car's roof, bouncing the helicopter onto its side, and an inferno engulfs both vehicles.

A shot shatters a van's side-view mirror close by. "Over there," Luxton says, pointing to where he thinks the gunfire is coming from.

Kat can't tell. Nor who shot down the helicopter. Nor who's attacking them now.

"G-go! Both of you," shouts Liz.

But where? With a deafening noise, auto safety glass rains down around them. Police swarm into the compound. Blue lights flash outside. There's no way out.

A crack of thunder explodes in Kat's head. All is silent. She feels heat on her skin. Her legs can't hold her anymore. The vans, the fireballs, the burning helicopter swirl in front of her. Her vision narrows to a tunnel, and all she can see is the horror on Luxton's face as two policemen, hands under his shoulders, drag him off.

FORTY-NINE

$$\diamondsuit$$

Thursday, 4:20 a.m., BST

The tang that catches her throat isn't smoke, but salty sea air. Kat coughs. She's standing by the porthole of a police launch, her hands wrapped around a cup of coffee, watching the belly of a half moon dip up and down with the rocking of the boat. She sees faraway ships' lights, but nothing that looks like land.

Inside, a pair of gray television screens on the wall of the small galley cabin are turned off. An empty bowl of soup, which she's just finished, is on the table with a soup urn, a pot of coffee, a basket of bread, a bowl of white sugar, a pile of cutlery, and salt and pepper shakers. The table's plastic top is chipped, and on one corner is a cigarette burn.

In the middle of the table, lying in a polyethylene bag, is her grandmother's ring, given to her mother, then loved and worn by Suzy and torn off her finger when she was shot.

There's only one of its kind, a big circle of silver with a square of tin on top, four tiny diamonds, one in each corner, and a figure-eight infinity symbol between them.

After Luxton and Liz were taken away, Kat was carried in a police van to a police station, where she was locked in a cell. The police guarded her with undisguised loathing, as if she were the cause of the death of their colleagues.

The conversations that she overheard were of shock, how a British military helicopter could attack a police checkpoint, about the police officers who had been killed, about politicians screwing things up, about Project Peace being a sham, about things going too far.

Just before midnight, the cell door was unlocked. Kat was taken to a helicopter that flew her to somewhere on the east coast, where she boarded the launch. They put her in a cabin and locked the door. From the porthole, she watched the launch put out to sea. Then the door was unlocked, and Kat was taken to the galley.

Max Grachev, in full police uniform, was waiting for her with soup and coffee. He told her that the helicopter attack had been carried out by a rogue military unit that supported Project Peace. The police had been ordered simply to arrest Kat and Liz. The helicopter crew intended to kidnap them.

Luxton and Liz were unhurt, but under arrest. Kat remained in danger, which is why they were heading for Europe, where she would be safer.

Now Grachev stands, arms folded, leaning against the wall. He has a bandage on the right-hand side of his neck. He walks with a slight limp. He's just placed Suzy's ring on the table.

Slowly, Kat opens the seal of the bag, puts her hand inside, feels the cold metal of the ring, and brings it out. She lifts the lid under which Suzy used to keep a tiny picture of them all: Mom, Dad, Suzy, Kat, Grandma, bunched together under the cherry tree on one summer's open day at the Lancaster orphanage.

The picture's not there. Instead, she recognizes a tiny powered circuit for a direct satellite transmission system. It might have been a small piece of decorative jewelry, but Suzy used it as a transmitter.

"Yulya wanted me to give it to you," says Grachev.

Kat picks up the ring and curls her fingers around its spiky edges. "Tell me," she says, her voice barely audible. "Friday night. All of it."

Grachev clasps his hands in front of him. "I knew Suzy was trying to find out about her father. John," he corrects himself. "I didn't know how dangerous gathering that information would be for her. Still, as soon as I got to London, I watched her. I didn't introduce myself. I doubt she knew I existed.

"I saw from our travel records that she was due to go to the concert on Friday evening. You are right. She didn't care about music. And it was a long way to go when she had no known connections in that area. There must have been another reason. I booked a seat as well. I didn't need authorization to go, so I went.

"Suzy arrived, preordered a gin and tonic for the intermission, took her seat, and sat through the first part, the Tchaikovsky, all the time acting perfectly normally. Then came the intermission. It was spitting rain, but still warm. Suzy picked up her drink from a ledge near the terrace door.

"I hadn't expected her to go outside. I thought, rather, that she was to meet someone at the concert. But she pushed open the terrace door enough to test the weather. She was looking out at something, very thoughtful.

"Quite suddenly, she left her glass on the terrace wall, walked down the steps, and started out across the lawn. She tried to make it look as if she were taking a stroll, but I could tell she was heading somewhere. I let her get as far as the sculpture just before the beginning of the footpaths into the marshes before following. But I misjudged the weather. It was darker than I thought, and Suzy vanished. I couldn't see her at all. There are two paths. You've been there, you know. One is a foot track that heads straight out into the marshes. The other is the grass track between the trees, which turns down past the pig farms. I headed down that one. The wrong one.

"I heard a shot, and I heard Suzy shout. I heard another shot. Then there was silence, and I began running toward her. By the time I got there, Suzy was dead, and the ring was gone."

He's not looking at Kat. He's avoiding her. "I am not proud of what I did next, but it was necessary. I ran back to the concert and sat through the second part, Beethoven's Ninth. Her empty seat was in view all the time. I knew she was dead. I knew I had failed to protect her. I have never felt less of a man in my whole life."

Kat steps across to the porthole, drawing in smells of marine fuel. She looks at her grandmother's ring in the glow of a back deck light.

Assuming its signal would have enough power to reach a low-orbiting U.S. military satellite, Kat now knows why Suzy would have gone to Suffolk, where the big skies and open coastline would give her a chance of a clean transmission. Suzy would have worked out that the time of the intermission matched the satellite's trajectory and that the concert would give her a cover. With rain clouds, she would have questioned whether she'd get a clear enough path. So she stood on the terrace, perhaps with a sense of destiny, but also calculating her chances of success. Then she must have decided to risk it.

Kat goes back to the table. Grachev hasn't moved. Neither of them speaks. Kat ladles soup into the bowl. It's vegetable and hot, and its burn goes right down her throat. Her body sucks it in. She breaks off a piece of bread, swirls it around, and eats as if there might be no more.

"Tell me, Max," says Kat, "why it would be necessary for a cop to leave a murder victim?" He doesn't answer right away. She rubs her right eye with the heel of her hand. "Unless it's to protect the murderer, who happens to be the cop's sister."

"I'm not so familiar with the British police. Loyalties are divided about Project Peace. We saw it at the checkpoint—"

"I don't want a lecture," says Kat. "Just answer the fucking question." She takes a spoonful of soup without taking her eyes off him.

"I knew about Stephen Cranley from the old KGB files in Moscow. I knew he was a friend of John Polinski and that he would have known about Suzy. He's an assistant commissioner, and he had the power to make sure things didn't get out of hand. I called him before returning to the concert. He told me to go inside and do nothing. Later that night, he called and said he was going to lead the murder investigation. He had arranged for it to be classified as international organized crime, which would automatically involve me."

"Did either of you know Yulya did it?"

Grachev shook his head. "Not then."

His cell phone rings. When he answers it, he walks to the porthole and looks outside. "How long . . . You're in contact . . . Fine. I'll deal with it then."

He ends the call with a pensive pause. "Sorry. We might have a problem."

"No, Max," says Kat forcefully. "No new problems until we've solved this one. When did you know Yulya killed Suzy?"

"Know?" he says loudly. "I knew when Yulya sent me the ring."

"And you didn't arrest her?"

"Grow up, Kat." He stiffens and holds his leg as he limps to the table and sits down. "Stop looking for easy explanations. It's very American. Either you're a friend or an enemy. We're different."

"I'm not interested," Kat says quietly. "Only in Yulya."

Grachev's hand slams down on the table. "There is not just one Yulya. There are Yulyas all over the world. You think RingSet can pull this off all by itself?"

"I'm only interested in one Yulya, your sister." She's been clutching the ring so hard that the sharp edges have cut into her and drawn specks of blood from her palm. "Did Stephen Cranley tell you that John Polinski is still alive?"

"He did, yes," Grachev says in barely a whisper.

"That Tiina's keeping him alive, but when Yulya takes over, he'll be killed?"

Grachev nods weakly.

Kat leans back in the chair. "So what did you plan to do about it, Max? Sit on your butt listening to Beethoven's Ninth?"

Grachev touches his lips with his fingers. His eyes move toward the porthole. Raised voices come from the deck. Grachev's phone rings again.

"How far? . . . Okay," says Grachev. The launch engine slows, making the cabin quieter. Kat gets up, goes to the porthole with Grachev. She hopes to see dawn, perhaps land, instead of blackness with the water indistinguishable from the sky.

Grachev ends the call, drops the phone into his pocket, and wipes the heel of his hand across his eyebrow. "The Americans know where you are."

"Shit," she mutters.

"They have an international warrant out for your arrest. They've sent a launch to intercept us." His hand touches his forehead, then runs around the cold metal rim of the porthole. "I was using whatever credit I have left to get you to Europe. But we're in international waters, and our use of this launch is unauthorized."

A silent streak of lightning cuts across the sky, showing up clouds so thick with rain that it seems they're being set alight.

Kat pushes past him to look out the porthole. A small olive green, flat-bottomed raiding craft comes into view. A U.S. marine sits behind an armored shield at the stern, manning a mounted machine gun.

FIFTY

Thursday, 5:07 a.m., BST

Marine Sergeant Mason is at the door, an M16 slung around his shoulder to keep his hands free, and his breath stale from a cigarette.

"You again," says Kat.

"You have to come with me, ma'am." He steps inside the cabin and to one side, giving her room to pass.

On deck, the smell of marine oil hangs in the summer night air. The moon breaks through the clouds and douses light onto the blackness of the sea, showing Nate Sayer on deck with Grachev, who steps into Sayer's space.

Grachev touches Sayer's chest with two fingers, but Kat can't hear what he says. She gets close enough for Sayer's answer.

"Did you ever ask yourself why Russians are always crying about their souls?" Sayer says. "Getting drunk or heading off to kill people? Or themselves?"

He's wearing a beige suit, white open-neck shirt, no tie, everything newly pressed and laundered as if he's dressed specially to bring Kat in.

"You think it's some kind of genetic conspiracy? No, it's because you don't try. You weep and drink because it's too difficult to think and act. What makes you think you can do anything to help Kat when you've messed up everything I've ever seen you try to do?"

He raises his eyebrows, pushes Grachev's hand away, and says to Mason, "Let's go."

Grachev doesn't move. He looks across to Kat, shaking his head. She has the ring and the jump drive with Suzy's History Book from the Media Axis computer. Grachev didn't search her, didn't even ask about it.

Mason's hand is on Kat's elbow as he guides her to a rope ladder that hangs down from Grachev's launch to the raiding craft.

She doesn't resist, but says to Grachev, "Europe—nice thought."

"Careful here, ma'am," says Mason. He climbs down first and keeps it steady for her at the bottom.

Four of them are in the raiding craft: Kat, Sayer, the marine at the mounted gun, and Mason at the helm.

Mason gives the engine enough power to raise the bow slightly, and as they round the stern of Grachev's boat, they see him leaning on the rail, looking down at the water, his expression leaden but pensive.

Wind hits her straight in the face. Sayer says something Kat can't catch. About 200 yards separate Grachev's launch from Sayer's.

Sayer's is bigger, an armed military vessel with a speedboat lashed to the deck and another raiding craft, she now sees, moored to the hull. As they come alongside, hydraulic steps are lowered from the deck of Sayer's vessel.

Mason gets off first, then Kat, then Sayer, then the marine, who ties down the machine gun. The two raiding crafts are left knocking hulls in the swell.

"You want some coffee?" asks Sayer.

"No," says Kat. "I don't want coffee. I want to know what's happening."

A throb from the engine vibrates the deck, and a gust cuts around the wheelhouse. Sayer walks to the stern, where the American flag is cracking back and forth in the wind and the engine noise is loudest. "The audio and visual activities on this launch are being relayed straight back to Washington," says Sayer. "This is the only place we can speak privately, and after that number you pulled with Nancy, we need to."

"Don't kid either of us," says Kat. "They're not sending you out here because there's trouble in your marriage."

As they were climbing the gangway, Kat began working out what she had to do. Some of the main shipping routes to Europe come from ports on Britain's east coast, the same area where Stephen Cranley still may have some influence.

Kat watched how Mason turned off the engine of the raiding craft. The mechanics aren't complicated. There's no key, only a button for power and a fuel lever. The deck of the launch is low enough in the water to jump into one of them.

The problem is Mason, watching from the gangway.

Dawn is coming up so fast that the sea is turning from black to silver. Once it's broken, escape will be impossible.

Sayer looks skyward; Mason, too, who checks his watch.

"Since that incident with your mom," shouts Sayer above the noise, "you've never trusted me, and I don't blame you. But that has nothing to do with what I have to say to you now. There's a bunch of people who'll tell you your dad's alive. Suzy thought he might be in some Third World labor camp. But he's dead, Kat. Your father is dead. And we've got to . . ."

His voice trails off against the cry of gulls swooping down over the stern.

He jerks his thumb toward the outline of Grachev's launch, which is disappearing into a low cloud bank.

"Grachev's a tortured soul. Can't get his tiny head around the thought that no one knows who the hell his father is. I met Tiina. You can see her in that Moscow photograph. Even back then we could tell she was a handful. She would have slept with a number of men."

"How do you know Dad's dead?" interrupts Kat, her voice nearly a scream to make Sayer hear. "Suzy believed he was alive enough to die for him."

Mason steps into a sheltered area behind a lifeboat to light a cigarette. Kat moves back along the deck to get above the raiding craft. Sayer keeps talking and moves to keep up with her.

"Suzy drove herself half insane. First she thought it was murder, then when she couldn't prove that, she got this crazy idea that John had been kidnapped."

"It's easy enough to fake a death in a plane crash," she challenges Sayer.

Kat tests the strength of the rail. It'll take her weight. She practices the escape in her imagination. Over the rail and down into the raiding craft without breaking an ankle; flip the fuel on. She can see the lever. Red button starts the engine.

"The day he died, your dad was in Lancaster with your grandmother.

It was a last-minute visit. No one knew he was going. No one could have planned such a professional killing so quickly. You tell me how you abduct someone with a reputation like John's. You'd need people to have taken control of the whole damned airport to do it."

"It's a small airport."

"Fine. But what do you do about the air-traffic controllers, fire crew, janitors, pathologist? Pay them all off?"

They did with Mom, thinks Kat.

The swell of the sea rocks the boat. A beam of cabin light catches a metal clasp dipping in and out of the water on the rope holding the raiding craft to the launch. Kat will have to jump, unhook it, and start the engine, all before Mason gets down to stop her.

"So if Suzy was nuts, why did she get murdered?"

"Because she had other information."

Mason, half hidden from view behind the lifeboat, head lowered, back to her, is talking to a member of the crew. Someone is smoking up front. Two people in the wheelhouse stare straight ahead.

"What do you want from me?" she says.

"I want you to let me save your ass. Together we can beat the charges against you. You were working for Cage. Cage is the U.S. government. You know about the file Suzy compiled."

A flickering shift of expression is all Kat needs. She's seen it before, in Sayer's study, the face, as it falters, feeling he's won and becoming lazy. Glancing down, out of the corner of her eye, she estimates the distance between the deck and the raiding craft.

"I don't have anything, Nate," she says.

"You got it that night in the embassy when Cage sent you in. You got it again from Media Axis."

Kat tilts her head toward him, feigning surprise. "Yeah, well, it's all made up, isn't it, Nate? That's what you just told me."

"You have it, Kat. And you're the only one."

"Bill Cage has it, not me," she says.

"Bill's being an asshole," says Sayer.

"What do you mean?" The breeze is up again. They're yelling in short sentences, voices raised.

"Head in the sand. Taking the Fifth. All that shit."

If she can land and keep her balance, she'll be ahead of them. She'll have to lean into the water to get the clasp, start the motor at the same time, and head for the fog.

"For John, for Helen, I'm trying keep you free. That's what this is all about, not letting you make the same mistakes as Suzy."

Kat's nodding. "Okay, Nate. I'm with you. Lot of things I don't know. But whatever it is you're after, I don't have it. And if I don't have it, does that mean you're going to throw me into jail?"

"Then let me know where it is. After the CPS is signed—"

Kat grasps the rail, tenses the muscles in her shoulders, and vaults over the side. She can't hear him anymore. Her eyes are on the raiding craft directly below, trying to match her fall with its shifting in the water.

She lands on the raiding craft's planked decking, falls backward, starts to get up, and slips on the wet planking.

Sayer shouts. A deck light snaps on, and Mason's shadow falls across Kat.

Don't look up, she tells herself. She scrambles back and reaches the cockpit. She glances up as Mason jumps down.

Kat barges into him. The marine falls heavily, hitting his upper thigh on a metal stay halfway down the hull. She hears a scream, thinks that Mason is hurt, but realizes it's her own scream from somewhere deep inside.

He's on his feet again, lurching toward her.

Kat leaps like a long-jumper, propelling herself across to the other raiding craft.

She lands in it, gets her balance, and scrambles to the stern. She pulls the mooring rope out of the water and unhooks it. The starter button fires the engine. Her hand is on the wheel. She has to get the boat moving to put enough sea between her and Mason.

Back in the first craft, Mason sees what Kat's trying to do. He uses the machine gun platform to lever himself toward her.

She eases the throttle slowly, making the gap too wide for him to jump between the two craft. Kat turns the wheel to get her bow away from the launch and head out to sea.

But the wheel is locked. No movement left or right. Two more marines jump down onto Mason's craft. No one's shooting; they don't think she'll get away.

There has to be a catch for the wheel—or a button. Something simple. Mason starts his engine and shouts a command. She glances up. A marine stands at the bow of the craft with a boat hook to bring Kat's raiding craft in.

The roll of low fog is thickening. Kat opens the throttle and leans out as far as she can, as if she's hard tacking on a sailboat. The craft tilts enough to change its path, fiberglass scraping on metal. She knocks Mason's craft to one side, slews in the water, and shoots forward.

Kat drops herself into the cockpit. She tries the wheel again. No give at all. She's heading out to sea at 15 knots and rising. Mason's craft casts off. He's at the wheel. Two marines are up front. They've drawn their weapons.

To her left, on the cockpit panels, there's a first aid locker. Farther up, two green bilge handles. In the corner, gauges for temperature, pressure, oil. In the panel above, a red button. Kat slips her finger over it but hesitates, as it doesn't seem to have anything to do with the wheel. She checks the boxes. On one side electronics, each piece neatly clipped to the edge: cell phone, Global Positioning System, short-distance radio, satellite transmitter, two flashlights, TV monitor. But nothing to free the wheel. On the other side, survival gear: ready-to-eat meals, wet suits, blankets, sleeping bags, parka jackets, helmets.

The craft hits a swell, jolting her. She looks back at the lights from Mason's boat. On her boat, there's Kat and not much else. On Mason's, there are three heavy men, a large-bore machine gun, its platform, and ammunition. She's a feather compared to them, but not fast enough to be free of them.

He's not gaining on her; she's not losing him, either. She doesn't know how much fuel she has, but if she keeps going, she'll just head farther out to sea. All he has to do is keep up with her.

Back inside the cockpit, she sees a piece of almost-transparent wire clipped to the bottom of the wheel. Right hand on the wheel, she reaches with her left to find the clasp and frees it, bracing herself to heave the craft around against the resistance of the waves. But it's power-steered. Feet astride and balanced, she turns back toward the coastline and eases on the power.

She runs parallel to the land, angling toward the fog bank. As she enters the fog, she hears the high-pitched throb of a helicopter.

FIFTY-ONE

———◇———

Thursday, 5:48 a.m., BST

Yellow streaks appear in the lead gray sky, throwing a dawn light across the water. She looks for the helicopter, but it's above the fog to seaward.

She's speeding past the curved, algae green, wooden timbers of a sunken boat's hull protruding from the mud like the arms of the dead.

She can't shake off Mason's boat and needs to find a place to land—the mouth of a river, or a stretch of shoreline near human life. The landscape is empty, with barely a tree, a sparse and desolate coastline of mudflats and marshlands. With the sea flat like a racetrack and the current moving north, she increases the speed.

Kat wedges herself in and switches on the GPS. The coordinates come up, meaning nothing to her until she orders up a map, which she zooms out until she can read clearly that she's off the east coast of Britain.

From the locker, she unclips the electronic gear and drops it into a waterproof bag and puts that into the survival bag with food, water, blanket, flashlight, GPS, and cell phone—all stored on the raiding craft.

She pulls out a jacket, bag, helmet, and goggles. She bundles up the jacket, stuffs it into the helmet, and straps the goggles around. From a distance, it would look like a human head. She secures it just to the left of the wheel, then tapes two gloves over the wheel itself.

Kat edges the craft inland, keeping her speed, until she's running just a few yards off the mudflats. Beyond that lies brackish water and clumps of grassy mud. She secures the survival bag to her back.

Inland, all she can see is water and marshland. She has no idea how deep or soft the mud is and whether she can walk through it.

She eases out the throttle a fraction more, feeling the craft accelerate. Then she jumps.

The cold shock of the water is more brutal than she'd expected, knocking air from her lungs. The bag on her back wrenches against her shoulder. She kicks to keep her head above water and finds her feet pushing into soft mud, knee deep.

Kat pulls herself free, rolls onto her back, hears the roar of Mason's engine, and glimpses lights as his craft speeds past her.

She swims the few yards to where mud, slime, and water meet and lets the water push her up and ground her.

She hears the helicopter again, and the dawn helpfully reveals it, a two-seater, like the ones used for traffic reports, flying fast and straight from the south about half a mile out to sea.

She clutches at clumps of grass and hauls herself up onto solid land. Then she sees another smaller river, more like a stream or canal. She half swims, half wades across. She crawls into a field, freshly harvested, grazing herself on sharply cut stubble.

A few hundred yards away, seagulls are following a tractor. Behind her, on what looks like an island, the helicopter is touching down next to a metallic, oblong building that looks like a warehouse.

Kat needs fog or darkness, but instead she's got a rising sun on a hot day. She gets the GPS from the bag, takes off its waterproof cover, and waits for it to tell her where she is. She came ashore on Sudbourne Beach and swam across the River Alde. She has more than a mile of marshes to cross before she gets to the nearest road. Inland farther is the village of Sudbourne. After that, there's a forest.

Kat slips down the green waterproof cover of the cell phone. It's a standard military-issue Motorola 358A, used by many agencies in the field. She snaps off the back, takes out the SIM card, closes the phone, and turns it on. As it boots itself up, Kat concludes from each message and symbol that, as soon as she uses it, the phone will be tracked by the Pentagon's Defense Intelligence Agency.

The only sign of human movement around her is the tractor.

With each step the land becomes firmer, but the cover less. Kat crawls most of the way, except when she wades through small, crisscrossing tributaries. At the fence of the field where the tractor is working, Kat wriggles forward on her stomach, breathing in the stench of manure. The field is dotted with shelters shaped like old aircraft hangars, tubes cut in half, with the pigs nesting down inside and roaming free inside the field. At each shelter, the tractor stops, the driver climbs down, takes a sack of straw off the trailer, and clears out the shelter. A dog runs alongside.

Kat slithers forward through dewy grass, unhooks the bag, pushes it under the fence, then squeezes under herself. To her left, there's a jumble of metal hanging from the fence like a wind chime. The tractor is too loud and far away for the driver to hear. Kat listens to the sucking-in of her own breath.

From behind, she hears the sound of the helicopter again, taking off across the water.

The tractor driver climbs up into the cab, reverses the trailer between two shelters. The driver is a woman, not much taller than Kat, with dark hair tied back and a long, serious face.

The helicopter begins a wide seaward loop, heading south to where Kat left the raiding craft.

Kat is on her feet, running. The ground is uneven, with puddles of water, soft pig and cow shit, and ruts made by the tractor wheels. She keeps her eyes on the farmer, who's kneeling on all fours, and when she starts to back out of the shelter, Kat drops hard to the ground.

The farmer moves to the back of the trailer, where she brings down a sack, slices open the top, and scoops out feed with a shovel. There's a cell phone sitting in a cradle just to the left of the steering wheel.

Kat keeps moving, but looks back, the sun in her face. When she reaches the huge tractor wheel, the dog, a brown and white foxhound, lopes toward her with a stream of high-pitched barking.

The farmer edges back from the shelter, hand on the low roof, helping herself to her feet. Her eyes are dark and alert, flickering briefly to the gulls with curiosity, then with fury to the approaching helicopter. She shakes the feed scoop like a weapon.

"You snooping bastards!" she shouts.

Then she catches sight of Kat, and her eyes stay on her while the helicopter roars back overhead and makes a loop for a return run.

FIFTY-TWO

Enormous eyes framed by a weather-beaten face, teeth yellow from cigarettes, keep Kat in sight while the farmer checks that all is intact on the tractor. She's wearing loose denim pants with pockets and a red checkered shirt. She wipes her mouth with the back of her hand, then rests both hands inelegantly on her hips.

"Is it you he's looking for?" she says. Her expression is of neither shock nor anger.

"I need your phone," says Kat, pointing up to the dashboard.

The eyes don't leave her. Nothing hostile. Nothing friendly. "That phone'll get us into trouble."

The driver peels back Velcro from a pocket in the right leg of her pants and brings out another cell phone, holding it out to Kat. "This one's registered in my dummy name, Margaret. Dump it when you've finished."

"Thank you," says Kat, hiding her surprise. She takes the phone, staying pressed against the tractor wheel, hidden from the helicopter. It's a regular Nokia, meaning its SIM card should fit the Motorola.

Margaret jerks her head skyward. "With him so skittish up there, you'd best go where he can't see you." She points to the shelter that she's just been clearing out.

"I just need to—" Kat begins.

Margaret raises a knotty finger to her lips. "I don't want to know who you are, what you are, or where you come from."

The dog paws Margaret's ankle. Margaret stoops down, crawls into the shelter, and beckons for Kat to follow.

"It doesn't matter, you knowing the dog's name, though," she says once they're inside, under cover. She picks up the dog; its tongue is all over her face. A sow is lying on her side at one end with a litter on her nipples. The straw is damp and smells of urine.

"Rufus has a gammy leg, so I kept him, when they made me get rid of all the other hunting dogs," she says. Her voice breaks, and she lets the dog jump out of her arms, out of the shelter, and back to the trailer.

She rearranges straw at the entrance. "My husband had twenty-five years with a clean license, a law-abiding citizen, then in the space of six months, his driving license was taken away because they said he kept breaking the speed limit. Nothing changed about the way he drove. They put a camera on every corner, then when they don't like someone, they find something you're doing wrong. They used speeding tickets to destroy him."

She points out toward the sky. "What I'm trying to say is that they'll get you in the end, but don't go without a fight. If he's your enemy, you're my friend. And that's all we need to know about each other. Now, hide up here until he buggers off."

Kat has a clear view on both sides out into the field. She fires up the Nokia and turns on the GPS she took from the launch. The Nokia shows a full signal with £100 of prepaid credit. She dials Bill Cage and listens to white noise and the twitter of a satellite.

It's been a day and half since he told her she was wanted on a federal double homicide rap, and since then, Sayer said Cage himself had been pulled in for questioning.

He answers, knows it's her because no one else uses this number.

"You okay?" Cage's voice is tired, strained.

"I'm fine," says Kat. "You?"

"The FBI searched my house and your apartment," he says quickly. Kat hears a distant siren. Cage is walking, and it's 1:30 a.m. in Washington. "Can you stay clear of Sayer until Sunday?"

"Believe me, I'm trying. What's with Sunday?"

"Once the CPS is signed, they might back off."

"Who's *they*?"

"I wish the fuck I knew."

"My dad—is he alive?"

Silence.

"Yulya Gracheva. She killed Suzy, right?"

Silence. The line's gone dead.

Kat lies flat, her face in the stinking straw, looking out at the shadow of the helicopter. It comes in hot and fast and lands heavily on the grass 150 yards away, near the tractor. Margaret walks toward it, hands on hips, as the door opens and the pilot jumps down. Kat can read the make—a Robinson 22—and the words SUFFOLK CONSTABULARY on the side.

Neither of Kat's phones would be secure. But would the response be this quick? Or has Margaret turned her in? From the body language between the two of them, Kat can't tell which.

FIFTY-THREE

---◇---

Thursday, 6:34 a.m., BST

The sow stirs and scrambles to her feet, scattering her piglets into the straw, shakes herself, and waddles to the entrance.

Kat uses the Motorola to go into an Internet search engine that matches English postal codes to locations on the GPS map, which is coming up with house names like Hill Farm, Stanny Farm, High House, Church Farm.

If Stephen Cranley had been transferred to the zone of East Anglia, he might have a home in the area. It's a long shot, but worth a try.

She types in BRITISH TELEPHONE DIRECTORY and gets to British Telecom, where she tries *Cranley*, initial *S*. She skips the street and city names and puts in just IP, the first two letters of the postal code.

The message appears: SORRY, NO KNOWN SUBSCRIBER.

Brick wall.

Outside, the pilot has both hands on Margaret's shoulders. Margaret knocks them aside angrily and steps back.

Kat uses the Nokia to dial Mercedes Vendetta in Washington.

"Hey, Kat, where you at?" So he's not locked up; it's hard to sound that mellow when you're in police custody.

"Hoping to speak to someone by the name of Leroy Jenkinson." She uses the lilt of Dix Street slang, like when they joke together.

"Anyone tell you that, they're looking at history."

"Your own history?"

"I don't do history."

"Past few days, you been behind bars?"

"What shit you talkin'?"

"I heard it."

"You heard shit."

"You been talkin' 'bout me to anyone?"

He sounds less mellow now. "Why I been talkin' if no one's been askin'?"

"I need straight talk, M," she says, her own tone hardening.

"I love the way you say my name."

"You heard about me being on a homicide rap?"

"I have not. But I do know you are not a natural killer."

"You heard about any shooting around any embassy?"

"Not that either."

"The cops been asking you about me?"

"They haven't. Should they?"

"You remember me telling you about my sister, Suzy?"

"You never stopped talkin' about Suzy. Wish I had a brother love me like you love Suzy."

"You heard anything about her?"

"We walk in different worlds. You know that. Why all the questions? You in trouble?"

"I'm fine."

"You wanna come by?"

"I'm outta town. I needed to know about those things, that's all."

Out in the field, the pilot and Margaret are still shouting at each other. A white car's winding down the road toward them.

"You sound like one worn-out babe," says Vendetta. "I tell you two things. My birth name *was* Leroy Jenkinson. But no cops have been round askin' 'bout me or you."

Nate Sayer lied to her. Or someone lied to him. Or Mercedes is lying to her. Or the FBI are onto Cage, but not Mercedes?

The car rounds a corner into the shade, a blue light rotating on its roof. Two uniformed men get out, dark pants, white, short-sleeved shirts. One walks over to the pilot and shakes his hand. The other's talking into a radio and pointing over toward Kat. As Mercedes has been talking, another name has come to her, the man who drove Liz to the parking lot, who spoke to her for five seconds with a pipe, a dog, an SUV, and an aristocratic English accent.

Simon Tappler.

"Gotta go, M," she whispers. "Love you."

She punches *Tappler*, initial *S* into the Telecom search engine.

Kat stays flat on her stomach, her face brushing the straw, nostrils fighting the stench, waiting for the search.

The cop from the white car finishes on the radio. Margaret gets back onto the tractor, points over in Kat's direction, lights a cigarette, and draws on it as if it's the nozzle of an oxygen tank. The pilot walks to the helicopter. The cops go to their car.

Kat's eyes are on the search screen. TAPPLER, S. W. CHERRY TREE FARM, BRAD-FIELD ST MARK, SUFFOLK, IP30 0EH. The map scrolls through until it settles on a speck about 50 miles inland from where she is now.

Gradually, the engine rumble of the tractor gets closer. Ice churns in Kat's stomach, and her defenses tighten.

It pulls up across the entrance to the shelter. Margaret jumps down with a pitchfork and a bucket of pig feed. She forks through the straw near Kat. "Keep your head down, and get up into the trailer," she says. "Lie flat. I'm going to cover you with pig shit and get you out of here."

FIFTY-FOUR

$\longrightarrow$

Thursday, 7:16 a.m., BST

They know you jumped into the water, but they don't know where," says Margaret, taking a tight left turn. "The pilot called the police when he saw me working."

They're in her battered green sedan, with torn seats and broken taillight. Rufus stands on a blanket thrown over the backseat, his nose catching the wind out of the window. Margaret's given Kat a wide sunhat, tilted to cover her face from the view of oncoming drivers.

Kat's told her where she needs to go.

They drive through a copse of trees, heavy with late-summer leaves, past a field of horses, and come out again into vast stretches of harvested fields and hog shelters.

"The Snape Maltings concert hall." Margaret glances hard at Kat. "They say a young woman was killed there on . . ." She lifts her hand off the wheel to her mouth. "Wait a minute. She was an American, and you're—"

"I'm from the States, yes," says Kat.

Margaret's eyes flit back to the road, her expression flat. They pass between a church on the left and a freshly planted forest of saplings. She slows for an intersection.

"You anything to do with it?"

"She was my sister."

Margaret turns right into a wider, better-surfaced road with markings in the middle. "I'm sorry."

Kat expects another question, but Margaret adds, "We mind our own business in this part of the world."

They travel in silence with a long stretch of forest on their left, bringing in smells of pine. Margaret slows where the road forks, checks for traffic, begins to pull out, then brakes so sharply that Rufus yelps and falls against the back of Kat's head.

Around the curve to their right is a police cordon.

Margaret turns the wheel left, away from it, and goes quickly until they're out of sight. Kat pushes Rufus out of the way and puts the GPS to the window.

"Fifty yards up, take the right fork in the road," Kat says.

The signpost at the fork reads BRADFIELD ST MARK—2.

"A couple of hundred yards through the village, turn right."

"Where do you want to go, exactly?" Margaret asks it like she already knows.

"Cherry Tree Farm," says Kat.

The foot eases on the accelerator. Margaret stares straight ahead, shaking her head. "Are you with Tappler's lot?"

"I need to find him."

Margaret's face becomes rigid. "Keep the hat. Keep the mobile phone," she says. "There's a farm track round the back of the Tappler house. You'll find a gap in the hedge. Go through that, keep to the right side of the tennis court. You'll come to a stone gardening shed which used to be a private chapel. You'll know it from the cross above the door. From there you get a good view into the house, kitchen to the left, dining room center, then living room. If the police cordon is because of you, and if you're associated with Tappler, then they might be at his house as well."

Kat gets out of the car. Margaret drives on.

Three vehicles are in the driveway: a dark blue Jaguar sedan, a red Mini Cooper, and a Toyota Highlander. The garden shed is derelict, with moss and weeds growing up inside it and a glassless window that gives her a view into Tappler's kitchen. The kitchen window is diagonally crisscrossed with small panes, topped by a sagging timber with maroon paint peeling off it. The sun's rising on the other side, and the kitchen's lit by a single overhead bulb. The house is older than anything Kat's seen in the States.

She sees Tappler first, right hand on the window frame, left cupped around the bowl of his pipe, sharp eyes scanning the garden.

Behind him, she recognizes Stephen Cranley, sitting at a table in the middle of the kitchen, ending a call on a cell phone. He gets up and rests a hand on Tappler's shoulder.

Cranley's expression is that of a man who has absorbed much in a short space of time but remains in control.

Her eyes scan what she can see of the rest of the room. Nothing lavish there. Wooden chairs, not even matching. The oven's to the left. The sink faces out the other side into the morning sun, which isn't over the house yet, so Kat's part of the garden remains in shadow.

A beam of sunlight hits her in the eyes. It comes from the far side of the house, where it's reflected off a driveway mirror put there to check oncoming traffic.

Cranley steps back from the window. He has a glove in his right hand, palm open, balancing a pistol, checking the rounds in its magazine.

It's likely cameras have picked her up coming in, and Cranley knows she's nearby.

Hands raised, Kat steps out of her cover. Tappler opens the door with Cranley watching their perimeter, gun at the ready.

FIFTY-FIVE

---◇---

Cranley and Tappler wait for Kat to wash up. Tappler's taken down a picture so that a computer can project images onto a plain white wall. The room is dark, with curtains drawn across the windows looking into the garden. There is an iron stove in the fireplace, with logs stacked on either side, and a bank of video monitors showing approaches to the house.

Before she filled the bathtub, Kat told Cranley how she found them, gave them the jump drive, told them to fix up a laptop to see if the data from Media Axis had survived. Tappler left out a set of his wife's clothes, pants and a green shirt, and explained that she and the children had gone to France until things quieted down. Kat's shoes are drying in the kitchen.

She walks downstairs, drying her hair with a towel. Cranley wraps his hand around the pot on the coffee table. "Freshly made, very drinkable, if you want some," he says to Kat, pointing to a chair.

She elects to stand. He shrugs, pours two coffees, takes one himself. He picks up the other cup from the edge of the stove and holds it out for her.

Kat nods toward the computer. "Anything?"

"Patchy," says Tappler. "Not everything. But something."

Kat sits down at Tappler's computer. "I should be able to get a clearer copy." She goes online, keys in her passwords, and opens the account to which she sent Suzy's History Book. She takes a sip of coffee, lets it seep into her, keeping her alert, despite every fiber crying out for rest. She watches the software work. The screen freezes, moves, freezes, moves again.

Cranley stands by the French windows, fingering the edge of the curtain, watchful as to what's going on outside, double-checking what he sees with the monitors inside.

The computer hourglass is frozen. Behind it, the screen appears to sweep itself like dunes being rearranged in a sandstorm.

Tappler cups his pipe in his right hand, pushing tobacco down with his thumb. His left hand hangs, swinging back and forward, brushing the back of his dog by the side of his chair.

"Shit," whispers Kat.

A familiar symbol appears in front of Kat. She recognizes the Chinese characters first, 参考, closes her eyes, and opens them again to see the whole message.

参考：hacktrap,1471 考：
CAPTURED BY
National Intrusion Computer Network Protection Center, Shanghai

Tappler glances up, his eyes thoughtful. Cranley drops the curtain, walks across, and looks over her shoulder. "Where does it leave us?"

"They are so, so good," mutters Kat. She unplugs the computer from the wall.

"Where's the router?" she asks Tappler, who gets up and walks to a desk in the corner, where there's a white, flat, oblong box with a small antenna.

"Disconnect it," she says. "Then destroy it."

Tappler pulls the router's connection from the electrical socket, puts it on the floor, and stamps on it.

"Does your oven work?"

Tappler nods.

"Put the router on a cookie sheet, stick it in the oven, and cook it."

Tappler nods again.

"Where's the jump drive?"

"Near the computer, behind the mouse pad," says Tappler.

Her eyes fall on it. Tappler goes through to the kitchen while Kat runs her hand around the edge of the computer, finds the USB port, connects the jump drive, and looks at Cranley.

"It leaves us with limited time. If they got that message into my system, they'll know where I logged on from." She shrugs. "Is this the area where you said you have some control?"

"I'm checking," answers Cranley, dialing a number on his cell phone, "whether I still do."

FIFTY-SIX

⟶◇⟶

Thursday, 9:23 a.m., BST

The computer screen jiggers, registering the jump drive. Cranley's talking on the cell and looking at the garden. Tappler returns from the kitchen and stands behind her.

"We found two sections clear from damage," he says. "Go to the search function and type in 'ACR was founded.'"

Kat presses the keys. The projector light comes on. She reads it from the screen. It's a corporate Web page, with pictures of laboratories and oil rigs.

ACR was founded in December 2002, and after rapid expansion, now directly employs more than 300,000 people in over 120 countries worldwide, with hub offices in Washington, Moscow and Beijing . . .

Tappler gives her time to read it, then says, "Stay in that section and put into the search 'premier provider.'"

In order to continue its role as a premier provider with proven capabilities, ACR has subcontracted research and development projects for gas and oil exploration in Central Asia to its subsidiary RingSet. These reserves are considered to be a useful contribution to the di-

versification of energy supplies, along with other areas of exploration, such as in Africa and Latin America.

"Now," says Tappler, "try 'Strongcross Sports and Community Center.'"
The highlighting shows the words. Kat goes back to the beginning of the
sentence.

In the last financial year, ACR donated US$29 million to Strongcross
Sports and Community Center in Iowa. RingSet gave the same charity US$19 million. RingSet profits for the previous year were US$7.8
billion after tax. US$2.6 billion went to ACR, whose overall profits
were US$51 billion. Seventy-nine percent of ACR's revenue came
from government projects with the Chinese, Russian and American
military.

"Who wrote this?" she asks.
"Suzy, probably," says Cranley, who's off the phone and joining them.
Kat reads on.

The Strongcross Center then donated US$2.3 million to Jim Abbott's
presidential election campaign. Four hundred thirty-six subscrib-
ers to the charity gave US$99,000 each, the maximum for individual
donations. Other donations from individuals, the charity and its off-
shoots, such as the Strongcross Swimming Team, went to state and
county organizations connected with the party and the campaign.

Kat's hand hovers over the keyboard.
"You get the idea?" Cranley's eyes flit up to the monitors, which show a
bicyclist crossing the entrance of the driveway. On another, a line of ducks
walk across the back lawn.
"I get it," says Kat.
"Now enter—" begins Tappler.
"Hold on," says Kat, pouring herself more coffee.
"The company specializes in leasing trade concessions areas. They in-
clude Voz Island, Felixstowe Port, and the Byford airbase."
She searches for RingSet and Voz Island.

She stabs her finger on the screen. "How far away is this airfield?"

"Fifty, sixty miles," says Tappler.

She puts in a search for Yulya Gracheva.

The screen swirls with merging colors, the software finds the name, but water has damaged too much data for it to produce an image.

Then Yulya appears in a video, but it's grainy, as if taken from a cell phone. She enters a door, stomping snow off her boots. She takes off a fur hat, down jacket, and gloves and rubs her hands together to warm herself.

The picture widens and becomes more clear. Yulya is in a large room, low ceiling, dim light, and half a dozen groups of people, standing against a wall, where the windows are frosted over, but letting in pale blue winter light. They are badly dressed, eyes flittering and mostly cast down to the floor.

She moves quickly and decisively as if she's in a hurry to go somewhere else. She summons one person from each group: an elderly woman; a young man; another but slightly older; a girl, about ten years old; a young woman—all dressed against the winter, faces reddened by cold.

They are ordered into another room. Each group must be a family. Hands reach out to stop the separations. Faces crumple, and the cries come over tinny and distorted on the recording.

Yulya follows them in. So does the camera. Yulya closes the door and shoots each of them dead, three rounds each, two shots to the head and one to the chest.

For a few seconds, the film goes to black.

"Who the hell took that?" mutters Tappler.

"A whistle-blower?" says Cranley.

Kat says nothing.

The screen lights up. The surviving family members are dressed in suits and overcoats. They're standing on the stage of a hall, holding up certificates. The picture suddenly changes. It's clear, no longer cell phone quality, showing a headline story in Russian onto which a translation is superimposed.

RingSet gives share options to Aralsk farmers.

Yulya and Tiina Gracheva are on the stage, applauding.

Kat remembers her dad and Suzy arguing once over the Iraq war, and her dad saying that Saddam controlled societies by killing and torturing half the people and rewarding the others.

The next section is a series of photographs of Tiina and Yulya with various world leaders. They are in the White House Oval Office with President Abbott, and again with his predecessor; with British Prime Minister Michael Rand; signing a memorandum of understanding on oil and gas exploration in the Kremlin; at a banquet with the Chinese president in the Great Hall of the People in Beijing; and again in China, signing a contract in Shanghai.

Every world leader of any worth apparently needs to know Tiina and Yulya Gracheva—and do business with them.

No wonder Suzy called her dossier The History Book.

FIFTY-SEVEN

Thursday, 9:37 a.m., BST

There's a map, hand-drawn and scanned in. Then it cuts to show a metal door with grille bars onto which is stenciled F-10689. Behind, through blackness, a beam of light shows up bits of a whitewashed back wall. The moving lens picks up a shackle around a wrist and then stops.

John Polinski's face is worn down by imprisonment. His eyes are sad, sharp, thoughtful, and he forces a smile. She sees traces of the campaigning attorney, the father being strong for his children, but grief seeps out until Kat can feel it roaring through her like a gale.

Her father speaks.

"I should be dead, but someone is keeping me alive. I am being held in a camp near an old Soviet military base in Kazakhstan. You've shown your bravery, but you have to stop. Even if I get out of here, they'll follow me and bring me back. Or decide to kill me. Much worse, Suzy, they will get to you."

His eyes are welling up, and his hand comes up as if the camera is a prison window, the manacle clinking loudly against the lens.

"You have a full life ahead of you, and you need to lead it. Don't die trying to change something that can't be changed."

Despite his defeated tone, John Polinski's powerful presence remains so tangible that Kat feels her father is close enough to touch; that if it's real and she can bring him back home, then she won't have to keep running.

The manacled wrist comes into view again, and a hand pushes a wisp of hair behind an ear. Fingers brush the bearded growth on his chin. The picture flickers and fades.

Kat swallows, keeps looking at the screen, because she isn't able to face Cranley or Tappler.

"Who saw him?" says Kat softly.

"Mike," says Cranley. "It took months to plan. Suzy wanted to go. He wouldn't let her."

"How?"

"He got a job at the port, then at the airbase, then as a cleaner on the plane. The planes ferry VIPs, and they don't keep that sort of staff at the other end."

Kat jabs her finger at the key to start the recording again. Nothing happens. She tries again. A black-and-white wave swishes onto the screen. She hears her father's voice breaking up. "I sho . . . be dead . . . old Sov . . . milit . . . stan . . ."

There's no picture now. Water has gotten into it.

Kat feels stripped down to the bone. She cups her face in her hands, and somewhere from deep inside herself, she lets out a loud, gut-wrenching cry.

FIFTY-EIGHT

◇

Thursday, 9:16 p.m., BST

Rain clears the skies, and the moon throws itself over the flat landscape like a spotlight. After twisting through villages, the road stretches straight ahead, interrupted by a small rotary, where roads lead off on both sides. To the right is a newly built housing complex. To the left is a high fence, and farther along, partly blocked by a cluster of trees, a watchtower marked by a small, single green light.

Kat gives herself only seconds to take it all in. She eases the powerful motorcycle into a track off the road, puts it on its kickstand, and leaves the engine running.

She slept the rest of the morning, then told Cranley what she planned. He didn't object and told her the flight schedules between Byford and Voz Island.

She asked him to use up some final favors to get Liz Luxton freed from wherever she was. She also formatted a cell phone SIM card, copied data over from the ruined jump drive, wrapped it in plastic wrap and poly-ethylene, and taped it to her back. Sometime, she might try to repair the damage.

She let Suzy's ring dry out, wrapped it the same way, and taped it inside the pocket of her pants.

With the jump drive ruined, intrusion into her Internet files, and Cage and possibly Mercedes compromised, the only place she's fairly sure Suzy's History Book is safe is on the hard drive in Liz's edit suite at Media Axis.

As the sun dipped, she got Tappler to run her down country lanes until she spotted a black-and-silver Yamaha 649cc V Star Classic motorcycle in a pub parking lot, with a black helmet locked to it.

She hot-wired it, and it took her about an hour to get to where she is now, a hundred yards back from the entrance of RingSet's airbase.

Allowing her eyes to adjust to the night, Kat crawls closer to get a better look. The fence has three layers. The first two are electrified, the outer wire with a weak current. The middle fence would be far more powerful, and the inner fence is a mix of barbed and razor wire. Two more watchtowers are visible; one to her left and one way across the runway, on the curve of the fence.

Part of the runway is lit up with activity. She sees the movement of people and hears their shouting above the drone of either a generator or an aircraft engine.

She slaps at a mosquito circling her cheek, picks out seed heads that have stuck to her sleeve, watches, plans, then gets back onto the bike and rides a couple of miles farther until she comes to a sign warning of road construction and sharp turns for half a mile. The road is more isolated. After curving away from her, it uncoils itself to become straight until being swallowed into the blackness of a forest.

While she's been there, only RingSet trucks have used the road, white with the blue logo, a single driver in each, and roller doors down the back.

Kat watches for two hours. When a truck goes in, a light is shined on the license plate, and the driver's palm is read through the driver's-side window. One goes in at seven minutes past ten; out at twenty-five minutes to eleven. Next hour; in at four minutes past eleven; out at twenty-seven minutes to midnight.

By then, after the country pubs have emptied, people have gone to their beds, and clouds have thankfully darkened the moon, the road lies quiet and empty. If they run all night, the next truck in is due in half an hour.

With no lights, Kat rides to the start of the roadwork, keeping the engine slow and barely audible. With wire from the bike's storage box, she straps two red and white cones to the backseat of the bike, together with a flashing orange warning light, and rides toward the junction.

According to her GPS, the left-hand fork heads to the town of Wood-bridge and then onto Felixstowe. The right-hand fork is a small side road going north. The next village is Campsea Ash. Kat puts a cone in the middle of the intersection with a warning light flashing and parks the bike along the side road, pushing it up the bank to give it elevation. She has a flashlight in her hand.

When she sees a truck's lights from half a mile ahead, she turns on the Yamaha's headlight. The truck driver flashes his lights against the glare. Kat steps into the road, swinging her flashlight back and forth. The truck slows. The sweep of Kat's beam catches on the cones. The driver's arm is up, shielding his eyes. Kat's in front of the truck, with her flashlight in his face.

She mustn't speak; a female voice would alert him. He mustn't see her; her clothes match no uniform from RingSet. She needs him to open the door, and then she hopes she'll be too quick for him, except she's not seeing some overweight man just waiting to retire at the wheel but a slender, olive-skinned figure, slightly unshaven, eyes irritated and alert, with the physique of an athlete, who can move fast, left hand on the wheel, and right hand somewhere else, reaching.

She lowers her flashlight beam to the ground, waving him around the cone. The driver's right hand comes up to the wheel, foot eases back on the accelerator, a finger to the forehead in recognition that all is normal, the expression of a working man relieved that his shift will end without incident.

When he's past, taillights fading into the night, Kat runs to the bike, starts the engine, kills the headlight, and catches up with the truck, careful not to let her engine rev too loudly. She coasts closer, staying in his side-mirror blind spot.

She gets the feel of his driving. He's safe, uses plenty of brake, and is slow to accelerate out of a turn. As the road straightens, she turns the lights on full beam, roars past, keeps going about half a mile, takes the next corner, turns the bike around, headlight on full beam, and heads back toward him, needle creeping up, eyes checking every second, 53, 67, 74, 80, 85 . . .

Kat's banking on a single, very human thing. The driver's on a salary. For Kat, it's personal.

The truck's coming around a corner, lighting up the crooked edge of a house, a fence, an orchard, a child's swing hanging from a tree, sweeping around the turn until the headlights settle back on the straight road, edges of light showing the overgrown bank, glare to glare with Kat.

He's doing 30. Kat's going three times faster. His hand's steady on the wheel. Kat's not shifting, either, coming toward him for a head-on unless one of them moves over.

Smoothly, he slows and edges over to the left. Kat goes to her left. She slows the engine and brakes, throwing red light out behind her.

He accelerates.

In the cab, he's shaking his head at the madness around him at this time of night. And just then, as his concentration is diverted, she brings the bike back into his path. He brakes on instinct, twists the wheel, and the front of the truck hits the bank, tilting it, then bouncing it back heavily on the road.

Kat jumps the bike, landing roughly on the grass bank, taking the flashlight and tie wire. The truck stops, hazard lights on, cab door open, and the driver leaps out. The Yamaha lies on its side, wheel spinning, engine running. Kat is close, lying down on the bank, legs splayed unnaturally.

The driver's flashlight washes over her. He curses in a foreign language. Kat's breathing is barely detectable.

She listens to his footsteps on the tarmac, then crunching into the grass. Kat's ready to make the split-second judgment, to know the moment when pretense will end and she can take him.

She shifts just enough for him to see movement, drawing him quickly in. The beam goes up and down her body. The driver drops to his knees, flashlight on the grass, head inches from hers. She can smell him.

Kat uncoils and hits the nerves above the sinus, blacking him out for long enough to knee his groin, then press her own flashlight into his ribs as if it's a weapon.

"Not one sound," she whispers. "Facedown."

He rolls onto his front. She pulls his hands behind him and binds them.

"Move and I'll kill you," she says.

In the cab, searching, eyes half on him, she finds tape in the door side pocket. In a toolbox on the floor of the passenger seat, she sees screwdrivers, pliers, a battery-powered drill, a rotary saw, and a Beretta 38, better than nothing, with a full magazine of 20 rounds. She unclips it, chambers a round, walks back, kneels astride him, and fires once into the ground an inch from his right ear. She unties the wire.

"Stand up," she orders. "Keep your back to me."

He gets to his feet, obedient but showing no fear. He's wearing a light blue jacket with RINGSET on the back and light blue pants with a dark stripe down the side. The back of his head, the line down to his neck, the shape of his features are sharp as if carved from rock. With his tanned, taut skin, he's a man who has worked hard in harsh weather.

His calmness chills Kat.

She senses what he's going to do and what she will do to stop him. She can only guess what'll make him do it. Maybe it's a condition of the job. Maybe he can't afford the shame. Maybe he comes from someplace he can't go back to.

Why does anyone risk his life?

A sky heavy with stars hangs above them. Droplets of sweat gather at the edges of Kat's lips. "Take off your jacket. Drop it to the ground," she says.

Kat lets the Beretta's butt settle in her hand. With a 38 it might take two, even three rounds to drop him.

A tilt of the head, hand on each side of the jacket, midway down, drawing it apart, smooth movements, doing all she ordered, but her insides are turning to ice.

As he drops the right side of the jacket, his hand hesitates. He shifts weight again. His fingers slide toward an inside pocket. Something's in there, but Kat can't be sure, although if it's a weapon, he'll be faster than her.

"Stop," shouts Kat.

He doesn't. She can't see what he's doing. Her finger's tight across the trigger, yet she can't pull it.

I do know you are not a natural killer. Mercedes' voice is in her head.

By the time she sees it's a gun, it's too late to do anything except throw herself to the ground. *Move, for God's sake! Move, damn it, don't you know how difficult it is to hit a moving human being!* she screams silently to herself.

The gunshot explodes through the quiet. In a blur, she knows she's not hit. His feet are rock-steady in firing position, not a muscle moving, and as Kat rolls onto her back, she catches his eyes, not focused on her, but at her as a target.

Kat fires four times, both hands clasped around the pistol butt to steady the recoil. He's down, face blown away like Suzy's, but the RingSet uniform unscathed except for green smudges of grass on the knees where he fell, which, if Kat cares to think hard about it, is exactly how she planned it when she pulled the trigger.

FIFTY-NINE

◇

Friday, 1:06 a.m., BST

His name was Marcel Lancaric. His relaxed face stares out at her from the ID card taped to the dashboard. Another picture's of a woman, blond bobbed hair, red overcoat, and silver gray stole, bundled-up baby in her arms, and a boy, four or five years old, in a Batman outfit, holding her hand and hugging a football.

Head in her hands, Kat focuses on the embossed Volvo symbol in the middle of the steering wheel, breathing in the metal and plastic smells of a new vehicle, swallowing to stop nausea from overwhelming her, and ordering herself to start driving.

The engine's running. The lights are on. FM radio plays easy-listening jazz. Fresh cigarette smoke hangs in the air, the butt stubbed out in an ashtray near where the Beretta was. Kat has two guns now, the Beretta 38 with 16 rounds left and his weapon, a smaller Beretta 21 with 5.

Kat's wearing the driver's blue RingSet baseball cap and overalls, has transferred all her stuff into the pockets, and has checked the SIM card taped to her back. When she pulls out, she doesn't look back. He's lying there, the same way Suzy was left lying in the marshes, except it's the back of his head that is unmarked and the front that is demolished.

She's been through his pockets for his ID and swipe cards to get into the base. She's searched the cab, the front bench seat, the sleeping bunk at the back. She's done other things, too, which she'll never be able to let rest. How, now, can she ever challenge anyone who's been involved in a killing, judge what they did with the corpse? How does she know that what she's done is right? A Mercedes-like answer floats into her consciousness: Killing happens when two people believe in what they do. It's as simple as that.

If Lancaric's daughter turns up one day to blow Kat's head away, Kat would understand, but still might end up killing her.

She turns the radio up loud, lets the truck pick up speed, follows the curve of the road, and soon she's on the straight road, running parallel to the fence of the base, where she sees a plane taxiing and the silhouette of a man signaling it to its stand. A drizzle starts. Wipers smear across the windshield.

She turns into the gate, lights flashing, late, needing to get in. She slows under a yellowish glow from the camp lamps, glad for the inclement weather. A single barrier is down across the road, with a guardhouse set back, two figures inside, breaking off from watching a soccer match. A spotlight shines onto the license plate. A scanner descends, jerks, and stops outside her side window.

She curls her fingers around a cloth soaked with Lancaric's now-cold blood. She peels it back, checking that the hand itself is unmarked. She swallows to stop herself from retching, keeps her eyes on what she's doing, and feels the stickiness of blood, not yet clotted, running into her sleeve.

She lifts the right hand, which was shockingly easy to sever with the man's own rotary saw, and holds it against the window glass, pushing it flat, until she hears a beep and sees the barrier shake and then rise.

She brings the hand down slowly, shaking, covers it with the cloth, and rests it on her lap as she drives slowly into the base.

Floodlights are on the plane she saw taxiing. She heads away from it, straight up toward low-rise huts, dimly lit, no activity, where she saw the trucks go before. A whistle blasts across the tarmac. Kat looks around, keeps going.

The whistle again. Kat glances to her right. The guard's so far away and looks so small against the front wheel of the plane, lights skittering around him, orange ones rotating on the top of airfield vehicles, straight beams from the aircraft wings, engineers' flashlights flickering around the under-belly, the fuselage lit up inside and on the ladder, where people are climbing up to get in.

He's waving at her, beckoning her over, and in her rearview mirror, she's being flashed by a jeep's headlights. Kat brings the truck around, dropping Lancaric's hand to the floor and pushing it under the seat with her free foot. She pulls the baseball cap further over her face, keeps the 38 on her lap, and stuffs the smaller Beretta into a side pocket.

The man at the plane's front wheel waves her in with a paddle, telling her to stop near the step, but she does it wrong. He yells at her, slapping his hand on the roller door at the back of the truck. "Back up. Back up. We need it close."

It's a Boeing 767, steps going up front and back, fuel truck parked under a wing, hydraulic platform with roped crate whining up toward the cargo hatch. Another slap on the back of the truck tells Kat she's close enough.

They have the key to the back. The roller door comes up, and there's movement behind her, making the truck shake. She's so far inside the airfield that she can't make out the perimeter fence, only the awkward shapes of trees outside in fields lit by flits of moonlight and darkened by rain clouds.

The reek of Lancaric's blood fills the cab. She shakes her head to clear the thought and looks in the side mirror. A line of men unloads boxes from the back of the truck. Rain splatters on the mirror and blurs the shapes. She lowers the window, wiping it clear, and she gulps fresh, damp air deep into her lungs like an injection of ice.

A hand slaps the side of the truck. The back door is rolled down.

"Okay, take her away."

The loaders are prisoners who hold their arms out in front of them while two men walk down the line, cuffing them.

Kat drives off. She's inside the perimeter fence, and she's not going to leave. No one seems to be checking, but that might change when she tries to get on the plane. And what about the truck? They've logged it in. When will they expect to log it out? Or does it have a parking bay on the base?

She drives into the moonlight shadow spread by an aircraft hangar and reverses into an unmarked bay, between two vans.

A splash of lightning brightens the sky. No one's watching her; she sees no cameras. She takes a nail from the truck's toolbox, crouches between the hangar and the truck, and lets air out of a rear tire.

Fifty yards along the wall, she sees a Dumpster. She finds the truck's jack beneath the chassis at the back, plans to jack it up, but changes her mind. The jack's covered in blue cloth. She unfurls it, puts the jack back, takes Lancaric's severed hand, and wraps it in the cloth. On a scrap of paper from the glove compartment, she writes, "Flat. Fixed in thirty minutes," and props it in the windshield with Lancaric's photo ID.

Kat walks along the hangar wall, drops Lancaric's hand into the Dumpster, then heads toward the aircraft.

Just about everyone working on the base seems to be armed. RingSet looks like it's run on the careless arrogance of gun culture. With its weapons, RingSet is unassailable, and anyone this deep inside the airfield is secure.

The 38 rests comfortably in her hand. Kat walks out swinging it like it's a fashion accessory. She picks not the back but the front steps, and takes them two at a time.

Kat counts only seven other passengers in the Club Class cabin. Three have RingSet overalls on like her. One is a woman. Two men are in jeans and loafers. Two other men are in jackets, pants, and open-neck shirts.

Kat takes a blanket from the overhead compartment, drops into a window seat, and pretends to sleep, careful to keep her gun and blood-flecked hands under the blanket.

"Do we have to go through customs?" mutters one of the men in jackets. He's sitting directly in front of Kat, hair curled down to the top of his collar, a black leather briefcase in his right hand, his left fidgeting in his pants pocket.

"Not here," says an older man next to him, an American with a southern accent. "Anyone who gets this far, they know who you are, and places like this you don't want to go around asking anyone's business."

A curtain hangs down, but not enough to cover the view toward the back, where the center seats have been fitted with shackle rings for each prisoner. They are led in, handcuffs unlocked, then locked again to the seats. None sit together. Each is in a middle seat of three, with powerful overhead bulbs shining in their faces.

The engines start up.

"Ammunition must be removed from weapons for the duration of the flight," instructs a woman attendant, moving down the aisle. Kat takes the magazine out of the 38, closes her eyes, sees Lancaric's and Suzy's faces melded into one, and hears the thud and hiss of the fuselage door closing.

SIXTY

$\Diamond$

Friday, 6:59 a.m., BST/1:59 p.m., Voz Island

She's been in the air for six hours, and Kat wakes to the trembling of turbulence, the sound of the seat belt alert, and the casual southern drawl of the pilot.

"Don't know how many of you folks have been to this part of the world before, but it's susceptible to a strange kind of dust storm. Think of a tornado that runs horizontal instead of vertical. And not just one; they come like tidal waves, one after another, gathering dust like rolling up a big carpet. The locals call it *boo-run*, which means 'strong wind,' but on the flight deck, we like to think of it as bad weather. We plan to get you on the ground before it hits, but once there, you might wish you were up in the skies again with us."

As they come in to land, white dust blows across a colorless landscape, which stretches beyond the runway, low huts, and fences toward a treeless horizon. Layers of heat rise up from the ground, creating a low haze everywhere.

The plane taxis to a stop, and the attendant opens the door. A blast of hot air rushes in.

A gust buffets the aircraft, and a guard in blue RingSet overalls, his face covered with a red scarf, stumbles into the cabin and rests his M16 automatic rifle against the bathroom door.

Through the window, Kat's been able to make out an airfield built in exactly the same style as the one at Byford, as if RingSet makes its camps the way McDonald's makes its restaurants. Perimeter fences with watchtowers run at right angles to each other. Just ahead is a control tower, and near the plane, a bulldozer equipped with a V-shaped plow pushes aside the white-brown dust that's blown around since the plane landed.

Between the plane and the fence are clusters of small, single-story buildings with sloping, eaved roofs, all coated in dust. People dotting the endless landscape have their heads lowered against the weather. There are no paths or roads that Kat can see, except for one being cleared by another bulldozer, at the end of which is a long, flat-roofed, whitewashed building, windows grimed up and dark doors facing out like motel rooms.

The pilot, in a white, short-sleeved uniform shirt, comes out from the cockpit, glancing disdainfully at the guard's weapon.

"We got you down safely," he says to no one in particular. "Now we've got to get back up again."

He gives the guard a sheet of paper and returns to the cockpit. The guard picks up his gun, rests it over his forearm. He walks farther back into the cabin, ignoring Kat and the passengers in her section, and begins checking the prisoners, holding a counter in his hand.

As if that is a signal to move, the passenger in front of Kat stands up, unclips the overhead compartment, and brings down a briefcase.

Shielding her lap from view, she clips the magazine back into the 38 and slides her hand into her pants pocket to put a round into the chamber of the Beretta 21 and secure the safety. Midflight, she also managed to wash her hands of Lancaric's blood. She eases herself into the aisle, eyes lowered; this is an atmosphere where personal space is not violated.

The passenger with the soft southern accent brings a scarf out of his briefcase and wraps it around his face, covering his mouth and nose. He heads to the top of the steps.

Kat is behind him. The sun is high in a cloudless, blue sky. She touches her face, thinking she's got an insect bite. It takes a moment to realize that her exposed skin is being stung by blowing dust particles.

"Better watch out," he warns her. "This used to be the Aral Sea. But the Soviets drained the water to irrigate cotton fields. It's now a wasteland of salt, sand, and crushed seashells that cut your face in the wind."

Kat follows him down the stairs toward four waiting jeeps, just like the ones in the picture: a driver, an armed guard, and the backseat for the passengers, with the RingSet logo of a bird of prey on the door.

Kat has memorized the map, and she has the cell number: F-10689.

A siren starts up. Two trucks with hydraulic ramps pull up underneath each of the plane's engines. The pilot's at the aircraft door, shouting, pointing out toward the weather. "Close the goddamn door!" he shouts. "Now!"

A dozen prisoners are walking down the steps. The aircraft doors shut behind them.

Loud, simultaneous commands come from the jeeps, guards slapping the doors to make the point. A jeep engine revs up. Somewhere in the distance, the wind whips up surface dust. The land seems to be rolling onto itself, threads of brown and white, gathering more and more, like a tidal wave.

The first jeep pulls away. Guards on the other two wrap their weapons. Kat's never seen weather like it, but from what people are doing, it looks like it happens often. In an instant, the buildings around her disappear from view.

Kat drops back. She's treading on half an inch of dust. It's scratching inside and hot through the soles of her shoes. She's under the wing, eyes half closed against the sting, mouth shut tight, hand feeling the way like a blind person.

One second, she's stepping through the storm's debris like mud, the next it's been blown away and she's hard on the tarmac. She touches the airplane's tire and feels its heat. A light from the wing shows up the dust, but the beam goes nowhere, as if it's shining point blank into a wall.

Above her the massive fuselage of the plane shakes and groans in the wind. Covers are going over the plane's engine cowlings. The way the pilots stay in the cockpit suggests they planned a quick turnaround.

After the storm dies, the plane will have to be refueled, and she doesn't see any refueling truck. The pilots will want to carry out a visual check for external damage. The rest of the prisoners will have to be taken off. Counting up, Kat reckons she'll have less than an hour to get her father out—if he's even in the camp; if she can find her way to the cell, get in, and get him back here.

Without warning, the wind drops, and with it the dust screen, so she has a sudden clear view. The jeeps are behind her. The prisoners are to her right, just beyond the aircraft wing, lying facedown on the ground. A guard stands over them with an M16 carbine.

As Kat begins to walk toward him, the wind whips up again. She keeps going. Grit blows against her face. The baseball cap lifts up from her head and vanishes. Her hand squeezes the butt of the Beretta, finger on the edge of the trigger guard. She fixes her sight on the guard; slight movement in the swirl, his back to her only four, five yards away, but the screeching wind so loud she has to get closer.

They say that after your first killing, the others come easier, and Kat knows what they mean. With the two at the Kazakh embassy, it was tears she had to stop. With Lancaric, she'd vomited, but that was because of the hand. With the guard looming ahead, whose face she can't even see, Kat is afraid of what she might have to do and what she might become. But it won't stop her.

He turns, startled to see her. Her finger moves inside the trigger guard. He sees the Beretta, but guns are commonplace inside a RingSet base. He's not hostile.

She points toward the plane, jabs at the RingSet logo on her overalls, and shows him a piece of paper with the cell number on it.

His head is scarfed, leaving only a slit for his eyes. He looks beyond her into the storm-filled blackness, shouts something, points to the storm, grabs her wrist, and leads her to the prisoners. He must think she needs to take one of them.

With her eyes half closed and her face stinging with sand, she sees only prone prisoners.

The guard takes the scarf off his head, steps behind her, and folds it around her head, tying it to allow her to see. Kat lets him.

She's barely noticing. Her eyes, moving along the line of prisoners, have stopped on a man she is convinced is Mike Luxton. She crouches down to be certain. Three days ago, while making her a daisy chain, she'd seen him double knot the same laces. She kicks them. No movement. She walks around to his head. There's no doubt in her mind. She pulls the scarf down from her mouth.

"Mike," she says, loud as she can.

No answer. Luxton doesn't move. She's about to put her lips to his ear when he lunges at her. His fingers curl like a lizard's tongue around her wrist, pressing her radial artery, doing everything he can to weaken her grip on the Beretta.

Sandy grit in her mouth, she can't find her voice. Kat throws herself backward, but those hands and arms, trained hurling bodies from trapeze to trapeze, are too strong. He shifts his weight, knees bent, keeping hold of her, drawing up his legs to get to his feet.

The guard's M16's coming up. The Beretta's slipping from her hand.

If Luxton gets it, the guard will shoot. And Luxton will shoot Kat, unless he recognizes her. Blinded by dust, deafened by the wind, working from every sense except sight, Luxton wouldn't even know the guard is there. He doesn't seem to know who she is—even that she's someone trying to help him.

Kat's focus is on her other gun, the 21, her left hand bringing it out from her pants and taking off the safety. Kat fires a round into the sky. Luxton doesn't slacken his grip, but his eyes meet hers under her scarf.

"It's Kat," she shouts, just as the wind lulls again. Dust drops to the ground. Vision clears.

Confusion flashes onto the guard's face. He isn't sure what to do. Kat has the 21 in one hand, held skyward, and now that Luxton's let go, she's regained control of the 38.

Kat stands up, both hands on the Beretta, pointing it at Luxton. "I got him. It's okay," she says quickly to the guard. She smiles.

The guard's face is dark, blotched with red, his eyes rough and blank; he doesn't know what she's saying. Kat smiles confidently, but over his shoulder, shimmering toward them, comes another rolling wave of sand.

The blow to her shoulder makes her cry out, and she feels the Beretta snatched from her hand. She's stumbling, arms out to break her fall, to keep her on her feet. Luxton barges past her, shoulder down, head butting the guard in the midriff. His cuffed hands swing together like a baseball bat and hit him in the face. The man's down on the ground. Luxton snatches the 38 from Kat and positions himself to fire.

"No!" screams Kat.

Luxton hesitates, and Kat is there, her hand on his arm. Luxton's expression flares angrily, but he obeys her.

"Tie him, then," says Luxton, keeping the Beretta straight on the guard's face. Kat undoes the scarf he gave her, brings the guard's hands behind his back, ties them. Luxton's on his knees, checking the strength of Kat's knot.

Then he lies facedown, arms stretched out, pulling the cuffs as far apart as he can. "Now, the barrel hard against the link," he says. "Shoot it through."

The sound of the gun blast is drowned in the roar of the wind. They can barely see each other. She thinks she hears him cry out, feels his hand on her arm, fumbling down to take her hand, fingers clasping over the Beretta, his lips against her ear. "Keep hold of me, and we walk," he shouts.

They move, leaning forward, the wind coming straight at them. If anyone else is around, Kat can't see them.

"We've got half an hour at best," yells Luxton.

"Before the plane goes?" screams back Kat.

Kat's only inches away, and she can just about make him out shaking his head. "No. Before we get killed. There'll be no way out of this place."

"But you came before."

He speeds up. His grip goes from her left hand to her wrist. "That took six months' planning. You can't just walk into a place like this."

"What about—"

"You want to see your father?" yells Luxton.

A bellow of wind knocks her back. Luxton keeps his balance. He's holding her upright, and as her head is jerked around by the gale, she feels the rush of a bullet passing within inches of her head. Something behind her is moving with purpose, while everything else is a random swirl.

She fires twice. She feels the gun buck, sees its spark. She hears the remnants of a man's cry whisked away by the weather as he's hit.

Luxton drops her wrist and runs back. The guard has fallen to his knees, curled like a baby, rocking from side to side, head bent forward like he's in prayer, jacket red with blood and his hand trembling around his neck, where her bullet has caught him.

Luxton takes the M16 and shoots the guard in the head.

Kat goes rigid. "You enjoyed that, didn't you," she accuses.

"You come to a death camp and expect no killing?" Luxton's down with the corpse, searching through the clothes, transferring papers from the dead man's pockets to his own.

Luxton brings her toward him, puts his lips to her ear. "The storm comes in cycles of three or four. We've had two lulls. We'll get two more if we're lucky. During the next lull, whoever freed him might be able to sound the alarm."

Kat nods, but pushes his hands away. "You know where my father is?" she shouts.

Luxton points the way they were heading, and just then the wind dies. The dust shield drops to the ground, and Kat's looking into Luxton's face, his eyes streaked and hard, the same man who four days ago guided her back from Balham and warned her away from all of this.

Like Kat, he wears a face that has crossed too many bridges too quickly. A few minutes ago, he was in a line of prisoners slated for execution. Now, all he wants to do is to get Kat to see her father before they both get killed.

His hand is on her head, the way a cop pushes a suspect into a police car. "Down," he says. "Down and don't move."

He keeps her face pressed into the ground as a jeep drives past. His calluses scratch the skin on the back of her neck, pushing forcefully, then relaxing and gently staying there until the engine sound dims. She looks up and sees the vastness of the steppe, lit by sunshine exposing them as a searchlight pins a fugitive.

His hand hesitates, hovers, and moves away. She feels his mouth press into her hair, then leave. They wait until the next surge of sandstorm comes.

When Kat gets to her feet, something sweeps through her, part warm, part cold, part antidote.

"Thank you," she says.

SIXTY-ONE

———————◇———————

Friday, 7:33 a.m., BST/2:33 p.m., Voz Island

Balloons of dust roll through the camp again, turning daylight to darkness, fresh air to choking fog, the swell of dust cloud darkening like a bruise, making Kat feel as if she's being engulfed by the ash from a volcano.

"This will be the last cycle," says Luxton. "It'll go on longer. Ten minutes perhaps. When it drops, we'll be exposed."

Luxton pulls on her wrist.

"Over there. That's where he was last time."

His hand is on a metal door of flaking black paint. Kat can see no more than a few inches ahead of her. She goes to the end of the building and counts them down: F-10687, F-10688, and, her heart locked with fear, F-10689, white stenciled letters, just like in the photograph. She feels down it, searching for the lock. Luxton touches her shoulder and shakes his head. She thinks he's telling her that it's unlocked, but only reads his lips, can't hear a word.

She pushes, but it's solid. Shoulder down, Luxton rams the door. Only the top edge gives an inch. The bottom is wedged.

Luxton's hand is pulling at the Beretta to shoot out the lock.

She puts up her hand to stop him and bangs on the door. Something's happening at the bottom, like a rat scrabbling a way through. She pushes, pushes harder, and she swears she hears a voice. The movement gets more frantic. Luxton's weight is with hers, and they break the door open, at least partway. Something's blocking it, but there's enough room for her to squeeze inside.

She steps into sudden quiet and blackness. The door is jammed by a pile of dust that has blown in and then been sucked back against it by the wind currents.

Kat reaches out, feels a wall of rough, concrete cinder blocks. She sweeps her hand in front of her.

"Hello?" she says hesitantly.

An unfamiliar sensation creeps over her, a tingling of the senses that has nothing to do with weather or the camp, but with a fear of her own personal emotions. She takes another step forward into silence.

The door gives more, and Luxton comes in, flashlight in hand, beam sweeping the room, picking up details of newspaper and magazine clippings on the wall.

The room is bigger than she'd imagined, 20 by 15 at least, a good height to the ceiling, with a bathroom off to one side, strip lighting on the wall, an air-conditioning unit, a writing desk with a separate lamp, a double bed made up with a white sheet, and a bedside table scattered with books. The bathroom is basic, but clean, with a grilled air vent.

Kat absorbs it all in seconds; not so much a prison cell as a motel room floating in hell.

Taped up above the desk, neatly arranged, dated pictures chronicle the rise of Tiina Gracheva to the very height of Russian money and power. In the week that Max Grachev was conceived, she stands as a young KGB interpreter with Kat's father in Red Square. Next to it, a different one of her father and Tiina duck hunting in Smolensk, just the two of them. Then they show Tiina, in uniform, as a senior official in the KGB; later in fashionable suits as a businesswoman; Tiina stepping out of a limousine; at her daughter's graduation; at a ribbon-cutting ceremony with Yulya outside an oil refinery; with the same daughter at a banquet in a chandeliered hall; only Yulya, nothing of Max or Lara.

Kat searches without subtlety: desk drawer out; papers on the floor; books' pages checked, then dropped; hands feeling under the bed; light switches on—no power; hands sweeping the mattress; sheet pulled back, crumpled, and dropped; bedside table drawer out, tipped over, dropped;

fingers inside the lamp shade; mattress upended; first pillow out of its case, shaken, dropped.

Luxton's hand is on her arm, but she shakes him off.

"We have to go," he says.

Second pillow, half out of its case, her fingers brush the corner of a piece of card, and Kat stops. She pulls it out.

"Kat," shouts Luxton. "He's not here. He was, but he's gone."

Her eyes are now adjusted enough to recognize a familiar photograph, crumpled, pushed from hiding place to hiding place, one edge torn, but everyone's there—Dad at the back; Suzy by his side; Mom leaning against the cherry tree at the orphanage in Lancaster, holding Kat's hand; Grandma Polinski behind them, with a blur of pink blossom at the back; the same picture Suzy carried in her big, ugly ring.

"Yes," she whispers. "He was here."

Luxton has her by the shoulders, propelling her out the door. The dust twists and dances, suspended.

A single shot cracks above the sound of the storm.

She senses Luxton behind her, sees the weapon flash at her again, but the shots are going wide. Then her attacker looms in front of her, closer than she expects, and she fires for the legs, which buckle. Two gunshots; not from her. They fall together, her cheek grazing against the rough cloth of his pants and the sand.

Luxton has his weapon leveled at the guard's head. Kat's face is inches from the guard's. He's short, stubby, not much taller than Kat. His eyes shiver, fingers splayed, head shaking side to side, no pride to play with.

Kat shows him the family photograph, her finger jabbing onto the face of her father.

"Where," says Luxton, then switches to Russian: "*Gde on?*" he shouts, pulling the guard up. He points through the dust cloud, and Luxton says, "Come on, then."

By now they're familiar with the cycles of the storm. In its last seconds, the weather becomes harsher. They have a few minutes, each moment getting darker and darker, the dust more abrasive.

They reach a row of whitewashed concrete cells, no windows, no doors, just iron bars, through which she sees a man, naked but for a couple of tiny threadbare rags that barely cover a quarter of his emaciated body. His feet are fettered, and his arms are wrenched up and tied to a metal ring in the wall above him.

From Luxton's flashlight, Kat sees a trickle of urine run out from under him, then as the beam hits the wall behind, she spots another man, but from the stench reaching her, he must be dead, and the patch that she first thinks is a massive bruise on his back is in fact a blackness of crawling maggots.

A rat with its baby in its mouth darts from the shadows and bolts between the bars to another cell. Hand on her mouth to control a retch: The rat was feeding on the human body, left to rot with her father in the cell.

"Keys," yells Luxton at the guard, who, still at gunpoint, fumbles in his pocket. Luxton snatches them from him, opens the door, and lets Kat go in.

As she steps forward, Kat sees a human shape, then its frailty, and as she recognizes her father, she also sees herself in his face.

Luxton takes John Polinski's body weight as Kat unties the rope holding up his hands. Her father's eyes are shut tight with pain. He feebly grasps the hanging ropes to hold the weight of his arms, the pain in his shoulder joints too excruciating for him to move them.

Slowly, slowly the stick-thin arms come down, and the crusted eyes open slightly.

Her father is in front of her, his face ash pale, lined and worn. Skin hangs over his cheekbones, and his shoulders jut out like tent stakes.

"It's me, Kat," she manages, sounding so stupidly formal.

The way his eyes, still sharp, dance around, she can tell he recognizes her, examining his daughter and the situation. There's no surprise, no great joy. It's as if, although he sees it's Kat, his mind is not used to dealing with happiness. His gaze moves directly to her face, testing himself, until he loses his courage and, shifting from love to furtiveness, he looks somewhere behind him.

John Polinski shakes. He's sitting on the earth floor now. His trembling hand touches his own face.

He holds out thin, shaking arms toward his daughter. Kat sinks to the ground to be with him, the drum of her pulse beating in her ears, as she touches first his fingers, then gently takes his hand, scared of the sores on it, but looks into his face and sees his eyes filled like never before at the sight of his daughter.

Kat cups her hand around his bony shoulder. Luxton's hands are around the other one.

Outside, there's only the guard, lying facedown, hands tied behind him. Visibility is still at a few feet. If anyone else is close, Kat can't see them, and they can't see her.

They carry her father out, then lower him to the ground next to the guard.

Luxton has the pistol on the guard. "Change him," he says, undoing the man's bound wrists one-handed.

She lifts the guard's torso, then his feet, while Luxton unzips his jumpsuit, pulls it off, and holds it out.

"Are you able to put this on?" he says.

Polinski nods. Luxton reties the guard, and they get her father to his feet and awkwardly pull the jumpsuit onto him. It's way too big, but it does the job.

"We'll carry you," Luxton yells at Polinski. He and Kat make a seat for him with their hands, and they set off in the direction of the airplane.

Kat's lungs are bursting; her lips chapped, hands crying with pain to take the weight of her father, feet clumsy on the shifting ground, hair blown into her face.

Without warning, Luxton stops. Visibility is so bad that a few steps farther, and they would have run into the underbelly of the plane. They lower John Polinski to his feet.

"Up there," yells Luxton, pointing toward the plane, his voice clear because the wind's gone quiet. The dust rustles as it settles, the brown gray screen dropping so she feels the heat of the sun on her face, eyes adjusting to clarity.

In the far distance are covered watchtowers. Vehicles begin to move. People emerge from shelter.

Near the plane, the engine of a fuel tanker starts up. The pilot gets up inside the cockpit, turns his back, and disappears from sight into the main cabin.

John Polinski bends, head hanging, his breath catching, resting hands on his knees. Kat sees how sick her father is.

Soon, as work begins again to get the plane refueled and off the ground, the three of them will become conspicuous. Two guards will be discovered, one dead, the other tied up.

The door shifts, then opens.

Luxton and Kat don't speak, but she knows what she should do, and Luxton is agreeing.

It has to be her, because she's a woman, and that's how things work.

A hose from the fuel tanker is being clipped under the wings. The cargo hatch comes down, and the cabin rear door opens—a head peering out to check that the weather's gone. Luxton kneels by her father, checking his pulse.

Kat runs up the steps as if she owns the aircraft. Two cleaners are in the cabin, vacuum cleaners humming down the aisle. She inhales the fresh smell of a place protected from the dust storm.

The pilot's leaning against the bathroom door, a cup in his hand, about to take a sip. He's average height, with gym-workout shoulders, a slight belly, strong hands, his mouth too wide for his face to make him good-looking, and there's no smile to be seen. He looks up at Kat and keeps his expression cool and demeaning.

"You the guy who flew us in?" says Kat.

His eyes shift from her face to the dust-smeared RingSet logo on her jumpsuit and back to her face again. He nods.

"What happens when the plane bumps into that shit we just had out there?" says Kat, jerking back her thumb toward door, turning her head enough to see through the curtain a small group of prisoners still in their seats, not yet having disembarked.

"We don't fly," he says.

"Where you from?" says Kat, taking a step to get right inside the cabin. He puts the cup on a ledge and checks a stain on his sleeve.

"Grew up on a farm in Kansas. Now I fly between dust storms."

Kat laughs, maybe longer than she should. "That's funny," she says. "I've never seen anything like it."

"Happens a lot in these parts, 'specially in the summer. Messes up the schedules."

"What about the plane? It got dust all up its ass."

The pilot grins at that. "Plane's pretty good." He affectionately pats the wall. "Flight plan's gone to hell. Waiting to get another slot."

"Doesn't seem there's a lot of traffic around to slot into."

He points upward. "Up there're the main routes from Asia to Europe."

Kat lets it rest there, just for a beat.

"I know we can't know who each other are, but suppose I call you John and you call me Jane?"

He shrugs, eyes roll a bit. "You can call me Dane. Denmark. That's where my grandparents came from. Everyone called me that as a kid. So where do you come from, Jane?"

"Lancaster, Ohio," says Kat.

The radio crackles from inside the cockpit. Dane checks his watch. "Excuse me. Only be a few seconds, but that could be our slot." He turns quickly as if he's afraid Kat might leave.

Kat motions for Luxton, at the top of the steps, to wait another moment.

The wing vibrates as fuel's pumped into it. Jeeps cross the camp, impossible to tell where they're heading. The cleaners work on the cabin. Another peek through the curtain: Two guards have come into the back and begun escorting the rest of the prisoners off. They don't act as if they know one of their workmates has been killed.

She looks back to the cockpit, sees Dane, headphones on, speaking into a mouthpiece and punching buttons. The prisoners and guards have left the main cabin. Kat signals Luxton, and he brings her dad in, pain in his face, but also wonderment. She points, and they disappear through the curtain.

Kat knocks on the open door. Dane beckons her in. He taps the arm of the copilot's seat.

"Roger," he says into the radio, flipping up a switch and another two on the ceiling. "Got it," he tells Kat enthusiastically. "One aircraft's coming in to land now. After that, if they can fuel us up in time, we've got a slot."

"How long'll that take?" says Kat.

"High pressure pumps, dual nozzle. Not long." His eyes are on a map screen now. He wants to be with her but not look at her. "I could ask what you're doing here," he says, "but I guess that could get us both fired."

"That's for sure," says Kat. "I'm getting a couple of sick folks onto the plane. I may not look it, but I'm a nurse." Her hand's across, touching his arm.

"A place like this, it's nice to talk to someone from back home."

She smiles. "You still got that farm?" she says softly.

"Hardly," he says. Calculations of weights and distances have superimposed themselves over the map. His eyes are on the numbers. "I lost it to the banks the year before I was due to take it over from my folks. It broke their hearts. I joined the air force, learned to fly, and ended up here, somehow. The job pays twice any major airline's rates. And we're told it's for the good and security of the nation. I hope to make enough to buy back the farm before my folks pass away."

He flits his eyes up to Kat. "So, there. You got my life wrapped up with a bow. You got one, too?"

"Good childhood," says Kat. "Like you. My dad died, and I went off the rails. You know, wrong side of the street kind of stuff. Guess a daughter loves her dad more than she thinks. Got myself together, trained as a nurse, then paramedic, and—hey—like you said, here I am, protecting my country."

She gazes through the windshield, watching the prisoners walking in a line, eight or nine of them, way across to the corner of the camp, their razor-clear shadows going with them. It's not just her dad, she thinks. She's got to get them all freed. Not this time, perhaps. But she'll have to come back.

She's paused enough for Dane to notice. The prisoners make an image that two decent people talking together should not mention. Dane's about to speak, but checks himself, and Kat says, "You got a wife, kids, or are you like me?"

"There she is," he says. The other plane kicks up dust on landing, slows quickly, and turns toward a set of steps on the runway.

"Had a wife," he says. "But I guess I'm attracted to women who don't much like a man when he's down. And you?"

"Not much good with men, up or down. I'm working with a guy right now who I wouldn't mind settling down with, but I don't think I've even registered with him, and you know . . ." The beginning of a lump in her throat makes Kat trail off. A figure steps in front of the plane and gives Dane a thumbs-up sign.

"That's our all-clear." He turns in his seat. "Where the hell's . . . Yeah, right, the name's classified, but I need my copilot."

Outside, the camp looks busy after the storm, and somewhere in that fenced-off wasteland, a copilot's being called, and someone's got to be finding a body.

She takes out the Beretta, rests it in her lap. He sees it when he looks up again from his instruments.

His face drops, begins a fast movement, but stops as Kat jacks a round into the chamber.

SIXTY-TWO

$$\diamond$$

Y ou won't survive," he says calmly, as if announcing light turbulence, but his smile fades, and his eyes sharpen into the hard glint of a man angry at being conned. He has a hand on each knee and is sitting bolt upright.

"I killed a man to get here," says Kat. "I'll kill one to leave."

"It's not about killing." Dane tilts his head to look out the side window. The storm has gone, and a breeze puckers the light surface of dust on the steppe like wind rippling water. Yellow outlines created by the afternoon sun make the landscape look less harsh.

"You fly us out," says Kat, "you'll get enough money to buy back your farm. And like you said, that's what it's all about."

"RingSet's not a company worth dying for, but I will not be responsible for the deaths of innocents," says Dane.

"You already are," Kat says.

He shrugs. "Kill me if you want, but I'm gonna clear the plane."

His gaze is aimed straight at Kat, way past caring about any feelings, including his own. "Okay, folks," he announces. "Everybody off, please, while we carry out an internal check of the aircraft." He clicks on a new monitor. It has multiple screens showing various camera angles of the interior main cabin.

John Polinski has a window seat in first class, his head lolling, his eyes half closed. Luxton examines his wounds and applies dressings from a first aid kit. The prisoners are all off, but the cabin staff and cleaners are still at the back. They obediently begin leaving through the jet's back door.

Kat's about to tell Dane to begin takeoff without the copilot, when a voice crackles through Dane's headset.

His face hardens. "That's the tower," he says. "They're onto you."

Kat slides down into the jump seat behind Dane, both hands holding the Beretta aimed at the back of his head.

She breathes in deeply, keeps her voice steady. "Then get us airborne." The surface of the runway looks distorted, melting in the heat and shimmering. In a plume of dust, two vehicles with yellow flashing lights come toward them from the direction of the control tower.

Dane takes off the headset, immerses himself in being a pilot. "Starting one," he says to himself, as the engine whines. "Starting two."

Luxton heaves the front cabin door closed, pulls the lever to lock it, and heads back to do the rear door.

"Fuel engine flow, okay. Gas exhaust pressure, okay." Dane's fingers play the overhead panel like a keyboard. The vehicles split up, one heading toward the end of the runway almost a mile ahead, one closer to the rear of the aircraft.

"Rear door's still open," says Dane, pointing up to a beeping red light.

"Go," says Kat, her voice pitched with urgency. "Take off with the goddamn door open."

"We can't pressurize."

"But we can fly. So fly."

Dane moves the thrust levers, making the empty plane vibrate. He shifts the rudder, and the aircraft turns toward the sun, yellow and swollen on the horizon. A third jeep veers, skids on the loose surface, and accelerates toward the end of the tarmac to cut off the aircraft's takeoff.

Sweat rivulets run down Kat's face. Dane looks flatly ahead, stops the turn, and gives the engines more power.

"Release brakes," he whispers. "A2 plus ten."

Kat catches a sudden movement in one of the monitors. The fuselage trembles, making the image shake, and Kat can't work out what's happening.

The aircraft's gaining speed. Sixty knots . . . 72 knots . . . 81 knots . . .

Dust hits the side windshield like a wall of rain. Blurs of rusting vehicles and low-rise buildings rush past. The land surface swirls into a cloud, and the jeeps become invisible. The runway, miragelike, changes from deep black, to yellow, to silver gray. The sky is storm-washed blue.

Then she catches something in the monitor. Another person moving toward Luxton.

Something familiar.

Luxton's arm is wrapped around the massive handle of the rear door that is half closed, shaking into a blur as the plane gathers speed.

He doesn't seem to have noticed the other person 20 feet away from him, who's drawing a gun. Through a twist of the hand on the weapon, the indistinguishable movement of body weight, then finally, when he turns, the now visible mustache, Kat sees that the man about to kill Mike Luxton is Simon Tappler.

No wonder they intercepted her at the house! No wonder Yulya found her at the concert hall! He would have known everything she was doing.

Tappler fires as the plane bucks. The shot misses. He steadies himself, hand on the back of a seat. Even so close, the plane's instability makes Luxton a difficult target.

Dane jerks his head up at the monitor. Kat's weapon stays steady on him.

Tappler fires again. Misses. The plane yaws, throwing him back against the open door. Air slipstreams suck out a pillow and a blanket.

"If I take off, he dies," Dane shouts over the noise of takeoff. "If I abort, you die."

A bird flashes in front of the nose. One twenty knots . . . 125 . . . 129 knots . . .

"We commit in twenty seconds," says Dane.

"Take off," says Kat.

Tappler grabs the back of a closer seat. In the monitor, he seems only inches from Luxton. He fires again, and this time Luxton lashes out and kicks the weapon from Tappler's hand. Another kick hits his face.

"Keep going," says Kat. She grips the butt of the Beretta, eyes darting between the monitor and the jolting of the nose on the runway.

"There," mutters Dane.

Just beyond the heat shimmer, two jeeps block the runway, one facing the aircraft, one backed up the other way. The sun flickers off the rearview mirror, showing a heavy machine gun mounted on the back.

"Committed," says Dane, pulling back the levers sharply, giving the engines extra thrust, and making the nose soar skyward. The plane shakes at the sharp angle of climb, wings straining to hold it against the extra pull of gravity.

Tracer bullets, curving beneath them, light up a path through floating dust.

Tappler scrambles to his feet. Luxton is buffeted against the door, being sucked away.

The aircraft dips sharply. Kat's sweat has gone cold and dry on her skin. The wings tip, and the ground rushes toward them. The whole fuselage tilts as Dane goes into a tight, low turn to avoid the tracers.

Tappler grabs Luxton's legs and pushes them outside the plane. Either Luxton will lose the strength of his arm, or the legs will be crushed by the vise of the door. The door shakes, sliding up and back, threatening to either slam shut or tear off.

"Keep us airborne," Kat shouts to Dane. She heads to the back of the plane. A lurch flings her against a seat. A line of tracer bullets arc above the wingtip. Beyond that she sees mountains capped with snow.

She keeps moving back.

The slipstream drags Luxton farther out of the aircraft. The door bumps wildly on its hinges. With his bare hands, Tappler is prying Luxton's grip from the hinge.

If Kat fires, she has an equal chance of hitting either. If the door isn't closed within seconds, they won't be going anywhere.

Tappler glances indifferently, as if he's been expecting her and doesn't care. She runs at him.

With each step she judges when she can do it—how close she is—how he will react.

His concentration becomes divided between Luxton and Kat. He shifts his body weight.

Too late.

Kat fires, first at the torso, then at the upper leg. That's when he crumbles and when she's onto him. Luxton, with arms trained for the trapeze, heaves himself inside, and in a single, elegant movement, swings around and bats Tappler out through the door.

Tappler plunges through a flaming trail of tracer rounds that drop out of range short of the fuselage.

With Kat anchoring him, Luxton pulls the door closed and locks it. The plane falls into an empty quiet, climbing more gently, calmly moving to safety across the infinity of the Kazakh steppe.

SIXTY-THREE

---◇---

The sun's glare catches her on the side of the face. A white blue sky stretches endlessly ahead, colors merging to the white yellow of the desert on the slight curve of the earth, and not a cloud anywhere.

Dane glances back at her. "That's the Caspian below us," he says. "The good news is that the flight plan was already filed, and it takes us back to Byford. The other good news is that no one is chasing us. Air traffic control is talking to us like nothing's happened."

"Meaning RingSet's told no one outside the Voz Island camp?" says Luxton.

"I'm only talking about air traffic control," says Dane. "But they've got us where they want us, either way. If we land at Byford, we're dead. If we go anywhere else, you get taken in for hijacking. They don't need to chase us."

"Where does that leave you?" says Kat.

Dane's long face changes in the sunlight, looking healthy, with a stubble that accentuates lines and a severity in the eyes. "The bank that took my farm is owned by ACR, and RingSet's an ACR subsidiary. Not much worse can happen to a man than having his whole life stolen from him."

"I saw worse, lots worse, in that concentration camp back at Voz," says Kat.

Dane looks away.

"You with us, then?"

"You made me a promise to buy back my farm. Sometimes life gets that simple. You don't want to keep your promise, then I'll decide my interests when the time comes." He flips a switch above his head and lowers his eyes to a display on the panel. "And I guess that'll be in about . . . five hours and ten minutes, when we reach British airspace."

Luxton walks up to the cockpit door. They talk softly in the doorway, their eyes on Dane. Kat trusts Dane, but she's not risking it. Either she or Luxton will be in the cockpit all the time.

"How is he?" she says.

"As good as can be expected." She glances down at Luxton's hand, which he's wrapped with a cloth, but is bleeding badly.

"Watch Dane," she says. Kat finds the first aid kit, comes back, and fixes Luxton's injury with antiseptic cream and a bandage.

When she's done, Luxton touches her elbow. "I didn't have time to say this before," he says, "but thanks."

"You, too," she says, waits a second, then asks, "Tappler?"

Luxton shakes his head, says nothing.

"Does that mean Cranley?"

"I can't imagine it."

"Cranley was with Tappler at Tappler's house. Just the two of them. I put in every damn electronic safeguard I have, yet I was still intercepted."

Luxton touches her face and runs his fingertips against hers. He takes her by surprise. But it's raw. She needs it. She's not stopping him.

"What does that mean?" she says.

"Let's work Tappler out later," he says. "I'll watch Dane. Go and be with your father."

John Polinski's breathing evenly, his battered body resting, eyes closing and opening, as if waking up. She wants to talk to him, to protect him, to learn from him. His sleeping frustrates her. Fatigue brings mad voices to her head.

If you're alive, why not Suzy? Why not Mom?

"Dad . . . ," she begins, before realizing his eyes are looking at nothing, that it's just his unsettled nerves. She rearranges a blanket to protect her father's neck from the chill of the air-conditioning. John Polinski shifts in his seat, and the blanket falls. Kat pulls it up again.

Kat lets John Polinski sleep. In the galley, she opens compartments, reads instructions, and soon surrounds herself with the smells of cooking food. When he stirs, she carries two trays through to the cockpit, then rests one next to her father's seat and taps his shoulder.

"You hungry, Dad?" she says. He opens his eyes slowly, blinks, taking in where he is, who Kat is. As if sleep has cured all, his face becomes electric. "Now, according to the menu, you have shellfish bisque soup," she says, mimicking a flight attendant. "Followed by corn-fed chicken with vegetable broth accompanied by crisp pancetta bacon. And there's apple brûlée for dessert, with a selection of fresh fruit and chocolates."

Her eyes are wet. She's not sure she can hold the tears; not sure she wants to. She takes his hand, scabbed with unhealed sores, so frail, but strong enough to curl around hers.

Reality draws sharply across Polinski's face. He pushes himself up in his seat, looks around, head jerking in panic.

"The man . . . I mean, who else . . . Suzy? Is she here?"

"She couldn't make it."

He blinks. "You know. Do you know? Did Suzy send you? She said someone was coming."

Clumsily, she leans across to him. "Here, eat. Get strong again," she says. She lifts the soup bowl to him, spilling some on his tray. She finds a spoon and hurriedly collects the packets of pepper and salt.

John Polinski quietly accepts his daughter's care, lets her set up the tray, unfurl the napkin, and pour water from a bottle. His left eye twitching, making the loose skin flex, he tears off a chunk of bread, dips it in the soup, and eats. He touches her cheek and says, "They moved me a week ago and put me in that cell. A man was shot just outside. They put his body in with me and tied my hands up, so I was hanging. Until then, I had a bigger room. I got used to it. A bed, a desk—"

"I know," interrupts Kat, when she should have let him talk.

He falters, a fracture of indecision in his eyes. "It's not the way it looked," he says.

"It's okay."

"No." His hand goes to her wrist. "I want you to understand. Those pictures on the wall—"

"I know," says Kat. "I know. I found this." She holds up the family picture from Lancaster.

"They were the conditions of my life," he says, his bony fingers taking a corner of the photograph, crow's-feet splaying out from his eyes as he squints to see it.

"Grandma? Is she still alive?"

"Yes. She's fine," says Kat.

"Still grumpy?"

"Still grumpy."

"We have to go see her. You, me, Suzy, Mom, we'll go down for Thanksgiving." Pausing, brow creased, he peers at Kat like a child. "Mom's passed away, hasn't she?"

A silent cry floats in the back of Kat's throat. He doesn't know. She'll have to start from scratch.

"Suzy, Mom . . ." she begins, and stops herself.

His bloodshot eyes contract into themselves, and he looks out the window.

He turns back, pushes himself up in his seat, and swallows. "Okay, Kat. Tell me. Start from the beginning."

As she speaks, Kat peels apart inside. Wall after inner wall disintegrates. Her story flows like water on arid land. Her father's attention nourishes her, the harsh black-and-white edges of her life bloom into color again, and she feels like she's on his lap in his study, secure and at home. Her eyes film over, and she talks blindly, missing nothing that needs to be said—regret, remorse, anger, the natural feelings of a daughter's human heart to her father.

When she tells him about finding her mother, then when she says she was murdered, John Polinski moves his head, acknowledgment in his eyes, but does not interrupt her flow. His face is worn, but it's soft and strengthening, drawing sustenance from her.

She tells him about the Kazakh embassy, about Suzy, the e-mail, the marshes, about Max Grachev, Tiina, and RingSet. When she mentions Bill Cage, there is a flicker of approval in Polinski's expression. With Cranley, he nods, and his lips move. And when she describes the photograph of the execution, he speaks for the first time. "Yulya," he says. "Yulya Ivanova Gracheva."

He brushes his fingers through his hair and looks around him as if, for a moment, Kat isn't there, and he's expecting someone else. He pulls his attention back. "Yulya is a terrible person," he says. "She spreads evil like . . ." He falters.

His jaw is trembling. "Suzy, you say. Now. Just last week."

"Friday night."

Drained of strength, his head drops. "Take the tray, will you?" Kat shifts the tray. "Friday night was when they moved me." His hands cover his face.

SIXTY-FOUR

---◇---

Kat finds fresh fruit in the galley fridge and takes a plate of it into the cockpit.

"We're over Germany," says Dane.

Luxton's stretched back, hands behind his head. The way he looks at her makes Kat feel warm, like she doesn't have to prove herself anymore. They've followed daylight, and the sun's as it was when they left. But instead of the meshing colors of the steppe, it's shining yellow at them behind a line of white clouds. In between, 30,000 feet below, it's so clear that Kat can see the outlines of houses clustered amid the summer green of mountains and fields.

"Above Holland, we'll cut an engine," says Dane, "and ask for an emergency landing at Schiphol in Amsterdam. We'll work out where to go from there."

Kat heads back into the cabin, tells her father, peels an orange, and hands a bit to him. He winces as his mouth, red with sores, reacts painfully to the fruit's acid.

"Sorry," she says. He chews and shakes his head, waves his hand that it doesn't matter. The sleep has energized him, rid him of the tiredness in his eyes.

"The St. Petersburg summit," says Kat. "How did you find out about it when no one else did?"

"Nate stumbled onto it," says Polinski.

"Nate?"

"Nate dug up all sorts of things. But he's not political. He didn't see what it meant."

Luxton comes out of the cockpit, leans between Kat and Polinski. "We're cutting the engine in a couple of minutes," he whispers. "There'll be a jolt and a lurch, and we'll lose a bit of—"

He doesn't finish.

Two windows next to Polinski's seat shatter. Freezing air sucks him from his seat and smashes him against the bulkhead. Kat grips her armrest, hooking her arm underneath, locking her foot into the side of the footrest, resisting the vortex of lost pressure.

She can't get to her father.

The airliner's nose dips sharply; flames leap out from the port engine through shafts of sunlight.

Through the open cockpit door, she sees a jagged hole in the side of the aircraft. Dane falls heavily onto the control panel. Luxton reaches for an oxygen mask dropped from the ceiling and puts it on Dane. He slaps his face, looking for vital signs. Dane comes around and wipes blood from his eyes.

Orange masks hang down all over the cabin ceiling. Kat puts one on. As she breathes, her senses come back. John Polinski is on the floor in front of his seat. A sucking, freezing gale sweeps away cups, trays, all roaring around her.

The plane wobbles and jolts, twisting in the air. Kat tugs at an oxygen mask, but it doesn't reach her father and snaps off. She braces herself against the back of a seat and heaves him up enough so that another mask can reach.

But he's unconscious, his breathing erratic, pupils dilated. She shouts, but all sounds are lost.

Slowly, fuselage shaking, Luxton helps Dane pull up the nose, but they're losing altitude. The starboard wing dips erratically, a fuel leak spraying out of it, and land rears up underneath them.

John Polinski coughs. His breathing rasps, then stops. His chest doesn't move. Kat puts her fingers to his neck and feels a weak pulse from the carotid artery. She lifts an eyelid; no reaction.

Her father's alive, but it might only be for a few seconds, unless she can get oxygen to his blood and then to his brain.

She breathes deeply, straining to fill her own lungs, and puts her mouth over his, tasting the sores, the dried saltiness of the sweat on his lips. She pinches his nose, shifts back his head, pumps her own breath into him. The chest rises, but drops again. He tries to breathe, but something's catching in his throat.

Hands under his shoulders, she heaves him onto the cabin floor and lays him on his side with his legs up. Seconds more, and his oxygen-starved brain will cease to function. She can't even use the oxygen mask, or he might suffocate.

Two fingers crossed together, she probes into his mouth, pulling out mucus and food that he's vomited up and is getting caught in his windpipe.

Her mouth is back on his, forcing her breath into him, again and again. Feeling a quiver of reaction from his lungs, she places both hands on his chest and pushes down to get the heart pumping more strongly. Breathing pumping, breathing pumping, breathing pumping, until her father coughs, spewing out more food.

His breathing stabilizes, and Kat straps on an oxygen mask.

In the cockpit, she sees Luxton tightening Dane's mask. The pilot has blood trickling from a head wound, his white tunic torn at the shoulder, the frayed edges blown about by wind.

Dane's hands are on the controls, struggling to keep the wounded aircraft airborne. His head lolls, eyes rolling, staying conscious.

Outside, a green mass of land lurches up toward them.

Dane speaks automatically into the PA system: "Six thousand feet and going down."

The airliner bounces on turbulence and throws Kat against the window. The sky darkens as they enter a cloud. The cabin fills with cold, misty air, curtains swing forward, showing the sharpening descent.

Dane increases throttle to the left engine, which whines, tipping up the wing. But when he tries the same with the right engine, the fuselage shudders. Flames, fed by leaking fuel, are streaking back from the cowling.

"Cut engine," mutters Dane, as if he's talking to himself. "Fire out. Put the goddamn fire out. Wind direction variation. Headwind component. Left engine, no retardation of thrust levers. Rate of descent?"

Lights surge with erratic electrical power, fade, and go off.

"Emergency power," says Dane. He seems oblivious to everything around him, hands weak from blood loss, moving back and forth, testing the panel, as the aircraft, section by section, dies around him.

"Both engines dead," he says, his voice softening with reality. "We're gliding.

"Both of you, life vests on, up front next to the emergency exit. I'm going to have to bring her down on water."

Kat pulls a life jacket over her head, puts one on her father, buckles herself into a seat next to him, and takes his hand.

"I'm here, Dad," says Kat. "Right beside you." He doesn't respond. Luxton's in the copilot's seat, hand on the controls, giving his strength to Dane.

Dane's faltering voice comes through the system. "Going down," he says. "Two hundred and ten knots. Thirty-two hundred feet."

The surface of the water underneath them ripples with tiny white, choppy waves. The air is cold, metallic, smelling of the sea. They hit low air turbulence.

"Allow for loss of headwind component," says Dane. "One hundred seventy knots. Nineteen hundred feet. Retain descent. Get her down to one hundred twenty knots."

Sunlight glazes over gray blue water. Wind noise becomes a high-pitched roar. The sea rushes toward them in flashes of sunlight, yellow, white, deep green, and slate gray, made darker and darker by the airliner, whose shadow encroaches above it like a lumbering, prehistoric bird.

She sees the green English coastline, then it disappears, and all Kat can see is water. Her chest tightens. Sweat runs into her mouth. Hands clasped, she grips the coarse fabric of the seat belt.

The first touch is gentle. The big, empty plane skims the surface, and the nose stays up. Water splashes through a gash in the fuselage onto Kat.

A crash vibrates right through the aircraft, knocking her back in the seat. The right wingtip slices the water, jarring the plane. The wing bounces up again, then dips, and the force of the water peels off its aluminum skin, creating a horrible, spine-chilling sound like a child's scream.

From the back of the plane comes a rumble like an earthquake, ripping at everything in its path. The fuselage twists, and the rear section breaks off.

Everything stops and settles. They are floating. Her father doesn't move.

Smoke from burning gasoline catches in Kat's throat.

As she unclips her seat belt, the cockpit door breaks away, and cascading water gushes in. It gathers her up, bumps her over her father, turns her, and pushes her against the gaping window. Her shirt rips on an edge of metal, and she's flung through, until suddenly, lungs bursting, she's floating in shallow water, the muddy sea bottom blooming clouds of silt around her.

She kicks to break the surface, takes a mouthful of water, spits it, and opens her eyes to see the huge white curve of the aircraft towering above her. It's only half submerged. They must be near shore. A tidal surge knocks her back. She grasps hold of a seat cushion, then two life vests. Gray waves smack loudly against the fuselage.

"Dad!" she screams.

The airliner's nose rocks. The windows are above sea level, but that means there's no way she can climb back up inside. She shouts out for Luxton. They've come down within sight of a coastline of mud and tufts of vegetation.

She has to get back to her father. Her hands flail against sodden human hair. Dane's face brushes her cheek, eyes bulging at her, his dead flesh still warm against the chill of the water.

She swims through the murk, knocking debris out of the way. Water laps into an enormous hole in the fuselage, and she sees Luxton, hands under John Polinski's armpits, keeping him on his feet, standing at the door on the edge of the cabin floor as if it were a cliff top.

He has a smile of survival on his face.

For a moment, it's as quiet as a cemetery, the sun casting a long afternoon shadow from the wreckage across the water.

Then seagulls start up, and their cries are drowned by a helicopter engine. A curve of machine gun bullets penetrates the fuselage skin just above Kat's head with such precision it's as though they were meant to warn rather than hit her.

Rotor blades whip up the water. The helicopter's side door is open, a gun pointing out. Treading water, Kat raises her hands to show she's not armed.

A military green launch, its propeller churning up brown mud and breaking the film of gasoline on the water's surface, appears in the gap where the tail has broken away from the fuselage.

Kat recognizes the Marine Corps emblem on the forearm of the man standing behind the mounted machine gun on the foredeck.

Even though it's broad daylight, the searchlight is on and in her eyes. Lamps underneath the launch cut through the smoky gray water to show the broken plane and its strewn contents resting on the water's bed.

She shifts her gaze toward her father and Luxton, who's examining the helicopter and the launch—the two separate guns leveled at them.

The launch turns sharply through the gap between the broken tail and the fuselage. Sergeant Mason's on the gun, with another marine at the helm. And Mason doesn't go anywhere without Sayer.

As the helicopter hovers, framed through the cockpit window, Kat sees Max Grachev, headset on, no uniform, but in a dark jacket and open-neck shirt, staring straight ahead toward nothing except the open sea and the horizon.

Kat takes in these faces with a new chill coursing through her. She realizes that the site of the downing of the plane must have been planned ahead by the entire group, waiting for their return.

Behind Grachev, in the chopper's open door, a tall, narrow-faced woman appears, booted feet pushed into safety sockets, both hands on a machine gun, blond hair kept back with a bandanna, unafraid to show the world her face.

Kat wipes the back of her hand across her mouth and stares up at Yulya Gracheva.

SIXTY-FIVE

$$\diamondsuit$$

Friday, 3:29 p.m., BST

A single-lane road with high grass banks and a potholed turning point leads back from the water's edge. It curves around, across two cattle guards, and through yellow fields of corn. A shower cools the air, creates a rainbow in the distance, then leaves.

Dane's body, wrapped in a black plastic bag and taped like a mummy, feet and shoulders roped down, bounces on a trailer behind a U.S. military jeep driven by Mason.

Kat is with Luxton in the back of an unmarked sedan driven by the marine who was at the helm of the launch. His uniform names him as Roth. Polinski is with Sayer in a second car, driven by Mason. Yulya and Grachev follow overhead in the helicopter.

Kat's eyes feel bloodshot, her body shattered by fatigue. She tries for a sense of emptiness, of relief, a sense that the job is mostly done and that she can't push it any further. Her quest has turned out to be for nothing much more than the truth and, pretty much, she's found it.

As they turn a corner at the top of the high ground, Kat sees in a side mirror the massive white protrusion of the crashed airliner, two helicopters overhead and three launches with British police in wet suits.

Luxton reads Kat's confusion. "There's been a deal," he says. "Yulya, Sayer, Russia, the United States, whatever. The British clear up the mess."

They're traveling on a wider road now, parallel with the coastline, under a canopy of trees. Sunlight through leaves dapples Luxton's face.

The vehicles turn left through a black metal gate in a high brick wall and past a lodge house. They drive along a narrow road of yellow asphalt through parkland of uncut grass; past a large, old, red brick house with high bay windows, narrow chimneys, and a carriage driveway; on past clusters of outlying sheds, houses, and stables; then around to a paddock where horse jumps, freshly painted in bright yellows, reds, and blues, have been pushed to the fence to make enough space for the helicopter to land.

It's coming down as they pull up. The rotor blade noise sends pigeons flying out from the woodland. Roth cuts the car engine, gets out, and opens Kat's door like a chauffeur. "This way, ma'am," he says.

As soon as Luxton's out of the car, he runs toward the helicopter. Liz, Grachev, and Yulya are still on board. There's the atmosphere of one of the RingSet camps—once inside, no need for cuffs. Whether victim or executioner, you are a player in a written master plan. They'll take you when they want, and no one will stop them.

Kat walks over to her father, who's leaning heavily on his car's roof, his sleeve ripped and hanging like a rag.

He looks up at her. "Are you okay?"

She nods. "And you?"

His breathing is short and shallow, and his skin stretches tight across his face. He lifts his hand to check a cut above his right eye, then wipes saliva from the edge of his mouth.

"It won't be natural causes that kill us today," he says, managing a smile. His concentration wavers, and his eyes move beyond Kat; she turns to find she's facing Nate Sayer.

The two men gaze at each other, eyes flickering between mistrust and a broken friendship.

Sayer doesn't move forward, just stands, his hands clasped in front of him, his head slightly lowered, his eyes flitting onto Polinski's and off again, not wanting to hold his gaze. He doesn't look at Kat at all.

"I'm not proud of what I did, and what I'm still doing. But it's keeping us all alive," he says.

"The day they took me in Lancaster—" Polinski's voice is raw and weak. He steadies himself against the car.

"I guided them there, John. If I hadn't, they'd have killed you."

Polinski says nothing. His head drops, drained of strength.

"After all we'd done together . . ."

Sayer's expression hardens. He steps forward, takes Polinski's elbow. "You were going too far. You knew it, but you couldn't stop yourself."

"Too far for whom?"

"You were my best friend, but—"

"Too far for whom?" Polinski repeats, shifting his weight, clutching Sayer's shoulder and wincing as pain shoots through him.

Kat puts her hands on his other arm. "Dad, don't," she whispers, her eyes darting angrily at Sayer. "Back the fuck off, Nate."

At the edge of the woodland, the engine of a backhoe starts up. It sends a young pheasant into the air.

Yulya jumps down from the helicopter. She arches her back, fingers hooked into her belt.

She's wearing a red shirt, faded blue denim jeans with a wide belt, and knee-length leather boots. She walks toward Kat. The way the sun catches her face makes crow's-feet crinkle across her face—youth, elegance, malice, and hardship, all mapped onto the skin of a beautiful woman.

Her eyes are alert, but gray and flat. Kat's seen the look in Dix Street on people who measure their self-confidence by how much they can destroy.

Yulya flips the butterfly safety button of a Beretta 9mm, the same weapon carried by the gunmen at the Kazakh embassy. She slips out the magazine, the extended version that carries 20 rounds instead of 17, checks it, and pushes it back in again.

Grachev gets out on the other side of the helicopter and walks to the fence on the far side of the paddock. The pilot stays in the cockpit. Sayer's face is dull, eyes drifting toward Yulya.

Across the paddock, Kat catches Grachev's expression, nervous, helpless, maybe. He makes no effort to stop what happens next.

Yulya's eyes linger on Polinski and Sayer, but it's Kat who interests her. She grips Kat's shoulder, backhands her viciously across her face with her pistol. "I should have done it before," she says. "That's for Alex."

She punches the gun into Kat's stomach. "For Vadim."

Kat puts her hands up in front of her to break the fall, but Yulya kicks them away, and Kat goes down. Yulya squats beside her, pulls her head up by the hair, puts her mouth close to Kat's ear and whispers, "Marcel Lancaric. Remember him?"

She pushes Kat's head back down. Her forehead hits a stone embedded in the soil, and she feels the blood damp in her hair. The sharp edges of Suzy's ring bite into her thigh through the jumpsuit. Her cheek throbs like a chain's cut across her jaw.

Yulya turns Kat onto her back as if she's a corpse and presses her knee into her stomach. Her expression is hard and functional, with no humanity, no conscience.

Kat strikes with both hands. Yulya blocks her, lands a blow on Kat just below her left temple, but when Yulya goes to strike again, Kat shifts enough to kick her behind the knee.

Yulya stumbles, and Kat scrambles to her feet. Yulya's raising her gun hand, steadying herself, eyes on Kat, satisfaction rippling down her face.

There's more than six feet between them, good for a clean shot, but too far for Kat to defend herself.

"Get back down," says Yulya.

Far away, Mason and Roth lift Dane's body down from the jeep and carry it to the edge of the woodland. The backhoe jerks backward, and its serrated blade cuts into the ground and tips damp soil aside.

Grachev walks a few steps across the paddock, leans on the fence.

Kat's down, as Yulya commanded. The grass is damp, smelling of horse manure. Yulya's shadow falls across Kat. The Beretta in her right hand targets her. It could be now, Kat knows, or it could be that Yulya wants to keep playing until she breaks Kat.

The biggest loss a psychopath can suffer is control, whether physical or psychological. Kat doesn't plan to let Yulya keep it.

"What does *soo-ch-car* mean," Kat says conversationally. "I'd really like to know. Is it Russian?"

Yulya's forefinger tenses inside the trigger guard.

"See, it's one of the last things Marcel Lancaric said to me before I shot him."

"It means *little bitch*," Yulya says quietly.

"That's right. That's what he called me. I said it was because of you that I was killing him."

The muscles around Yulya's brow tighten. But if Kat's read her right, Yulya won't kill until she's regained the ground.

"He also said you thought you were a hot babe in bed. But guys say it's like screwing a beached whale."

"Shut up," whispers Yulya.

"So that's why he never let you fuck him."

Grachev takes his hands off the top bar of the fence, lets them hang.

"You are an idiot," says Yulya. "Just like your sister."

Her face is smooth and stiff, not yet ready to pull the trigger. Kat moves an inch on the ground. "That's funny," she mocks. "That's exactly what Marcel said about you. Yulya Gracheva was so dumb she—"

The shot comes, but not from Yulya.

SIXTY-SIX

---◇---

Friday, 4:03 p.m., BST

The bullet strikes the fence post next to Kat, sending wood splinters into the air. The second one splits a stone near Yulya's feet, throwing sparks.

As Sayer stops firing, Grachev puts three rounds through the open helicopter door, hitting the pilot, then shifting his aim slightly to let off two shots at the backhoe driver, who must have been at the very limit of his range. The driver slumps over the wheel.

Mason, pulling his pistol from his holster, moves for Grachev.

"Leave him, Sergeant," shouts Sayer. Confusion crosses Yulya's face.

"Drop it, Miss Gracheva," says Sayer. "If you kill her, I'll make damn sure your whole world dies."

Yulya doesn't move. Nor does Sayer. If Yulya shoots, Yulya dies. The call is hers.

Mason's next to Sayer, covering Yulya. Roth has stayed on the other side of the paddock, his carbine checking everyone.

"Hand over Suzy's file," says Sayer to Kat. "If you don't, Mason will search you for it."

Kat reaches to the small of her back, tears off the tiny package that she taped there in Tappler's kitchen the evening before.

"It's not all there," she says, holding it out. "Water damage." Sayer takes it, unwraps the polyethylene, pulls a cell phone from his pocket, slips in the

SIM card, turns it on, and walks over to Grachev. He shows Grachev what comes up on the screen.

Grachev nods.

Yulya rests her weapon on her folded arms. Mason offers Kat a hand and helps her up from the ground. A cluster of midges fly into her face, and she swishes them away.

Grachev walks over to Kat, his limp from the bombing noticeable, and takes her out of earshot. He leans his rifle against a fence post. "We have the copy in your Internet file. The FBI has the two copies you gave to Bill Cage. Tell me there are no more copies."

"There are no more copies," mimics Kat.

"Thank you."

"Well done, Max," says Kat dryly. "Good work for a cop whose sister tried to kill him."

Grachev's tone becomes soft, persuasive, frustrated. "You will do now what you refused to do on Monday when I talked to you in the park. You are still alive because Nate Sayer is here. He has stopped Yulya from killing you. I don't like Nate, but I have an agreement with him; think of it as an agreement between Russia and the United States. Yulya lives, and you and our father live. We keep the SIM card. Sayer's vehicles have diplomatic clearance to go to Heathrow airport. From there, you will go to Washington. This time, do exactly as I say. I'm asking you to save our father's life."

"You're evil, Max, like her."

"I have a duty to my family, to my country, and to what is right. If you ever find a situation when these three duties agree with each other, let me know."

He begins to walk toward Yulya. Kat catches him by the shoulder, pulls to spin him around. "What are you saying, Max? You doing it to please Mommy? You can't just—"

"That's the arrangement," says Grachev. "In better times, maybe later, I can get to know you as a sister to love and admire, but not now. It is impossible."

"Kat, drop it." The interruption comes from Sayer. "For Christ's sake, just this once, drop it."

"No, she won't drop it." Even breaking with fatigue, John Polinski's voice commands. "She's my daughter. We see things through."

Grachev picks up his rifle and walks toward the line of cars. After Polinski's outburst, no one is speaking. Grachev's engine fires up in the silence. As he pulls away, his window comes down, and he glances at Polinski, then Kat. He doesn't look at Yulya. Then he is gone, down the long driveway.

Kat moves to her father and takes his hand. Sayer joins them. "Who picks up the pieces, John, when people like you and Kat see things through?" he says, his voice soft but angry. "Who makes the compromises? People like Max and me. That's who—when the idealists are saving the planet."

Polinski shakes his head. "Who was it who said bad deeds carried out by good men are all the more evil, because they know better and do it anyway?"

"You never looked deep enough to see the damage," answers Sayer.

Polinski doesn't reply. His balance goes, and he stumbles. Sayer catches him by one arm, Kat by the other.

So Yulya goes free. There's something crazy about the past few days, and she's just going to watch Suzy's killer, with Suzy's History Book, sashay out of it all. But there's something sane about what Sayer's telling her. Her dad's alive, and Yulya was going to kill him. On the surface, it's a good deal. The only thing is that Kat's working out a way to make sure it doesn't happen like that.

"Nate's right, Dad," she says with a forced smile. "Let's call it a day."

Polinski's eyes drop to the ground. His hand grips Kat's.

Kat looks across to Sayer. "I'll ride with you. Dad and Mike can ride together."

SIXTY-SEVEN

◇

They leave Yulya at the paddock and hit heavy Friday-evening traffic heading south along the expressway to London in a two-car diplomatic convoy, American flags flying on the hoods. Sayer's in the backseat of the lead car with Kat. Mason's driving. Polinski and Luxton are in the car behind, driven by Roth.

There's a lot to say, but no conversation. Kat tries to read Sayer's face, but he's giving her nothing. Kat's calculating. She reckons she's got until London. After that, it'll be too late.

They stop at a mall. Sayer buys Kat, Polinski, and Luxton towels and fresh sets of clothes. They don't shower, but in the mall bathrooms, they dry themselves and change.

"Mason was only half right," says Sayer after they set off again. He holds up the bag with the cartridge case Kat found in the marshes. "It's not a 7.62. It's a 9mm, from a Russian sniper rifle called the VSS. It's silenced. Pretty rare gun, based on the 7.62, but ramped up to take the 9mm round."

"Yulya's?" asks Kat.

"No evidence of that. It's not the most accurate long-range weapon in the world. Five hundred meters, at best. But it packs a wallop. The slug's designed to go through body armor, but it doesn't mushroom and disfigure like a normal bullet. They started using it in Chechnya. Made forensics and body identification easier, apparently."

"Who pulled the trigger?"

"It doesn't matter. Like I said, you've got to stop."

"Have you got the weapon?"

"No. And stop asking. Stop thinking."

"Max and Yulya get away?"

"Max is clean. He was working with me. The Russian government will handle Yulya."

"You and he cut a deal?"

"He saved Yulya. I saved you and John."

"And those people held in Kazakhstan with Dad—"

"Shit happens."

"And the lies? Are you going to live with all the fucking lies?"

His eyes flit out to the road, then back at Kat, brow creased. "Sergeant, pull over at the next stop, will you?" Mason pulls in. The second car follows. Sayer gets out. "Come with me, Kat," he says.

He walks up a grass bank to a field. Sayer rests one hand on a fence post, waiting for Kat to catch up.

"I couldn't say this on the boat when I wanted to, so I'll say it now." He jabs his finger against Kat's shoulder. "The next time you fuck with my marriage, I'll hang you out to dry."

Kat knocks his hand away. "Suffered some collateral damage, did you?"

"Nancy's in Washington," says Sayer, his tone quieter.

"Good for her."

"It's what you said to her that sent her."

Kat shrugs. "She won't leave you, if that's what's worrying you. That's what she told me, anyway."

"The house there was broken into."

Kat turns her head toward the field, lets her eyes follow a path toward a copse of trees.

Mercedes Vendetta, thank God for him, has done what she asked and broken into Sayer's R Street house.

"Anything taken?"

"They only did the safe. And only you know what's in there."

"I seem to remember it was insurance. If you go down, others go down with you."

Down the bank, Mason's leaning on the hood of the car, eyes alert toward the expressway. Roth has gotten out of the second car. He watches inward, toward the field.

"John'll go down," he says. "I did bad things for him, even if he didn't know it. Suzy, too. Or her reputation. She worked closely with John."

"Others?"

"Others, too. Powerful people."

"Who?"

"Doesn't matter to you, Kat, because it won't get you Suzy's killer."

"I did it, Nate. I had your safe broken into."

Sayer's eyes flare. He's guessed or he wouldn't have wanted to have talked to Kat away from the car and Mason.

"I don't have to give those files to anyone," says Kat. "Or maybe I do. It's your call."

"How? Who? Was it Cage?"

"It was private. You'll never get to it."

"Without me, you'd have been dead. John'd be dead, too. And this is how you repay me?"

Vendetta's still free, or Sayer wouldn't be so rattled. He'll piece it together sooner or later. But what's he going to do? He'd have to deal with Vendetta himself. And Kat can't imagine Sayer walking down Dix Street.

"No one needs to go down," she says.

"And?" Sayer swallows and calms. He drums the fence post with his fingers and keeps his eyes on Kat, who says nothing. "You want Yulya?"

"Yes."

"I can't help you."

"I don't want help. Take Dad with you," says Kat. "Get him checked by a doctor. Take care of him. Protect him. Let Mike go. Just don't stop us." She holds out her hand, palm flat. "And leave the shell casing with me. It's the only evidence I have."

Sayer gives her the plastic bag with the casing. Kat pushes it into her pants pocket. He turns his back to her, goes down the bank, talks to Mason, who opens Luxton's door, and points up to Kat. Luxton gets out and walks toward her.

From the high ground at the edge of the field, Kat and Luxton watch Sayer's convoy leave. She waves to her father. He waves weakly back. He's too far away for her to see his face.

"Well done," says Luxton. He leads. They cross the field to a footpath that takes them through woodlands.

"Is there somewhere we can go, rest up, work things out?" says Kat.

"You're looking at it." Luxton's setting the pace, knocking branches and high plants out of his way. "If we go to a hotel, we're marked, even if we pay cash. The computer will alert the authorities if our ID puts us as living closer than a thirty-mile radius, if our credit card doesn't match the car number, if our biometrics don't match."

"Why are we walking so fast then?"

"If Tappler was bent, it means Cranley might be bent, which means Liz—wherever she is—she's in trouble."

He doesn't say *if she's still alive*, but it hangs with them. He stops at the edge of the woods. Twenty yards ahead is a main road, hood to trunk with cars backed up against a rotary. On the other side is a gas station; beyond that a shopping mall with the parking lot packed. It's Friday evening. The place is jumping.

"Wait here," says Luxton.

"Wait! I need to know what you're thinking."

"To get a vehicle and go to London."

"And when you get there, what are you going to do?" Her hands are on his shoulders, shaking him. His face is cut. The bandage on his hand is dirty with dried blood. His eyes look as red as hers feel. "How does that help you find Liz?"

His hand goes onto hers. There's anger in his touch, affection, too.

"You're chasing your sister's killer," he says. "I want to get to Liz before I have a killer to chase."

Kat puts her knuckle to her mouth. "Yeah," she says softly.

Luxton points across the road to the mall. "I need a car. I need a phone. I need money. I need weapons."

"This is England," says Kat. "Guns are illegal."

"There's a place. It should be empty, no one expecting us."

SIXTY-EIGHT

$$\diamondsuit$$

Friday, 8:40 p.m., BST

Luxton and Kat are five miles from Cherry Tree Farm in Bradfield St. Mark in a Land Rover SUV that Luxton stole from the mall parking lot. Luxton's driving. They have cash taken out of ATMs from three different cards and four cell phones. One is neutralizing the Land Rover's tracking system. Another's been used three times: a call to Liz, then one to Cranley. Both calls were put through to voice mail. Then, Kat switched the SIM card and made a fast call to Mercedes Vendetta. He picked up. She told him what she needed. They buried the phone, with its SIM card, three feet down in soft earth to weaken the tracking signal.

They drove through a small town where the TV screens showed President Jim Abbott with Prime Minister Michael Rand, a shot of them at the door of an English country house, with the caption underneath ABBOTT AT CHEQUERS ON EVE OF SUMMIT. The Russian, Chinese, and other leaders are due to be at Chequers for dinner, too. The signing is to take place at the historic palace of Hampton Court, just outside of London on the Thames River.

The sports screen showed fans draped in the red-on-white cross of the English flag, outside the stadium, laying out sleeping bags for the night. The England–Brazil final was to kick off at 1:00. The CPS signing was scheduled for 12:45.

A rolling caption beneath the news screen said a cargo plane had crashed into the North Sea, with no casualties.

Luxton slows, but drives straight past Cherry Tree Farm. Lights are on in the kitchen and the living room where Kat, Tappler, and Cranley watched Suzy's History Book. The curtains are half drawn. A light's on in the bathroom upstairs. The Toyota Highlander is gone. The Mini Cooper and the blue Jaguar are still there.

Tappler's house is exposed across a freshly harvested field in the front, but protected by a wooded garden and high trees in the back. It's set back from the road in the village. It's partly isolated, but not enough to make it a perfect retreat. Their advantage is that Kat has approached it before. The problem is that Cranley and Tappler saw her.

Luxton's also been there. He went in through the front door, and Tappler showed him how his security system worked. Luxton knows the field of view of the cameras, the pressure pads under the lawn and the driveway, the infrared cordon across the garden and the front approach. He knows the code on the wall pads, one inside the front hallway, one by the back door. He knows he will have 20 seconds to punch in the six-digit code. That's if Tappler hasn't changed it or if it doesn't rotate automatically.

He knows that inside the main house, where Kat went, visitors see a rambling farmhouse, welcoming, shabby, outdated. But in the garden sheds outside, he knows that Tappler keeps an arsenal.

If it weren't for that, they wouldn't be here. They have everything they need except guns.

Luxton parks on a farm track half a mile up the road. They leave the cell phone connected in the hope the vehicle stays invisible. They walk back toward the house. It's dark, and there's no moon.

They enter the village along a narrow road, with cottages on one side and open land on the other. Kat can make out a building and soccer field goalposts. At an intersection, there's a school on the right, two thatched houses on the left, and straight ahead, slightly to the left, is Cherry Tree Farm.

About 200 yards to the right is a bigger road with steady traffic. To the left, the road runs down a hill and curves away. The hedge that separates Tappler's house from the road has a gap for the path leading to the front door.

The storehouse, where the weapons are, lies 50 yards up the driveway, beyond the vehicles. Luxton doesn't know if the buildings are individually alarmed or linked to the central system inside the house. He does know that Tappler separated the weapons into two caches.

His automatic rifles and sidearms are in a locked metal cabinet in the room at the back of the building. When Tappler showed them to him, Luxton saw 5.26mm light machine guns, AK-47s, M16s with M20 grenade launchers, Heckler & Koch 7.62 automatics, and others.

The ammunition was kept in an air-conditioned cellar accessed through a trapdoor hidden by a rubber mat on the floor, together with two M72 LAW rocket-propelled grenade launchers.

Tappler revealed the weapons to gain trust—proof that he would oppose the CPS, with violence, if necessary.

Kat moves ahead of Luxton, skirts around the edge of the property toward the back of the house, the same way she did before. Luxton stays across the road.

She watches the garden. She watches for a shadow cast by movement across a lightbulb. The garden is hued with light from the house. She can see an outline of the long brick storehouse with its skewed, mossy, tiled roof where, if Luxton is right, they can arm themselves.

Her cell vibrates. It's a message from Vendetta, who confirms that he has the SIM card Kat gave him on Dix Street and he's in the place where Kat told him to go, a café on P Street, with soft chairs and Wi-Fi, where people hang out for hours at a time.

Kat sends a text message to Luxton. He responds immediately.

Luxton's good. He's quiet. She doesn't see him until he's lit up for a beat by a flash of the orange sidelights of the Mini Cooper as he unlocks the vehicle with a message programmed by Kat and sent from his cell phone.

All those years back, she used the same system to get into Nate Sayer's safe. If you get the frequency right, there's no difference between a cell phone and a car key.

The Mini's interior light comes on. Luxton opens the glove compartment, gets what he needs, and closes the car door. Tappler's wife, away in France with the children, had left the remote to turn off the house alarm in the car. Even if there were an automatic code rotation, the remote would have kept up.

For a second, spotlights flare on in the garden, then die. An alarm inside the house beeps. Then there is quiet. Luxton walks up the driveway to the storehouse. There's been no beep, no flare from the storehouse. The alarms aren't linked, and Luxton hasn't seen it. They don't know where the cordon is.

There's no time to text. Any moment she could stand on a pressure pad under the grass, but Kat runs across the lawn, and when she's close enough, she shouts to Luxton.

He stops. She reaches him and explains. They go to the house.

The back door has two locks; one computerized, which has been opened by the remote, and one Yale cylinder deadbolt, which Kat opens in less than ten seconds.

They step inside. Both of them are familiar with the house. There's no sound. No one there. The lights are on, but the windows are closed.

It's been just over 24 hours since Simon Tappler drove Kat through country lanes until she found a motorcycle to steal. She spent almost three hours watching the RingSet base at Byford before killing Lancaric and boarding the plane.

Luxton closes the door quietly behind them. They are in the kitchen. No alarm goes off. There's a stuffiness in the air, thicker than for a house that's only been left empty for a day, something that catches in the back of Kat's throat.

Luxton pushes open the door to the living room. The smell becomes more pungent. "A lot of questions answered," he says flatly.

Cranley's body lies behind the sofa with a sheet draped over it. He's been shot in the back of the head.

SIXTY-NINE

The back lawn, which slopes uphill from the house, ends in an apple or-chard, and this is where Kat and Luxton bury Stephen Cranley's body. They don't speak. There is no ceremony. The grave is shallow.

Afterward, Luxton finds the keys for the storehouse and heads out. Kat closes the kitchen door and opens the window to clear the mustiness. She sees a light flashing on the landline phone—the voice mail.

"Stephen, Simon, are you there? It's Liz. Phone me as soon as you c-can."

The message is time stamped 5:23—seventeen hours ago. Liz left a num-ber, but Kat doesn't use it. Instead, she calls Bill Cage.

"Cranley's dead," she says.

"How?"

"Tappler shot him."

"Where are you?"

Kat doesn't say. "What's happening with the CPS?" she asks.

"Abbott's in England. If he signs, we lose. If he doesn't, we survive."

"In Washington?"

"Nobody's moving. The cops, the military, Congress, business. Every-one's waiting, like an African town riding out a coup."

"Two things." She recites the number Liz left. "First, trace it. I need to know exactly where she is. Or was. Then, set up a secure route for me to call it."

"Okay."

"And there's a guy you need to see. Large, black, slightly crazy eyes." Kat gives Cage the address of the café on P Street.

For the next hour, Kat strips and reformats Tappler's laptop. She practically builds a new computer that cannot be tracked. She's so immersed that the opening of the kitchen door makes her jerk around.

"Take your pick," says Luxton. He lays a Colt 45, a Glock 18 automatic, and a Heckler & Koch 9mm MP5 submachine gun on the table. "The rest are in the car. I'll bring in some other stuff in case we need it overnight. Then I'll reset the alarms."

Kat slips a power cable into the laptop and boots it up. Luxton washes his hands. Cage calls back.

"It's a cell phone," says Cage. "Right now, it's on the third floor of the central Media Axis building in London. Give it sixty seconds from when I hang up. I've rerouted your line. You will be secure for at least three minutes."

"Thanks," says Kat, ending the call. She looks up at Luxton. "Liz left a message on Tappler's voice mail. Cage tracked her."

Luxton pulls out a chair, leans on it. "Where is she?"

"Media Axis. Or at least the phone is."

"Jesus," he says. "How?"

"I've fixed it so we can make a secure call to that number." She holds out the landline's handset to him. He takes it.

"Untraceable?"

"For three minutes. But I need two minutes with her."

Luxton dials. Kat saw some feeling in Luxton when he made her a daisy chain, although it was tempered by mistrust. But now, as he talks to his sister, he is awash with humanity. Kat leaves the room to let them talk, but a minute later steps back in again, and Luxton is wiping a tear from his cheek.

"Speak soon," he says.

As he hands the phone to Kat, she asks, "Is she—?"

"Yes," he says.

"Liz?" says Kat, taking the phone.

"What c-can I do?"

"How safe are you?"

"Everyone's waiting until tomorrow. Stephen Cranley got me out of jail. I'm at work."

"Can you get into the edit suite where I left Suzy's file?"

"Yes."

"You got a pen?" Very slowly and precisely, Kat dictates to Liz the code to get through the digital walls she put around Suzy's file. Liz repeats it back. Kat tells Liz what she wants. "Once you've done that, separate it off, copy it, and send it to this e-mail address."

With the call ended, Kat leans back in the chair, puts her feet up on the table, and covers her face with her hands.

"Will it work?" says Luxton.

"Your sister will create a masterpiece they will never forget."

"Thank you," he says.

"For what?"

"Getting me out of that Voz Island hellhole."

"Thank you for getting us here."

He laughs briefly, perches on the windowsill, lights a cigarette, and looks out over the garden. There's a moon of sorts draping it in a hazy glow. "This must be the safest house in England tonight," he says, exhaling so the smell of tobacco smoke drifts across to Kat.

Kat thinks of her call to Cage, the vehicle, and a million other ways they could track her here. But they're armed. She has a plan. As Luxton says, this is the last house they might think of coming to, and she's decided, once they find Liz, what she is going to do.

She picks up the Colt, waits for him to finish his cigarette, then takes Luxton by the hand, leads him up the stairs, to the bedroom where she'd bathed and changed the day before. She closes the door and puts the Colt on the bedside table.

"Lie down," she says softly. "Don't speak. Just do as I ask."

She lays him on the bed and takes off his clothes. She doesn't speak, nor does she take her eyes off his. His body is firm, and she can see the strength in his shoulders. He lets her take control. She takes off her shirt, sits on top of him, leans down, and kisses him on the mouth, enjoying the lingering smell of nicotine and the taste of male sweat. He cups her breasts with his hands. Then she stands up, slips off her pants, and leans over him, letting her nipples brush across his mouth. She sees teardrops trapped inside his eyes.

She puts him inside her, puts her mouth on his, takes each hand and entwines his fingers in hers. She clutches him to her, as close as two people can get, and when she feels him quiver and she begins to come herself, she lets out a little cry, closes her eyes to blackness, knowing that whatever happens tomorrow, nothing will destroy the common ground they've just created.

She rolls off him and lies next to him, letting him cradle her, thinking she needs to rebuild herself into a woman again before she goes out to fight Yulya Gracheva.

SEVENTY

$\longrightarrow\!\diamondsuit\!\longrightarrow$

Saturday, 6:23 a.m., BST

World leaders will begin arriving at Hampton Court Palace shortly after 1:30 to attend a reception in the Great Hall among 16th-century Flemish tapestries that illustrate the biblical story of Abraham.

An orchestra will play a mix of multicultural music from the Minstrels Gallery that overlooks the hall. After the signing, delegates will move out to the gardens, where they can talk privately among orange trees planted by King William III, Prince of Orange, and lime trees planted by King Charles II in honor of his Portuguese wife, Catherine of Braganza.

Alone in the kitchen, with Luxton asleep upstairs, the Colt 45 within arm's reach, Kat reads through the itinerary for the CPS signing. Cage is due to call at any time. He should be ready to send her data from the SIM card kept by Vendetta, the raw material from Suzy's History Book. Kat will load it into the laptop. Then, Cage will secure the line for her to call Liz, who will send across the parts she has edited.

In all, Kat reads, 187 world leaders or their representatives will attend. Many are flying there by helicopter from Heathrow airport. Others are driving in from London. Rogue nations have not been invited. A few states have boycotted.

For the signing itself, the leaders of the three primary powers, the United States, China, and Russia, will sit in the center of a long wooden table.

Other leaders will be on their flanks, ranked not alphabetically but by the size of their economies.

In the center of the room will gather leaders of the world's most powerful nations. On the fringes will be the weakest. Behind political leaders will sit business leaders. Tiina Gracheva from RingSet is listed as a representative for Russia.

The signing is due to take fifteen minutes, with Abbott, as leader of the world's biggest economy, making the last speech. When he ends, the signing begins, then over on the other side of London, the England–Brazil match will kick off.

At this stage, CPS delegates will be joined by community representatives from their countries, chosen by lottery. In the United States, one lottery winner has been the Strongcross Sports and Community Center from Iowa.

While delegates mingle, images of the game will be superimposed around the tapestries, on dark wood walls, and across the lawns, onto enormous screens erected in the gardens.

In the evening, the British prime minister will host a reception at Downing Street for the Brazil and England teams—whatever the result.

Kat checks several sites and keeps her eye on the television. There's nothing public about Abbott's precise itinerary, except that he's at the prime minister's country house near a village called Princess Risborough in Buckinghamshire—about a hundred miles southwest of where she is now.

No one matters except Abbott. Kat doesn't have much political instinct, but she can't see how Abbott can sign, especially with Tiina Gracheva in the room, once confronted with the images from Voz Island.

She answers the phone. It's Cage. "I'm ready," she says, tapping the Accept key on the laptop. A green light flickers on the laptop, and the download begins.

"It's big. It'll take a couple of minutes," says Cage. The download begins.

"Is Abbott using Marine One to get to Hampton Court?" asks Kat, referring to the presidential helicopter.

"Yes. He leaves Chequers at 11:35. Due at Hampton Court at 12:00."

"Early."

"That's how Abbott likes it."

"Can we get into Marine One's communications?"

"Audio or video?"

"Video. We can't get through at Chequers, because it's run by the British. But we have a brief window when he's on Marine One."

"I'll check."

"One more thing. Javier Laja's cell number. The right one. The one he'll have until he goes onto the soccer field."

"That'll be done."

"Any word from Dad?"

"Not directly. He's with Sayer, and he's safe. Sayer's sitting on the fence and holding his breath like everyone else, I'd imagine."

"Dad's the evidence," says Kat.

"Exactly. Sayer will use him or destroy him. Depends how the wind blows."

"Hold on," says Kat. The download finishes. She opens it to the picture of Yulya she first saw a week ago at the Kazakh embassy. "It's good, Bill. It's good," she says excitedly. "We'll talk in half an hour—after I have the stuff from Liz."

Kat now has one full copy of the file on the reformatted hard drive. Through the kitchen window, she sees a glimpse of dawn. It'll be a long day, but by the end, Kat will either have won or be dead.

She dials Liz Luxton.

"Ten sections," says Liz. "All about twenty seconds. Ready to go. N-now."

Kat presses Accept on the laptop. The download only takes seconds. Before Kat flips open the file to check, Liz says, "Things are d-difficult. I've got to go."

A photo comes up: Yulya about to murder the peasants. Liz's line's dead. Kat redials. A voice says "Incorrect number."

Luxton's hand is on her shoulder.

"What?" she asks, more brusquely than she intended.

"The police are setting up a checkpoint at the intersection," says Luxton calmly. "Come upstairs."

Kat takes the Colt. Luxton's got the Glock 18 and the 9mm. The bedroom light is off. Luxton kneels on the bed's rumpled sheets, ducking his head where the beamed roof slopes down. He points through the gap in the curtain without moving it and moves back for Kat to look.

Two police cars, blue lights turning, parked diagonally, hoods together, block the northbound lane. Officers with flashlights stand on the south-bound lane. It's early. There's no traffic.

"Over to your right, on the electricity pole at the corner of the school playground," says Luxton. It takes a moment, but Kat sees a hidden video camera there, pointing straight at the entrance to Cherry Tree Farm. "I missed it," he says.

Kat looks to her right and sees an English village at dawn, the people not yet awake.

"It might be the camera. Might not," says Luxton. "They could have found the Land Rover. They could have intercepted your calls. They could have been tracking Liz."

"Even tracking Cage," adds Kat. "Or it might have nothing to do with us."

"Maybe," says Luxton. "But in minutes, we could be under siege." He slides off the bed. She lets him take her hand and lead her downstairs.

SEVENTY-ONE

◇

Saturday, 7:01 a.m., BST

The Mini Cooper is registered in the name of Jennifer Tappler. It's licensed until December 18, was bought less than a year ago, has a 1.6-liter engine, and a tank full of gas. In the back is a torn schoolbook, a model airplane with a broken wing, and a party whistle, along with a floral blue car seat.

Luxton is wearing a yellow jacket with POLICE stenciled on the back below the insignia of the Port of Felixstowe. "It was hanging in the shed," he says, as Kat gets in. "The port carries weight around here. So it might be useful."

Kat keeps the laptop and phones with her. She looks behind. A blanket's on the floor. She leans back, feels the reassuring shapes of the weapons underneath.

"I reckon it's been set up by local police," says Luxton. "If it's a Project Peace issue, they won't do anything until the big boys arrive. The Mini Cooper's a locally registered car. There'd be no official record of Simon Tappler leaving the country. There might be none of Jennifer and the kids being gone as well. It's summer. People travel."

Luxton drives out slowly, turns right, and heads down the hill and around a curve to the left, where the road narrows even further and dips between high banks thick with high summer grass.

He keeps to side roads, going north. The farther they are from London, the safer they are from detection. He takes a byway that winds past two farmhouses, where dogs bark and tractors have left the road thick with fallen manure and harvested straw.

He drives for more than an hour. The landscape becomes horizon-flat, greens and yellows, dotted with buildings and trees, but no hill or slope for as far as the eye can see. He turns into a track that leads to a forest and stops.

"Keep going," says Kat.

Luxton looks at her curiously.

"Put us under the trees," she explains. "Cover from satellite cameras."

Luxton gets out, leaving his door open. Crisp air fills the small car. He lights a cigarette, walks into the trees, walks back again, paces around. The cell phones and their SIM cards may be compromised, but she'll have to use them. Tappler's laptop is so old, it has no means of wireless transmission outside the house.

Six hours from now, Abbott will leave in Marine One to go to Hampton Court. Eight hours, and he will have signed the CPS. If they drive toward London, they won't get past the first big checkpoint.

Luxton opens the back door, brings out a light machine gun from the back of the car with boxes of ammunition. He's found a hidden place on flat ground where they can see to the horizon on all sides. To the west, mist rolls low across the fields. To the east, the rising sun creates a pink glow in the sky.

If anyone approaches by land, it'll be along the track they've just driven up. He'll see them a mile or more away. If they come by air, the Heckler & Koch 13E can damage aircraft up to 400 meters in the air.

Luxton props up other weapons against trees around the car. If there's going to be a siege, he wants it on his own terms.

Kat opens her door, swings her feet out, sets up the laptop, and opens the file Liz sent her.

It's brilliant.

Liz has created ten minifilms, five of them straight from Suzy's History Book. For the others, she has used a fast image technique of juxtaposing images of Abbott against the results of his policies. Yulya is killing the farmers. Yulya and Tiina are handing out share certificates to the surviving family members. Abbott is meeting Tiina at a White House ceremony. Abbott shares a split screen with Yulya.

Faced with a split-second decision while looking at the deaths of unknown people, a U.S. president might do nothing. But if he's associated with the picture, things will look different.

As Kat copies the files onto the cell phone, Luxton's shadow appears above her. "If they're tracking us, they could come at any time. If they go into Tappler's house and if they find Cranley's grave and put two and two together, then I guess we have another hour before they come. What I suggest is we wait an hour. You send the files. Then we split."

Kat leans on the hood, the Colt and an AK-47 automatic next to her. Luxton is at the edge of the trees to the back of the vehicle. They each have a 180-degree field of view. Kat faces east into the sun. She watches the early-morning pink turn to a blue summer glow. She watches a tractor start up more than a mile away, its sound reaching her seconds later. She smells Luxton's cigarette smoke drifting through the woods toward her. She sees a car wind down a faraway road and disappear between a cluster of buildings.

She plays back to herself Liz's last words. *Things are d-difficult. I've got to go.* Kat told Luxton what Liz said.

When she closes her eyes, she hopes to see herself curled up with Luxton, moonlight dancing through the curtains. But she sees Dane's body, bumping against her in the sea, and the fuselage looming up against her. So she keeps her eyes open and fixed on the farmland in front of her.

No aircraft is in the sky. No vehicle comes toward them. She hears Luxton's footsteps on fallen leaves. "I'll watch. You concentrate on what you're doing," he says. He stands six feet to the right of the car, where he can see westward through the trees and keep the wide field of view to the east.

She calls Cage. "So can you get the pictures to Marine One?"

"No," says Cage.

At first she doesn't take it in.

"Did you say 'no'?" says Kat. Her voice is raised enough for Luxton to look around. His eyes are steady, not hoping for the impossible, like Kat.

"They've put a blanket alert on all signal traffic. They're aware of a general threat to disrupt the signing of the CPS, but not a specific one involving you."

An intercept on a general threat involves millions of Internet activities.

The intelligence agencies will have authorization to break through passwords and encryptions at will. They will work on words, voice signatures, cell number IDs, IP addresses, vehicle movement, thermal-imaging signatures, biometric and iris data. If you're suspect and you move, they will track you and stop you anywhere in the world.

Kat knows. Cage knows. They've been there and done that.

Cage is telling her that the plan won't work. In calculating her response, Kat thinks back over the past week, from the moment she saw the photo of Yulya at the Kazakh embassy.

"Friday?" says Kat. "Aliya Raktaeva, trade secretary at the Kazakh embassy, was working for you. Suzy was here in England with data she'd compiled in order to expose and destroy the CPS. She was also working for you and with Stephen Cranley. She sends the data from a ring that was specially engineered. You send me in to get it on what should be a routine job. But Suzy has been betrayed—probably by Simon Tappler. Yulya sends her men into the embassy to intercept the file. They kill the staff. They copy the data onto a SIM, but fail to erase it from the hard drive. The rest of that night's history."

"All of that's correct," says Cage, "but—"

"So my point is that Suzy was out on the marshes to send the data directly to a satellite. No risk of Internet intercepts."

"Yes, to an FCA low-orbiting satellite," says Cage. "That way only we get access."

"Each orbit is about ninety minutes?"

"Ninety-eight minutes."

"And that's why Suzy chose the marshes on the east coast. To meet the satellite orbits under a big sky."

"Our bird is two hundred thirty-seven miles up. It bounced the signal straight onto our dedicated paths on the NSA's geosynchronous bird fifteen thousand miles up. We brought that straight down into the Kazakh embassy."

"When's the FCA satellite due overhead next?"

"Where?"

Kat gives him the name of the village they passed through. She waits. Luxton grinds a cigarette butt into damp ground. Seagulls dip and wheel over the fields.

"They work in twelve-minute windows. You've just missed one. So the next is 11:04 British time. Then 12:42. After that 2:20. Then, 3:58, and so on."

"We have two slots before Abbott's on board Marine One."

"Kat," says Cage patiently, as if he's let her go this far but has to stop her now. "Hear me, please. I can't get it to Marine One."

"From an NSA satellite, they just might."

"And how do you plan to get the file there?"

"Same way Suzy did." She has the ring out of her pocket, balancing in the palm of her hand.

"You have her ring?"

"Yes."

"How?"

"Later," says Kat. "But will it still work?"

"It should."

"If we go for the 11:04 slot, can you talk me through?"

"Lay it flat, and see how the corners are chiseled out to take the SIM card. The diamond has been switched—it's difficult to see with the naked eye—to make an antenna. It's also the on-off button and allows contact with the satellite, which locks on and draws up the data."

"How do you know it's working?" says Kat.

"You don't. You can't even test the signal strength. They tell you at the other end that it's come through clean."

"Suzy's did."

"Then this should. But put the best images first in case the transmission gets lost."

Luxton keeps his vigil. The sun is burning off the mist. It has the makings of a clear, hot day. A perfect day for a soccer match. A fine day to sign an international treaty. A harvester combine works a field just over half a mile away.

Kat wants to be ready in forty-five minutes, well before the satellite passes overhead. She arranges the files in alternate order, makes sure that Abbott's face is in the first one. She slots the SIM card into the ring.

She imagines how it might play out: how Abbott will see the images and how his instincts will kick in; how every leader wants to ensure his place in history and how Abbott will decide on his; how he will consult quickly with his advisers on how to withdraw from the CPS for the most credible reason.

Kat gets up, walks to Luxton, drapes her arms around his shoulders from behind, and says, "Thank you."

He keeps his eyes fixed ahead. "For what?"

"For being here for me."

He turns around. They're not on common ground. He's angry and distant, like when she first saw him. "I'm here for Liz," he says.

Kat's about to respond when she hears a bleep from one of the cell phones. She breaks off, goes to the car, where the door is open, with the phones lying on the front seat. The bleep comes from the phone she used to call Cage.

The message is a picture.

SEVENTY-TWO

$\diamond$

Saturday, 8:52 a.m., BST

The image lasts fifteen seconds, a moving picture panning across the faces of five people: Nate Sayer, Mason, Max Grachev, Liz Luxton, and her dad. Their arms are pulled behind their backs, probably cuffed. They are sitting on a floor that looks to be made of concrete. They are squeezed next to each other. They all have bare feet. Liz is in a white tank top covered with an unbuttoned red shirt and jeans. The others are wearing the same clothes as Kat last saw them in: Sayer neat, but crumpled; Mason in uniform; her dad with the guard's outfit from Voz Island. Grachev has only the blue shirt, the jacket gone.

Their heads are bent down, their eyes on their laps. Yulya's giving them no chance to show defiance. On the final frames, when the camera zooms out, Kat sees a high wall, brick at the bottom and corrugated steel above. The picture isn't wide enough to show the roof. The building must be large.

Someone else has the camera. Yulya's standing at the edge of the frame, tapping a pistol barrel against her right knuckle. She turns to the lens and says, "Kat, wait for my call." Then the picture goes to black.

Kat walks over to Luxton and plays it back to him. "Wait for the call," he says. "And keep watching east." He walks to the edge of the woods, his back to Kat. He takes a cigarette out of the pack, puts it to his lips, doesn't light it, takes it out, drops it to the ground, grinds it in with his foot, squats down, his weapon leaning against his knees, puts his chin in his hand, and looks westward.

Kat has Suzy's ring ready to transmit. As soon as the slot opens, Kat will decide. Seventeen minutes later, the call comes.

"Mike," says Kat. Luxton doesn't go to Kat. He moves into the position where he can take over her watch and see as much as possible over a 360-degree sweep. This time, the lens is straight on Yulya's face, no background that Kat can make out.

"Kat," says Yulya. "In other circumstances, you and I could be good friends. I like you a lot. You remind me of myself. You and I aren't to blame for the situation we find ourselves in."

She smiles. It shows up a dimple on her right cheek. "So I want you to listen to what I propose. Is the line clear enough?"

"It is," says Kat.

"All you have to do to resolve the situation is nothing. After one o'clock this afternoon, once the CPS is signed, you can do what you like. You'll feel good about it because you will have saved four lives. They're your lives to do with as you will. Lose them or save them."

Yulya's counted wrong—Grachev, Liz, Mason, Sayer, and her dad. Five. Not four. Kat hopes it's a mistake, a sign that Yulya's frayed and weary.

The camera jerks quickly away from Yulya to show the five hostages, exactly as they were lined up before. Then comes a distorted crack of gunfire that blanks the screen for a few frames, and when it clears, Mason is slumped, his head falling onto Sayer, whose face contorts into an expression of horror.

A man pulls Mason out of the line. Kat recognizes him as Viktor, from the marshes. Mason's not dead. Viktor grabs hold of his arm, pulls him out of frame. Mason screams in pain. Kat hears two shots in quick succession.

"Like I said," says Yulya. "You have four lives to save. All you have to do is nothing, and they will live."

After Mason, Kat guesses, Yulya's next target would be Sayer, moving gradually upward in magnitude, in terms of who means the most to Kat.

The next picture proves Kat wrong again. John Polinksi, his hands shaking, holds a pistol to the head of Max, his son. Viktor holds a gun on Liz.

"The rules are simple, Kat," says Yulya. "I will know if you do anything at all, which includes sending data to low-level satellites, chatting with Bill Cage, anything, then I will order your father to kill Max. If he doesn't obey within five seconds, Viktor will kill Liz. Once that's done, we'll start again. Do you exactly understand the rules?"

SEVENTY-THREE

$\diamond$

Saturday, 10:03 a.m., BST

Luxton smokes, sitting on the hood. Kat walks up and down next to the car.

"Take me through it again," she says. "From us all leaving the paddock."

"Max left first. Alone," says Luxton. "Then we left in two cars, and Yulya stayed behind. Liz was at Media Axis, a hundred miles away. Liz and your father are the real hostages. We don't know about Max and Sayer. They could be decoys."

"Max is real, I think," says Kat. "Yulya tried to kill him with the bomb in his apartment, and he'll always be a threat to her control of RingSet."

"Makes sense," agrees Luxton. "And Max worked with Cranley."

"But then again, so did Tappler," Kat argues against herself.

"Tappler needed money, but Max is a millionaire."

"Which leaves Nate as a possible decoy. He could have had Liz taken at Media Axis. He calls Yulya the minute we leave him with my father."

"What about Roth, the other marine? What happened to him?"

"They killed him straight off. They didn't need him. They only needed Mason to make a point."

Kat replays the short film. She freezes the frame on Sayer's face. He's looking down, his hair a mess, showing baldness on the crown that's usually covered. "Whoever he's working for, would Nate really let Yulya kill Liz, my dad, and Max in cold blood?"

"Go on," says Luxton.

"Whatever the situation, Nate's a hostage. Everyone who works for Ring-Set is. They all work under a shadow of violence." Ideas rush into Kat's mind. "How many airfields does RingSet own?"

"Byford's the big one."

She zooms into the picture, making it even more grainy, and jabs her little finger at the screen. "Hard floor, corrugated steel wall. Could be an airplane hangar. Yulya hasn't gotten so far without being careful. She's not worried about us knowing where she is. She's more worried about getting out quickly when she needs to. I'll bet you she's at Byford. As soon as the CPS is signed, she's flying out with her mother. She'll either kill her hostages or take them with her and dump them at Voz Island."

Luxton says nothing. He packs up the light machine gun, lays it in the back of the car, draped with the blanket. He opens the trunk, brings out a Remington 870 pump-action shotgun for blasting open doors, and lays it on the backseat. He keeps one small M72 disposable antitank rocket launcher in the trunk and moves one to the backseat, together with four loose grenades. He wedges two more grenades between the passenger and driver's seats. He lays an AK-47 on the passenger floor side, and checks and chambers rounds in the handguns and the 9mm automatic and puts them on safety.

"We go?" asks Luxton.

"Yes."

As soon as Suzy's ring links with the satellite, Yulya will know. If Kat speaks to Cage, Yulya will know; anything electronic, Yulya will know. The only element of surprise they have is to kill Yulya at the base. Kat's been there before. She has a plan.

She sets the laptop and three phones a foot away from the right tire and covers them with light earth and damp leaves. She hesitates on the fourth phone. If she uses it to neutralize the car's tracking system, Yulya might know. If they use the car without it, chances are, no one's tracking it. She slips the SIM card with Liz's edited films into Suzy's ring, closes the lid, and makes sure the tiny button is in the Off position.

"Am I right?" she checks with Luxton. "Yulya will know where we are from the phones. But she doesn't know which vehicle we're in."

"Yes, but no way of knowing for sure."

"We'll have to risk it," says Kat.

"So we have no communications at all?"

"That's right."

"It's two hours away," says Luxton. "You drive."

SEVENTY-FOUR

◇

It took less. Kat drove fast. There were no checkpoints.

Kat and Luxton are on a patch of high ground in thick, overgrown grass, watching the entrance to the Byford airfield. When she drove in on Thursday night, it was dark. Today is bright, under a huge blue sky, and security has been ramped up. A sliding antiterror barrier is across the entrance. Two watchtowers have gone up just inside the gate.

For a hundred yards each way from the gate, an extra layer of fencing has been built. You'd have to cut through four sets of wire, each alarmed and at least one electrified. The central fence is topped with concertina wire.

Four guards are at the gate, two patrolling, two inside the control room. The main TV screens are turned off. A bank of monitors is on.

Beyond the fence, a passenger aircraft is parked at a stand, with steps running down from the rear and front doors. Another is taxiing down the runway toward the central area. Kat's just watched it land. To its left are four aircraft hangars, three huge, oblong buildings and one long and narrow, with a roof that curves almost all the way to the ground. Yulya's unlikely to be in there. The curving roofline doesn't fit with the picture Yulya transmitted. That leaves three hangars to choose from.

Civilian traffic on the road is light. The last car came more than ten minutes ago. The RingSet trucks are steady, the same type as Kat hijacked.

But some have an extension on the driver's cab to make room for a sleeping bunk behind the seats. That's the type Kat's looking for.

Kat and Luxton slip back farther into the undergrowth and walk half a mile back to the junction where Kat intercepted Lancaric. The Mini is parked 200 yards farther on. Some of the weapons they left in the car. Some Luxton's loaded onto the car seat and pinned the blanket across them.

Kat stays off the road, lying in a culvert with fast-flowing water soaking into her. It gives her a direct line of fire into the place Luxton's walking to.

He's wearing the yellow jacket with POLICE and the insignia of the Port of Felixstowe embossed on the back, the RingSet logo on the sleeve. He carries the car seat and sits with it on a bank at the side of the road. He picks a stem of grass and chews it.

Kat is 75 yards away. The MP5 is good up to 200 yards.

She hears a truck. It has the bigger driver's cab. Luxton stands up, lifts the car seat with both hands, and begins walking. As the truck nears, he flips out his right thumb to hitchhike and points to the jacket's logo. On Thursday, Lancaric was by himself. This truck has a passenger, a man in a dark jacket, tie, and shirt.

The truck slows and stops. The passenger lets down his window.

Kat's trying to cover Luxton. Her angle to the windshield means she wouldn't be guaranteed to hit the driver. And it's better to have him alive. She adjusts her aim to the head of the passenger, but the wheel is in the way. She goes for the central torso of the passenger. The decision takes less than a second.

Luxton puts the car seat on the ground, turns, and points back toward the Mini, hood up, broken down. The driver refers to the passenger, who's shaking his head.

The exchange lasts fifteen seconds.

Then something happens. Kat thinks it's in the conversation, but she can't be sure because she can't hear what's being said. Luxton climbs up on the step of the cab, draws the Colt, shoots the passenger, and holds the weapon to the driver's head.

Kat scrambles up, crosses the road, and stands right in front of the truck's windshield, weapon on the driver. Luxton runs to the passenger side, drags out the passenger's body, carries it to the ditch. As Luxton rolls it in, Kat glimpses the face. It's Lev, the man who tore down her pants on the marshes, whom Luxton swore to kill.

Luxton lifts the weapons in the blanket from the car seat, puts them on the passenger seat, climbs in, shifts himself and the weapons to the bunk space behind, and puts the Colt to the back of the driver's head.

Kat climbs into the passenger seat and sees how cleverly Luxton shot Lev. No round went out through the chassis or the window.

"Wait," she says.

Luxton keeps the gun on the driver. Kat runs to the ditch. Her hands are in the water underneath Lev's bloodied torso, where she is searching for his cell phone, and finds it in his pants pocket.

She bloodies her hands getting to it, but the phone's stayed dry. She rinses off in the water, jogs back to the truck, and crawls into the bunk. The roof's just high enough to sit. Luxton is hunched up against the cab wall. They are hidden from outside view, but Luxton's breath would be warm on the driver's neck.

Luxton glances at her. Kat'll do the talking, calm and in control.

"You get us inside, and you'll be fine," says Kat softly.

"They'll kill me," whispers the driver. He's no Lancaric. Or he knows about Lancaric. His eyes dart everywhere. His hands tremble. A man has been shot dead next to him. It's one of the most effective forms of persuasion.

Kat scrolls through Lev's call register. She stops at an entry labeled "YG." Is that Yulya Gracheva?

SEVENTY-FIVE

---◇---

Saturday, 12:05 p.m., BST

No one'll kill you if you drive normally," says Kat. "You've done this before, so when you get to the gate, look straight at the iris scanner, and lower
your window for the palm print."

The driver pulls out and accelerates slowly. The empty road ahead has
a heat haze on it, which spreads through the fence onto the surface of the
airbase.

"What's your name?" asks Kat.

"Sam," he whispers, so quiet that Kat can't tell his accent.

"Good, Sam. Now just relax. Who's going to win the soccer match?"

Sam doesn't answer.

"Your kids'll be watching it, I bet," says Kat.

Sam stays quiet.

"That's okay, Sam," says Kat. "Not nice to think of the family at times
like this."

Sam's hands grip the wheel. His wrists are taut. Sweat gathers under his
hairline.

"Are they expecting Lev? Or did he hitch a ride with you?"

"I don't think so. I just gave him a lift." He's English, with an accent like
the farmer's, Margaret, who drove her to Tappler's house. His eyes flip up to

the rearview mirror, meet Luxton's, and flip back again. His face shows total terror. Any guard worth his salt will detect it.

"I'm for Brazil," says Kat. "But I'm an American, and I've got a bit of a crush on Laja."

In the mirror she sees him smiling quickly to please her. "Yeah. Brazil," he says.

Sam downshifts and indicates a right turn into the base. A red sedan is coming toward them, an England flag flying from the roof. Sam stops to let it pass.

"I'm lying down now," says Kat. "Just go through the gate like you have a hundred times before."

She covers herself with a blanket and curls like a fetus. Her right thigh has a grenade pressing into it. She slips the MP5 beside her. It's too big to use in her cramped position. Her hand wraps around the Glock 18 handgun instead. If she uses it, she's dead anyway.

Luxton pulls a driver's protective screen up between himself and the back of Sam's head. He can't be seen from outside. He stays sitting, pressed against the cab wall.

The sun swings around, its warmth magnified by the window glass. The air brakes kick in, and the truck jolts to a halt. Sam doesn't speak. The guards say nothing. A machine bleeps. Metal scrapes on metal as the antiterror barrier moves down. Sam edges the vehicle forward, then stops. Another antiterror barrier comes up from behind, boxing the truck in.

A phone in the guard booth rings. It's answered.

Fifteen seconds pass. Nothing moves. No one speaks.

Kat looks through a crack in the blanket. Luxton looks toward her. His expression is unexcited.

Thirty seconds pass, then a rap of a hand on the door. "Lev Chichagov? He's down as traveling with you," says a voice. It's accented, probably Russian, like Lev.

Christ. She closes her eyes. What would Kat have done in Sam's position? Try to jump the cab, see if she could get the door open before Luxton fires, and take her chances among the four guards.

Sam doesn't. He lifts his right hand off the wheel and jerks his thumb backward. "He was held up at the port," he says. "Said he's getting the next one."

"There's no 'next one' listed here."

"Then he was wrong, I guess. Here," says Sam. "Check my phone. Here's the message from him."

Ten seconds pass. Kat can't see what's happening. She imagines Sam's hand hanging out the window, offering up his phone.

"Okay, go ahead. The aircraft's loading now."

The front barrier slides down. The truck moves ahead slowly. Breathing again, Kat levers herself up enough to look out the side window onto a vast expanse of airfield. Four hundred yards to her left, she sees one of the hangars. Beyond that are the other three.

"What was the plan with Lev, Sam? Where were you to drop him?"

"He didn't say. Just a lift to the base, that's all."

Sam's eyes skit up to the mirror. They're losing their fear. He's calculating Kat's vulnerability. He's concluding they won't shoot him inside the base.

"Slow down and give me your phone," says Kat.

Sam keeps driving. Luxton responds by noisily rechambering a round.

"Slow the fuck down, Sam," says Kat, "and give me your phone, or he'll kill you and toss you onto the tarmac."

The truck jerks to a halt and starts up again. Sam passes his phone to Kat. She dials Bill Cage. "You got a caller ID on this?" she asks when Cage picks up.

"Yes."

"You hear that, Sam? That's my boss in Washington. This base is illegal, and in the next hour, it's going down. Your choice whether you spend the rest of your life in jail or become a national hero. If you don't believe me, press redial when I'm done."

Sam says nothing.

Kat speaks to Cage. "Do you have my location?"

"Byford airbase."

"What visuals?"

"0.3 meter resolution."

"You see four aircraft hangars?"

"Correct. You're in the truck fifty yards inside the gate."

"Right. Forget about the narrow hangar. East to west number the others: one, two, and three."

"Got it."

"What signals from the hangars?"

"Mixed. Nothing specific."

"Thermal imaging."

"Negative."

"Shit," whispers Kat. "I'm calling a number now. I need an immediate location ID when it picks up."

She presses the Send button on Lev's phone for the address book ID marked "YG."

It rings.

"Triangulating," says Cage.

It keeps ringing. The truck is crawling. Sam turns so Kat sees the tail of the aircraft, then the steps leading down from the plane's tail door.

It keeps ringing.

"Nothing yet," says Cage. "If it picks up—"

"The gatehouse is watching us," says Sam.

Still ringing.

"If it goes to voice mail, we lose it," says Cage.

A figure at the top of the aircraft stairs beckons Sam to drive toward him.

"Go," says Kat, "as slow as you can."

The hangars disappear from view. They're heading in the wrong direction, now perhaps 300 yards from the aircraft and closing. Even going at ten miles an hour, they'll be there in less than a minute.

It goes to voice mail.

"Sorry," says Cage.

"She's got my dad," says Kat before she can stop herself.

A fuel tanker pulls up under the wing of the plane. Two guards step out to meet the truck. Lev's phone rings. The caller ID says "YG." Kat picks up, but doesn't speak.

Yulya's speaking angrily, in Russian.

Kat says nothing, keeps the line open. Cage is still there on Sam's phone.

"Number two," he says. "She's in the middle hangar."

SEVENTY-SIX

---◇---

Saturday, 12:14 p.m., BST

The hangar doors are open, showing a wide, gaping entrance through which Kat can make out the shape of a smaller aircraft inside. Against the midday sunlight, it's too dark inside to see more.

Luxton taps his yellow Port of Felixstowe jacket. Kat nods.

"Sam," he says. "Stop thirty yards from the plane on the apron. Then turn around one hundred and eighty degrees, so the back doors face the aircraft. Then unlock the back roller door."

"You need manual unlock as well."

"Then give it to me."

A glint of silver on the plane wing sends the sun straight through the windshield into Sam's eyes. He puts his hand up. "I don't have one."

"You do," says Luxton quietly. "If there's an accident, you have to get them out, don't you, before the police come."

Sam says nothing, just hands Luxton an electronic key.

"Slow and stop now," says Luxton. "Keep the engine running."

He turns the truck in an even curve. Luxton slips into the front seat. As Sam stops, Luxton opens the door and jumps out. He's carrying the Colt and takes the submachine gun that Kat's been using. Kat climbs over into the passenger seat. In the side mirror, she sees Luxton run around the back of the truck.

There's a beep when he tries the door, but it doesn't open. Luxton's exposed to the guards by the plane. His jacket will give him a few seconds' protection. He slaps his hand on the roller door. Kat glances at Sam, who's staring straight ahead.

She hits him with a vicious blow to the face. "Unlock it!"

Sam turns to her, his eyes soft, frightened. He's unable to make a decision, and words won't work. Kat smashes his left wrist against the steering wheel.

She draws on every ounce of cold cruelty she can find. "Unlock it, Sam." With his right hand, he presses a button under the dash.

Kat watches through the side mirror and the windshield. The guards step forward, confused. Luxton shouts something in Russian. He comes into Kat's view. He's carrying two weapons. The yellow jacket is open. He's relaxed, sweeping his arms about.

One of the guards on the ground brings up his weapon. The guard at the top of the steps is on a cell phone call. He goes rigid.

Luxton shoots him first. Then he shoots the two guards on the ground. Kat sees the glint of ejecting shell cases. Six in all. Two rounds each target. Silence-shattering explosions, which spread throughout the base. Kat checks the watchtowers and the gatehouse. Nothing. But they have seconds to take it to the next level.

Luxton opens the driver's door, pulls Sam out, and gets in. Kat presses redial on Lev's phone, gives it to Luxton. Luxton accelerates smoothly, brings the truck around in a long curve toward the middle hangar.

Yulya answers on the second ring. She starts screaming questions in Russian again.

The truck's 350 yards from the hangar, picking up speed.

"Lev? Lev?" shouts Yulya.

Luxton replies in Russian. Thirty seconds, and they'll be there. A spotlight shines inside the hangar. Kat sees two figures. The plane's a Gulfstream executive jet. There's a helicopter behind it. She can't see any hostages.

"Lev—"

"This is the British police, Miss Gracheva," says Luxton, switching to English. "It's over. You and your men—"

The windshield shatters. Luxton falls over the wheel. The truck slows, and Kat's screaming out, "Mike! Mike!" Her hands are on the wheel, dragging it under his weight. The side of his head is bloodied. He's lifeless, but his foot's locked down on the gas pedal.

A second shot hits the cab wall above Kat's head. The truck's veering in a circle, about to lose balance and tip.

Kat leans across Luxton, pushes up the door handle. As the door gives, Luxton shifts, but not enough to bring back the wheel. She screams again, primal and deep, to gather all her weight. She pushes him out onto the tarmac, doesn't look back, doesn't want to see.

Kat has control of the wheel. Another bullet hole appears in the driver's side window. She flinches and ducks. The window's safety glass spiderwebs and cascades inward.

Kat glimpses Yulya at the door of the hangar with a rifle. Hunched down behind the wheel and dashboard, Kat stomps the accelerator to the floor.

A round hits the engine block. Two more fly high, over Kat's head.

Yulya's nearly in front of her. Kat edges the wheel to hit her. Yulya jumps aside, and the truck goes inside the hangar. The searchlight sears Kat's retinas. She turns her head from it and hears a new burst of automatic fire.

The truck skews around to the right, its back tire shot out. Kat tries to correct the pull, but she can't. The truck's skidding in a tight circle. She breathes in burned rubber and sees the hangar swing around in front of her, the wing of the Gulfstream, a glimpse of the helicopter, wooden cargo crates stacked by the walls, a crack of light from the closed doors at the other end. She hears gunshot echoes.

She eases off the gas to get back the balance. From the handling, she judges that the tires of two wheels are blown. She can't see Yulya. But she sees Viktor, his face playful, like Yulya's, alight with a cruel grin.

Then framed in the windshield, she looks straight into the eyes of her father, watery, his expression old, understanding, proud. He, Sayer, Liz, and Max stare up at her from less than 100 feet away, tied up, unable to move, directly in the path of the truck.

SEVENTY-SEVEN

$$\Longrightarrow$$

Kat accelerates, swings the wheel hard left, and pulls on the hand brake. The truck tips. The back lurches around, and the vehicle goes up on two wheels. Kat slides across the seat, adding her weight to the momentum. A spinning tire sweeps an inch past Sayer's face and hits a cargo crate, which bounces the truck farther over. It crashes onto its side. The windshield bursts. An air bag pushes Kat back against the seat, twisting her head around.

The truck rolls onto its roof and settles. The cab frame buckles. The air bag deflates, leaving nylon tangled around her. Kat's lying on the dented inside of the roof. The glove compartment springs open. Papers scatter. A grenade tumbles onto her stomach. She feels the barrel of the Remington shotgun. Ashes from Sam's cigarette butts fall onto her face and get into her mouth.

Straight ahead of her is the undercarriage of the Gulfstream jet; to her right, a stack of crates. Her left hand hangs out the window, wedged because of her position. She can see Sayer's legs and the bare feet of Liz next to him.

The truck didn't crush them. She's bought everybody a few more minutes of life. She remembers herself pushing Luxton out of the cab—wounded or dead, she doesn't know. She thinks of Sam and feels sorry for him. She sees the three guards by the plane, falling to Luxton's gunfire, one after another. She summons Mercedes Vendetta. *Don't go battling guilt.* Yeah, right. Don't regret. Don't think back.

She manages to turn her body slightly, taking off pressure from the Remington pressing into her left hip. She smells gunpowder. But no one's been shooting inside. It must be the potassium nitrate from the air bag. She smells tire rubber and gasoline, and she sees a stain on the concrete as it leaks from the tank toward her.

But the concrete in front of her darkens with something else. White sneakers with a red streak up the side appear, red socks, and the hem of fresh blue denim. She tries to look up, but can't get the angle.

Yulya crouches right down so that Kat can see her properly.

"You okay, Kat?" she says softly. "Don't worry, we'll get you out."

Kat doesn't speak.

"The way they maintain these trucks, sooner or later, someone was bound to have an accident," says Yulya.

Yulya speaks into a cell phone. "We've got them," she says. "No. Fine. Leave us." Yulya closes the phone. "You heard that, Kat? We'll end this my way."

She leans her rifle next to the cab windshield. Kat can tell what it is from the wooden buttstock, skeletonized with two carved holes in it—a VSS, Vintovka Snaiperskaja Spetsialnaya, or special sniper rifle, the type Sayer matched to the round used to kill Suzy, the type used to shoot Luxton, the type deliberately brought into Kat's field of view to taunt her.

Yulya lifts up Kat's left hand, with Suzy's ring on it. Her tone becomes soft and friendly again. "Oh my God," she says. "The family heirloom." She rests Kat's fingers delicately on hers like a manicurist. "What I'm going to do is save the ring, then get you out of here."

Yulya's fingers tighten around the ring. Kat resists. Yulya lets go and steps back an inch. "Oh, Kat. Dear Kat. How I do like you." She moves out of view and stands up. "Viktor," she shouts.

She doesn't need the ring from Kat to kill her. She killed Suzy first and took it after. But she wants to break Kat before killing her. She'll do that by making Kat watch her father and the others die. As Kat judged, Yulya wants a ceremony, a ritualistic series of deaths, ending with Kat.

Yulya squats down again. "Why don't we do this like a visit to the dentist?

Viktor cuts the ring off your finger while you relax and watch TV. They're signing the CPS now. Why don't we watch it?"

Kat shifts another inch, freeing up her right hand pinned underneath her. A large, wide screen is lowered in front of her. She sees the hands of the two men carrying it, but not their faces. They lean it against the cargo crates. A wire trails from the left-hand edge.

The picture shows Hampton Court's Great Hall filled with politicians, some seated, some standing behind a long, dark, wood table. Three raised lecterns at the front are decorated with the national flags of the United States, China, and Russia.

The image flickers and the screen splits. On the left is the London soccer stadium, looking like a huge silver spaceship with a sword-thin, glistening arch curving over the field. Outside, fans draped in the red-on-white cross of the England flag pace around. Inside, the crowd cheers as the England team runs onto the field.

Delegates at the CPS ceremony look up as the three presidents of the world's official new superpowers step forward to take their places at their individual podiums. Abbott's face is rigid and serious. He's wearing a charcoal gray suit with a pale blue shirt. He touches his earpiece. His eyes drop, but he doesn't break his step. His hand goes into his jacket pocket, and he brings out a pen.

The camera cuts away to others in the hall. "See there," says Yulya. Her finger is on the right-hand screen, just above a small, attractive, middle-aged woman in a white pantsuit, sitting behind the Russian president. "That's my mom. She'll be saying a few words after the signing."

In the top right-hand corner, a digital clock tells Kat it is 12:56:14. The ceremony is due to end in less than four minutes.

"John," shouts Yulya. "Do you see her? Remember fucking her and ending up with Max? Do you see Mom there, Max? First time you've ever seen Mom and your real dad together."

Yulya's sitting on the floor, arms drawing up her knees and a pistol hanging loosely in her hands. She's next to Kat, engrossed in the screen. Viktor sits on the other side. He has a double-bladed knife, plain on one edge and serrated on the other. He takes hold of Kat's left hand.

"Your buddy, Lev," Kat says to Viktor, "he's dead. She told you, did she?"

As Kat speaks, she pushes her right hand down to her hip and gets her fingers out of their cramped position. She makes sure the shotgun's safety is disengaged.

Viktor grips her more tightly and splays out her ring finger, separating it from the others.

Kat's fired a Remington 870 in training. But that was with earmuffs, breakfast, a good night's sleep, and a target at 35 yards. She knows it can be a destructive and decisive short-range weapon. She knows the barrel digging into her waist, which she's maneuvering toward Viktor, is only 18 inches long. She knows the gun's loaded with seven cartridges of double-ought buckshot, because she watched Luxton load it. She knows the end of the barrel is hidden by the air bag nylon, and she knows the safety's off. What she doesn't know is that the shotgun's rigged with an automatic-fire capability.

Viktor lowers the knife blade toward her finger. Kat pulls the trigger.

Four cartridges fire at point-blank range, cutting through Viktor in succession as the heat of the barrel burns her from below. The roar takes her hearing, but Viktor disappears into a mist of white and red, his left hand still holding Kat's. She crawls out of the cab. Unhooks herself from Viktor's mangled body. Coughs on the smoke. Sees Liz choking on gunsmoke but unharmed.

Automatic gunfire hits one of Yulya's men, lying wounded on the ground. Far away, Luxton is propped up against the entrance of the hangar. He fires again. Another man falls. The hangar goes quiet. Completely silent.

There's no sign of Yulya.

SEVENTY-EIGHT

$$\longrightarrow\!\!\diamondsuit\!\!\longrightarrow$$

K-kat, over there," shouts Liz. "His knife."

Kat sees Viktor's knife wedged under a box. She gets it, kneels, and cuts the ropes holding the four hostages together. She cuts the bonds around Sayer's hands, then gives him the knife to free the others.

She picks up the shotgun. Luxton looks weak, but is still standing. From the blood on his head and shoulders, Kat can't work out where he's hurt. He doesn't move. Maybe he can't. Maybe he's covering her.

"Where is she?" Kat shouts to him.

She turns and turns, taking in the hangar in 360-degree sweeps. She should have three shells left in the Remington, but it's only an effective weapon close-up, and the hangar's cavernous.

Her father pushes himself to his feet. Sayer's helping Liz up. Grachev looks at no one, but walks stiffly toward the shattered cab of the truck.

The TV set, damaged by gunfire, has gone blank. But she remembers seeing it at 12:56:14. She breaks into a run.

"The cell phone," she shouts to Luxton. "Did you—"

The phone's in his bloodied, outstretched hand. She takes it on the run and emerges on the vast, hot, quiet apron of the airfield. The last satellite window opened at 12:42. Plus twelve minutes before it closes makes 12:54. And they've driven seventy miles south, which will make a difference.

It must be about 12:58. She's missed any chance of getting the images to Abbott before he flew to Hampton Court, and it's two minutes from the CPS signing.

The sun's so strong she can't see the phone's keypad properly. She punches Cage's numbers anyway.

Cage picks up. "Kat, Kat. Are you okay?"

"Yeah, I'm fine. Everything's fine. Did we miss it?"

"What the hell's happening there?"

"Did we fucking miss it?"

"No. There's been a delay."

"What do you mean?"

"We've got three minutes and the satellite window's still open."

She lowers herself to the ground and sits cross-legged. Three minutes on a day like today is two lifetimes.

"I'm playing you a live feed from Hampton Court," says Cage.

Kat cups her hand to block sunlight from the tiny LCD screen of the cell phone. It shows Abbott onstage, hands on each side of the podium, turning, talking to the Chinese president. He laughs, turns back, and glances at the lectern.

"You ready?" asks Cage. "Stay absolutely still. If you move you'll risk losing the uplink."

"Go," says Kat, pushing the Unlock button on Suzy's ring.

"Coming through," says Cage.

Kat hears an engine noise from somewhere straight out of the sun. She can't see it. She can't put up her hand as a visor. She can't move because of the ring.

"Kat, to your left." Cage's voice is sharp, close to panic. "Vehicle."

"Are the pictures coming through?"

"Move!"

A jeep's coming straight toward her. It's marked with the RingSet logo. Yulya's driving, her hair windblown under a red hat.

"Kat!" Cage is screaming now.

She glances back at the screen. "Is it through?" Then back at Yulya, whose left hand's on the wheel, her right holding some kind of weapon.

Kat doesn't move. She holds the ring absolutely still. "Can Abbott see it yet?"

The jeep's engine roar drowns Cage's response. Through heat-haze ripples, Kat sees Max Grachev outside the hangar with a rifle resting on the hood of a truck, white flashes jumping from the barrel.

One moment Yulya's face has the shape of a smile. Then a flame curls around from the back of the vehicle, and suddenly the jeep's engulfed in fire, and Yulya is screaming, her skin stretched across her face like a mask.

But the jeep keeps coming toward Kat, a streaking ball of burning fuel from the punctured tank.

Yulya jumps clear, tumbling over the tarmac, the flames around her like a water line, her front untouched but her back burning. She lets off two rounds in Kat's direction but they fly wide, then she rolls on the airfield apron to try to put out the fire.

"How we doing, Bill?" Kat hasn't moved.

"Signal disruption," Cage replies. "You okay?"

"How much they get?"

"No way to tell."

The sunlight makes it impossible for Kat to see what Abbott's doing.

"Is Abbott reacting?"

"No."

Kat's not going to move until The History Book is delivered. Her mind is on the prisoners on Voz Island, on the families separated and murdered, on Suzy's dead but perfectly serene face staring up at her in the morgue with her skull torn out by one of Yulya's bullets.

Yulya's prone, legs splayed like a sniper, less than 200 yards away. Only a stream of black smoke cuts across her line of vision. Kat hears the crack of rifle fire.

"Update, Bill." Her voice is tight. If she reaches for the Remington by her side, makes any movement at all, the transmission will fail. Yet if Yulya hits her, she'll move anyway and the transmission will fail.

"Six seconds."

Another crack. A whining ricochet from ten feet away.

"Four seconds."

Two shots. One skips fifteen feet from her, the other two feet.

The wind's blowing the smoke higher, clearing Yulya's line of sight.

"It's in," says Cage. "Move. Move. Move."

Kat rolls to her right as a five-round burst chews up the surface where she's been sitting. She picks up the Remington and moves forward, right, then left, to deny Yulya a clear shot. For her buckshot to be lethal she has to get within thirty yards of Yulya.

But fifty yards out the jeep's fuel tank explodes. A wall of hot air hits Kat, and her right foot jars against something on the ground. She trips, topples forward with heat surging around her, breaks her fall, and the Remington smashes from her grip, skids along the ground, and fires off a burst of its last three rounds.

Kat scrambles to her feet, taking refuge in the new, thicker smoke cloud from the burning jeep. She runs with the smoke, her throat rasping, her eyes stinging, trying to get behind Yulya, except Yulya's watching, staying exactly where she is, because as soon as the smoke clears, Yulya will kill Kat. It's just a matter of time, seconds only, which is why as the sunlight jumps through the burning haze, making the colors around the airfield textured and strange, Kat sees Yulya waiting, confident of her target, her lips turned into a smirk of victory.

Kat has one weapon left. As she runs, she tests it on her fingers. It'll work, but only if she gets close enough to use absolute force.

She circles, putting the burning jeep between her and Yulya, and she can see clearly back toward the hangar, where Grachev's still leaning over the truck hood, his rifle silent. The same man who killed the helicopter pilot at the limit of his range, whose shots blew out the jeep's tires and ripped through its fuel tank, cannot bring himself to fire directly on his sister.

But that doesn't make him useless.

"Max," she screams as a gust of wind suddenly clears the smoke.

Yulya's gaze shifts to Kat, rifle raised, then back to her brother, who has her in his sights. Her moment of hesitation is enough for Kat to vault onto the jeep's charred hood, and use its bounce to hurl herself at Yulya. She crashes into her headlong, and as Yulya tries to regain her balance, Kat punches her in the neck, making sure the sharp edges of Suzy's ring cut through the skin.

As they hit the ground, Kat punches harder, twisting the ring's metal and pushing it through soft tissue until blood jets out, flooding over her, and Kat knows she's ruptured one of the carotid arteries.

Kat holds Yulya to stop her struggling, and, as her strength goes, Kat pulls her head up by the hair, bringing them face to face. Through trembling and fading eyes, Yulya manages to concentrate on Kat. In those last seconds, her arrogance stripped, her lips moving without the smirk, a softness covers her face, as if she's a little lost and surprised.

Kat drops Yulya's head and stands up, her hands soaked in warm blood. She's flooded by a terrible sense of fury that Yulya's dead but nothing's resolved. She needs to do more.

She hooks her foot under Yulya's body and turns it so the back of Yulya's head is against the ground and her face is staring up. She wipes her hands on her clothes, picks up Yulya's rifle, checks the chamber, and puts the barrel against Yulya's forehead.

A hand falls on Kat's shoulder. She shakes it off. Grachev holds both shoulders gently. "It's over, Kat," he says. "She's dead. It's okay."

She lets the gun fall and Grachev hold her, lets him absorb her rage. Amid the smells of blood, oil, and fire, and the feel of sunlight on her face, Kat waits for her trembling to subside, for serenity to take its place. But before it does, she hears static in her earpiece and Cage's voice.

"Kat, you there?"

"We're okay here," she says, stepping back from Grachev.

"Are you watching Abbott?"

"In a second." She runs back to where the cell phone's still on the ground. She looks down at the cell phone. Abbott's speaking. She clicks up the speakerphone's volume. "Even with high energy prices, the American people have made our economy the envy of the world," the U.S. president is saying. "But keeping America competitive requires affordable and secure supplies. And that is why I am proud that the United States is a leading partner in the Coalition for Peace and Security."

Abbott's right hand goes up to his earpiece. His eyes sweep the room, rest on the Russian president, then go to Tiina Gracheva, then back to his lectern.

Kat hears Cage's voice. "He's seen his autoprompter. He's reading from the hard copy of the speech. We're telling him to pull out or the pictures will be superimposed on the soccer screens."

Abbott brushes the lapel of his suit. "However," the president says haltingly, "the gathering today is designed to examine the finer details of the coalition . . ."

The Russian and Chinese leaders look down sharply at the prepared text.

". . . agreement of all partners to ensure—"

"He's pulling out," says Cage. "It's done."

"Good job, Bill," says Kat.

She doesn't end the call, doesn't know what to feel, so she gets up and walks over to the jeep.

Grachev looks down at his dead sister. Tears run down his face. Kat steps forward, arms outstretched.

"It's okay, Max."

His embrace hurts. She's bruised all over, and her side stings. She feels his deep crying.

Behind them, Kat sees Luxton lying on the ground. Liz crouches next to him. She's sponging his face. Kat's father is propping himself up with an arm around Nate Sayer's shoulder. They walk together out of the hangar.

Gently, Kat steps away from Grachev. "Go see your dad, Max," she says.

Grachev walks robotically toward John Polinski. It's then that Kat notices the guardhouses are deserted.

"Everyone's cut and run," she says to Cage.

"The police are on their way. We're delaying them. But you've got about fifteen minutes."

Enough time. Kat keeps walking. It's wonderfully quiet, with smells of aircraft fuel mixed with the English harvest. Birds dip and weave through the big sky, streaked with silver clouds.

"The signing delay. How did you do that?" asks Kat.

"The CPS schedule was contingent on the start of the game. I got Javier Laja's number like you asked, called him, mentioned your name. He said sure. He made up some sexy soccer star bullshit for a few minutes. It bought us enough time and, well, anyway, the pissing contest's over, and we've won."

At the beginning of what Cage says, she's laughing inside because of Javier Laja. At the end, she thinks of Suzy, her mom, her dad, Cranley, Max, Mike, Liz. She sees the faces on Voz Island.

"Yeah," she shouts, and can't help herself. "Who's won, Bill, and at what fucking cost? Just tell me that."

She throws the phone to the ground and feels dryness in her mouth.

SEVENTY-NINE

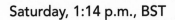

Saturday, 1:14 p.m., BST

Kat walks over to her father. He's standing with the help of Grachev and Sayer. She takes his hands in both of hers. She holds them for a few seconds. Her father is too weak to speak. She doesn't know what to say. Suzy always handled Dad better than she did.

She looks at Sayer. "Take care of him, Nate?" she says. "Bring him home safely."

Sayer nods.

"Bring Suzy home, too."

Sayer nods again.

"Bye, Dad. See you in Washington," she says awkwardly.

"Thank you," he whispers.

She digs into her pocket and brings out the VSS cartridge that Sayer gave her. "Max, if you're still a cop, get this matched to that rifle. There'll be some trail to Yulya, and I want it on record that Yulya killed Suzy."

Without waiting for a response, Kat kneels and embraces Liz. "You're a big star. You made it work."

Liz is still cradling her brother. "F-fuck them for m-making us do it."

Luxton props himself up on his elbows and says something to Liz, who helps him to his knees, then his feet.

Yulya's shot grazed Luxton's left temple and made him black out. But he knows what he and Kat are to do next, because they decided it in case they ever got this far. They lay Yulya's body across the back of a jeep, and Kat drives to the airliner. She and Luxton load the bodies of the three dead guards in, too, then drive into the middle of the hangar and stop under the wing of the Gulfstream.

They unload the bodies. They carry Mason onto the jeep. Kat drives out to Sayer. "We need to get him home, too," she says. Luxton and Sayer lift Mason's body onto the tarmac. Sayer covers his face with his jacket.

Luxton and Kat take the jeep back into the hangar. Luxton pulls the M20 grenade launcher out of the wreck of the truck cab. He leaves two grenades in the jeep and another in the cockpit of the helicopter.

Kat closes the hangar door until only a narrow gap remains open. Luxton fires a rocket-propelled grenade into the fuel tank of the Gulfstream.

As they walk away, a fireball gathers inside the hangar. The walls burst open, and a sheet of flame leaps skyward, then subsides.

She says good-bye to Luxton at the deserted entrance of the base, walks down the road to the Mini Cooper, drives to Heathrow airport, and leaves the car in the long-term parking lot.

Bill Cage has had Kat's clearances restored and fed her biometric and iris readings into the British security system. Kat buys new clothes, showers, and eats. The TV screens show the 2–1 Brazil victory over England. The CPS signing has been delayed for technical reasons. A gas explosion at a private airfield on the east coast has destroyed a hangar, but there were no injuries.

She boards a flight to Washington. At Dulles, she catches a cab to Dix Street and gives the driver $100 to wait. It's just past ten at night, and Vendetta answers the door.

"What you been doin', girl? That shit you told me to keep been all over TV."

Kat stays in the doorway. He has whiskey on his breath. "Thank you, M," she says. "Thank you so much."

He peers at her face. "You got yourself cut up, there, above the eye." His finger hovers by her face. Then he steps back, opens the door for her to come in. She shakes her head, kisses him, draws in the smell of tobacco, whiskey, and hashish.

"You got those things from the safe on R Street?" she asks.

"I got 'em."

"Can I have 'em?"

"Can I have you?"

"Yeah." Kat kisses him lightly on the lips. "Maybe tomorrow."

Vendetta laughs, leaves the door open, and comes back a moment later with a supermarket plastic bag, heavy with documents. "You scare me like no one on this street ever did. But that don't mean I don't love you."

Kat smiles. She feels good, knows it will only last a minute. "Me, too," she says. She brushes his cheek with the back of her hand.

The cab drops Kat at her apartment. It's been searched, but neatly, and she doesn't care. In the mirror, she looks at the cut above her left eye and another on her right cheek. She showers, wraps one towel around her and dries her hair with another. She makes herself coffee, perches on a kitchen stool, paints her nails a softly hued burgundy to offset her blond hair, and watches TV.

A Red Cross plane has landed at Voz Island.

When her nails are dry, she dresses in loose beige pants, sneakers, and a burgundy top. She takes time with the lipstick and eye shadow.

She hesitates about Suzy's ring and decides to leave it on her workbench. She picks up the supermarket bag. On the way out, she sees a handwritten envelope amid the junk mail, recognizes Cage's writing, and leaves it on the floor.

It's balmy outside. She walks up to R Street, past her dad's house, crosses the intersection, presses Nancy's doorbell, and speaks into the intercom.

She holds out the bag as Nancy opens the door. Nancy's not surprised. Nate must have told her everything. She looks drawn, but welcoming.

"Hi, Aunt Nance," Kat says. "Nate asked me to put these back in his study."

"You know where it is," Nancy says warmly. Kat runs upstairs. The safe's open. She puts the bag inside and locks it.

Kat's twenty-four years and a few months old—nearly eight days older than she was last week, when she went into the Kazakh embassy. She's done all right, but there's a lot she doesn't know about the world. Nancy's waiting for her at the bottom of the stairs.

"You know, Aunt Nance. If you're . . . I mean, it's a nice night, and I wonder . . . you know . . . I'd just like to walk and talk with someone, if you've got time, that is."

Acknowledgments

Many people gave their time to make *The History Book* possible. Roger Whittaker and Lengya Cheng explained computers; Amanda Gunn and Grahame Wylie showed me the skills of a video editor; Dr. Togzhan Kassenova guided me through Russia and Kazakhstan; others, who would prefer not to be named, gave insights into the world in which Kat finds herself; and the BBC, which sends its reporters to places other broadcasters rarely venture, has allowed me to work in Kazakhstan, Washington, and beyond, where I met people and found ideas.

Claire Bolderson, Liz Jensen, Cait Murphy, Lisanne Radice, Mary Sandys, Ed Stackler, Tanya Warnakulasurya, and Adam Williams guided and advised on the manuscript.

My thanks to the team at Warner Books and particularly to my editor, Les Pockell, whose incisive input improved the book no end.

A very special thanks to my agent Simon Lipskar who worked on *The History Book* from when it was merely a five-line concept on a piece of paper and enthusiastically supported it throughout. Without you, Simon, it would never have been published.